BRIAN S. LEON

HAVOC RISING

RED ADEPT PUBLISHING
Unlocking New Worlds

Havoc Rising
Copyright © 2014 by Brian S. Leon. All rights reserved.
First Print Edition: May 2015

ISBN-13: 978-1-940215-47-1
ISBN-10: 1940215471

Red Adept Publishing, LLC
104 Bugenfield Court
Garner, NC 27529
http://RedAdeptPublishing.com/

Cover and Formatting: Streetlight Graphics

Not a word of retreat. You'll never persuade me.
It's not my nature to shrink from battle, cringe in fear
with the fighting strength still steady in my chest.
I shrink from mounting our chariot — no retreat —
on foot as I am, I'll meet them man-to-man.
Athena would never let me flinch.

—Diomedes to Sthenelus on the battlefield at Troy,
The Iliad, Book V, Homer

PROLOGUE

May, 2011, New York City.

IT WAS TUESDAY, AND THE city was alive on a pleasant spring afternoon—a perfect day for Mazeen Fawaz to become a god. After weeks of training and months spent isolated from those he loved, his sacrifice was about to pay off. After peering out the dirty window of his dingy apartment at a ratty patch of grass covered by bags of garbage, the young man placed an innocuous-looking metallic disk into a recess on the bottom of his watch then gathered his backpack and left his rathole of an apartment in the Red Hook housing development in Brooklyn. Though he was scared and nervous, and perhaps even a little excited, a sense of purpose and duty kept him focused on his task.

This is it. He pulled his backpack's straps tight, locked the door behind him, and braced himself for the thumping bass that always reverberated through the hallway no matter the time of day. The noise wasn't as bad as the acrid and pungent smells, though.

The first water taxi to Manhattan wouldn't leave until 2:20 p.m. That would give him two hours to pick up a small but significant package that awaited him at a hotel and get to the museum nearby. The seemingly innocuous device inside the package would take him just a few minutes to assemble. He ran through the steps of the plan repeatedly in his head as he made the short ten-minute walk in the bright sun down Dwight Street toward the ferry docks.

As usual, the terminal and the water taxi were crowded with shoppers from the furniture store, which allowed him to pass mostly unnoticed. Mazeen was in his early twenties and not bad looking

1

by Western standards, but his dark complexion was unmistakably Middle Eastern. He regularly shaved to further remove himself from scrutiny, but just being Arabic in New York got him sideways glances, and people often moved away from him on the ferry or subway. He didn't care. It fueled his courage for what he was about to do.

He didn't try to avoid eye contact, even though most of the people he encountered did. Maybe it had nothing to do with his appearance — just New Yorkers being New Yorkers — but he knew that if he tried to look away he would come off as shifty and suspicious. He was already concerned that his constant tugging at his shirt because of his profuse sweating would attract attention.

Just act casual, he kept thinking as the ferry made its twenty-five-minute journey across the turbid water of the East River to Manhattan. The cliché made him smile a bit as he walked up to the upper deck for "fresh" air. He found the idea ridiculous — that the foul air out on deck would be any better than in the stuffy salon below — but at least there would be a breeze.

Everything about New York City made him uneasy, from the odd-looking twin-hulled ferryboat, painted like a giant yellow taxicab, to walking the crowded streets amongst the giant buildings that blocked all sunlight and sense of direction. He had to keep reminding himself that his ordeal was nearly over as the ferry docked at the foot of Lower Manhattan's vast concrete monstrosities.

At the Wall Street subway station, Mazeen caught the Five Train north to Grand Central and then the Six Train to the East Seventy-Seventh Street station as he'd done so many times before. In an effort to calm his racing heart, he tried to focus on his mother and sisters, picturing their faces. When he found that giving way to thoughts of his mission, he redirected his thoughts to the promises that had been made both by him and to him. The entire trip passed by in a blur.

He climbed the stairs from the Seventy-Seventh Street station and emerged in front of the massive redbrick façade of Lenox Hill Hospital. He glanced into the emergency entrance as he passed under its green awning. The hospital was calm now, with only a few people waiting and a vacant gurney in the hall, but he suddenly imagined the bloody chaos and broken bodies that would soon overwhelm the small facility. He tried to convince himself that what he was about to do was of little consequence compared to the reward he'd been promised.

The constant noise from the endless stream of vehicles, the ubiquitous construction, and the whistles and sirens echoing among the buildings faded to a dull hum over the next block and a half, and the never-ending throngs of humanity disappeared from view. He tried to refocus on his task, but he couldn't get past the images of a man carrying a limp young girl with a bloody stump for an arm or a small boy, covered in his mother's blood, screaming inconsolably. He shook his head to try to clear it. Sweat began to dampen his shirt again, and doubt started to creep back into his thoughts. It took considerable effort to force back the growing uncertainty as he continued.

He walked down East Seventy-Seventh Street toward Park Avenue, feeling a bit better because he had something else to focus on—he would pick up his package just up the street at The Mark Hotel. Security on the subways and ferries was too tight these days to risk carrying even the arcane type of bomb he was about to use.

Even he didn't fully understand the explosive his benefactor wanted him to use, and he had trained in bomb making with those al-Qaeda zealots for weeks in Yemen before coming to New York. Of course, it was one of his benefactor's creations, which meant it had little in common with normal explosives.

Part of the device, a featureless metallic disk about the size of a silver dollar, had been on a shelf in his apartment when he'd first arrived—right where she'd told him it would be, in plain sight. He didn't even need to build the bomb. All he had to do was keep the disk under his watch until he put it into the disk drive of a laptop that would be left as a package for him—under a false name—near the target, place the computer in his pack, and walk into the museum. There would be no obvious detonation device, no external wires, no timer, nothing suspicious. She'd told him it would trigger automatically once he entered the building.

Mazeen suddenly recalled with vivid clarity the first time he'd witnessed her power. The man had failed to deliver a message due to the presence of police activity in town. Despite his pleas for forgiveness, she simply extended a hand, and the man folded in on himself as if he were a paper cup being crushed. What remained was smaller than the soccer ball Mazeen had carried as he watched in horror. Then, he learned, she killed the man's family, too. That act stood in stark contrast to the lavish generosity she was also capable of when people achieved the goals she'd set for them. It was said that she

3

was immortal and could even grant immortality if she chose. In fact, if he wasn't sure she would never lie to him, and if he hadn't witnessed her power firsthand, he might have doubted the bomb would even work. But she'd assured him that he was chosen specifically because the reward would be significant—not an afterlife with some number of virgins, but one in which she promised he would be reborn as a god, maybe even like her.

Mazeen might have looked like a Muslim in appearance, and in public, he acted like one, but he wasn't one. He couldn't have cared less about Allah. His benefactor, not Allah, had saved the lives of his mother and sisters. To protect them and keep them safe, he'd have given anything to be like her.

Mazeen would never forget the terror he'd felt the night the earthquake had killed his father and destroyed his family's small mud-brick home just outside of Bam. He couldn't find his father in all the rubble and began to panic. He felt weak and helpless when he finally found his mother and tried—and failed—to lift a collapsed wall from her crushed legs. The memory of her weak voice urging him to dig through the rubble to get to his baby sisters, whom her body was protecting, haunted him. Even now, years later, he had nightmares about it. If not for her—his savior, appearing as if from nowhere to effortlessly toss the broken wall away and then take them in and provide for them—they never would have survived. But while it was true he owed her a debt, taking care of his family far outweighed any gratitude he felt. The reward she'd promised him for this act would ensure that he would never be so weak and helpless again. He quickened his pace, renewed. Today was going to be a good day.

Mazeen crossed Park Avenue and veered toward the elegant brown-brick edifice that housed The Mark Hotel on Madison Avenue. As he entered the stark, ultramodern lobby, he pulled a clipboard out of his pack and walked across the garish black-and-white-striped marble floor to the austere black reception desk.

"I need to pick up a package for a Mr. Anthony Mendez," he said in exactly the way he had practiced for weeks, trying for an air of New York nonchalance.

The apathetic young woman at the desk, wearing a severe black blazer with white trim, ducked behind the counter and produced a flat package, slightly less broad than a pizza box, with a tag on it. She didn't bother to view the tag or even glance up at Mazeen. He took the box and walked out. *I could have had a third eye and green skin.*

Less than half a block later, he stopped between two buildings and walked down the outside stairwell to the alley below to duck out of sight. He opened the box and took out a laptop, pulled the metal disk from under his watch, and placed it into the disk drive. It fit perfectly, which made him smile and instantly erased any doubts he'd had. He put the computer into his backpack and zipped it closed, left the clipboard and box behind in the alleyway, and climbed back out to the street. The instant he walked back onto the sidewalk, he became paranoid that someone might have seen him. It took an act of sheer will for him to calm his fears, reminding himself that, so far, he'd done nothing wrong as far as anyone could tell. Even so, he couldn't stop his hands from trembling.

His pulse quickened again when he saw the trees lining Fifth Avenue, and the closer he got to the museum, the more his hands shook. He grabbed the loose ends of his shoulder straps and daydreamed as he walked in the shade of the trees along Central Park and Park Avenue. He imagined what kind of god he would become. Would he be able to manipulate matter and energy the way she could? Maybe he would have the power to see into the future, or fly, or both. No matter—as long as he didn't end up like that monstrosity Kesed that she kept around like a pet.

As he approached the queue of school buses and tour buses on the street in front of the Metropolitan Museum of Art, Mazeen paused. This close to his target, the full weight of his mission hit him like a brick. She had promised him he would be reunited with his family soon. Only then would he be able to protect them properly from any disasters that might ever happen again. He focused on his twin sisters—now ten years old—and his crippled mother and forced himself forward.

The gray-stone, monolithic structure of the museum loomed ahead like a mountain. Its imposing neoclassical façade was dotted regularly with small black windows at street level and high, arched windows between colonnades above. Street vendors and artists lined the wall under the windows along the south wing of the building but stopped just before one of the long, narrow fountains that flanked the stairs at the main entrance. The museum was not as crowded as it would have been earlier in the day but was still teeming with parents chasing—or dragging—kids and pushing strollers, museum patrons, groups of schoolchildren, and throngs of visitors in tour groups. He

5

stepped into the security line just inside the door to have his backpack checked, and as he waited, he worried about when it would happen.

The longer he waited, the more his pulse and mind raced. The whole world slowed, and he began to sweat and shake more violently than before. He fought the doubt that began to creep into his mind. He noticed one mother, just inside the Great Hall, trying desperately to convince her screaming boy that the museum would be fun, while just beyond, a group of young girls near his sister's age gathered hand in hand, singing, as they waited near a queue of maybe twenty more children and their chaperones. Dozens more faces of all ages and races stared down at him from the balcony above. When he finally glanced up the line to the spot where he would check his pack, he suddenly couldn't handle not knowing when the bomb would go off.

What would happen if she'd lied about the bomb, or worse, about his reward? No. She would never lie. What if it didn't go off, and she thought it was his fault? Would she take it out on his family?

He took a few leaden steps closer to the guards' station. When his turn finally came, he stopped short of the table and wiped sweat off his forehead with a shaky hand. All at once, questions entered his mind — questions he had not until this point even worried about: why here? What was her purpose?

A tall African-American security guard walked over to him. "You okay, son? You don't look too good. Why don't you come over here and sit down for a second and catch your breath."

He stared at the guard and lost his composure. His eyes wandered past the columns and down the Great Hall again as he felt the adrenaline build. She had her reasons, and he had his. He had to trust her.

Mazeen thought of his sisters playing near their mother one last time then bolted past the security guard into the Great Hall of the Metropolitan Museum of Art, shoving people and knocking over a stroller as a blond woman screamed.

He made it only a few steps before a tremendous pressure began bearing down on his entire body, and then all at once, the world folded in on him in a blinding flash of light that enveloped the entirety of the Great Hall.

CHAPTER 1

The Same Day, San Diego, California.

AS A THIRTY-TWO-HUNDRED-YEAR-OLD GUY WHO protected humanity from all manner of brutish and nasty creatures, dealing with sea lions and obnoxious wannabe fishermen should have been a cakewalk, right? *Yeah, not so much.* At least, not that day.

I'm going to kill him. I watched the other boats anchored and drifting around the kelp beds off La Jolla and shook my head. *I'm going to strangle his fishy ass and use him for chum. What the hell is with all the damned sea lions?* Everywhere I looked, there was another one, including two bulls, six cows, and at least that many young ones — and that didn't include the seals that pestered us. *There are at least thirty boats out here, and I'm the only one dealing with the damned dogs.*

Things weren't going well on that particular charter. First off, my clients were late. Secondly, the wind was up, blowing at least ten to fifteen knots, which was about double what the forecast had suggested. Wind made casting a fly tricky, especially for amateurs. I had already untangled flies a dozen times from the antenna on the canvas-covered top that shaded my steering console, and I'd unhooked flies from my jacket another half-dozen times. Fortunately, no hooks had penetrated skin. Then there was the guy puking off the bow as his two buddies laughed at him. There was no mercy in fishing.

The fish were cooperating when the guys could actually get the fly beyond the engines, but the damned sea lions were playing havoc with the fish once they were hooked, plucking them off my anglers' lines as if they were freakin' raspberries at a U-pick farm. Mercifully — for the fish, anyway — they weren't getting hooked often.

7

Holy crap. I hate these days. Thank Zeus it's almost over. "We got about twenty minutes left before we need to head in," I said, ever hopeful that the guys would have some sympathy for their seasick friend and just call it off early.

"I sure would like to have caught one of those yellowtail while we were here," replied the bulkiest of the trio of clients, with an attitude. He had a belly that his very expensive and scientifically developed fishing shirt—fresh from a catalog—strained to contain, and his cigar breath made me a little queasy. His pudgy face was the color of a cooked lobster, and every time he took his hat off to wipe back his thinning hair, the stark tan line nearly made me laugh. I could deal with that crap, but the guy hadn't managed a cast longer than fifteen feet all day, and now he wanted one of the most demanding fish you could catch in Southern California. *Yeah, right.*

Of course, it was always a guy like that who set a world record—no concept, no clue, and no skill, but all the luck in the world. That was fishing, and that was why I usually loved it: anything could happen. But today, it was just irritating.

When we finally got back to the charter dock at the landing on Mission Bay where I kept my boat, the sick guy stumbled away even before I'd finished tying her off. His fancy fishing shirt was stained colors never seen on anyone healthy, and the odor that wafted off him as he staggered up the dock was indescribable.

The other two gathered their rods, cooler, and camera gear, and the beefy guy handed me a ten-dollar bill, giving me a half smile. "It sure would have been nice to land a few more fish, Steve." His tone suggested I hadn't done enough—a sentiment backed up by the measly tip. "But I guess that's why they call it 'fishing' and not 'catching.'"

That was the statement of someone ticked off about not catching any fish but wanting to seem like an experienced angler—I knew that from my many years of fishing all over the world. Being stiffed on the tip didn't bother me because I didn't do that job for the money, but I freakin' hated that saying. "Well, maybe next time we won't have so many dogs to contend with," I said as I began to stow loose gear and collect the day's trash in preparation for cleaning the boat. "If you'd have hooked that yellowtail you wanted today, you never would have landed it."

"You may be right, but it still would have been fun. See you next time." He waved dismissively as he walked down the dock.

If there were any justice in the world, he would jam that seven-hundred-dollar four-piece fly rod into the railing on the way to his rental car and turn it into a ten-piece toothpick. That didn't happen. I spent the next few hours cleaning out the custom twenty-six-foot center console boat I chartered, trying to figure out how the guy had gotten vomit underneath the cap rail. I mean, jeez, I had to contort myself just to get at it with a brush.

As I scrubbed, a familiar voice came from behind me.

"Rough day out there, Cap'n Dore?"

The boat rocked a bit, but I chose to continue scrubbing rather than turn and face him. "Now, how the hell would you know that, you squid's dick?" I scrubbed just a bit harder. "Why on Earth were we the only ones harangued by sea lions all day? There had to have been three dozen boats off La Jolla, and I got to host the Pinniped Fest, you fishy-smelling jackass. And get your slimy hands off my clean boat."

"Aw, come on, dude," my visitor said in a conciliatory tone. "Those guys would have killed anything you landed today, and you know it. Clymene was just making sure they didn't get any spawners."

"Well, how come you didn't at least warn me about the wind? I mean, I expect NOAA to get the weather wrong, but for cripes' sake, don't you control it or something, being an all-powerful Sea Titan and all?"

I finally turned around to see my weathered old friend straddling the cap rail of my boat with one foot on the dock and the other dangling inside it. As usual, he was wearing a hideous shirt, unbuttoned to his navel. The shirt was some bizarre combination of yellows, reds, and greens, like something out of Picasso's acid trip, but at least it fit him. A massive, bushy, dingy-white beard covered his chest.

"Could that shirt get any more obnoxious, Ned?"

My beach-bum friend—Nereus the Titan, Protector of the Sea, in self-imposed exile in Southern California—always made me think of Santa Claus at the beach after a two-day tequila bender. And it figured that Clymene, one of his many sea-nymph daughters, was encouraging the fish-stealing pains in the ass we'd encountered that day.

"Did the dudes leave any beer behind?" Nereus asked, ever hopeful.

I'd never been much of a drinker because, frankly, I just never liked the taste, so any spare beers would have gone to Nereus. However, he was out of luck. I shook my head, and he sighed.

9

Despite being a Protogenoi, or Old One, one of the many powerful otherworldly beings that came to our world from time to time, I considered him a friend and always gave him the stuff that got left behind.

"You got any cheese puffs left in your bag, then?"

"No beer and no cheese puffs, Ned, but I think I have some corn chips if you want them. And I've got water if you want it," I added, trying to sound generous.

Ned had laid himself back to bask in the sun on the wide cap rail along my boat's starboard bow and closed his eyes. "Water? Ugh. No way, man. You know what fish do in that stuff?" He made a face as he got comfortable. "But I'll take them corn chips. Oh, you hear about the bombing earlier today?" he asked as I tossed the bag at him.

I expected it to smack him and then bounce onto the dock beyond, but instead, he caught it as if he'd been watching me the whole time, though he never even opened his eyes. His action made me smile, and I shook my head, impressed, as I resumed cleaning.

"No, you know I don't have a regular radio onboard. Middle East somewhere?" I just assumed he was making conversation, but I probably should have known better, given who he was.

"Nah, man. New York City." He opened the bag of chips. "Metropolitan freakin' Museum of Art. Suicide bomber. Kablooie. Took out seventeen people, injured another thirty-three. They can't find any remains of the bomber or the bomb. Not even residue, man. Nada." He was munching loudly as he spoke. "Happened right at the entrance. I guess none of the art got damaged, but some kinda cool old cup was stolen while they were sortin' stuff out. Thief totally ransacked some sheik's private collection that was on loan to the museum. Curators said it was the least valuable item in the collection and just a simple bronze cup, but I'm hearin' different, dude."

I climbed off the boat with my gear and began to spray the two rods I'd brought and break them down. I loved days when people brought their own gear because the cleanup was fast. The only problem was today it gave me time to wonder about the bombing. I'd seen a lifetime of bombings, many lifetimes in fact, but Ned wouldn't have brought up a mere suicide bombing if it didn't relate more directly to him and, by extension, to me.

"So?" I asked. "What are you hearing? And I assume you don't mean on the news." I finished the rods, zipped up my gear bag, and walked off the dock.

Ned flip-flopped along behind me, talking through a mouthful of corn chips and getting crumbs in his long beard. I could smell them upwind. *Ugh.*

"Cup was special," he managed to spit out with a spray of crumbs. "And, dude, you know I don't watch TV or nothing. You humans sensationalize everything, man. I just got a vibe that somethin's happenin'."

I had been involved with seemingly benign situations turning out to be ominous — and vice versa — for millennia, so I knew better than to jump to conclusions just because Ned had a hunch. Heck, for all I knew his hunch was a reaction to too much skunky beer, sun, and stale cheese puffs.

"Well, if you're right, I'm sure I'll hear about it soon enough from Athena." I put the gear in my truck. "I'm heading home and getting some rest. And, hey, find out where I can get a couple of nice white sea bass for my guys on Friday, would ya? They're good guys, and I know they'll release them."

"I dunno, dude. I'll see what I can do. Take 'em easy." He strolled off toward the seawall at the end of the marina, munching as he went.

CHAPTER 2

WHILE I WAS DRIVING THE short distance home down Rosecrans, the news of the bombing was still all over the radio. I flipped through a couple of stations and got the gist of the story, which was basically what Ned had told me: suicide bomber in the entrance to the Met, fifty people either injured or dead.

The odd part was that absolutely no remains of the bomber were recovered. They couldn't tell what kind of device had caused the explosion, even though surveillance videos showed the guy bolting through the Great Hall and then *whammo*.

The detail about the cup was a brief side note—clearly not considered significant beyond the fact that it made the story that much weirder. Every major tourist attraction, airport, train station, bus depot, and government building across the country was on lockdown, and all I could do was wonder if we were having a repeat of 9/11. As horrible as that had been, at least it was a purely human event. I only hoped that the attack in the Met was as well.

By the time I pulled into my driveway in Roseville, on Point Loma just a few miles from my boat, I knew it was much worse than a terrorist attack. Unless some museum worker wanting to complete his cups-of-the-world collection had snagged it, it was too coincidental— odd bombing and odd theft. I didn't believe in coincidences. I did, however, believe Ned's assessment that the cup was more important than they knew or were admitting. It had to have been, or he just wouldn't have cared. And that was all I needed to raise my hackles ever so slightly. It certainly wouldn't be the first time an artifact of profound and frightening supernatural power had been judged as insignificant simply because mundane humans just couldn't see or feel the object's true nature. The fact that I hadn't heard from Athena or her Metis Foundation only meant that things hadn't quite reached catastrophic proportions for all mankind yet.

That was when I noticed the lights were on inside the den of my small house. *Crap.* Apparently, I was wrong about the catastrophic thing.

I hated when she showed up like that, and I was also still a bit grumpy from the tough day fishing. After I opened the two-car garage, I drew out the process of putting my stuff away, out of pure defiance. I dropped a garbage can lid and banged around a bit to emphasize the fact that I was home but not coming inside.

After delaying the inevitable as long as I could, I closed the garage, kicked my boots off, and walked inside. The door from my garage opened up into my meager little outdated kitchen, which was separated from the den only by a counter and some cabinets.

"Honey, I'm home," I shouted. No response. I plodded toward the den — sweaty, fishy, and hungry — and there she was, sitting on the arm of my leather chair, picking at the stuff on my fly-tying desk. As usual, she was dressed to the nines in a formal gray lawyer-type high-powered business suit, her fiery-red hair pulled into a tight bun at the back of her head. Her flawless beauty combined with her inexorable manner would have been intimidating enough in a boardroom if she ever dared show it in a mundane setting. I could also see the raw power she embodied as a kind of intense blue-white aura around her, which beings like her specifically hid from humans because our minds normally couldn't handle it.

She was one of the most powerful of Ned's fellow Protogenoi brethren still here in our world, and she was stunning to behold in every way. Even her voice was beautiful, and I was the only human she'd ever allowed to see her in her true form. I had seen men fold in total acquiescence to her disguised presence and instantly agree to whatever she might ask of them. Those poor fools unlucky enough to witness even a portion of her power and force of will would have gladly sacrificed themselves for her.

I'd worked for her for over three thousand years, so I knew better, and thanks to one of her gifts to me, I was also immune. I stood behind her, hands on hips and a bit bone weary, staring at the various fly-tying head-cement stains on my carpet, trying to figure out the best way to address her, given that I knew why she was in my den. I always knew why she showed up, and it was never good. That was just my nature.

"I will never understand your fascination with the remains of dead animals," she said, dragging a fingernail through the feathers, fur, and flash material I use to tie flies. "There are far easier ways to catch a fish if you must do so." She tossed a bright-blue bucktail back onto the desk, finally turning her head just enough to see me. Even in profile, her face was perfect, far too perfect to be human, and I could see the brilliant blue of her eyes flare with an intensity rivaled only by an electrical discharge. "I take it everything is now arranged to your satisfaction in the garage, Diomedes?"

"Well, sometimes you just gotta shift stuff around," I said offhandedly. "Haven't you ever looked at something and thought, 'Wow, that's really annoying there—I just gotta move it right now'?" I made my way back to my bedroom, mumbling, "I've got some stuff in my den I'd like to move right now," as I took my shirt off.

To be honest, I wasn't really irritated at her, but rather at the situation. Part of me wanted to just go back to being a normal mortal man, but a significant part of me knew what was at stake and refused to let me back down. I longed for the days when the worst thing I had to think about was riding into battle with my men at Troy. But apparently, like my father before me, this entity sitting in my den favored me above all others, so she chose me to fight against those creatures and beings that normal men could not.

My benefactor never cared about the emotional or physical wear and tear that I felt, because she wasn't human. Far from it, in fact. While she'd been known by many names over the course of history, I first knew her back in ancient Greece as the Goddess of Wisdom and Warfare. Immortal or not, I was still human. Given that she was from another plane of existence, I never fully understood her motives, but since she was always intent on protecting humankind, I never really cared why she did what she did.

For the past half century or so, Athena had run the Metis Foundation, one of the most well-respected think tanks in the world. The foundation's primary focus was finding peaceful solutions to human conflict, and they were pretty good at it. I knew her efforts included the Fourth Treaty of Paris, the Treaty of Versailles, the Treaty of San Francisco, and that whole NATO thing. In fact, I Googled "list of treaties" once, just for fun, and realized she'd had a hand in just about every one that came up. My work for her involved less civilized solutions to much less human issues.

"Don't be so brash, Diomedes," Athena said, her steely voice reverberating in my head. "We have business to discuss."

"Can it wait until I'm clean, or is it something I can do smelling like dead fish?" I yelled. I started the shower and hopped in. When I finished a few minutes later, I put on some sweats and a T-shirt and came back out front to where I could hear her banging around in my kitchen cabinets.

"Don't you ever have anything to drink here?" Athena asked before I could make it down the hall.

"Hell, if I knew you were coming I'd have baked a cake. Now, what's up this time, Athena?" I was pretty sure it was going to involve the New York thing, but I never quite knew with her. "And why can't you at least bring food when you come over?"

"Fine, if it will allow you to focus," she said, her voice becoming more stern as the aura of her power surged ever so slightly. "What would you like to eat?"

Score one for me. I walked into the kitchen and leaned against the counter next to her as she stopped searching through my cabinets and glared at me, her blue eyes alternating between the color of the deep ocean in bright sunlight and its shade right after a storm.

"How about Chinese? I know a good place. They have awesome wonton soup and an outstanding shrimp with lobster sauce. Ooh, maybe some pho. Do you like Vietnamese? I know a good place for that, too." I liked to see how far I could push her before she got really mad.

Her eyes began to glow an intense blue, and her aura flashed so brightly I squinted involuntarily.

Time to stop. "Pho is good. There's a place right down the street," I said, lowering my voice while staring down at the counter to avoid eye contact.

"It will be here as soon as they finish it." She walked back into the den. "Can we get down to business now?"

I had no idea if she'd really ordered or how she might have ordered. I also had no idea how she expected the food to get here. As far as I knew, the place didn't even deliver. Even after three millennia, the limits of her abilities were beyond me.

"I presume you've heard about the suicide bombing in New York." Athena shifted her weight from one leg to both while placing her hands flat on my counter. She stared at the cracked Formica in front of her. "There's more to it than the mortal authorities know. Are you familiar with this?"

She produced a photograph from her jacket pocket and passed it down the counter to me. It was a mug shot of a funky hexagonal vase made out of a dull grayish metal. A museum tag in the lower left corner read "Beaker with etched decoration." It couldn't have been more than six inches tall, and it flared out at the top like the horn of an old-fashioned gramophone. It had a few designs etched into it, but altogether it was unremarkable. It was just an old bronze cup.

"No. Should I be?" I said, shaking my head as I slid the picture back.

"It's more than it appears. Are you familiar with the legend of Jamshid?"

"The Persian king, fourth ruler of the world, controlled angels and demons and invented wine — that guy?" I was unable to think of any other Jamshids off the top of my head.

"Correct. Among his accomplishments was the creation of a cup." Her deadly serious countenance might have been frightening the first two jillion times I'd seen it, but now it just underlined the importance of the situation. "A cup that—"

"That supposedly allowed the user to see anything that happened anywhere in this world or any other. Yeah, yeah, yeah. I thought it was supposed to be a crystal ball, not a cup. And I would have thought it would look nicer than an old beer can. I mean, I know lots of guys who seek wisdom in a six-pack, but come on." I wasn't really thinking straight, and I was kind of worn out from fishing five days in a row.

"How long have you and I been doing this?" she queried, glaring at me, a deep furrow forming over her brow. "Three thousand two hundred and eleven years, isn't it? Have you really forgotten what happens to objects from the immortal plane when handled by normal mortals? And have I ever given you reason to question me before? Honestly, you're behaving like that ass Achilles."

The nasty comment about Achilles was just uncalled for, but as she said it, she eyed me the same way a lioness watched its prey just before it attacked. Her eyes glowed intensely. As she closed the short distance between us, I unconsciously stepped backward into the refrigerator. I should have known better than to screw with her when she was that tense. I'd watched her waylay thirty soldiers in seconds at Troy when she was only mildly perturbed.

Then the doorbell rang. *Whew.* Thank Zeus for delivery.

CHAPTER 3

I GRABBED THE PLASTIC BAG CONTAINING the noodles and soup from the confused Asian kid at the door, tipped him a ten—the only cash I had on hand—and returned to the counter to mix the pungent broth, noodles, tripe, and tendons with a liberal helping of sriracha. My boss watched me without reaction, much as I imagined a scientist would have viewed a petri dish, as I prepared the soup and began to eat.

My boss. Of all the Old Ones I'd dealt with over the years, she was by far the strongest I'd ever seen. While she beat Ares in combat on numerous occasions thousands of years ago, I hadn't seen her use more than a mere hint of her powers since our days at Troy. Even then, for reasons still unknown to me, she began to appear in corporeal form less and less often and instead began channeling her power through me. With her help, I bested both Aphrodite and Ares in combat and killed every warrior I faced, even when I was wounded or the odds were otherwise insurmountable.

She told me she'd chosen me because my honor, courage, and wisdom in battle impressed her even when I was a young boy fighting in the War of the Epigoni. Even so, I knew I wasn't her first choice to become her immortal emissary. Originally, she chose my father, Tydeus, one of the greatest warriors of his time. Finding him eating the brain of a fallen enemy on the battlefield at Thebes as he lay mortally wounded, Athena rescinded her offer and let him die for committing such a dishonorable, inhuman act. I never knew about that until she told me some centuries later. I was horrified by the idea that my father would have done something we Greeks viewed as heinous and utterly dishonorable. Given my father's reputation prior to that, I understood why she picked him, but I also understood why she rescinded the offer and let him die instead.

17

I took it as a great compliment that she chose me in his stead. Just after the war ended, in my tent on the beach at Troy, she offered me immortality in exchange for acting on her behalf in all matters pertaining to the protection of humankind. She explained that her strength and power would inextricably bind us forever.

Her overwhelming offer sent my mind racing through the stories about legendary heroes, like Heracles, Perseus, and Bellerophon, and their tales of sacrifice and suffering. I felt dizzy and even sick at the surreal offer, so I refused.

I changed my mind after the tribulations that Aphrodite inflicted on me in revenge for wounding her and nearly killing her mortal son Aeneas. The so-called Goddess of Love prejudiced my wife against me, so I could not go home again. I tried desperately to enter Argos but could not because the men who'd usurped my throne and bedded my wife kept attacking me at her orders. Finally, after weeks of anguish, faced with the prospect of never seeing my wife and family again and wandering aimlessly at the hands of a powerful but petty being for the rest of my days, I decided to take Athena up on her offer to protect mankind from such creatures.

If only I'd known a tenth of what I knew now, I probably wouldn't have waffled so long before I accepted her offer. I had no concept of the variety of beings that existed alongside us, or the true extent of the world, nor did I have any idea how tenuous mankind's position was. I discovered that heroes like Heracles and Bellerophon were more than legends — they were my predecessors. Yet I remained, having survived far longer than any others of my kind.

While I stood there in my kitchen eating the pungent soup, I could feel a buzz begin to grow in my head as visions of centuries spent pursuing the stuff of nightmares raced through my mind. Everything — from other Old Ones trying to subjugate humanity, to the seemingly endless creatures, also native to our world, that simply didn't like humans — flashed through my head like a slide show. I saw creatures — Paranthropoi, or Parans for short — that people believed were mythical or legendary, such as vampires and the races of fae that were so numerous even I didn't know them all.

Those memories just made me feel old, at first, but then part of me recognized the fact that my experiences made me dangerous and very good at my job. I was a Guardian — the bulwark that stood between humanity and anything that would try to alter it.

All at once, the electric surge of Athena's power stabbed at the very core of my mind, and her voice echoed in my head, snapping me back to the problem at hand. While Athena filled me in on what she knew about the bombing, I got the feeling that the situation could prove troublesome, mostly because I'd been around long enough to understand the devastating potential objects like this Cup could have, even if used for a noble cause. It was a good thing I was such a highly trained troubleshooter.

I excelled at clandestine operations, intelligence gathering, and combat. Some historians even credited my theft of the Palladium at Troy as the first commando raid in history, and I could no longer keep count of the number of special-operations groups I'd been involved with around the world. I was as deadly with the archaic weapons I grew up with as I was with an assault rifle, and I had over three thousand years of training and experience in every type of combat that humans, and most nonhumans, could devise. And right then, my instincts were screaming that the mortal authorities knew nothing about the true nature of the Cup situation.

"You need to find who took it and get it back before they try to use it to assassinate a dignitary, disrupt world economies, or worse." She flashed a predatory grin.

"How long do you think we have? If it really was the Cup of Jamshid, then certainly whoever took it knows of its power and thinks they can use it. Can you find out anything more about the limits of its abilities? That may help us figure out what they want it for. Meanwhile, I'll work on who took it. I'll head out tonight. Oh, and do you have anyone set up who can get me access to the investigation?"

"You'll meet with someone from Homeland Security there in New York," she said, sliding an official-looking Department of Homeland Security folder over to me. I could have sworn she didn't have it two minutes earlier.

"Your contact's name and information is in there. I'll be in touch as we find out more about the Cup."

She didn't need me to inform her about my progress. We were linked by more than just her power, though she allowed me to function on my own and respected me enough to interact with me face-to-face, rather than in my head, for most things. Having someone else bang around in your head never worked well for the one hosting. Just look at what happened to Joan of Arc, for Pete's sake.

Athena walked out of my kitchen toward the front door, and I followed.

"What, no 'Good luck'?" I quipped.

She glanced back around the door at me and smirked. It was a playful look that could have easily waylaid a lesser man. "There's no point in involving Tyche in this. Her mother is still upset with you," she said, smiling, and closed the door behind her.

Man. Beat the crap out of one immortal's mortal kid and wound her in the process, and they never let you live it down.

CHAPTER 4

RETRIEVED MY PRIMARY GEAR BAG from my loadout room, which was just my mostly converted walk-in closet in my bedroom. I still kept some clothes in it, but various kinds of weapons took up most of the space. The pack contained a special tactical vest, both of my swords, several knives, emergency gear, my laptop, some black combat clothes, and two sidearms: a SIG Sauer P226 Navy and a Glock 21. It also contained enough extra ammo to make a militia jealous. Even though I knew it would be ready to go, the old soldier in me still took the time to make sure everything in the bag was in order.

Once I was done with my gear, I pulled out a pair of slightly wrinkled khaki pants and a white button-down oxford shirt from the small part of my closet not dominated by weapons and gear. I wanted to dress respectably, figuring I was entering into a full-on Department of Homeland Security investigation that would be further mired by the alphabet-soup crew—FBI, NSA, CIA, DIA, NYPD—and who knew what other agencies. Besides, putting more pressure on Athena's inside man would not go over well, and I needed to give myself an edge by wearing something more respectable than boat shoes, shorts, and a T-shirt. I was not about to wear a tie, though. I was only willing to do so much for humanity.

The last thing I did was pull my Way Stone out of the safe in the closet floor. In the hands of a normal mortal, it was just a highly polished river stone, but in the hands of someone with power or a connection to the plane it came from, the Way Stone glowed a soft greenish color and would open the Telluric Ways—the energy highways along ley lines all over the world. The stone opened a hole in the fabric of space that connected it to some other spot on Earth, enabling me to travel the entire world in a matter of minutes.

Once I got onto Interstate 8, I chose to head east toward one of the two nearest gateways. The particular point I was headed to sat at the base of the mountains about forty miles east of San Diego, just outside a casino parking lot. My other option was just about as far, only it sat to the north along I-5 in the middle of Camp Pendleton. Leaving my truck in the parking lot at the casino was a much more reasonable option than abandoning it along the side of a road at a Marine Corps base, especially with the nation's terrorism-threat level so high.

For me, and for most humans who could use the Ways, traveling along them was a bit random and kind of a shot in the dark, with some minor exceptions. I knew the Ways functioned by creating a link between any two spots on a given ley line. If I wanted to cross to a spot not on that line, I first had to get to a spot that was on it. I also knew from experience that the energy in the Ways would fry anything battery operated if it was powered on when a person entered. But that was all I knew about how they operated. For getting from place to place along them, I had learned a few major paths fairly well over my lifetime, and my route to New York was one of them.

I left early, arriving at my jumping point at about three in the morning because I wanted to get to New York at dawn, and with the time change, I figured it'd come out perfect. I left my truck in the adjacent casino parking lot and marched off into the foothills to find the exact spot I used as my main gateway.

It didn't take long at that time of night to get away from prying eyes near the small Indian-run casino, and I walked to the familiar area—a valley several hundred yards from the lot—unnoticed. The only sounds I could hear in the still night air were cars racing along the interstate a few miles away. While the ground was rocky and uneven, I knew the terrain well enough that I didn't really need the small Maglite I carried. Still, it would have been a really ignominious start to get to New York with a sprained ankle. With my free hand, I pulled my Way Stone out of a pocket on my vest.

In the darkness of the foothills, with only a sliver of moon offering any real light, I had to rely on the intensifying glow of the stone to tell me when I was close to the portal. In the daytime, thanks to the ability Athena gave me to see through veils, I could see those doorways even if they were closed. In sunlight, it was like gazing through crystal-clear but choppy water—no matter how I looked at it or cocked my head, all I could make out was a heavily rippled version of the rocks and desert behind it. The distortion was the effect of the energy from the Telluric Ways pushing in on our world. To find the Way in the dark, however, I had to use the stone's glow to get close and then watch for the warping of my flashlight beam as the light passed through it.

The stone's smooth, glowing surface got significantly warmer once I was in front of the Telluric Ways. I made sure I knew specifically where the portal was, put my flashlight away, rubbed the stone, and focused on opening the portal. I pictured it mentally as opening a door, and the choppy water congealed into a brilliant light.

I stepped into the light and, as always, was instantly overwhelmed by a barrage of energy that assaulted my senses of touch, smell, and even taste. It shut down my sense of hearing except for a persistent thrum that vibrated my entire being. All I could see inside the Ways was a pure white light that flooded in from all around me as I walked along the ley line. It felt like just outside the Ways, only magnified a thousandfold. The coolness of the arid desert at night and the earthy smells of the rocks and dry dirt became so concentrated that I could taste them, and all other sensations were lost.

The overwhelming sensations, as well as the vibrating thrum and uniform illumination, made moving through the Ways disorienting when I first started to use them. I had no sense of direction, but I quickly learned that if I just put one foot in front of the other, I'd advance. As I walked, I knew that each new smell, temperature change, and feeling was a different portal off the line, but I couldn't read their energy signatures well enough to know where they let off. Most of the fairy folk, or fae, could navigate the Telluric Ways like a highway, complete with markers and signs. I, on the other hand, had to wait until I encountered a familiar energy before I stepped through it, or I risked ending up in some random place. The portals I knew best gave off sensations that mimicked those of the locations they opened upon.

I recognized my first door not only by its warm, dry temperature, earthy and herby smell, and relaxed vibe, but also by the fact that it was only ten steps from the point where I'd entered. The gateway opened onto a nexus point in the desert just outside of a small town in Northern Mexico called Caborca. From there, I could open a path in any number of directions, including the one that took me straight to New York and right into Central Park along the tree line on the south edge of Pug Hill. Anyone not specifically watching me when I passed from the Way into the park would think I simply walked out of the trees. The portal into Central Park felt exactly like New York — busy, intense, and prickly with an oppressive barrage of smells of food, car exhaust, cement, and people.

By the time I made it through, it was half past six in the morning, and the streets had not yet gotten crowded with the morning commute. I figured I had just enough time to find a hotel room and make a quick stop for a bagel before I needed to meet my contact at the museum.

Finding a hotel room wasn't hard. I chose one at Fifth Avenue and Eighty-First Street because it was the closest to the Met, but I almost fainted when they told me the room rate. The simple brick façade made it blend in with the rest of the block without much fanfare, so I'd assumed it was a modest hotel. Once I was inside, however, the extravagant lobby's cool marble floor, gilded crenellated molding, rich wood paneling, and fragrant leather chairs revealed otherwise. Athena was probably going to kill me when the charge appeared on my Metis Foundation credit card, but what the hell — I was worth it.

I had arrived way too early to check in, but the front desk clerk offered to keep my bag for me until the room was ready. Before I handed my bag over, I ducked into the hotel's business center and locked the door behind me so I could gather the things I'd need from my pack. I took the folder Athena had given me, a jacket, my Metis Foundation ID, the SIG Sauer, and one of my knives, which was a short tanto-style blade made for me by a Dvergar who taught Japan's greatest bladesmith, Masamune. Sharp didn't even begin to describe it. I hadn't needed to sharpen it in three hundred years.

I strapped the knife to my calf under my pants, put my gun into a shoulder holster, threw on the light windbreaker, and then checked my bag at the front desk. I still had plenty of time to grab a bagel and lox, so I strolled down Eighty-First Street.

CHAPTER 5

WHILE I SAT AND ATE one of the best onion bagels I'd had in years at the shop on Second Avenue just south of Eighty-First Street, I opened the folder to check out whom I was supposed to meet up with.

Her name was Agent Sarah Wright, who, according to her bio, was a five-foot-eight-inch-tall brunette with gray eyes. There was no photo in the file, but I figured that her height and gray eyes would make her easy to spot.

I took my time eating, and before I left the bagel shop, I asked one of the employees for some honey. All they had was a squeeze bottle for tea drinkers, but it would have to do. I pocketed the bear-shaped container, left five bucks behind, and headed back up Eighty-First Street to the museum.

Once on Fifth Avenue, I pushed my way past the sea of photographers, reporters, camera crews, and at least twenty news trucks clogging the street, until I got to the barrier tape blocking off the entire sidewalk in front of the museum. It took me a minute to get the attention of a few overworked cops trying to maintain the perimeter, and I flashed my official-looking Metis Foundation ID badge at them. Surprisingly, they let me pass without too much scrutiny and then directed me over to the mobile command center, which had been set up in four trailers just to the right of the museum's entrance.

As vast as the circus was outside the tape, inside it was worse. It reminded me of an anthill. In addition to the trailers, there were ten vans of varying sizes parked anywhere they could fit. Some of the vans were nondescript black or white vehicles, but most bore the markings and license plates of various federal and state agencies. There must have also been another dozen police cars and trucks spread between both ends of the museum.

For every car, truck, or van, there had to have been at least a half-dozen people milling about, talking, or moving with purpose in various directions. If there was any order to this chaos, I sure couldn't see it. I cringed a bit when I saw that the mobile command center — four trailers, each sprouting a bumper crop of antennas and satellite dishes from its roof — was the most heavily populated area. To make matters worse, none of the trailers appeared to be marked, so I walked up to most officious-looking guy I could find in the crowd and introduced myself.

Dressed in a cheap, wrinkled suit with an NYPD detective's badge hanging from his breast pocket, he was busy berating a crime-scene tech about some kind of protocol, and he completely ignored me. From all my many years serving in militaries around the world and throughout history, I understood chain of command. I also knew that mid-level drones, like that guy, lived to rain crap down on anyone on a lower rung, especially after they themselves had been doused in crap. Above all, I had no illusions about the stress levels of everyone involved in a potential terrorist attack on US soil. But I had very little patience for blowhards and bureaucracy, and after three thousand years of being mostly self-reliant, I did not play well with others — or so I'd been told. It took an act of will to rein in my irritation, by controlling my breathing and staring at my shoes, while I waited.

Finally, after a few minutes, it was my turn. "Whaddya want?" he practically spat at me.

My first reaction was the desire to punch him in the throat. Fortunately, reason won out. "I need to see Agent Wright of DHS," I said as flatly as I could and then pulled out the folder and opened it, pretending to read down the page. "Agent Sarah Wright, to be specific. My name is —"

"I don't give a shit if you're Fiorello La Guardia himself. Do I look like some kinda liaison officer?" He pronounced *liaison* like *lie-ay-zon*. "You're at the wrong trailer, buddy. Ask the guys over there." He pointed with his thumb over his shoulder at the trailer farthest from us.

I weaved my way through the crowd over to that trailer, which actually did have a very small sign taped right next to the door that read "Interdepartmental Liaison," among other things — though, in my defense, it was written in tiny, sloppy script. I walked up the steps into the trailer to find it empty except for one mousy woman with short gray hair. She was busy typing on her cell phone and talking into her headset.

"Can I help you?" she said without taking her eyes off her phone.

It took me a second to realize she was actually talking to me.

"I'm a consultant with the Metis Foundation. My name is Steve Dore, and I'm looking for DHS Agent Sarah Wright." I tried not to sound incompetent after she'd caught me off guard.

She glowered at me as if I'd just killed her dog. "What agency did you say you're with?" she asked, clearly annoyed that I'd disturbed her. She was probably playing Angry Birds.

I flashed her my most winsome smile. She must have been immune because not only did she keep her clothes on, but she didn't even smile back. I wasn't bad looking for a guy who was born in 1230 BC. In fact, I looked exactly the same age as I had when Athena had made me immortal—anywhere from thirty-five to forty. However, I was still over three thousand years old, and interacting with people, particularly women, made me feel it.

It probably didn't help that I had no interest in fashion or style. I kept up with the times, but only as far as I was comfortable. For the most part, I'd always had a beard and moustache, though I kept them short like my hair. While I'd been told I was ruggedly handsome and outdoorsy, I'd always considered myself plain because of my swarthy skin, straight dark-brown hair, and simple brown eyes. Anyway, I was getting used to rejection over the past hundred years or so.

"I'm here to meet with DHS Agent Sarah Wright," I repeated.

"I'll call her, and she'll meet you out front," she said dismissively. Clearly, she was busy, and I was taking up valuable time. *Gotta make those green pigs pay.*

I walked out front to wait and began to survey the museum's grand front façade. It made me think about when the Met was founded back in 1870 and what a big deal its opening was to the city. It had originally opened in a small building way down Fifth Avenue, but the art collection grew so fast they had to move it three years later into a private mansion, and then they built this place.

The building had actually begun as a hideous red-stone gothic disaster that they fortunately covered up with its current design and finally finished to huge fanfare in 1902. Unfortunately, I was off dealing with issues during the Second Boer War in Africa, so I had to read about it in the British newspapers we got weeks afterward, but I had seen the museum before its current incarnation and again when I got back to the city a year after its grand opening.

As I began to think back to what the rest of New York had been like a hundred years ago, someone walked up behind me. I spun around to see... gray eyes. Funny what you notice first.

She was attractive enough to require a double take but not enough to make you stop and stare, at least not dressed as she was with the sleeves of her shirt rolled up, no makeup, and sweat stains under her arms. With her dark hair pulled back in a partially disheveled ponytail, hands on her hips, and wearing latex gloves, she was all business and apparently less than thrilled to be interrupted. I was batting a thousand so far.

"Steve Dore?" she asked without offering a hand.

"That'd be me, yes," I answered, trying to mimic her all-business tone. "Agent Wright, I presume?"

I didn't dare try my charming smile on her, for fear of taking yet another blow to my ego so early in the day. Still, there was something about her that kept my attention, and my reaction surprised me. I didn't even want to think about how long it'd been since my last real date. Dates? What the hell was I thinking? I had to focus, dammit.

Trying to keep things professional, I approached her and offered my hand, which she ignored. I let it hang for a second and then let it fall. *Stee-rike three...*

"What can I do for you, Mr. Dore? I'm a little busy, in case you hadn't heard." She waved a hand toward the museum before returning it to her hip.

"I'm from the Metis Foundation. I was told I needed to see you as an aid to your investigation."

"Leave your ID with Margaret, and she'll get you a visitor's pass," she said, pointing back inside the trailer, her tone starting to relax a bit.

I walked back into the trailer. It took me a few minutes to get Margaret's attention away from her phone, but I won out in the end by pretending my ID badge was a bird flying around. The pure of heart always prevail.

When I finally re-emerged, clipping my visitor's pass to my jacket collar, Agent Wright was in a heated phone conversation. I tried to look as though I wasn't listening in as I waited for her to finish, but it was hard not to overhear. While I didn't hear my name specifically, I did hear the Metis Foundation mentioned several times.

She clearly was not happy about my presence. She hung up with an exaggerated jab at her cell phone and stared at the ground for a moment before facing me as she rubbed her forehead. She had taken her rubber gloves off.

"I'm not here to cause trouble," I said, trying to sound conciliatory. "In fact, I might be able to help. I specialize in stuff that's... well, not normal. I promise not to get in the way, and I'll be out of your hair as fast as I can. I swear." I held my hand up.

"I'm sorry. It's not you." She sighed. "It's just this thing is a jurisdictional clusterfuck, and the last thing I needed was one more group to coordinate with. Follow me."

She strode toward the museum's entrance at a good clip, weaving through people like a skier on a slalom course, then crossed under the second line of perimeter tape surrounding the stairs up to the main entrance and flashed her ID at the guard. I flashed mine as well and followed, trying not to fall too far behind. She had the gait of a damned cheetah.

"You don't need to worry about me," I said as I caught back up to her. "I'll be in and out before you know it, and I'll provide you with any pertinent information I find. I just need to see both crime scenes and all the video footage for two hours before the event, if I can. Oh, and I prefer to work alone."

Unless mundane people really carried out the bombing and robbery independently and randomly, I was sure I'd find some evidence — or better yet, witnesses — to show me who, or more precisely what, had done the crime. The only problem was that the witnesses I was searching for wouldn't willingly show themselves to anyone, including me, without the right motivation.

I didn't expect to find any physical evidence, even of the supernatural kind, because the crime-scene investigators would likely have taken everything, no matter how small or insignificant, so I was putting all my money on a witness. Just as importantly, however, I needed to see the scene myself. I'd seen enough explosions in my lifetime to know the difference between man-made, natural, and supernatural detonations.

"Not a chance, Mr. Dore," she said without sounding distrustful. "We just got word that an extremist terrorist group called Jundullah is claiming responsibility for the bombing. And there are already dozens of crime-scene investigators in there from at least five different governmental agencies. I can get you copies of the security footage, and you're welcome to walk the scenes. Please just stay out of everyone's way."

We rushed up the steps and into the main entrance, and the place was even busier inside. Halogen work lights had been set up on stands all around the Great Hall and aimed down from the balcony above, illuminating every conceivable inch of the immense space with a harsh, hot, and unnatural white light.

At least two dozen crime-scene techs scrambled around on their knees, picking at the marble floor and taking photos, while another dozen scoured the columns and walls with specialized magnifying goggles and metal detectors. Just behind them stood the brass, pointing and second-guessing everything the techs were doing. I doubted they were trying to be obtrusive, but it was a high-profile incident, and I could imagine that nobody wanted to screw up. To make matters worse, the strong lighting heated the area to near sauna-like conditions, making everyone miserable, especially the techs in their biohazard suits.

The smell inside the Great Hall assaulted me at once—it was a cross between ozone and an electrical fire, but there was no scent of charred flesh at all. There were five more biohazard-suited investigators photographing and working around the specific area where the explosion had occurred. My first impression was that it was like nothing I'd ever seen before.

"Put those on, and wear these, but try not to touch anything," Agent Wright said, handing me shoe covers, rubber gloves, and a dust mask. "If you feel the need to touch something, call me, and I'll get you permission. I'll be in the security office."

She handed me her business card and marched off into the fray. As she left, she stopped to speak to the first person she encountered—a tall, lanky man in shirtsleeves with his tie thrown over his shoulder. As she spoke to him, she pointed back at me, he nodded, and then she continued on her way. The guy glared at me and furrowed his brow until another person, covered head to toe in a biohazard suit, approached him and demanded his full attention.

That was my cue.

CHAPTER 6

TRIED TO EXAMINE THE SCENE of the explosion, but other than physical damage, I didn't see much. But even with the volume of techs scouring the area and blocking my view, I was able to come to a few conclusions.

The origin of the blast was obvious: a scorched spot about two feet wide at the center of a circle of busted marble tile that radiated out along the floor over a diameter of maybe twenty feet. The epicenter was about halfway between the four giant limestone colonnades at the entrance and the information desk. Anything inside that area was cracked or destroyed, including all four of the colonnades, part of the adjacent wall to the north, and most of the information kiosk. Predictably, every window along the front and in the entry doors was shattered, and glass was everywhere inside the Hall.

What I didn't see was more telling. There were no small pieces of rubble or any debris of any kind within the blast area, not even broken glass, which was everywhere else. I doubted that even the army of techs could have been that efficient at collecting evidence. It was as if everything in that area had just vanished, including—from what I overheard—the bomber's body, along with three others that were still considered missing.

The part of the information kiosk that had been within the blast radius was also missing, but just outside that area, papers, pamphlets, and maps—all unburned—lay scattered about. Then there was the glass, which was all *inside* the Great Hall, not blown out as I would have expected.

Unfortunately, I'd witnessed my fair share of explosions, IEDs, and suicide bombings, and this was unlike anything I'd ever seen before—by extremists or anyone else. While the bodies had been most certainly removed the day before, there was very little blood

31

left behind and no bits of body on the walls, as when other suicide bombers targeted crowded places.

Initial reports suggested that fifty visitors had gotten caught by the explosion, but there was a total lack of carnage. What blood was present was well outside of the apparent blast radius and was most likely from flying shards of glass or bystanders blown into walls, the information kiosk, or the colonnades opposite the entrance.

According to the reports on the radio, the injured survivors and dead bodies they did find were massively battered and had countless splintered and shattered bones, as well as lacerations from broken glass, but they were all otherwise intact. No one was blown apart.

They were the kind of injuries that would come from intense shockwaves following massive explosions rather than from proximity to any kind of bomb I knew of. The blast must have been hot, too, because it left a scorch mark at its origin point. The charring on the white-and-yellow marble floor didn't spread far, though, so the explosion couldn't have been hot enough to incinerate the bomber. Plus, a simple fire wouldn't have interfered with electronics the way this blast had.

The TV news was already reporting that the surveillance footage showed a blinding blast just before the cameras and all electronics within the building fizzled out, but I'd know more when I reviewed the footage myself. So, what had happened to the bomber? My first guess was lightning bolt because that was the only thing I could think of that could cause a highly localized blast intense enough to burn and crack marble and *possibly* incinerate several bodies. Its impact could also throw bodies around like ragdolls. However, a lightning bolt didn't fit because none of the survivors or any of those killed showed any signs of being struck or even had electrical burns. And as hot as lightning was, it wasn't hot enough to disintegrate a body, let alone four. Plus, I couldn't figure out how it would have gotten through the building without destroying the domed ceiling, which was still intact way overhead.

None of these clues pointed to a conventional IED or even a natural phenomenon. That meant that I wouldn't learn anything by just poking around the Great Hall. I'd have to wait until the interviews with survivors were completed to find out any more details about the explosion, and I didn't have time for that.

I scanned the crowd of investigators but noticed only normal mortals. The ability that Athena gave me to pierce veils and glamours also allowed me to see auras of powerful beings, such as some fae and wizards and witches. In the case of magical veils, I saw the haze of magic around the hidden item or individual. I couldn't perceive the glamours used by many fae, so I just saw the fairy as it appeared naturally, despite whatever deception it may have been trying to cast.

Those beings who possessed and controlled real power — Old Ones such as Athena or my friend Ned to a much lesser extent — couldn't mask it from me, so I saw their auras. The auras of the power emanating from magic users such as witches and wizards were directly related to strength: the stronger the magic user, the brighter the aura. In the case of the Old Ones, I saw both their auras and their true appearances, which in some cases were so overwhelming that they could have been devastating to a mortal mind. Some beings, such as Athena, were benevolent and appeared as simple but powerful humanoids, while the forms of others were more consistent with their natures. True evil was indescribably grotesque. My ability protected me from any damage those visages might have caused and prevented me from being controlled or manipulated as well. My perception was not a power I had to activate; it was simply how I saw the world.

I began working my way to the south end of the Great Hall, keeping my eyes open as I walked. In a building as old as the MET with that many artifacts, I knew there were other beings around, especially certain types of fae, and I had to find them to see what they knew about the bombing. The task wasn't going to be easy. First, it was daytime, and second, the place was teeming with people — neither of which made finding fairyfolk, particularly brownies, easy.

The various types of short fae collectively called "brownies" were actually common. They usually lived in houses and might do chores at night if the residents were nice to them. Brownies — which belonged in the Seelie, or Light Fae, category — tended to tolerate humans and even help them from time to time, unlike their Unseelie, or Dark Fae, brethren. Unseelie Fae despised humans.

Since brownies hated to be seen, they hid behind veils that made them invisible, and they only came out at night, but they could also cast glamours that gave them the appearance of all kinds of household objects. There were a few different kinds of brownies, including Hobs and Hobgoblins, and I was hoping to find the former because the latter were more dangerous and conniving. Either way, they all loved honey.

I reached into my pocket to make sure the squeeze bottle I'd swiped from the bagel shop was still there. It had leaked. *Great.* Now my pocket was a sticky mess, and my rubber glove was covered with goo. Well, at least it was on the glove and not my hand. *Gotta appreciate the small victories in life.*

Before anyone started watching me, I snuck out toward the Greek and Roman art collection, just past the Met Store in the Great Hall, and then skirted around the library to the European sculpture and decorative arts exhibit in the middle of the main section of the first floor. I tried to walk as if I were just another investigator as I progressed through the exhibit hall, keeping a watchful eye out for anything out of the ordinary. There were fewer investigators wandering around the museum the farther I got from the Great Hall, and none of the techs I encountered gave me a second glance once they noticed the ID badge on my jacket.

I was meandering toward the medieval art collection when a collection of ivory statues over a mantel, at the rear of a small room displaying seventeenth-century French furniture, grabbed my attention. The room was laid out to resemble a period parlor complete with gilt armchairs, a red-velvet-topped gaming table, a parquet wood floor, heavy draperies, and all manner of horrendous decorations that I'd hated even back when they were originally in vogue. The ivory pieces, however, were just the kind of items I was seeking, and that room was the perfect place to find a Hob.

The carved figures over the mantel flanked a gaudy clock set in the belly of a gilded horse. They were mundane in nature, but on an end table next to the fireplace was a small, bearded man twisted into some kind of bowl. *Bingo!*

I was sure he was casting a glamour, but it just looked like an impossible yoga pose—Upward Facing Soup Tureen. I stepped over the velvet rope cordoning off the room, walked over to the fireplace, and tapped on the end table near the little fairy's feet. The small figure opened one eye but didn't move. I tapped again.

"I can see you, Hob. I need your help," I said quietly and then pulled out my goo-covered hand and spread my fingers between my face and the Hob. "Man, what am I gonna do with all this damned honey? It's just ruined this jacket. I'm going to have to throw it away."

With that, the little man's other eye opened, but he still didn't move. I could see him eyeing my dripping fingers. His mouth opened, and he licked his lips a bit.

"I'll just have to head to the bathroom and wash my hands and clean this jacket." I crossed back over the velvet rope and walked to the bathroom right around the corner from the exhibit.

Once I was in the bathroom, I checked the stalls to make sure I was alone, locked the door, placed the squeeze bottle of honey on the sink, and waited. It didn't take long. I began to scoop the spilled honey from my jacket pocket with my gloved hand, dripping the sticky amber liquid on my shoe, the tile floor and all over the sink, muttering to myself. The door opened just a bit for a few seconds. I left the bottle of honey in the sink, along with my gloves, and crossed to one of the stalls, keeping my back to the sinks, but I didn't close the door behind me.

The bathroom door opened again and closed just as quickly. In one of the mirrors, I could see the little Hob hopping from sink to sink toward the honey. I waited until he'd started to eat before I faced him. I didn't move. I just watched as the pot-bellied, garden gnome-like figure stood in the bowl of the sink, scooped up the honey with his pudgy hands, and shoveled it into his mouth, smacking his lips in obvious delight. It was like watching a dog eat peanut butter — drippy, gooey peanut butter. It was gross.

I cleared my throat, and the Hob froze. I didn't know if he was trying to turn invisible or if he was trying to morph into a bowl again — neither of which would have hidden him from me — but he took on the same pose he'd held in the exhibit as I walked closer.

"I can still see you," I said, trying not to seem threatening. "On my honor, I will not harm you. The honey is yours, but I am very much in need of some information."

Finally, the little guy squinted at me. He was tall for a Hob, maybe a full two feet in height. He wore red boots and blue denim overalls decorated with a purple hippo. He had his bushy beard tucked inside the bib of the overalls, probably so he wouldn't eat it as he inhaled the honey. He was completely bald, which was fortunate, given how much honey was on his head. He even had honey in the one monstrous ear I could see.

I mimicked his pose, and his eyes widened. "I told you I can see you," I said in a pleasant tone, careful not to sound too disrespectful. "I'm not mundane."

At that, the Hob relaxed his pose, faced me, and began digging the honey out of his ear and eating it. *Ewww.*

"Waste not, want not," the little brownie said when he noticed my revulsion. "Waste not, want not; waste not, want not. Besides, it's the best stuff anywhere, and it's been a while since I've had any." He continued cleaning off his bald pate and repeating, "Waste not, want not; waste not, want not."

He was starting to irritate me with the whole "waste not" thing when he suddenly stopped and gazed at me. "Are you a Guardian?"

"I am. I am Pallas Athena's, and I am currently called Steve Dore."

I learned long ago that Rule Number One in dealing with any nonhuman creature—and some humans for that matter—was to never under any circumstances give out even part of my real name. For those who knew how to use them, like some Parans and most witches, true names were intrinsically tied to their bearers and could be used against them in all sorts of nasty ways—if not for personal gain, then as currency. True names could be used to enact curses or track—or even control—the individual. Names were linked to identities almost as intimately as blood.

"I simply need to know if you saw what happened at the entrance of this building yesterday or know anything about what was stolen or who or what might have taken it. On my word as a Guardian, I only wish to determine if what happened bears specific consequences beyond the mundane to the mortal world I am sworn to protect."

The Hob eyed me for some time. Actually, he alternated between eyeing me and eyeing the honey. I could tell he was nervous—he was far jumpier than a Hob would normally be, in fact. All fae hated answering direct questions, and they rarely gave direct answers, but this guy stopped eating the honey and began looking at the door as if something were going to barge through it at any second. He even developed a twitch in his bushy left eyebrow. It didn't help that I was asking for very specific information, which was inherently valuable to fairyfolk. But that was why I'd brought the honey.

"All you want to know is what I saw?" he asked, now eyeballing the honey exclusively. It didn't escape me that he left out the parts about what was stolen or who took it, trying to change the deal a bit. The twitch stopped instantly, and I could have sworn he was drooling a little. It was like watching a crack addict waiting for his fix.

"Did you see what happened at the entrance at the time of the bombing, or do you know anything about what was stolen or by whom?" I asked again, being as specific as possible. While they never lied, fae had a nasty habit of being vague and misleading if you gave them a chance.

"I saw nothing. I was guarding my charge when the walls shook," the Hob said, glancing around furtively. "I saw nothing, but I felt a foul, unnatural magic."

A foul, unnatural magic. That definitely ruled out anything mundane. "And what of the item that was stolen? Did you see anything or anyone beyond the normal mortals here that day or prior to that day?" I hoped to find out if he had seen any of the Old Ones or any unfamiliar Parans. "Answer me these last questions, and I will leave you alone to enjoy your honey and return to your collection. They are particularly fine pieces, by the way, in pristine condition for items so old."

With these guys, "thank you" would end a conversation in a heartbeat, but flattery could work wonders. I walked closer to the door to reinforce the idea that I would leave as soon as he told me what he knew, and I noticed that the damned thing was still locked. I wished I knew how they opened doors without actually unlocking them. It was a trick that would have come in very handy on my more clandestine operations.

He started hopping from foot to foot, glancing quickly from the door to me to the honey. "Um, yes," he finally said, grabbing the squeeze bottle in a bear hug and jumping to the floor with the graceful ease only the fae can pull off, especially carrying an item so substantial relative to his size.

"Well, what was it?" I asked through clenched teeth while throwing my hands up and cocking my head.

"You said that was your final question and then you would leave!" he screamed at me. "On your honor, you swore!" He began to hop around as if his feet were on fire, hugging the bear-shaped bottle so tight the top might pop off.

Great. "The deal for the honey was three-fold, and you have given me but a single answer, Hob. Do not renege on me." I bared my teeth a little, but rather than snarl, I tried to smile to hide the fact that I would have preferred to punt him across the bathroom. I wasn't sure it worked.

The Hob froze instantly and peered up at me without raising his head. I could see by the sheepish look in his eyes and the pout of his lower lip that he knew I was in the right. If I had let him go at that point, it would have implied I accepted a change to our original deal. He stood stock-still for a long moment and then suddenly began to bounce around like a kitten high on catnip. "We-kuff," he said, spinning around like a top. "We-kuff, we-kuff, we-kuff, we-kuff."

I had no idea what he was saying or what it was supposed to mean, but if his purpose was to try to irritate me so badly that I'd just let him go, he was succeeding. "What the hell is 'we-kuff'?"

The Hob just kept bouncing and spinning around, hugging the bear-shaped bottle like some sort of dance partner.

"What is 'we-kuff'?" I asked again, losing my patience.

"No more questions!" the Hob shouted and then suddenly stopped spinning.

"Fine. Don't tell me." I waved my hand dismissively at him. *To hell with the little bastard.* "What the hell does we-kuff even mean?" I mumbled, mostly to myself, as I walked to the door, unlocked it, and ran upstairs to see where the Cup had been stolen.

The little shit blew past me in a breeze that ruffled my jacket. *Fucking Hobs.*

CHAPTER 7

TOOK THE STAIRS NEXT TO the library up to the second floor and followed the sounds of cameras clicking and people talking. There were more and more people the closer I got to the ruined case where I assumed the Cup had been displayed.

The case was a plain glass-and-steel cabinet illuminated by a single halogen light suspended from the ceiling, mixed in among various other similar cases in a gallery of paintings and photographs just to the left of the museum's main staircase. According to tags on the glass cabinets next to the shattered one, they were all part of a recent temporary exhibit of a collection of Middle Eastern objects on loan from a Sheik Abdul Aziz Al Hamoudi. At the moment, the Middle Eastern artwork was scattered throughout the museum; its more permanent home was under renovation.

The displays in the area were all benign, except for the one case surrounded by yellow tape, smashed glass, and people in biohazard suits. Three forensic investigators were busy collecting evidence in the form of a continuous stream of photographs. They were taking pictures of the glass on the ground from all angles, the items on the floor around the case where the "beaker" used to be, the hall, the remains of the case itself—anything and everything. They were probably not the first crew to do this today.

I stood back to watch. Nothing was unusual—just an ordinary smash-and-grab—but I did notice three surveillance cameras spread around the hall. Whoever took the Cup would have to show up unless the cameras had been fried along with all the other electronics. At the very least, I might be able to see someone casing the display before the explosion.

After surveying the other objects in the collection to make sure nothing stood out, I walked across the gallery to the balcony overlooking the Great Hall. As I peered down, no details stood out beyond the scorch marks and the circular pattern of the blast. From this perspective, the site of the explosion bustled with life, and the Great Hall echoed with all the activity, but I had little real information.

The three techs behind me tried to stifle their laughter by quickly taking a few photos. Had I done something funny? I checked my shoes for toilet paper but found none.

I decided to head back downstairs via the main staircase and then find Agent Wright to get the security footage. As I skirted the investigators, trying hard not to impede their progress, I kept noticing furtive glances in my direction, and one of the techs even snorted a laugh. I surreptitiously checked my fly. It was up. *What the hell?*

I walked back downstairs by the most direct route, digging at my teeth — in case there was food stuck there — with my hand over my mouth and keeping an eye out for any other brownies. I didn't see a single one, nor did I find anything else that struck me as unusual, even in my teeth.

I was pretty distracted and self-conscious at that point, so it took a second for the total lack of anything unusual to dawn on me. With sudden clarity, I realized that whatever had happened there was actually very far from normal. There had to be more than the one Hob in this museum, but clearly something had scared the brownies away from their treasures, even those outside the area of the robbery. Of course, it didn't take much to scare a brownie, but I needed to see those security tapes. I knew that there was some sort of magic involved even if I had no clue what "we-kuff" meant in brownie-ish.

I pulled out my cell and the business card and dialed Agent Wright's number. She picked it up on the fourth ring.

"Agent Wright? This is Steve Dore. I'm finished with my walk-through. If you have copies of the surveillance tapes, I'll pick them up and get out of your hair."

"Ah, Mr. Dore. Okay." She sounded distracted. "Head to the security office, and I'll have them make you copies. The office is to the left of the entrance. Just follow the signs."

I tried to slip downstairs, avoiding investigators, but more and more people sniggered as I passed. It was like running an obstacle course with randomly moving barriers. I stumbled twice, but I finally made it, paranoid as hell and completely perplexed.

The chaos of the security office snapped me back to reality. There must have been twenty people jammed into a room meant to hold four. I counted six museum security guards, twice as many people in shirtsleeves trying to look important—whom I took to be agents of various government organizations—and a handful of techs and cops who all clearly wanted to be anywhere else. I couldn't blame them, because the steamy place stank like body odor and hot electronics.

The dark space was full of monitors—some black and white, others infrared—which offered the only real light in the room except for a couple of work lamps hung under the desks so techs could work on whatever was down there. Another wall was full of electronic equipment with flashing red and green lights and wires strung to several rolling cabinets full of machinery marked with DHS and FBI labels.

A cacophony of voices coming from any number of the guys in shirtsleeves trying to talk over each other, or into radios or phones, echoed through the small area and drowned out every other sound but the techs clacking away on keyboards. I could only guess that they were trying to restore the systems that were blown during the blast. Everyone else in the room looked overwhelmed except Agent Wright, who was standing in the middle of the crowd watching one particular technician intently as he worked. Only two of the cops eyed me when I approached the doorway, and they both glowered, suggesting that another body was unwelcome.

Despite all the electronics I did see, conspicuously absent from the room were any computer hard drives. Those were probably down in the basement somewhere. This room was for daytime monitoring and quick response.

I studied the screens until I located the one for the gallery upstairs where the Cup had been, and I noted its number and designation. I also checked the ones that showed the Great Hall and the other entrances. Whoever had stolen the Cup must have passed through at least one of those fields of view at some point.

Agent Wright began an animated discussion with a tiny wisp of a man in a museum guard's uniform. She towered over the poor guy, who kept jerking back as she poked him in the chest. After a moment, she pointed out the door where I stood and noticed me standing there. She waved me in and finished up with the guard. He left, wide-eyed and sweating profusely. It could have been from the chewing out or the fact that it was about four degrees hotter than the sun in there with all the people and electronics. Everyone was sweating, including Agent Wright.

"St. James, grab me a copy of the security footage for the past seventy-two hours," she said to an older, bald—but well-built— African-American man with a bushy gray mustache, who was suffering a lot less from the heat than everyone around him. He was also dressed in a museum guard's uniform. He and the other guards appeared to be at the beck and call of the agents in the room. "And bring it to me outside. It's too damn hot in here, and I need some air."

She glanced in my direction and arched her eyebrows as one corner of her mouth edged up in a partial smile, which I took to mean she wasn't entirely irritated to see me. "Follow me," she said, walking out past me.

I followed her outside to an area behind one of the museum's fountains, grateful to be out of there. Again, everyone watched me the entire time we were walking. Enough was enough already. If I wasn't already so self-conscious, and if it had been anyone other than Agent Wright, I might have asked if there was anything odd about me. Instead I just stood there, paranoid.

Fortunately, within a few minutes, the guard named St. James made his way out to us with a thumb drive, which he handed to Wright, and then disappeared back inside.

Agent Wright eyed me and sighed heavily, clearly worn out and frustrated. "Did you find anything helpful?" she asked hopefully, handing me the drive.

"Not in so many words, Agent Wright. No." I was glad to have something to focus on other than my paranoia. Unfortunately, my ego kicked in instead. "I highly doubt this was the work of terrorists, but I expect I'll see a lot more on these disks. I have a few people I need to talk with here in town before I leave. I promise I'll call you with any information that may help you. I appreciate the help, and so does the Metis Foundation." I was trying to sound more valuable to impress Agent Wright.

"It's not my first time working with the Foundation. But it is the first time I was told to accommodate one of their investigators by the Undersecretary of Homeland Security for National Protection and

Programs. Clearly, somebody trusts you."

Athena had some pretty impressive contacts. Agent Wright smiled at me, and despite what was going on around us, my pulse quickened just a bit. Then I got self-conscious again and figured I should quit while I was ahead.

"Thanks. I'll be in touch." I started to head back toward the liaison coordinator's trailer to get my ID back. I glanced over my shoulder and noticed that Agent Wright was watching me walk away.

"Um, Mr. Dore," she called, which brought a grin to my face. Inside, I was pumping my fist.

"Mr. Dore, wait," she said, walking after me.

I was simultaneously excited and terrified by the idea that she might actually like me. While at one time in my life women had practically thrown themselves at me, over the last few hundred years I'd rarely been pursued by women who didn't want to kill me. I stopped and grinned back at her, trying to act coy.

When she got to me, she reached around and pulled something off my back. *What the hell?* She smirked into her hand, trying to cover up her amusement, and handed me an old decal — some sort of industrial warning placard. It said, "Danger: Gas Vent Below," in bold red letters on a white background.

My mouth fell open as I grabbed for the decal. She just laughed. Despite being disheveled and sweaty, her laugh revealed how attractive she really was. Even though she was laughing at me, it was worth it for the briefest of moments. Then I stared back down at the sign and thought, *Fucking Hob.*

"Tha-thank you, Agent Wright," I said, trying not to croak.

Fucking Hob. I tried to get out of there as fast as I could and immediately ran into some poor tech carrying a heavy plastic case. I managed to remain upright, but the tech spun around and fell, dropping the case with a thud that made everyone in the immediate area stop and take notice. I tried to retain what little dignity I had left by helping the guy up before I continued on my way. That was what I got for upsetting a brownie.

After I retrieved my ID, I used the walk back to my hotel to regain my composure. It wasn't the first time a Hob had screwed with me, and it wasn't likely to be the last. *It's just what they do. Still, fucking Hob.*

CHAPTER 8

ONCE I GOT BACK TO the hotel and finally checked in, I was a little surprised to see a room that was pleasant, slightly outdated, and nowhere near as luxurious as I'd expected, given its price. Of course, my room was at the lower end of the hotel's price scale and didn't have a view of Central Park. The whole space was decorated in pinks and tans, and the color scheme really set my teeth on edge. In fact, the only part of the room that justified the price was the immense and opulent marble bathroom that was like something right out of a spa.

I pulled out my laptop and got comfortable at the desk. I took a few minutes to make a list of cameras I needed to pay attention to and inserted the thumb drive. The drive had over sixteen gigabytes of data on it, so it took the better part of an hour to find the views I wanted, but once I did, I began with the earliest footage from the regular camera nearest the Cup's display case. I let it play, fast-forwarding through the moments when no one was in view. Over the course of the next few hours, nothing more than people passed through the frame, many of them stopping to view the display that contained the Cup. Even though I could see through veils, I couldn't see things on film that the film couldn't pick up, so I was hoping that whatever had taken the Cup wasn't covering itself.

Finally, after about six hours of watching without a break, an interesting detail showed up in the field of view. The time stamp on the image read four o'clock in the afternoon two days ago—the day before the explosion. Nothing had entered the screen for several minutes, and then two emaciated, long-limbed, small humanoid creatures bolted from the Asian Art Gallery overlooking the main stairs, through the area with the Cup's display, and down toward the Greek and Roman art on the second floor. If I didn't know what

I was seeing, I might have mistaken them for ugly kids, but I knew instantly that they were Hobgoblins. Less than a minute later, a tall figure appeared, slowly making its way along an identical path to that of the Hobgoblins until it stopped at the glass cases in the gallery. It didn't walk so much as shamble.

Once it was completely in frame, I froze the image. I couldn't see an aura or any sign of magic in the video, but it definitely was not human. It might have been at one time, but it sure wasn't anymore.

The figure was well over six and a half feet tall, was dressed in an expensive suit, and had to weigh close to three hundred pounds. Its arms hung limply at its sides, unnaturally still, and it plodded along as if it were being pushed and might fall over at any time. It might have been someone possessed by a controlling entity, or it could have been a zombii or even some sort of golem. If I'd seen the figure in person, I would have known for sure.

In possessions, a spirit resided within a host, but the host remained the dominant figure. I saw possession as two pictures superimposed over each other with one clearer than the other. Zombiis, on the other hand, were simply people controlled by magic, so even though they acted like possessed people, I'd only have seen the one figure surrounded by a magical haze. Golems were creatures made entirely from other objects, sometimes including parts of dead bodies, and held together by powerful symbols and sigils that caused the entire creature to give off an aura of magical energy.

Given that the creature had made it into the museum without much scrutiny, I seriously doubted it was a golem. Both the zombii and the possession would account for the "foul, unnatural magic" the Hob had claimed to feel, however.

I let the video run and watched the thing stand in front of the Cup without moving—not just standing still but eerily motionless. Statues could have taken a lesson from the guy. The nonaction occurred for ten minutes before the image became pixilated and nearly blacked out. It scrambled for a few minutes and then came back. As far as I could tell, the giant form never even shifted. Finally, roughly a minute after the camera fritzed, the shambling mound lumbered back toward the main staircase. I checked the time stamp, searched the other cameras, and found him walking down the stairs. I kept switching camera views to see if the guy interacted with anyone or anything along the way, but he didn't. I couldn't help feeling as though I was missing something.

Shifting my focus, I viewed the grainy images from the infrared cameras. There was only one IR camera near the collection that included the Cup. Unlike most Forward Looking Infrared — or FLIR — cameras, the ones used by the museum were set up to record in gray scale with hot images showing as bright white blobs on a cooler gray or black background. People were vaguely humanoid white blobs in the images, but the cameras could not record detailed pictures, just temperature differences.

I matched the time stamp on the IR camera to the one that showed the shambling giant. He appeared as a massive white ball in the frame, far larger and less humanoid than he would have if he were human. He was either giving off so much heat he would have been a walking furnace, or it was an energy signature. Given people would have noticed a two-hundred-degree furnace walking past them, I settled on the idea that the creature was giving off a huge amount of energy. Either way, he was decidedly not human. That meant my theory of it being either a zombii or a possession was wrong. I was back at square one.

As I watched, the white blob steadily increased in size until another significantly smaller humanoid figure appeared at the edge of the frame, coming from the main staircase. Then, as the smaller form approached the giant, the white blurs of both figures began to merge until most of the screen flashed white. This point in time matched the spot at which the regular security camera faltered. Whatever the smaller form was, it was veiling itself from normal view but not masking its heat signature. And clearly, both figures were connected somehow. But what was I seeing? The footage was getting more and more confusing as I watched.

The image on the IR camera stayed mostly white for three full minutes, according to the time stamp on the footage, before softening back into two indistinct blobs and then to one sizable blob and a smaller humanoid one again. The humanoid form drifted back toward the main staircase and off screen, followed by the broader blob about a minute later, just as it had in the regular camera's footage.

There were no IR cameras in the Great Hall or along the main staircase, so I couldn't track the smaller form past that gallery. Using the regular camera footage, I searched every entrance and exit for unexplained openings and then tracked the giant form into and out of the Cup's gallery and up and down the main staircase, through the Great Hall, and outside. Never once did it turn its head, look around, raise its arms, or do anything other than shamble. People nearby gave it a wide berth but paid it little attention beyond that.

Making some rough comparisons with relative heights from the two different cameras, I estimated the shorter figure was nearly two feet shorter than the shambling giant. I froze the best image of the giant I could find and e-mailed that to Athena along with a clip of the IR footage that showed the figures merge and then separate again. I also e-mailed the photo of the giant to Agent Wright, hoping she could get e-mail on her phone. Within minutes, I got a call from her.

"We saw this guy already," she said in a businesslike tone. "All the cameras malfunction about the same time he's in the area of the cup, but we can track him straight to and from the gallery upstairs but never around the site of the explosion. What'd you see?"

"Call it a hunch. Do me a favor. I assume you guys have facial-recognition software. Have your people do a search for this guy from noon until just before the explosion the day of the bombing. And based on your statement, I assume you guys consider the IR footage at the time he's around the gallery upstairs completely useless?"

"In general, yeah. That is one big brick wall of an ungainly man, though," she said, sounding a bit friendlier. "So you think this guy is involved?"

"I'm not sure if he was behind it, but he was definitely involved. He's on camera in front of that missing cup for quite some time in footage from two days ago. I haven't finished checking yet, but I'll bet you dinner tonight he's in front of it the day of the explosion, too. Run his face through your DHS databases to see if you find any matches, and let me know."

"I will, and you're on," she said enthusiastically. Hopefully, it was the chance of having dinner with me, and not the possibility of a lead, that was making her giddy.

"I'll be in touch if I find anything else," I replied, grinning broadly, and then waited for her to hang up, feeling vindicated and oh, so much better about myself.

CHAPTER 9

THE ONLY THING LEFT TO do was to wait on Athena's information. It was closing in on late afternoon, and I knew she would get back to me no matter the time of day, but if it wasn't soon, I was going to have to cancel the next morning's charter.

My thoughts shifted to the oddness of the scenario—the giant, shambling figure emanating massive amounts of energy and the smaller humanoid figure veiled from view. I ran through it over and over in my head for a few minutes, trying to think of what might be involved, when the little Hob's cryptic word came to me—"we-kuff." At the same instant, there was a knock at the door.

I answered the door and was only somewhat surprised to see Athena standing there. The instant appearances were more impressive when she did them across multiple continents. She was dressed in a black pantsuit with a white shirt that somehow made her flaming red hair, which she was wearing in a tight braid on the back of her head, more vibrant than usual. Her eyes were brilliant blue and sparkled like gemstones, and the smile on her face suggested she was pleased with my progress.

"Oh, it's you. Nice of you to drop in. I take it you got my e-mails?" I walked back to the seating area. I didn't exactly invite her in, but I did leave the door open for her.

"Nice place you've chosen, Diomedes. I hope you don't expect me to pay for it," she said, following me across the room to sit down.

"Hey, it was the closest place I could find, and I'll be out of here by morning. Besides, I know who, or actually, what, stole the Cup."

"Do tell," she said, eyeing me sideways, waiting for my answer.

"The big figure is a Wekufe, so I assume the small one in the IR footage that merges with him is his Kalku," I said, trying to impress her.

"So it would seem," she replied without changing her expression

48

at all, as if what I'd said was common knowledge.

Undaunted by her reaction, I pressed on. "I know that a Wekufe is an entity composed of pure energy that functions like a battery and that a Kalku is a Mapuche Indian shaman powered by the Wekufe, but that's about all I know. I've never faced them before."

"The Kalku provides the Wekufe a human body and thereby a way to create havoc among the living. The pair bonds almost symbiotically. You should know that independent of the Wekufe, the Kalku might already be a powerful wizard, made even stronger by its association with the entity. And you cannot actually kill the Wekufe. You can only disperse its energy until it finds a new Kalku. Underestimate the pair at your own risk." She got up, put her hands behind her back and began walking to the door.

Apparently, we were done here, so I followed, contemplating what she'd said. I'd faced magic users before, but none that were supercharged or carried a cup that could warn them I was coming — assuming the shaman knew how to use it. "Great. Any other good news?" I laughed, trying to hide my concern.

"I assume the human authorities believe the IR footage is anomalous?" she asked without turning back.

"Pretty much, yeah."

"Can you find this Kalku and retrieve the Cup?" she asked with one hand on the doorknob.

"That's why you pay me the big bucks," I replied, shrugging my shoulders. In truth, it was routine. I was used to going after monsters; I just didn't like it when they were unfamiliar ones.

She bowed her head curtly, and the terse set of her lips rose a little at one side into a knowing smirk, suggesting she believed me, but the squint of her eyes suggested I had better do this quickly. "Stay in touch, and let me know what else you find out," she said, opening the door to step out.

"Oh, DHS said some terrorist group is claiming responsibility, so that's the direction the official investigation will head," I said, and she nodded as she walked down the hall.

My cell phone rang. It was Agent Wright. By the time I'd answered it and looked back up, Athena was gone. *Typical.*

"Agent Wright, did you find anything?"

"You could say that. First, the techs confirm that person was also present just before the explosion. He was in an area near the display case, not more than fifteen feet away, when the bomb exploded, and the cameras short-circuited. Second, we got a probable initial ID on the guy, but it doesn't make sense, so we are continuing to check against all our databases."

"What do you mean it doesn't make sense? Did you get a match or not?"

"Well, yes and no," she replied with some hesitation.

"Okay..." I replied, drawing the word out.

She sighed heavily. "One of the security guards, a serious football fanatic, claims to recognize him. Says he's Joaquin del Rios, a.k.a. Jack 'the Ripper' Rios, the retired football player. You know, the middle linebacker for Oakland up until forced retirement for too many concussions two years ago? Swears he saw him both days in person and wanted to get an autograph, but museum policy forbids employees harassing patrons for personal reasons."

"Wow. I didn't expect that one. He should be easy to track down, but what's the issue?" Her identification threw me, considering I was sure the hulking creature was a Wekufe.

"Well, Rios is dead," she replied, exasperated. "Died last week from a brain hemorrhage. Made the news and everything. Something about the controversy around head trauma in professional football players."

"Hey, he was from somewhere in South America, right?" I hated Oakland, living as I did in San Diego, but I had to keep up with the competition in my division. "I recall something about him being the first professional football player from his country."

"Yes, he was from Chile. Hold on a sec..." The sound grew muffled, and I could tell she was covering the phone.

I was right! It was a Wekufe, and it was wearing Jack Rios as a suit. Then my spirits sank when I realized I'd never be able to collect on our bet. How in the hell could I ever convince her the dead guy was involved in stealing a magic cup, which was likely covered up by a supernatural bomb? *Sometimes it sucks being me.*

I walked over to the desk and sat heavily in the bizarrely shaped mesh chair. Over the phone, I could still hear the conversation, but it was too muffled for me to make anything out so I waited patiently, drumming my fingers on the desktop while I tried to devise a way to explain the Wekufe that would sound both believable and sane.

I cradled the phone between my shoulder and cheek and then pulled my gun from its holster under my arm. I ejected the clip and the chambered round then disassembled the gun, laying the parts on the desk in front of me.

"Sorry about that," she said. "I just got news from US Customs that they have no record of him entering the country, and the local medical examiner just talked to the coroner in Santiago and verified that Rios is indeed dead. They're faxing us a copy of the autopsy report right now. There's no way that was him in the museum." I could hear the frustration in her voice.

"What about the bomber—any word on him? Witnesses said he was a young guy and looked Middle Eastern." I figured there was no point in telling her that yes, that really was the dead former football player, and no, the bombing was not a terrorist act. People loved the concept of myths and legends but mostly because deep down they believed they weren't real. Knowing humans were really at the bottom of the food chain changed a person's reality, and for law-enforcement types, that could be very bad. They needed to believe that everything they saw had a rational explanation. I began to reassemble the gun as I listened.

"Nothing yet, but we never really got any good images of him," she said. "We're checking video cameras along the street just to make sure, but that takes time."

"Okay. Look, I've got some people to talk to, but if you find anything, let me know ASAP." I had absolutely no doubt she'd find nothing that would make any more sense than a dead football player as a potential suspect, but I wanted to seem positive.

"Ditto. Oh, and I guess I owe you dinner. Whoever that guy is, he's clearly connected to this mess somehow. I won't get out of here until late, though, if that's okay."

Holy crap! My thumb slipped off the recoil pin and spring as I was inserting it back into the slide, and the spring caromed across the room, ricocheting off the wall somewhere over the bed behind me. Either she'd made a connection without me making up some bizarre story to link that hulking figure to the bombing, or she really did like me. I didn't question it. I wasn't about to push my luck and find out it was just that cops didn't believe in coincidences.

"Ah, yeah, that's fine. Just swing by my hotel when you're done. I'm at the Stanhope Park," I said, desperately trying to keep the excitement out of my voice.

"Yikes—it must be nice to work in the private sector. I'll be in touch."

It took me five minutes to locate the damned spring and pin.

CHAPTER 10

BEFORE MY DATE, I HAD something I needed to do. Like most sizable cities, New York City had a serious Paranthropoi population. Hell, I knew of a huge population of goblins and trolls alone, and at least three giants — and they didn't play football. Most of them lived in the underground tunnel system inhabited by the mole people — the homeless humans who took shelter there. It was not a nice place. It was even less nice when you actually knew what was down there. If some supernatural puppet creature and its human-wizard puppeteer were in the city, then some creature down there would know it.

I began to gear up in my hotel room, starting with pulling on my tactical vest. It was a Blackhawk Omega Cross Draw vest that I'd had specially fitted over my cuirass. The armor was impenetrable and weighed little more than a few ounces. Hephaestus had made it ages ago, and Athena had given it to me. The vest itself was an upgrade from my days in the US Navy as an operator with the SEAL Team Development Group, the Navy's counter-terrorism unit, also known as Team Six.

In fact, most of my gear consisted of modified or updated versions of what I'd used with them. When I needed modern weapons, I still preferred the SIG Sauer and the Glock from my SEAL days. I strapped my Sig to my right hip in a specially designed speed-draw holster and holstered the Glock on the right side of my vest. I stored one of my Dvergar-made knives blade-up in a special sheath on the upper left side of my vest while I strapped the other to my left thigh. I kept a smaller knife in my right boot and an Emerson CQC-6 folding knife in a pocket in my battle dress uniform pants, or BDUs. I also carried a couple of flares and two flash-bang grenades in my vest pockets, and I rounded everything out with a halogen Maglite, a small LED Maglite, knee and elbow pads, and several spare clips for each sidearm.

I threw my swords into a cheap canvas duffel bag to keep them inconspicuous. During most missions, I wore them on my back. They were kopis-style blades given to me by Athena, three feet long and slightly curved. As sharp as my knives were, the swords made them seem dull. With enough force, they could cut through the pressure hull of a submarine.

The last thing I did was wrap my hands and wrists in a few feet of thin leather strips. They were far less restrictive than gloves, and the leather helped me maintain a solid grip on my weapons, especially when they were wet.

When I finished gearing up, I shrugged into a trench coat. It was awkward, and I probably appeared peculiar, like a hunchbacked flasher, but I learned long ago never to go into battle ill equipped. Fortune might favor the bold, but she rewarded the prepared. I ran straight down the hotel stairs, out a side entrance, across Park Avenue, and into Central Park.

I walked south through the park toward the Ramble, making pretty good time. I passed a handful of joggers and a few walkers, but only the walkers gave me a double take before they crossed to the other side of the path. *Smart people.* Once I got close, I walked off into the woods toward a significant rock outcropping. The trees were flush with new spring growth, which provided excellent cover from prying eyes.

There had always been rumors and conspiracy theories about caves and underground facilities in Central Park, but they were based on a kernel of truth. There was indeed a massive tunnel complex under the park, with one entrance just yards off a main jogging path in a substantial granite formation near the Loeb Boathouse. Its main inhabitants were goblins, and they kept a fairly sophisticated veil over the opening. The veil didn't actually disguise the cave so much as cause passersby to not notice it.

Goblins weren't skillful magic users, but like many Parans, they could manipulate humans a bit. Unlike most true fairies, who could turn invisible at will, goblins—who were not fae at all—could not. Instead, they just played with the human brain, specifically the visual cortex, by secreting some sort of chemical. It was a complicated trick to pull off, and not many creatures could do it. That type of veil was so difficult, in fact, that while goblins could keep people from seeing them, they couldn't keep anyone from smelling them. In any foul-smelling area in Central Park, if there wasn't a dead body, goblins were to blame.

The goblin cave connected to the other tunnels that wound through the city's bedrock along dozens of miles of pathways and caverns. They even linked to the subway system in several places. It was the least conspicuous way I knew of to get through the city, and I figured anyone who took a valuable museum piece and knew about the tunnels would use them to escape or hide out. With the exception of the trolls and a group of nasty Kobolds, most of the residents of the tunnels were harmless unless provoked, and I might be able to coax out some information that could prove useful for finding the Kalku and his Wekufe.

Whatever substance the goblins used to block normal people's vision had no effect on me — plus, I'd known about this cave for nearly two hundred years — so I quickly spotted the entrance along the back side of the granite hill. The opening was only about four feet across, so I had to crouch to enter and then drag my duffel bag through after me. It was incredibly dark and musty and had an overriding scent of dog crap, but once I was inside, the cavern opened enough for me to stand up comfortably. It was still light out, so if I was lucky, not much would be awake down there yet.

I took off my trench coat and pulled the swords out of the duffel then stuffed the coat in it and tossed the bag just inside the entrance. I pulled out my LED Maglite and followed the path before me, keeping my eyes and ears open.

The tunnels were mostly natural formations, fissures running through the bedrock in and around New York City. Some of the tunnels were carved out of the granite, but I had no idea when or by whom. The tunnel I was currently traveling through was natural and, though no more than three feet wide, was easily eight feet in height and got taller the deeper the cave descended. The only problem with it was that because of its proximity to the lake, the floor and walls were wet. Combine that with the nearly 15-percent downgrade and the occasional four - to six-foot drops, and footing could be treacherous.

After about ten minutes of slow going, I pulled a crude map out of my vest pocket. According to the goblin who had given it to me years ago, the path to the subway tunnels should have been just ahead. It wasn't. If I couldn't get through to the subway tunnels, I'd have to go right through the heart of the main goblin camp and then through the Kobold settlement. While an individual or maybe even a few goblins could prove helpful and possibly provide information, blundering into the heart of their home would be considered rude and aggressive and probably end all hope of help from them, not to mention piss them off. Wandering into the Kobold colony would probably earn me an invitation to dinner — as the main course.

As I shone my flashlight to examine the tunnel wall to my left where the fork was supposed to be, a unique gibbering echoed up from farther down the tunnel. I didn't speak goblin, but I recognized the language. *Oh well. I guess it's inevitable.* Hopefully, they knew something about the Wekufe or Kalku.

From around the next corner, two goblins appeared, engrossed in conversation. They didn't even react to me at first, even with my flashlight on, but as soon as they noticed me, they froze and glanced at each other surreptitiously.

Goblins were short, ugly humanoids with long arms and stubby legs, brownish-green skin, and lots of pointy little teeth. Since they were mostly subterranean and nocturnal, their eyes were gigantic. And then there was the smell. Public restrooms seemed sweet by comparison.

These two were dressed in clothes from a 1980s hair-band video. One wore zebra-striped spandex pants and a torn white tank top with neon-colored bandanas tied around his head. The other had black pants and no shirt but wore a leopard-print jacket that had to have been made of plastic. I had to stop myself from laughing.

I could smell them releasing whatever it was that veiled them until the acrid scent became so thick that I started coughing. Finally, after what had to have been three or four minutes of the goblins' unsuccessful attempts to confound my eyes and fade into the walls, I waved.

"Hello," I said in between coughs. "I was wondering if you could help me. I'm a bit lost."

They just blinked and stared at me, mouths agape. Their eyes were impossibly wide, but neither said a word. Living in New York, I knew they would understand English, but I was hoping one or both could actually speak it, too.

"Yes, I can see both of you," I said, continuing to cough. "Look, I have this map that a goblin made for me years ago, and I need to get to the abandoned tunnels. It shows an entrance right around here somewhere." I pointed at the wall to my left with my light.

Goblins aren't the sharpest knives in the drawer, and those two were closer to spoons. A few seconds later they both just screeched a high-pitched yowl approaching the range of an air horn, and turned tail and ran.

Crap. I chased after the wailing goblins, keeping an eye out for possible left turns, until the tunnel opened onto a low, dark cavern that echoed with excited gibbering. My little light only projected a narrow beam, but the echoes made the space sound vast, and if the smell was any indication, there were dozens of goblins living right there.

I popped a flare and tossed it, and the gibbering changed to shrieks as lots of goblins skittered about to get out of the way. Man, I hoped it was only goblins I was hearing.

"I mean no harm!" I shouted. The last thing I needed was to set off a full-blown goblin riot and send them scurrying down every tunnel for miles, alerting everything of my presence. My eyes started watering from the stench. I placed one hand under my nose.

"I just ask safe passage to the abandoned tunnels," I said, trying not to sound too threatening. "I'm lost."

The screams and the skittering died down, but the gibbering did not. I counted eighteen goblins, though it sounded as if there were dozens more just outside of my field of view.

Finally, an enormous goblin about my height made his way into the light of my flare. His shiny, solid-black eyes had to have been the size of grapefruits. He was dressed in jeans that had been ripped and reworked to fit his stubby, muscular legs, and to top things off, he wore a Yankees cap. In one hand he dragged an adjustable wrench about four feet long.

"Go," he said in fairly clear English, and pointed back the way I'd come with a freakishly long finger that had a wicked nail on the end. "Now."

"Whoa, whoa, whoa," I said, backing up with my hands up. I made a deliberate show of turning off the Maglite, but I didn't leave the area illuminated by the flare. "I just need to pass through here. If someone would show me where the tunnel I'm looking for is, I'd be very grateful. Very grateful, indeed."

He stopped and blinked his giant eyes at me. Even with that ugly a face, I could tell he was thinking. He cocked his head to one side. "What you have?"

"I don't have anything with me, but I'll get you anything you want. Look, I need to get going. I have to find a Wekufe and his Kalku before they disappear."

"Ah, explosion in museum in park day before," he said, shaking his head knowingly. "They come through here like you, last evening. Kill Etwe, Finfa, and Otha. You chase dem?" He pointed into the darkness at something I couldn't see.

"Yes, I am chasing them, and I will catch them and make them pay if I can find them."

"Kalku very powerful, but Wekufe strong, too. Dey surprise us, kill without warning. Goblins not fighters, not prepared. Otha my brother." His giant eyes became watery. "You catch, you kill?"

Suddenly, I was completely surrounded by goblins. They were swaying slightly, just beyond the light of the flare, which was near to burning out.

"I promise I will capture the Kalku if I can, but I cannot truly kill the Wekufe, and I will only kill the Kalku if I need to. He has information I need. But if you request it, once I have the information I require, I will bring the human back to you for your punishment if what you say they did is true. And I will carry out whatever measure of justice you require. I so swear. But I need to move now."

Part of my job was to be an emissary to the other races with whom we humans shared the world. Sometimes it meant that I had to mete out justice to maintain a balance. In the case of unprovoked murder, I would gladly have returned the culprit for punishment. I might not have liked all the other races we shared space with, but I treated them with respect. There was a single exception to that policy, though: I'd kill every vampire on sight if I had the chance.

He eyed me suspiciously for a few seconds, and then his face softened. It was the goblin version of a smile. "Very well. Skeefa will guide you. If you catch, you bring back. Dead or alive."

In the failing light of the flare, the giant goblin turned and focused on something back in the crowd. He spoke to one of the smaller goblins dressed in overalls behind him. "Skeefa, take him where Kalku go yesterday. Be fast."

He turned to me. "We make deal. We hold up our end, you hold up yours. Go." He dismissed me with a flick of his wrist as the flare died and the cave reverted to total blackness.

I switched on my light and saw the small goblin in kids' overalls bobbing and weaving in front of me. He waved for me to follow. "My name Skeefa," he squealed. "Come, come. Let's go." And he took off like a shot.

At first I lost him and was momentarily frustrated, but once we were out of the giant cavern and back into a tunnel, my little LED Maglite provided plenty of light, and I could follow him. For such stubby legs, the guy could fly. Flat out, thanks to Athena, I could run a forty-yard dash in just over a second, and I could keep that speed up for ten minutes without collapsing, but I was just barely keeping up with the little guy. Although we ran for less than two minutes, we must have covered at least a mile by the time he stopped. The goblin pointed at a wide crack in the wall of the tunnel off to the left.

"Kalku go dis way, through here." He bobbed up and down and bared most of his pointy little teeth in what was probably a grin. Those guys could give a shark dental envy. "Don't know after dat." The little guy was so ugly he was almost cute.

"Thank you," I said. "I will bring him back."

To call the crack in the wall a tunnel was generous, but apparently it was the path I needed to take. If that Wekufe could make it, as broad as he was, so could I. I ducked through and squeezed along for just a second, having to unfoul the swords on my back from the craggy rock twice in the tight passage before it opened up.

The air on the other side was cooler, though more metallic and oily and tinged with the distinct odor of rotting flesh. The ground was also flatter. I swung my light around and found I was standing on a carved stone ledge alongside a pile of unused subway tracks.

As I tried to figure out which way to head, gravel crunched heavily to my right, followed by a grunt that could have come from a rhinoceros. I wheeled my light in the direction of the sound, and a long, dark shape swung right at me.

CHAPTER 11

A S FAST AS I WAS, I never stood a chance. The blow caught me straight across the chest with a metal-on-metal *thunk* that echoed through the area like a gong and sent me flying backward through the air. I landed on my butt on the rough, uneven, rocky ground, but other than dropping my flashlight, I was okay. Thank Athena for that cuirass. I was now in total blackness except for a tiny area, fifteen feet away, illuminated by my dropped light.

I didn't have time to take stock of what had just happened. On instincts honed by more than three thousand years of combat, I rose to a crouch and began moving to my left through the darkness. Not knowing what or how many I was facing, I pulled the Sig from my hip. I trained the gun on the area where the anonymous creature's blow had come from and fired twice at about head height, hoping the muzzle flash might blind it temporarily. The gun's report echoed like thunder and, for the briefest of moments, lit the area around me like lightning.

The flash revealed a massive, upright, humanoid creature with a thick arm wielding what I thought was a very long stick. The thing bellowed an inhuman roar that rattled on and on as it reverberated off the rock walls, rendering me nearly deaf for a moment. Fortunately, the flash—and possibly the shots—threw it off enough that its next swing sailed high and missed me, but it was close enough that I could feel the breeze across my scalp. I tucked and rolled farther to my left, trying to circle wide to avoid being cornered, desperately trying to hear over the ringing in my ears in the darkness. To make matters worse, that thing could clearly see in the dark, and I couldn't, and I only had the one flare. Plus, I had no concept of my surroundings other than an assumption of size that was based on the echoes.

I crept along, unable to see and hear, as I dug into my vest for my halogen Maglite. Switching it on, I aimed where I'd last seen my attacker. The intense light surprised it, and it dropped its weapon—a ten-foot-long section of subway rail—with an explosive, metallic clang, threw its right arm up over its face, and let loose another deafening roar.

It was a troll, and judging by its bellows and the fact that it instantly attacked me rather than simply trying to catch me, it was pissed. As I circled, it was hard to miss the fact that its left arm was missing just below its elbow, and its right leg was badly burned and damaged below the knee with a jagged bone jutting through the flesh of its calf. The injuries were fresh, probably inflicted by the Kalku the day before. For all the troll knew, I was the same intruder, coming back to finish it off.

Just great. Despite its injuries, the dull black creature was easily twice my height and built like a linebacker. Its freakin' legs were thicker than my chest, and given time, it would heal completely, including regenerating its missing arm. In the meantime, it was seriously injured and trying to defend its territory from a threat.

Without hesitation, I fired three rounds into the center of its mass just below its raised arm. I would have aimed for the head, but it consisted of a relatively small cranium and a thick skull and was currently shielded by that log of an arm.

The nine-millimeter rounds hit the troll's chest in a tight cluster but didn't even penetrate its skin or even faze the creature, so I slid the gun back into its holster and worked on my next brilliant idea. Trolls had hides as thick as a walrus's, covering a mass of even denser muscle. I would have had to use armor-piercing rounds and a high-powered rifle to do any real damage with a gun.

To make the situation even worse, my bright halogen lamp was not only making the troll angrier but was also forcing it to keep its arm up to protect its one and only weak spot—the eyes. Keeping low, I crept sideways, trying to get a feeling for the space we were in. I knew the cavern was broad, but I couldn't risk taking my light off the troll to look around. Twice the troll blindly swung out at me, trying to connect, but I was too far back and too low.

I feigned a quick juke to the left, screamed to get its attention, and then dived back to the right to get around it. As I pushed off, my footing gave way on loose rocks, and I skidded on my back right into the troll's feet.

The troll immediately raised its injured leg and stepped on me. Its gigantic foot caught me square in the chest, pinning me to the ground. Even with a healthy leg and all of its weight behind it, the troll could never have bent my cuirass, let alone crush it, but I was still stuck. I dropped my flashlight, grasped its heel with one hand and its toes with the other, and lifted and twisted the injured limb until the troll let loose a high-pitched screech and lost its balance, falling to the ground with a crash.

I grabbed at my flashlight as I rolled free and got my feet under me. Without caring about the direction, I scrambled to get out of the troll's reach. Once I was out of range, I noticed two stacks of wooden rail ties and rails up against the cavern walls and a pile of pea stone, for leveling the ties, a few feet away. I was now at the dead end of some sort of abandoned storage chamber for the building of the original subway system. The old underground rail line I sought had to run somewhere nearby. I just needed to find my way out of this cavern.

As the troll clumsily got back to its feet, I saw the crack I'd come through just over my shoulder. Above us, the ceiling disappeared into the darkness, and all manner of loose stones littered the uneven, rocky ground. The oblong chamber was no wider than twenty feet at its center. The cavern's mouth lay some sixty feet away—fifty feet beyond the troll that currently blocked my path to it. Now back on its feet, the beast formed a perfect roadblock, stumbling around trying to avoid my light as it swung its arm blindly trying to find me.

At least I had a better sense of my surroundings. I pulled out one of my swords and kept the flashlight aimed at the troll's face. It continued to swing wildly at me but never came close to landing another blow.

Trolls were bloodthirsty, violent, and indiscriminate in the carnage they created, but this would hardly be a fair fight. I'd never had an issue with killing, but I didn't relish killing an opponent that was simply defending itself, not to mention severely injured.

I crouched and waited until it took another wild swing, and then I jumped, spinning my sword around to plunge it into the creature's unprotected chest. I connected solidly right at the neck, ramming the sword to its hilt and slicing down as I fell to the ground. Given that the troll was probably twelve feet tall, I had a good four feet to drop, which cut the poor creature in half, neck to groin. Its entrails slid out onto the stone floor into a rank and steamy mass around my feet, up to my knees.

Fortunately, the force of my attack made the troll fall backward, away from me. It was dead before it fell to the ground with a jarring thud, its badly broken leg twisted awkwardly underneath its bulk. The metallic, rotted smell of troll offal at my feet filled the chamber, nearly gagging me. Knowing it would have eventually healed from its injuries, I felt bad for killing it, but I just didn't have any other choice.

I pulled the sword free from the troll's gut and then wiped it off on the pile of old wooden rail ties before returning it to its sheath on my back. I found the light I'd lost when the troll hammered me with the subway rail, and I picked it up. I glanced back at the troll's missing arm and damaged leg and then headed out through the cavern's mouth, wondering how strong the Kalku was to have done that kind of damage.

CHAPTER 12

QUICKLY FOUND THE OLD ABANDONED subway line just outside the troll's cavern and then switched back to the smaller light and fitted it with a red filter as I progressed. I didn't want a blazing torch giving me away fifty yards up the tunnel. Plus, the filter helped preserve my night vision. I didn't bring night-vision gear because I knew there wouldn't be enough ambient light to magnify.

The old subway tunnel continued unobstructed for quite some time. The uniformly carved circular passage was about ten feet in diameter with narrow gauge track laid along the floor, probably to accommodate the hand trucks used to cart people, tools, and debris from the dig sites. This was definitely not one of the working lines.

After an hour of creeping across level ground, the tunnel sloped upward somewhat, and the air soured and warmed. It was a foul combination of sweat, fire, and rotting food, and I could make out random noises, too. The sounds were indistinct — the odd cough and metal scraping metal — but there were no voices. I had to be getting close to one of the areas inhabited by the mole people, where hopefully, I could at least find out if the Kalku had passed through. I began to hear the faint but distinct reverberation of the subway through the walls. The closer I got to the source of the sounds and smells, the more the ambient light increased. It got bright enough that I didn't need my flashlight anymore, so I switched it off and returned it to its pouch. I made it to the end of the tunnel and found a spot where part of the wall had collapsed, forming an opening with the source of light coming from the other side. I ducked behind the left edge of the fissure then crouched down and stuck my head out just far enough to peer out.

The crack opened onto a massive cavern with warm, fetid air reeking of human waste. Pits, drums, and an old barbeque grill held bonfires that were each surrounded by a few people. At least I was hoping they were people. They were all sitting remarkably still, and each one had an odd black haze around his or her head. My first thought was that it was some kind of magic, but it was greasier and somewhat sloppier than my previous experiences with enchantments.

I counted twenty people around six fires, none closer than forty feet to one another, and the closest one to me was easily seventy-five feet away. I could make out three other exits from the giant cavern. I sat and watched for a few minutes, taking stock of the situation. Absolutely no one shifted more than to cough, not even when a high-pitched, metallic clatter began rattling up a tunnel to my left about a hundred feet away.

I lowered myself to the ground and began lizard-crawling slowly toward the nearest group, staying as low as I could and close to the cavern wall. This back part of the cavern was pretty dark, but I didn't want to start a panic—if that was even possible. I had little doubt that these folks had seen more bizarre stuff than me come through the crack I'd emerged from, but if they were under some sort of spell, they still might attack an intruder on sight. Given the surroundings, even if they just panicked, some of them could get seriously hurt, too.

As I crept closer, my suspicions were confirmed. Each person— and they were definitely people—had a variety of implements within reach: axes, wrenches, hammers, and all manner of old railway tools. I crawled up to a fifty-five-gallon drum lying on its side about thirty feet from where three men and one woman were seated on crates and pallets around a small fire. A makeshift spit spanning the flames held a variety of burnt lumps. From my vantage point, I could see all the people had matted and tangled hair and were dressed in tattered and dirty clothing and covered in sweat, dirt, and soot, but no one moved or talked—they all just stared blankly into the fires. Every single one of them was sallow and malnourished. This close, I could also see that the greasy haze that covered their heads oozed instead of flowing the way normal magic did. I had the impression it was amateurish— powerful but still unpracticed. That feeling was reinforced by the fact that the fog was very loosely connected to the individuals, moving and warping around them rather than secure and tight to the head.

At one point, a lone figure pushing a cart shuffled into the cavern from the tunnel—the source of the racket. No one cared; they just kept their gazes fixed on the fire pits. It was as if they were all stoned. I was sure it was some kind of magic, but I wasn't sure how to help them or even if I could.

Of course, the guy had to steal a cart with a loose wheel. Its rattle on the stone floor reverberated off the cavern walls like a train. I couldn't see what was in the cart, but the man pushing it — with his matted beard, torn and dirty jeans, plaid shirt, and ratty, drab-olive government-issue jacket — had the same thousand-yard stare and dark halo as the others. He shuffled past everyone toward a tunnel directly across from me and disappeared down the passageway. Seconds later, the deafening clatter stopped.

I could hear a voice echo up the passageway the cart guy had disappeared down, though I couldn't make out what it was saying. Given the total lack of response from the cavern's residents so far, I decided to risk it and get up and make a move. I slowly rose from my prone position and just stood there, waiting for some reaction. No one flinched. I took a few steps toward the passageway across from me. No one noticed. I did a little jig. No one even blinked.

What the hell? I walked to the group closest to me and approached an old woman. I stood behind her and cleared my throat. I waved my hand in front of her face. Still, no one budged.

Her eyes were completely milky white and opaque. All three of her companions were the same. This close, I could definitely tell that the quasi-nebulous greasy black haze around their heads was ill formed. Still, it had to be magic, and the miasma was the residue of the spell.

A spell suggested a magic user, and that likely meant the Kalku had come through here at some point. Either that, or it was a total coincidence that these people ran into another sorcerer. Granted, group mind control wasn't usually part of a shaman's magical repertoire. They mostly focused on divining or healing or communicating with spirits, but then, this situation had the feel of someone who wasn't that familiar with mind-control spells.

I hurried after the cart pusher and stopped at the entrance of the tunnel when I heard a low chanting. The cart pusher reappeared in the passage, without the cart this time, and began to approach me. Like the others, his eyes were clouded over, the haze surrounded his head, and he shuffled right past me without concern.

The dogleg in the tunnel he'd emerged from was illuminated by flickering light from somewhere farther down. I could smell the fire, and it was fragrant, almost pleasant, like burning herbs or incense. The chanting was mostly unintelligible, and the few sounds I could make out as words were in a dialect I didn't understand. It sounded vaguely Spanish.

My mind raced. Could the Kalku still be here a day after stealing the Cup? Why would he have remained in New York? I pulled my Sig, ejected the clip, and replaced it with a fresh one as quietly as I could. I'd only used a few rounds, but even one extra bullet could be vital in a fight.

The problem was I had no idea how far back this pathway extended or what it opened onto. Plus, if that was the Kalku, the Wekufe had to be very close. I wasn't familiar enough with either to be in a position to have to take them both on at the same time in a close-quarter battle. And I had no idea if he had hostages or more of those zombiis with him or even if it was the Kalku at all.

My only option was to draw out whatever was in there. I surveyed the main cavern for a position that provided good cover and a full view of this lighted passageway. To my far left, about thirty-five feet away, was the last entrance into the cavern, obscured slightly by a partially collapsed ceiling. The crack I'd come through was directly across from me while the path the noisy cart guy had used was far off to my right, more than a hundred feet away and on the other side of all the bonfires and zombiis.

The wall between the partially collapsed passageway and the lighted passage was curved just enough that I'd still have direct line of sight between the two positions. If I took up a position just behind the fallen rocks at the mouth of that cave, the bonfires would be behind anyone or anything that came out from the lighted passageway.

I ran to the mouth of the collapsed tunnel and ducked behind the rocks. I couldn't hear or smell anything odd down the passageway behind me, so I figured I'd take my chances. I got into a combat kneeling position and pulled my Sig.

"Hey!" I shouted at the top of my lungs, hoping the entranced people wouldn't suddenly decide to come to life. I waited for a few seconds, and the chanting from the tunnel abruptly stopped. The chanter knew I was there.

CHAPTER 13

"YOU IN THE CAVE, STOP what you're doing, and come out with your hands over your head!" I shouted. *What the heck — it works for cops on TV.*

I didn't dare take my eyes off the tunnel, but I could tell none of the other cavern dwellers had stirred. A low, hushed voice and a rocky scraping sound emanated from inside the tunnel after a few minutes.

My plan was simple: identify who or what was down that passage, take it out quickly if necessary, and try not to die in the process. The best-case scenario was also the worst — it would indeed be the Kalku, and he'd still have the Cup.

"Come out calmly, and we'll resolve this situation peacefully," I yelled. "No one needs to get hurt."

At that, I began to hear shuffling coming up the passage. It was a slow but steady sound that increased in volume. I still couldn't see anything, though.

"We know you're in there. Make it easier on yourself and just come out." I figured I could throw out the "we," since who or whatever was down there had no idea how many of me were up here.

As the shuffling got louder, a shadow emerged from the tunnel mouth, followed abruptly by a substantial figure. It shambled out into the open, looking around deliberately and then focusing directly on my position behind the rocks. It was a man well over six and a half feet tall, probably weighing as much as two seventy-five, with "football player" written all over him.

Although the thing was dressed exactly as it had been on the videotape from the museum, it was encased in a brilliant red aura that flared to white along its edges. The emanation conformed to the shape of its body and was so intense it was as if someone were holding a flare behind him. I could make out an intricate covering of softly glowing tattoos all over rotting skin, including up along the neck and face and down its forearms and hands. Bright bands of what I assumed was energy were escaping from places where its skin was torn or cut, and its eyes glowed radiant white. In fact, most of its head glowed as if lit from the inside like a jack-o'-lantern.

Its gaze never left my hiding spot as it moved farther out, stopping maybe six feet inside the cavern. While it knew exactly where I was, it didn't act all that concerned. Once it stopped, it simply stood there staring at me with those glowing white eyes. I knew I couldn't kill it, so my only hope was to hit it fast and hard and weaken it before I had the misfortune of finding out exactly what this thing could do.

I squeezed off three quick rounds into its head, spraying bits of bone, rotting flesh and brain matter into a nearby bonfire with a sizzle. The spellbound people around the fire didn't move, and the creature didn't falter even though the shots had removed most of the right side of its head, leaving only the glowing mass underneath. The parts of the right side of its face and skull that remained attached hung down onto its shoulder and chest like the peel of a banana. Only the left eye, cheek, ear, and jaw were still intact.

I lowered my aim and put three bullets in the left side of its chest, where a person's heart would be. Gaping wounds opened in its chest and back as the bullets passed through its rotting corpse and into the rock behind it. The hollow-point bullets I preferred were designed to create massive damage, but that thing barely noticed, and they were passing through its form so easily that I now had to account for any of the mole people that might end up behind the creature. Still, if I could do enough damage to the Wekufe's human shell, then maybe that would weaken its presence and limit the Kalku's power before I had to face him, too.

I took aim at the Wekufe's massive left shoulder, making sure the area of impact behind it was clear, and fired four more times. The shoulder blew into shreds, leaving its arm dangling by the clothing that covered it, and a bit of rotted flesh.

Despite the damage, the thing didn't react at all—no show of pain, no building anger, nada. It just stared at me with what was left of its mangled head, with a near-blinding glow emanating from the missing parts. The other wounds glowed so brightly white that the bonfires behind the creature were dull by comparison. Even as the flesh fell away, none of the energy dissipated or bled off but instead just held the humanoid form it wore. *Screw it.* At least it wouldn't be able to swing at me with that tree trunk of an arm if I did finally piss it off.

That was when the zombii-like residents of the cavern got up, grabbed their weapons, and headed toward me. *Yikes.* In addition to the Wekufe, I now had two other issues to deal with. First, assuming the Kalku was still down that tunnel, I had to prevent him from escaping, or I'd risk losing him and my only link to the Cup. Second, I was about to be attacked by a group of people who were not acting of their own volition.

On a field of battle, my attitude was unwavering: *Never let an enemy live.* Thanks to Quintus Smyrnaeus, it had become a highly contested piece of battlefield lore. I felt no remorse for Ilioneus that day long ago when the old Trojan implored me for mercy and I killed him instead—we were at war, and he, at least, was acting of his own accord. But the mesmerized people in the cavern were not at war, and I'd been entrusted with protecting normal mortals from any creature or being that would do them harm. Yes, I could have easily killed those people, especially in their present lackadaisical state, but they were innocents.

I thought about backing farther into the crevice I was in to create a bottleneck for my attackers, but it would also have created a barrier for me if the Kalku tried to make a break for it. My only real option was to take the fight to the zombiis. I put my Sig back in its holster, got up, and sprinted at the nearest person.

I covered the hundred and fifty feet between us in just under two seconds. The guy I ran for was not only the closest to me but was also on the opposite side of the cavern from the Wekufe, which was now just over a hundred feet away. He was a middle-aged man in poor health wielding a maul, and I punched him with an open hand to the chest so fast he never had a chance to react. He fell backward, dropping his weapon as he landed with a thud.

Without slowing, I picked up the maul, smashed it against the floor to break off the heavy metal head with a gunshot-like crack that sent sparks flying, and attacked the next zombii. I used the wooden handle to disarm him then spun it around and brought it under his legs to knock him over. I broke the pickaxe off the end of his weapon and then started to work with both handles, disarming and incapacitating the remaining cavern dwellers as quickly as possible.

I tried to do as little damage to them as I could, focusing on limbs, but contact with the hard wooden handles at my speed tended to break their already brittle bones. I met no resistance from anyone, and it took me less than a minute to put a stop to all of them.

Having worked my way across the cavern to disarm the zombiis, I was now standing among the bonfires, about ninety feet behind and to the right of the Wekufe. I tossed aside my makeshift clubs as I once again faced the energy creature wearing Jack Rios as a suit. Despite my actions, it still hadn't taken a step or changed from its original position. Seeing the twenty people on the ground around me, I made a mental note to have Athena send in medical help later. They didn't deserve to get hurt, and I hated it when people took advantage of weaker individuals — it really pissed me off.

I focused on the Wekufe and made a show of pulling my swords out over my shoulders, sliding the flawless metallic blades from their leather scabbards with only a soft, bell-like knell. It had to turn around to focus on me again, its mangled arm dangling uselessly at its side and its ruined head and gaping wounds glowing from its true form underneath.

"Let's go, Sparky. You and me." I crouched low, holding my swords out to my sides with the tips down. I slowly circled back to my right, dragging the tips of my blades over the stone floor, creating sparks. I was being dramatic, but mostly I was wasting time, trying to get the thing to make the first move.

It wasn't working. All the Wekufe did was track my movements, constantly turning to face me. Once I had reached the point where the Wekufe was between me and the tunnel it had emerged from and was less than fifty feet away, I stopped, spinning the swords low. I had no idea what this being was capable of, so I wasn't sure what type of defense to prepare. Not that I was a purist, but I figured it was best to keep my options open until I had a better idea.

"What's the matter? You afraid of me?" I said.

The problem with most nonhumans was that they didn't have human emotions. This thing very well may not have had any concept of fear or even an ego to bruise. It wasn't going to stop me from trying, though. If I could somehow get a rise out of the magical battery, then I'd know I was in its head. "Good God. You stink, too. Is that fear or just a lack of hygiene?"

In the blink of an eye, the glowing form of the Wekufe, visible at its head and along its wounded shoulder and arm, flared with a white-hot intensity as some sort of force erupted through it and threw me like a rag doll against the cavern wall behind me. Force is a simple function of mass and acceleration, and I covered the twenty-five feet damn fast. I smashed into the wall with a jarring thump, my armored back taking most of the blow, but the impact jerked my head back against the rock. I fell to my knees, seeing stars, but managed to keep my swords in hand.

I shook my head to clear the cobwebs and steadied myself with my swords as I tried to focus on the Wekufe. I couldn't be sure if that attack had come from the Wekufe directly or from the shaman somewhere behind it, using its power to magnify the effect. Either way, with my bell rung, three hazy versions of the Wekufe now stood about seventy-five feet away amidst a host of stars and tweeting birdies. *Nice.*

"Phew! You two guys are gonna have to wait. I gotta deal with him first," I said, pointing my right sword at the middle Wekufe as I got to my feet.

I shook my head again. The stars receded, and the three burning figures started to coalesce back into one. As my vision cleared, a small man in a poncho and a bizarre feathered headdress was standing just behind and to the right of the Wekufe. That was not good.

CHAPTER 14

THE LITTLE SHAMAN REMINDED ME of a Native American version of Moe Howard from *The Three Stooges*, except that he was wearing a dark-brown poncho with a white geometric pattern. His odd headdress was bright orange with a red design along its length, and a full plume of long feathers sprouted along his forehead, projecting up and over his head. Including the foot-long plume of feathers, the guy couldn't have been over six feet tall and was easily a hundred years old.

He drew alongside the Wekufe, and the energy spirit began glowing far more intensely than it had a few minutes earlier. As the fiery-red glow increased around it, the energy began to spread toward and then envelop the Kalku, who was now standing less than a yard away from the creature. That had to be bad. Plus, it really bothered my eyes and made my splitting headache worse.

"You sure you don't want to talk this whole mess out?" I asked, staring down at the ground to save myself the discomfort of staring into the blazing light surrounding the pair. "No need to make me kick your ass. All I want is the cup you took and maybe to know why."

The glow in the room flared, causing me to squint as my feet left the ground again. This time I only had a few feet to fly before I smacked into the rock wall behind me, so the impact was much less than before. Not only did I manage to keep my head from snapping back upon impact, but I also landed on my feet.

I was never very good at diplomatic solutions. I took two steps forward for momentum and threw the sword in my right hand at the Wekufe as hard as I could and then sprinted right, knowing that a magic user couldn't focus a spell on me if I kept on the move. The sword impaled the Wekufe low in the chest and passed straight through, releasing a huge, noiseless flash of light, but the creature

72

still managed to stay upright.

The Kalku raised his left arm in my direction and extended it toward me, his hand twisted into a claw. I stopped just long enough for him to focus on my position and then took off again, continuing to my right, trying to flank them. I drew my Sig as I ran. The light in the cavern began to dim as the flames from the bonfires at the opposite side of the cave were drawn toward the Kalku and Wekufe and then diminished. I could see the witch doctor gathering the energy from the fires as a ball of flame engulfed his clawed hand.

Oh, shit. The cavern lit up as the bonfires blazed again, and the diminutive shaman's hand unleashed a spout of yellow flame the diameter of a telephone pole and struck the spot where I had been, shattering the rock wall into rubble. He then drew the blaze sloppily around the cavern like a flamethrower, charring and cracking rock as he tried to catch up with me. He flailed around like a lone fireman trying to control a high-pressure hose. His inability to control the spell precisely slowed him down, and it was clear he had limited experience with offensive magic.

I continued to move, without slowing, toward the wizard. Once I was some forty feet to the left of him, I jumped straight at him with my sword raised overhead and my Sig aimed roughly in his direction. He was still dragging the gout of flame around twenty feet behind me, trying to catch up. In the instant it took me to cover the distance between us, I emptied the clip from the nine millimeter into him. Everything happened so fast that he barely reacted as several bullets tore through his chest and neck. I could still see his eyes trying to track me when I brought the sword down on his head, splitting his skull and extinguishing the flame instantly.

I landed with the Sig pointed at what was left of the wizard's head and pulled my sword free. His limp body slumped to the ground in a bloody pile with bitter smoke rising from his clawed hand and outstretched arm.

The moment the little man collapsed, the Wekufe began shaking violently just a few feet away. I dropped the empty Sig and pulled my Glock from under my right arm as I angled back toward the tunnel the wizard had come down. Before I could dive into the passageway for cover, the Wekufe exploded.

Oddly, the wet, leathery ripping of Jack Rios's body rupturing was the only sound it made as the warm remains pelted me. It was like popping a balloon—a massive, rotted-meat balloon—which was kind of gross and not at all what I'd expected. The energy that had emanated from under the thing's skin was just gone.

Once I'd scraped the bits of rotting flesh off me, I sheathed the sword, holstered the Glock, and retrieved the Sig, replacing its spent clip. Bits of Rios's body covered every surface within the cavern, including the walls and all of the mole people, some hundred feet away. I stood staring down at the dead Kalku. *Dammit.* It didn't bother me that I'd killed the guy—he attacked me first—but so much for finding out why he took the Cup or even where it was. I stalked cautiously down the tunnel, keeping an eye out for my other sword. I found it stuck six inches into the rock wall at the dogleg. I checked the blade's reflection to see if I could see what was at the end of the tunnel. Nothing moved in the reflection, but I left the sword in the wall just in case and rounded the corner with the Sig in a combat-high position, moving toward the light.

The source of the light was a fire pit and two torches set into the walls of an alcove. A shopping cart filled with rocks and scrap metal sat just inside the small chamber, and a large animal-skin bag slumped against the far wall next to a wooden walking stick topped with a hat like Clint Eastwood's in those Spaghetti Westerns. A broad double circle was drawn on the rock floor with some kind of chalk to one side of the fire pit. Around the concentric circles was a series of geometric shapes and glyphs similar to those on the shaman's poncho. At the very center was an ugly bronze cup filled with red liquid.

Bingo. I knew wizards used circles for conjuring or containing magical energy, but I didn't see any active magic or energy exuded from these circles. Since the guy who would have activated them was now dead, I wasn't worried about springing a trap.

I grabbed the vessel, and at once, the dull patina of the Cup took on a mercurial sheen. It was actually quite beautiful. The red liquid congealed into a mirror, but rather than a reflection, an image of my boat at the dock back in San Diego appeared. I stared for a few seconds then figured I'd better not mess around with something I didn't understand. I picked up the skin bag from the floor along the wall behind me, dumped the fluid into the fire, creating an odorless sizzle and an ominous cloud of red-tinged steam, and tucked the Cup into my bag.

From up the passageway, I began to hear muffled moans, along with scraping and shuffling from out in the cavern. I figured the mole people must have been coming out from under the Kalku's spell.

I carefully collected everything else and threw it into the fire pit, hastily scuffed up the drawings on the floor to make sure no one could use them again, and left the alcove. As I passed my sword in the wall, on my way back into the cavern, I removed it and returned it to its sheath. Most of the people were indeed starting to move, regaining their senses and moaning and groaning. It reminded me how much my head hurt. I rubbed my hand across the back of my head and found my short hair matted over a golf-ball-sized lump. My fingers came back covered in blood. The wound didn't feel that bad, but I knew that scalp lacerations tended to bleed profusely. I was sure I had a concussion, and my head felt as if it had been used as a gong. At least my vision was back to normal.

I holstered the Sig and massaged the lump on the back of my head as I approached the most alert of the group — a youngish man who was trying to sit up. He held his jaw while blood trickled from his mouth. As I came close, I could see him watch me with a furrowed brow and squinted eyes for only a second while he rubbed at his bruised mouth. His movements were deliberate and slow as he regained his wits.

"You okay?" I asked.

"Will be," he moaned then spit out a mouthful of blood and a tooth.

I felt bad about that. He didn't even bother to look around. I spent the next few minutes helping the others and taking stock of the injuries I'd inflicted. Nothing worse than a few broken bones and loose teeth, but I felt like an asshole for hurting them. That quickly gave way to anger at the Kalku for using them and placing them in harm's way. Good riddance to the little shit. Athena would have to live without knowing why he stole the Cup in the first place.

By the time I was finished checking, the first guy to wake up was standing tremulously, gazing around at the others, wide-eyed, with his eyebrows high on his forehead.

"If you'll tell me the fastest way out of here, I'll go get help. I promise, no police," I said.

"Don't need no help. We kin take care of ourselves. Out's that way," he said, pointing at the opening the noisy cart pusher originally came in through. He never once tried to make eye contact. I'd have killed that Kalku again, if I could, for making me hurt those people.

The mangled remains of the shaman made me grin as I remembered that I needed to get him back to the goblins. Noticing the pieces of Jack Rios all over the cavern, I decided that they were entirely unidentifiable to anyone who didn't already know what they'd been part of. It could have been considered desecration, but given that none of the remaining parts were much larger than a cell phone, I decided it was best to just leave the incalculable number of pieces where they were.

As I looked from the remains back to the injured mole people, I figured I'd be better off just getting out of there before those guys started asking questions. I grabbed the bloody mess that was left of the Kalku, wrapped the poncho around the parts of his head and upper body, and pitched him over my shoulder. I threw the skin bag over my other shoulder, pulled out my flashlight, and returned the way I'd come. First, I'd drop the body off with the goblins, and then I'd get the Cup back to Athena.

CHAPTER 15

'D THOUGHT THE KALKU AND Wekufe would be tougher. The Kalku had been powerful but woefully inexperienced. I'd expected someone capable of creating the kind of complex explosion that had happened at the museum, not a little guy behaving as if it were his first day with the training wheels off. There was no way he was the mastermind behind this whole thing.

After verifying with the goblins that the body I had was indeed the man who'd caused them trouble, I presented it to them and left. I had no desire to know what they intended to do with it.

Of course, the duffel bag with my trench coat was missing from where I'd left it inside the cave entrance. I was sure no one would notice me walking across Central Park at nine o'clock at night, dressed in black with two swords on my back and a couple of guns, and what appeared to be a dead goat hanging from my shoulder. Covered in what was left of Jack Rios, I probably reeked like a dead goat, too. It all just added to my pounding head.

It turned out—much to my chagrin—that no one noticed. While I did cross paths with several people—including one old woman, on an electric scooter, feeding and talking to the raccoons—no one paid attention to the smelly, armed nut with the dead animal on his back, even after the recent bombing. Thank God New Yorkers were so jaded. I even managed to sneak up to my hotel room without raising any alarms, by waiting for the night clerk to duck into the restroom. Once in my room, I locked the door and grabbed my phone to call Athena. It was a few minutes before ten. The message light on the room phone was blinking, and I had a message on my cell as well. It had to be from Sarah, which probably meant I'd missed her.

My head pounded as I dialed. Athena answered on the third ring. "And?"

"I got the Cup back. The Kalku is dead and the Wekufe is... whatever it is that happens to him when his Kalku is dead." I started to undo my vest to take it off, and a piece of the Wekufe fell on my boot. "Um, really odd that the guy stuck around, don't you think?" I rubbed my head.

Nothing so far made sense, but my head hurt too much, and my stomach felt too queasy as I thought about my date. I couldn't figure anything out right now. But I did notice it took Athena a few seconds to respond to my statement. I'm sure she knew I was apprehensive.

"Good work. And yes, very odd. I'll have Octivius and Dechion pick it up from you shortly." Overall, she seemed pleased.

"I kinda figured the Kalku and the Wekufe would be tougher. Other than slinging me against the wall and trying to incinerate me, they were pretty tame. Clearly, not used to combat—magical or otherwise."

"Not completely unpredictable. A Kalku is basically a shaman," Athena explained. "Their abilities usually lie within the realm of healing and prophecy. The Wekufe is like a battery. Once the shaman connects to it, his abilities magnify, and they often become capable of causing sickness and even death. You say he tried to incinerate you and managed to throw you, I assume using some sort of spells?"

I put the phone on speaker and brought it into the bathroom with me to start cleaning up. "Yeah, why?" I asked, finally stripping out of the vest.

"Well, Mapuche shaman aren't usually proficient in that kind of magic, and the Wekufe has no abilities except for whatever physical attributes the body it is given possesses. It just functions to supply its Kalku with the energy it needs to cast spells."

"The Kalku was trying to pull off some kind of magic with the Cup, and he had twenty homeless people under some sort of mind control. We'll need to get them some medical help if we can." I splashed water on my face and then dabbed a cold wet washcloth at the lump on my head.

"I don't know that he would have had the ability to control his visions in the Cup," Athena replied. "And there's no way he should have been able to control or even manipulate a person, let alone many people. That makes no sense."

"Well, he projected a lot of power," I said, jerking and wincing as

I tried to clean the dried blood from the tender area at the back of my head. "He picked me up like a rag doll, tossed me twenty-five feet, and then generated enough fire to shame an M202 FLASH. I mean, he cracked rock, for cripes' sake, and all while apparently controlling those people. He wasn't particularly adept at combat, but he had some ideas about it. Look, I'm headed back late tonight. We can talk more about it later. It's done with."

Poking at my wounds and talking about how I'd gotten them wasn't improving my mood, and all I could think about was the phone call from Sarah probably asking why I'd stood her up.

"Very well. Be at my office tomorrow morning," she replied curtly.

"Nah, I'm supposed to be on the water tomorrow. Can it wait until I get back around three?"

"Fine, but no later than half past." She hung up.

I checked my messages. Both were from Sarah. One saying she was running late and the other saying she doubted she'd make it after all, but she might have news about the bomber, and she'd call later if she did.

At first, my heart rose, and then it sank again with the next beat. I hadn't stood her up—she was going to stand me up. Given the gravity of the situation, I completely understood. As I stood there, disappointed, I wished the world I lived in wasn't so arcane. Sarah and all her colleagues had no idea that nothing they were doing really had any bearing on this event. I'd wrapped it up for them in a few hours, and they would never know. And we could have our date.

A knock at the door snapped me back to attention. I peeked through the peephole but couldn't make out anything but black material.

"Who is it?" I asked, ducking to the hinge side of the door, ready for it to slam open.

"Oc and Dec," replied a deep rumbling voice. "You're expecting us, Tydides."

I opened the door and peered directly into the chests of two of the most titanic guys I had ever seen, even bigger than Ajax was. They were a couple of Athena's Spartoi, the warriors created from dragons' teeth, nearly seven feet tall with pale white skin, amber eyes, and shaved heads and surrounded by a glowing energy that suggested they weren't human.

I was six feet tall and just over two hundred pounds. World-class athletes would have killed to be in my shape, but these guys made me feel like a pimply teenager in gym class. They were mirror images of each other, dressed identically in black silk suits that probably cost more than my boat and were so well tailored I couldn't even tell if the guys were armed.

And she had the nerve to complain about the hotel I'd chosen. Boy, did my head hurt.

"Come on in. I'll get you the Cup," I said, but they didn't move. I shrugged. "Suit yourself."

I dumped the contents of the goatskin bag onto my bed and fished through them until I found the tarnished old vessel. I held it up for the mountainous bookends, and its dull metal finish came alive at my touch with an otherworldly mercurial sheen. I put it back in the bag and walked over to hand it to them.

I didn't know for sure, but given that the Cup was a man-made magical object, I was sure Athena would give it to the Hermetic Order of the Golden Dawn, the Odin Brotherhood, or a similar organization for safekeeping.

"Here ya go," I said, feeling somewhat relieved. For a second, I even tried to believe it could be that easy.

They took the bag and left without saying a word. Side by side, they took up the entire hallway, but despite their enormity, they moved easily. *Good grief.*

As I closed the door, I wondered what they'd be like in a fight. I recalled sparring with Ajax during the funerary games at Troy and how easy it had been to predict his moves because of his size. But when he connected... *hoo boy.*

The phone rang.

"Steve?" Sarah asked. "I hope I didn't wake you."

"Nah, just touching base with the Metis Foundation's people here in New York and cleaning up. Sorry I missed your calls."

"Oh, no problem. You said you'd be out. Did you find anything? Because we've made some headway."

"The ID of the bomber?" I asked, suddenly feeling energized. "You mentioned you might have a lead."

"Well, not a name," she said enthusiastically, "but we have some video of his movements over the past month. We haven't been able to match his face with any state or federal IDs yet, but we have facial matches of him on the ferry from Brooklyn and the subway up to the museum, including yesterday before the explosion."

I was impressed by how keyed up she was by this information. It wasn't that I didn't think she was good at her job, but I liked that something as simple as finding a facial match got her fired up. She was committed, and I could relate.

"It'll take us a while longer to check private security cameras to verify his movements that day, but since he came through Brooklyn, we'll spread our search there as well," she continued.

"That's good news," I said. "I wasn't as productive."

It was a lie, but I didn't think the truth would go over very well. Plus, I really didn't want that Cup back on public display. If the Kalku really was the one behind all this and discovered what the Cup was, then it would only be a matter of time before a more informed person — or entity — came to get it. It was better off in the hands of people who could protect it.

"I didn't really find much at all — just some eyewitnesses in the park who described a guy who could have passed for a football player, but that's the extent of it. In fact, I think I'm going to head back to San Diego tomorrow and let you guys handle the rest of it. But if you wouldn't mind staying in touch if you find the bomber's ID..."

"I doubt that will be an issue," she replied. "I'd be willing to bet we find a bit more within the next twenty-four hours. Should I contact you through the Metis Foundation or directly?"

"Just contact me directly, but either way works. It was a pleasure meeting you, and I appreciate your help. Good luck chasing this guy down."

"Got it. Remember, I still owe you dinner," she added.

"Next time I'm in town." I couldn't help but smile at her admonition.

We hung up, and I began cleaning myself up and packing my gear bag so I could get back home. It'd been a long day, and the upcoming one wasn't going to be any shorter, although it would be far more enjoyable.

The problem was, I couldn't shake the feeling this thing wasn't really over and that the real culprit was yet to be found. How had a Kalku controlled magic beyond his talents as a shaman? What was he trying to use the Cup for? Why hadn't he just gone home? And why was there a separate — but clearly connected — bomber? Though I supposed, given that the Kalku could control people, it made some sense: he could have just fiddled with the guy's mind and sent him in as a diversion.

Then there was the whole question about the nature of the bomb itself. How did a shaman with no obvious combat experience create a magical incendiary device that sophisticated? Too many questions and not enough answers.

CHAPTER 16

I USUALLY GET DOWN TO MY boat two hours before a charter, so I was at the dock at four in the morning. I'd only had a few hours of sleep after I took the Ways back from New York, and I was still thinking about the Kalku and the Cup as I put fly rods together, strung them, and attached flies to tippets. I was so distracted that when Ned hopped aboard it actually startled me badly enough that I fumbled my four-hundred-dollar titanium pliers overboard.

"Dammit, man. You could give someone a heart attack, sneaking up on them like that," I said. "Get my damned pliers, would ya?"

"Jumpy much, dude?" Ned laughed.

He pointed at the water and at Elvis, the bull sea lion that frequented our landing and mooched fish carcasses, with my pliers in his mouth. The battle-scarred old pinniped flipped the pliers onto the boat, barked loudly enough to wake anyone still asleep on their live-aboards, and then took off. He had a new blue-and-white Tady 9A lure stuck in his flank. *Man, I hate sea lions.*

"Just got back from that mess in New York. And now I gotta fish all day," I replied, even crankier than I'd been five minutes ago. "Why don't you go pull that lure outta Elvis's ass and leave me alone?"

"Dude, you're going fishing!" He said it as if that in and of itself should have been enough to cure all ills. Maybe normally it would have been. I just shrugged in response.

"Word is you wrapped it up, man," he said, flashing me a smile so wide that it glowed in the first light of dawn. "That's what I hear, anyway. So, what's eatin' ya? And don't worry about Elvis—he's got a collection of lures that would make a tackle shop jealous. I sell 'em on the interwebs from time to time for sardines and beer money. We share the 'dines, and I get the beer." He winked at me.

"Ah, it's not the fishing," I replied, stopping my preparations to look at him. "Yeah, I got the Cup back and got the guy who stole it, too, but he died before I could talk to him. There's still stuff that doesn't make any sense. That's what's bugging me. You know anyone in Brooklyn?"

"Died before you could talk to him?" he said with a single hearty chuckle. "I hear tell you exercised your usual brand of diplomacy on his ass. But I might know someone in Brooklyn. Why?" Ned dug into my cooler. "You ain't put the beer in there yet, man."

"How many times do I have to tell you I don't provide beer? If they want it, they can bring it. I was hoping to get a little more information about the guy who blew himself up. He traveled up from Brooklyn to the museum the day of the explosion, but the Feds have no record of him from any kind of ID. If you knew someone in Brooklyn, then we could ask him to ask around, maybe find a lead, maybe ID the guy. It just bugs me, okay?"

I was being curter than I intended, and I really did need Ned's help. In my world, Ned was the guy who always knew a guy. I was hoping he'd know someone or something that kept up with the supernatural happenings in Brooklyn. After all, he clearly found out about what took place in the tunnels under Central Park pretty quickly. That didn't really surprise me. Goblins were wicked gossips.

"Gotcha. I'll check, but it'll cost you—and not just my fee," he said, smiling that white smile again. "You know, dudes who traffic in information ain't cheap. I'll let you know when you come back. Oh, before I forget, you might find a white or two at the Imperial Beach kelp, on the shallow side near the dinosaur cage. And you better release 'em, too, or I'll plague your ass with dogs." He waved at me over his shoulder as he walked up the dock.

I sighed and watched the flag on top of the hotel across the bay to check the wind, hoping to find it calm for a change. Wouldn't that be nice?

It was a beautiful day on the water, and by the time we got back into the bay and motored toward my marina that afternoon, I had put the Cup and the case out of my mind. My anglers, an accomplished husband and wife, were on their game, and we actually found the white sea bass. One of them would have been a world record on fly, which would have been a feather in the cap of a great day, but it was better than that. Having fished with this particular pair of anglers for several years, I knew they had no desire to kill fish, even for a record. So the wife got it, they took a few pictures, and without a second thought, we let the fish go. The time I took making sure the fifty-pound fish was safely released got me a two-hundred-dollar tip.

As I tied up at the dock and began to clean up, the buzz of the great day began wearing off, and I had to sit down for a minute. My head started to hurt again, my stomach wouldn't stop growling, and my back was a bit sore as well. With a sigh, I checked my watch: almost three. Maybe I could finish up with Athena and be home by five. Maybe pigs could fly, too.

I finished cleaning the boat and my gear a little slower than I'd planned, mostly on mental autopilot, and before I knew it, I was on my way to the Metis Foundation's offices downtown near the baseball stadium in East Village. The Foundation occupied a one-hundred-thirty-year-old Victorian mansion that was completely out of place on the corner of Thirteenth and Island surrounded by condos and construction.

As I walked into the waiting room, I realized that most of my shirt was covered in fish gunk. I probably stank. I was nose-deaf to fish smells anymore. This was going to be fun.

The Metis Foundation's offices were as opulent as the building was out of place. While the outside screamed "antique," the interior was as modern as it got—all glass and steel. Standing in the reception area always reminded me of being at an aquarium.

The reception area itself was about fifteen by twenty, with a steel-and-black-leather sofa to the left, a "floating" glass-and-steel stairwell leading up to a highly polished black door to the right, and a somewhat forbidding brushed-steel receptionist's desk in the middle.

As I approached the desk, it was hard not to stare at the giant wall of glass that isolated what they call "the bullpen." Inside, dozens of people swarmed around low-walled cubicles or open desks, but the massive bank of monitors and screens that occupied every inch of the three-story wall at the back of the room captured my attention. It was tiring just watching the constant human activity through the wall of glass. The camera feeds from all around the world, charts, graphs, and data displays made me feel old—I was born in an age when our greatest technological achievement was bronze. To make matters worse, everyone was dressed in business formal attire, and I stood out like a sore thumb.

Most of the people who worked there were just that: people. But a few were different. I knew of at least two Seelie Fae—a tall, blond female Elf and a male Yaksha—and several members of the Hermetic Order of the Golden Dawn, the organization governing natural-born witches and wizards. I wasn't sure what else Athena had working there.

I approached the fresh-faced, rigid, blond young woman behind the desk. I was there often enough that most of the people knew me, but this girl was new. Instantly, her face began to scrunch up in disgust, and she grabbed for a tissue. "Can I help you?" she asked, her eyebrows knitted in a forehead of deep furrows.

Smelling the way I did, I was guessing she thought I was lost. "I'm here to see 'the boss,'" I replied, throwing air quotes.

She stared at me for half a minute before she finally reached for the phone. "Dere's, ah, a man, here to see you," she said into the phone, holding her nose.

Beyond her, in the bullpen, I could see a couple of younger employees who recognized me, stifling laughs as they watched. I beamed at them and nodded my head ever so slightly.

"Yes, ma'am. Yes. Right away." She hung up the phone and gawked at me. "She said to go right ub."

I jogged up the floating stairway to my right. The door at the top appeared to be shimmering black glass, but it was far more. I always wondered if it might actually be partly alive. Living or not, whatever it was, I doubted even the Pelian Spear or my swords could penetrate it. As I reached up to knock, the door slid open to reveal the Elf.

She was tall—over six feet, maybe six-one—and could easily pass for a supermodel except that her skin was so pale it resembled ivory, but warmer. Her hair was so blond it appeared white in some light, and she always wore it so that it covered her pointy ears. But what got me were her eyes, which were an intense shade of emerald green—the whole eye, not just the iris. And while I respected her immensely as Athena's very capable right hand at the Metis Foundation, I lived to harass her like a sister. The fact that she didn't understand any of it made it that much more fun.

She smiled as I walked in, and then she smelled me. "Whoa," she said, nearly dropping the papers in her arms as she tried to cover her nose and step back at the same time. "Smells like you tried to mate with a sciaenid about five hours ago." Elves: always precise, and no sense of humor.

"It was a white sea bass, and I was reviving it to let it go." I narrowed my eyes at her and entered the room.

"Humans," she said, shaking her head as she returned to her desk just inside the doorway. "The sciaenid is the race of croakers, including the local *Atractoscions*, or white sea bass as you call them."

Her reaction to me was nothing new. I knew it came from her total lack of understanding of what it meant to be human, and not from animosity, and it was exactly the type of reaction I lived to elicit from her.

"They're fish, not a race, Brey," I said, dragging out her name to annoy her. Her name was Breygivila, at least the part of it that I knew, and she hated when I shortened it. "And I let it go." I would have stuck my tongue out, too, but that was a little too childish.

Once I was a few feet into the room, the door silently slid closed behind me, giving me the illusion of being isolated and contained. On this side, the door behind me was currently crystal clear, as were the interior walls, with the exception of a single polished-black wall along the room's far side, which partitioned Athena's office from the space I was standing in. The whole forty-foot-long room fully occupied the small second floor of the building, and at the moment consisted of a broad, open space taken up mostly by a wide glass-and-steel conference table surrounded by a dozen chairs made of steel and black leather.

The clear wall gave a view directly down into the bullpen and to the wall of monitors beyond. This room always creeped me out because every part of the structure gave off a faint glow of energy as if it were alive, and I knew that it could somehow change its features, including its layout. And while the space was currently soundproofed, I'd experienced it set up so that we could hear everything going on in the bullpen below, too.

When I turned from harassing Brey, Athena was standing in front of me. She was wearing a white-on-white pantsuit that made her fiery hair — in a single loose braid over her shoulder — stand out even more. The monotone outfit also accentuated the preternatural perfection of her pale skin.

"Smells like you kept it in your pocket," she said seriously, her nose wrinkled and her eyes squinting. "Artemis would be very disappointed that you let such a fine prize free after the effort of your hunt." Athena can make an expression of abject horror seem attractive. "And it's about time. Didn't you check your phone messages?"

I had completely forgotten to turn my phone back on at the boat. *Oops.*

She entered her office through a doorway that just appeared in the shiny black wall, and I followed. Her office was stately but simple, anchored by a bizarre desk that combined elements of stone, steel, wood, and glass. Her chair resembled a steel throne and looked about as comfortable as an iron maiden. Luckily, the two leather chairs opposite her desk were not as severe.

"Ah, no. Sorry. And that's probably why Artemis doesn't fish with me," I replied. "Besides, what's so urgent? Somebody steal the Fork and Knife of Jamshid now?"

I sat down with a flop in one of the chairs, which I had no doubt was made of some exotic leather that cost more than most people made in a year. I was tired and hungry, and Athena's briefings had a way of taking forever, but her intense, irascible gaze and the terse set of her lips told me this thing was far from over.

"Octivius and Dechion are dead," she said, reaching across the desk for an elaborate letter opener. "We found what was left of them earlier today outside of New York. They didn't make it far after they picked up the Cup from you. And yes, the Cup is missing again. So let's go over everything. *Again.*"

I was dumbstruck. While I didn't know them well, Oc and Dec were part of Athena's most elite unit of Spartoi, specifically formed from dragons' canine teeth. No mortal could have stood up to them and survived, let alone killed them. And to kill them while they were expecting trouble would take someone or something powerful. While I wasn't a fan of the Spartoi's simple tactics and lack of ability to improvise, I hoped Oc and Dec at least died swinging.

When my eyes refocused on her, Athena was pointing the letter opener at me. It was carved from the claw of one of the dragons she'd killed and whose teeth likely included the canines that formed Oc and Dec and made up the bulk of her army of Spartoi. It was probably sharp enough to peel shavings off the stainless steel parts of her desk. I got the point. She wanted to make sure I wasn't forgetting anything.

She didn't actually need me to tell her what I knew, but she really did try to stay out of my head as much as possible. I had to remind myself that these detailed debriefings helped me maintain that aspect of our relationship, so although tedious, they were worth it. I spent the better part of the next few hours going over every single moment of my time in New York, from the places I'd gone to the people and creatures I encountered. I also mentioned that I had Ned chasing down a lead in Brooklyn.

"I want you back in New York as soon as possible to follow up any and all leads that might develop with regard to the bombing and theft, and I don't want you working alone on this," she finally said.

"Aw, come on," I protested. Having Oc and Dec killed had spooked her enough to want to saddle me with a couple of her oversized goons. "How long have I been doing this now? I don't need a babysitter. Your Spartoi are tough, but they're blunt instruments. Not the sharpest sticks in the pile — no offense. I don't need some lumbering hulk hanging over my shoulder, scaring people while I work. If I have to, you know I can call in backup. Hell, Abraxos and Duma can reach me within minutes anywhere in the world."

I knew Athena would have issue with my first choice of support. Duma and Ab were brothers and probably the most trusted allies I had. But they were Peri, legendary and deadly Anseelie Fae. Both the Seelie and Unseelie Courts considered them traitors, and most races would turn them over instantly or report a sighting just to avoid diplomatic issues with either court. I didn't care. If I needed help, they'd be the ones I'd call.

She stared hard at me for a few silent minutes until I relented. "Okay! If you are so inclined, have your guys on Ready Five," I said, rolling my eyes. I acquiesced just to move things along. Besides, Ab and Duma's help aside, having an army at my beck and call might be useful in a pinch.

Athena placed the letter opener on the desk, sat back, and tented her hands with her index fingers resting on her chin. To my surprise, she actually backed off.

"Maybe you're right. I'll hold them off for now, but remain in constant contact on this. Clearly, as you feared, the Kalku wasn't the worst thing after the Cup. I could well imagine there may even be several parties interested in its recovery."

Damn. I was going to have to cancel my charters for the next few days at least.

CHAPTER 17

RETURNED HOME AND STARTED TO reassemble my gear. In addition to my usual complement of firearms and edged weapons, I pulled out the Pelian Spear. I didn't know if I'd need the spear or not. At eight feet long, it was more of a battlefield weapon than a close-quarters one.

It was originally a gift to Achilles's father, Peleus, from Hephaestus, Athena, and the centaur Chiron and—like my swords—in the right hands it could penetrate anything. More importantly, a victim who was impaled upon the spear was pinned to this world, which was particularly useful when I was dealing with dimension-hopping Protogenoi or other teleporting creatures. And it called to its wielder, so it could always be recovered. Unfortunately, it was unwieldy to travel with in public, so I used a special PVC tube covered in fishing-tackle-manufacturer decals and destination stickers so that I could pass it off as a fishing rod when I had to bring it along.

I spent several hours going over my supplies, down to all the straps and buckles and making sure I had charged batteries for my flashlights, cell phone, and handheld GPS unit. Once that was done, I packed everything into two duffels and decided to grab some sleep for a few hours before I left for Brooklyn. Maybe I was being a bit obsessive, but given the nature of the things I'd gone up against, retrieving the damned Cup the first time, and the fact that two of Athena's best Spartoi were killed for the thing, I felt it best to be overprepared this time.

At four in the morning, a pounding on my door awakened me. I figured if it was someone I needed to worry about, they probably wouldn't have knocked, so I just plodded to the door and answered it. Even before I flipped the light on outside, I could tell by the portly outline and the shadow of the enormous bushy beard that it was Ned. He was wearing a black Hawaiian shirt decorated with images of old woody-style station wagons, surfboards, and pink-and-green flip-flops, and it was completely unbuttoned around his prodigious belly. He also had a six-pack of beer in one hand.

"I have got to get you a cell phone," I said, yawning, and wandered into the kitchen.

"No way, man," he said as he entered the house, glancing around outside before closing the front door behind him. Once he was inside, he switched the outside light off and then peered again through the peephole and rechecked the locks. "With those things, anyone can reach you anytime they want."

"That's the point. So why are you here?" I was not happy about being woken up, but I knew Ned wouldn't have done it if he didn't have what he thought was a good reason.

"Got news, dude," he said, finally joining me in the kitchen, popping open a can of beer. "You know what a Lar is?"

I clenched my jaw, exhaled heavily through my nose, and crossed my arms over my chest, and he shrugged in response.

"You mean the old protector spirits that used to guard Roman cities?" I asked. "No, never heard of them. Seriously? Is that what you woke me up to ask?"

"Sorry, man. Didn't know what you knew, dude. Anyway, apparently, Brooklyn has one, a powerful one. Some of the old Italian families still keep it going through regular food offerings and the upkeep of its shrine. My contacts say if it happens in Brooklyn, the Lar knows about it."

"How do I find it?"

"Holy Cross Cemetery. Its shrine is at the entrance on Tilden. Bring something nice." He winked at me.

I was contemplating whether the information was worth being woken up for but decided it was just Ned being Ned. "Great. Anything else I should know?" I sighed.

"Yeah, man. I'm gettin' word of some heavy hitters moving in the same circles as you, lookin' for that Cup." His voice softened. "I heard they even ripped apart a couple of Athena's personal-guard dudes. I'm gettin' bad vibes, man. Lots of bad vibes. I say we go down to Fiji for a while and lie low till this mess gets sorted. I know this sweet little bay that has some tasty waves on the south side. Even has some bonefish, too, dude. Be better for your health, ya know what I mean?"

"I'm aware of what happened to Athena's men. But those bad vibes you're getting are exactly why I can't just run off, nice as that sounds."

"Suit yourself, man," Ned said, shrugging. He downed the beer he was drinking, burped, and opened another can and just stared at me.

Ned knew I would never shy away from any fight, no matter the odds. But more importantly, he knew I would stop at nothing to get that Cup back before more people died.

"What do you know about these so-called 'heavy hitters'?"

"Not much," he replied, taking a long pull on the can. "Way I heard it, some terrorist group outta Iran is lookin' for it, and they got some kinda Paran help. Word is it's them that killed Athena's guard dudes. Also heard tell a powerful thaumaturgist was behind the original theft." Ned burped again and exhaled deeply.

"Aw, man—seriously," I said, fanning the beer smell away. It took me a few seconds to get enough breath back to continue. "Terrorists working with Parans, huh? Maybe Agent Wright was on to something. And a powerful magic user makes sense, given the nature of the explosion."

"Who's Agent Wright?" he asked, raising his eyebrows as he opened yet another beer.

"No one you need to worry about," I replied, encouraged by the thought that Ned's information might just give me a legitimate reason to keep working with Sarah. "Just stay low, and I'll catch up with you when this mess is over. And hey, watch my boat, will you? Any beer you find is yours."

After finishing the rest of his six-pack, Ned flopped onto my couch and began snoring instantly. Unfortunately, my mind was now racing, and I was wide-awake at quarter of five. With the three-hour time difference between here and New York, I figured I might as well get moving.

I drove back out to the casino parking lot east of San Diego as the sky began to lighten and walked down to the little valley to find my usual gateway to the Telluric Ways. I pulled the warm Way Stone from my pocket, opened the portal, and stepped through. I exited outside the Mexican village then opened the next gateway into Central Park.

From Central Park, I caught a cab to Brooklyn. On the way, I called Agent Wright and left a message letting her know I was back in town and asking if she'd made any progress. With not much else to go on at that point, I was hoping that a lead on the bomber might give me some insight about whomever he worked for.

I knew nothing about modern Brooklyn, so on the long and expensive ride, I asked the cabbie for a hotel recommendation. He suggested a bed-and-breakfast off Rutland near Prospect Park. In a place as old as Brooklyn, that kind of lodging was likely to be home to one or more brownies, which could prove useful. And if the place had been a home for some time, its threshold would be particularly strong. Many nonhumans couldn't cross over a home's threshold without an invitation. Most people were familiar with that aspect of vampiric lore, but it applied to much more than Strigoi and Moroi. If a house protector such as a brownie was also present, it could reinforce that threshold like a supernatural electric fence. It would be an extra bonus layer of protection.

The cabbie let me out in front of a building that resembled every other one on its tree-lined street—a three-story bowfront Victorian row house made of redbrick, with a basement at ground level and a steep stairway up to the narrow French front doors. It was partitioned off from its neighbors by a short stone wall.

This was an old neighborhood. I could feel its age, yet it appeared peaceful and pristine and a complete contrast to the hustle and bustle of Manhattan just across the bay. By sheer luck, they had a room available, and I was able to settle in quickly.

My room was at the back of the house on the second floor and had a pair of twin beds opposite a nonworking fireplace. It was a neat and comfortable space with a pair of chairs flanking the fireplace and a view out over the garden. I threw my bags on the bed closest to the windows and started unpacking.

While I was organizing my gear, my phone rang. It was Agent Wright. "Back already?"

"Yeah, well, to Brooklyn, anyway. I'm aiding in the recovery of the cup now. Any more info on the bomber?" I was hoping she'd be okay telling me even though my official part in the bombing investigation was over.

"We still have no ID on him, but we've got a pretty good map of his whereabouts leading up to the bombing," she replied apologetically.

She spent a minute outlining the basics of what they knew about the bomber's movements up to and including the day of the explosion.

Despite what they knew about his movements around Manhattan, they still had no idea what part of Brooklyn the guy came from.

"Well, since I guess it's now part of my job, do you know anything more about the cup that was stolen?"

"The cup?" She was clearly surprised. "No, sorry. Our priority is finding the bomber and any associates. The police and the museum are dealing with the theft."

It was hard to explain to mortals that even the most mundane-seeming object could be quite powerful and deadly in the wrong hands. I once witnessed a demon lay waste to an entire battalion of soldiers using only an old bone.

"Well, what about the terrorist link? Isn't it possible that whatever terrorist organization claimed responsibility for the bombing stole the cup for some religious purposes?" I was on a serious fishing expedition, but given that I currently had nothing, I figured it couldn't hurt to ask.

"The terrorist angle is being explored by other agencies at this time," Agent Wright said, using an official tone.

Her sarcasm made me snort, and I could hear her laugh, too. The problem was I didn't know what else to say to keep the conversation going.

"Well, good luck finding a lead on Mr. Boom-Boom," I finally said after a long silence.

She laughed a little louder this time, which made me smile.

"Mr. Boom-Boom, smartass?"

"You got a better name right now? I'll call you when I find something," I said, smiling.

"*When* you find something? I can't tell if that's arrogance or confidence." She chuckled.

"Neither. I'm just an optimist. I'll be in touch," I said and then hung up.

After surveying the gear on the bed, I grabbed my Sig and slid it into a shoulder holster, pulled it on, put my CQC-6 in my pocket, and strapped a tanto knife to the inside of my calf under my pants. Even though it was almost summer, the air still held a chill, so I pulled on a light jacket, stuffed an image of the bomber — from the video — into a pocket, and stopped at the desk in the lobby to ask where I could find a good Italian deli.

I spent the rest of the morning purchasing a bag full of cured meats, good buffalo mozzarella, bottles of expensive imported olive oil, and balsamic vinegar, as well as six types of cookies and a loaf of bread that was so fresh you could smell it fifty feet away. I was going to need it to appease the Lar properly in order to get its help.

Once I had my offering, I walked to the Holy Cross cemetery, a dozen blocks down and a dozen more over from my hotel and right in the heart of Flatbush. The area was a working-class part of Brooklyn that used to be made up of mostly Italian-American and Jewish neighborhoods but had become a true melting pot over the years and was now home to ethnic groups from around the world.

The entrance to the Holy Cross Cemetery off of Tilden Avenue was a monumental stone double archway adorned with a Chi-Rho cross, capped with copper flashing and an oversized traditional cross. It was clearly a Roman Catholic resting ground. Just inside the archway and to the right was a small building, which I assumed was some sort of office, with a few cars parked next to it. The cemetery itself was beautifully kept, and the trees were covered in new spring growth, casting a serene and peaceful atmosphere over the area. A grassy expanse with gravestones and bushes flanked the entrance then gave way to a dense stand of trees and more graves. If it weren't for all the dead people, it would have made a great park.

With no one in sight, I set the bag of food on a stone ledge on the back of the entrance's central pillar. Above it was a bas-relief carving of a man wearing a tunic and a laurel wreath. He had a spear in one hand and a horn in the other, and below him was a wicked-looking serpent.

I walked toward the nearest stand of trees and began reading grave markers, keeping an eye on the bag. After about twenty minutes, the shuffling sound of someone crossing the grass behind me finally drew my attention.

I was surprised to see the Lar with a heavy rake in his hands, dressed like a groundskeeper. His nametag read "Joe," and he looked like an old Italian grandfather — a hawk-like but regal nose, a receding hairline of pure white hair, and a slightly stooped back. He moved easily, despite his aged appearance.

He wasn't veiling himself, but Lares usually didn't since they appeared entirely human. The aura of power he emanated came from the area he protected. This one was particularly powerful, which meant he'd been there a while, and the descendants of the families that had originally summoned him still supported him and would ask for his protection by presenting him with gifts and offerings like the ones I'd left at his altar. Still, it was odd for a *Lares Compitalicii*, or a town protector, to be in a cemetery.

"Can I help you find someone?" he asked in a heavy Italian accent without looking at me, raking at the grass but not gathering anything.

"Sto cercando per voi, onorato custode," I replied in Italian, letting him know I was seeking him. I bowed my head in deference to him and his authority here.

Most types of Lares weren't particularly strong beings anymore — people just didn't believe in them the way they once had. They used to be protectors and guardians of homes and villages and any number of other objects and locations and were very similar to brownies. The Lares that protected whole communities, on the other hand — like this one — wielded an awful lot of power but were bound to use it only in protection of their territory.

Joe would likely know everything that occurred in his protectorate and at one time would have done things like help crops grow, provide water, and even stave off illness. Generally, Lares were benevolent unless something supernatural threatened their community. Given that Joe's altar was in this hundred-and-sixty-year-old cemetery, he wasn't really old by fae standards, but the area he protected was massive. If some being came to Brooklyn to do harm, it'd have to deal with him. And if people in his community were up to no good — say, planning a bombing, for example — I had no doubt he'd know about it.

"We in America, we speak English here," he replied. "Why you look for me?" Joe kept raking at the grass and didn't make eye contact.

"I need your help trying to find someone," I said, hoping to earn his trust.

He stopped raking and peered at me through hooded eyes. "How can I help you, *custode*?" He used the same word for me that I'd used for him. It meant guardian. At least he knew who I was. "You try the phone book, or maybe try that Google thing?"

"Those won't help me. This person blew himself up in the Met the other day. I think he lived somewhere here in Brooklyn, and I think he was working with a powerful shaman. But there seems to be more to the situation. An object of special significance and power was stolen, too. I thought you might be able to help me find where the bomber lived — if he did live here. That way, I would at least have a starting point for finding out who wanted the object and why."

The Lar walked around a few headstones and approached me. Standing only a few feet away, he stared at me, his mouth pressed tightly closed while he leaned heavily on the rake with both hands as if it were a staff. "Meh. Maybe. Maybe no. What you bring me?" He tipped the top of the rake toward the altar.

An enormous serpent slithered over to us with the bag in its mouth as I gestured back toward the altar. The reptilian creature reminded me of a legless dragon, maybe fifteen feet long with a broad, laterally compressed head, more like a *T. rex* than a typical snake. As it approached us, its coloration blended first with the black pavement it passed over and then with the grass we were standing in. That was just all kinds of icky.

Instantly, I reached for my gun, but just as quickly, Joe placed a steadying hand on my shoulder. He simply shook his head, his mouth lifting at one side into a smirk. The serpent stopped at Joe's feet and dropped the bag from its jaws then coiled up to my right, watching me with its beady, reptilian eyes, which were at my eye level. It swayed slightly back and forth, its jaws agape just enough to reveal a nasty set of teeth.

"Just some food," I replied, suppressing a shudder and trying not to sound or seem too concerned about the giant snake in front of me.

The Lar waved his hand as if he were shooing flies, and the serpent lowered itself back to the ground and slithered off to disappear among the grave markers and trees behind me. I couldn't help but watch the creepy scene, partly out of vigilance and partly out of curiosity. A creature of that size should not have just disappeared that easily. I had to suppress another shudder.

"You bring me any jujulena or cucidata?" he asked, dropping the rake and picking up the bag.

"I think there should be some of both, along with anise cookies and a special biscotti." I put my hands behind my back and watched him as he dug through the bag like a kid picking through his sack at Halloween.

"Bah, I don't like the biscotti. They make it too sweet here. Ah, sopressata and felino! *Bene, bene, bene!*"

"I was told the biscotti was more traditional and very good. That's why I got it." I silently watched him continue his exploration of the bag. "Do you think you could help me?" I finally asked after a few minutes.

"What was his name?" he asked while he continued to riffle through the bag, releasing the aromas of fresh bread and cured meats.

I was glad my offerings worked, and it was actually fun to watch him pick through the items so excitedly. I only hoped his enthusiasm didn't wane as soon as I told him I had little information about the kid. "I don't have a name. All I have is a rough image from a videotape. I know he used to take the water taxi from Red Hook across to Manhattan, but that's all." I looked down at my feet, hoping the tiny bit of information I had would be enough.

If he was as powerful as I thought, I doubted he even needed the picture. I handed him the print from the surveillance cameras. He stopped digging, grabbed the picture, and scanned it for maybe half a second before passing it back. It couldn't have been more than a glimpse, and then his attention shifted back to the bag. I shook my head as I took the picture back, figuring I was wrong.

"I thought as much," he replied, digging back into the bag. "Ah, good mozzarella," he said, holding one of the fist-sized balls of cheese under his nose and inhaling deeply. "The boy lived in the Red Hook Houses, in Building Nineteen on the corner of Dwight and Verona on the first floor. The unit was not his and had not been occupied for some time before he arrived. Be careful. That place is a warren of violence and misery." With that, he stopped searching the bag, picked up his rake, and let out a sharp whistle.

"You've been very helpful," I said, ecstatic I finally had a solid place to begin. "This is my first visit back to Brooklyn in some time, and despite my purpose here, I've enjoyed myself. It's become very nice. If ever I can be of service, you have but to ask." I was careful not to thank him, but I wanted to show my respect. It was hard to do that and not sound like a total kissass.

Out of the corner of my eye, I noticed the serpent slink up behind the Lar. Joe held up the bag, and the legless creature grabbed it and glided away across the manicured grass, through the trees and headstones, back into the cemetery, and out of sight. This time I couldn't suppress the shudder. Everything about that snake was just wrong.

"You should also know there are other... nonhuman things concerned with this boy, as well. I have done my best to discourage them, but I was alone in doing so. Until now. *Buona fortuna, custode.* I hope you find what you look for." He waved his hand as he followed the serpent back among the graves.

CHAPTER 18

I DIDN'T KNOW MUCH ABOUT THE Red Hook Houses except that they were the second-largest projects in New York and home to around six thousand people, give or take. The area was rife with all types of crime and not what anyone would call safe — especially at night. But the location made sense if the bomber wanted to stay off the grid.

I left Holy Cross and returned to my bed-and-breakfast. In my room, I double-checked my Sig and tucked my Glock into the waist of my pants at the small of my back, making sure my jacket covered it. It wasn't the best place to carry a backup, but it worked. I made sure I had a spare clip for each gun in my shoulder harness, threw my cell phone into my jacket pocket, and left.

It was already four in the afternoon by the time I headed back outside. I didn't want to spend the better part of an hour hoofing it, so I grabbed a taxi. The driver did a double take when I told him to drop me at the corner of Verona and Dwight. I didn't know if his reaction was because I was white or because I was crazy enough to go to that area. Either way, I took it as a bad omen.

About twenty minutes later, he let me off along Dwight Street just down from the Verona intersection and in the shadow of the mammoth, looming brown-brick structures of the Red Hook Houses. The sheer magnitude of the housing development was overwhelming. It was four blocks square and composed of at least two dozen six-story buildings with an institutional bearing. It was a town unto itself. I hadn't known what to expect, but the reality left me puzzled. Sure, there were bags of trash and random litter on the sidewalks, but the lawns between the buildings were green and well maintained and all the trees had fresh growth, giving me more an impression of big city than ghetto. Nobody behaved in a cautious or shifty manner, nor did the mostly African-American people that passed seem alarmed or

100

even concerned by my presence... from a distance, anyway.

As I approached the entrance to Building Nineteen at the far northern end of the complex, things changed dramatically. I nearly gagged at the smell of dozens of bags of garbage on the sidewalk waiting for pickup. Even though no one was visible around the building, I had the distinct feeling I was being watched. It could have just been someone peeking at me through one of the windows, or I could have just been paranoid, but I couldn't tell either way for sure, so I just kept walking as if I belonged there.

Up close, the structure was in poor condition, especially the entryway. What had likely been an entry buzzer system at one time had been pried apart and mostly destroyed. The door barely hung in its frame, and the windows around it had either been taped over or replaced with cardboard. I had to make an effort to pry the door open.

The heat and humidity in the entry hall, created by hundreds of people living in cramped conditions, hit me like a fist. The smell in the dark corridor overwhelmed me. It wasn't a disgusting odor, exactly, but rather an overpowering combination of spices, foods, smoke, pets, people, garbage, waste, mold, and any number of unidentifiable odors. Only a few of the lights in the long hallway actually worked, and one flickered constantly. Somewhere in the building, a radio was thumping out bass. Televisions blared, people yelled, and kids cried.

From the information the Lar had given me, I knew the apartment I needed to locate was on the first floor, but there had to be sixty apartments per floor, and I doubted anyone would tolerate me knocking on doors and asking questions. I walked down the corridor, making a mental map of how far apart the doors were to try to judge apartment size while making note of the units that were silent. It was easier than I thought. Some of the residents left their doors open, probably in an attempt at improving ventilation, I saw a few residents leave or enter, and various kinds of noise emanated from behind other doors, leaving only three quiet apartments along the hall.

I decided to risk it and knock on the doors to the noiseless units. At the first one, I got no response. At the second one, my banging agitated a poor woman who had just fallen asleep after working a double shift. She screamed so loudly at me that several neighbors popped their doors open on their chains to see what was going on. I tried to apologize but found it easier just to move on and pretend to leave.

Once the ruckus had died back down, I approached the third quiet apartment. As I knocked, an African-American boy around ten years old opened the door of the apartment across the hall and stood there dribbling a basketball. He was wearing an oversized T-shirt and shorts so long they could have been pants. I grinned at him as he watched me warily.

"I don't think he's home," the boy said. "I ain't seen him in a couple of days. He's crazy anyway. What you want with him? He in trouble?"

"Is he an older Hispanic man who weighs about three hundred pounds?" I asked, hoping the kid would describe the bomber instead.

"Nah, man," he replied, bouncing the ball. "Dude that lives there be young and look like he come from Iraq, except he ain't got no beard. You a cop? What he do — beat somebody for making too much noise?" He snorted.

"No, nothing like that. And no, I'm not a cop. Do you know his name?"

"Nah. He always keep to hisself," he said, shrugging his shoulders. "If you ain't a cop, why you looking for him? He owe you money?"

"No, it's just important that I locate him. Did he ever have friends over?"

"Not that I ever seen. I told you, he crazy. I ain't telling you nothing else."

"That's okay, you've been very helpful so far. Why don't you go inside now?" I said, trying to usher him along so I could break into the apartment.

"Nah. Can't dribble in the house. Wakes up my baby sister."

"If I give you ten bucks, will you go back inside?"

The kid stopped dribbling and stared at me for a few seconds.

"Twenty bucks," he finally said, sticking out his chin and tossing the ball between his hands.

"Fine." I pulled some money out of my wallet. Normally, I would never flash money in a place like that, but I was far from normal. I handed the kid two tens. "Now, will you go back inside? You'll be safer that way."

"I knew it. You gonna kill him!" the kid responded excitedly.

"No, I'm not. In fact, he's already dead. Now go back inside," I pleaded.

"Whatchu mean, he already dead? Somebody else cap his ass?"

"Look, kid, I gave you twenty bucks, now just go back inside." I was beginning to worry that our conversation would attract unwanted attention from other residents. I glanced down the hall to make sure we were still alone, and my jacket fell open, giving the kid a good view of the gun under my arm.

He barely even registered a reaction. "That a nine?" he asked matter-of-factly.

What's up with kids these days? "Yeah. Now go. Scoot!" I said through clenched teeth, waving him off.

The kid let out a sigh and bounced the ball back toward his door. Just before the kid closed the door completely, he looked up at me. "My brother went to talk to your guy the other day on account of all the noise he be making in the middle of the night. I heard the shouting through the walls, and then everything got real quiet. I ain't seen Maurice since, but Momma say that's 'cause he had to go do a job. Maurice ain't never left on no job without saying bye to me and my baby sister." He spoke softly, the tough street-kid attitude slipping away.

"I'm sure your brother's just fine, kid," I replied, a little upset with myself for being so abrupt with him. "Go on inside, now."

The kid closed the door, and I made sure the hall was still clear. Satisfied I was alone, I pulled the Sig then pressed my shoulder to the door and shoved hard. It didn't budge. There were only two deadbolt locks in addition to the knob, but apparently, it had been reinforced. *To hell with it.* I took a step back and performed a *tactical entry.*

The door flew open on its heavily reinforced hinges, with a thud that echoed through the hall. A normal door would have come right off, but this one stayed completely intact and hinged. I dropped down on one knee, raised my gun, and was instantly assaulted by the intensely sweet smell of decomposition and the buzzing sound of swarming flies.

Behind me, the kid's door opened on its chain across the hall, and I immediately swung the door closed, covering my mouth and nose with the back of my gun hand. He may have been used to seeing guns around there, but I'd be damned if I was going to expose him to a dead body, especially since it might be his brother.

The curtains in this space were drawn, but there was still enough light that I could see. The ten-by-ten room was entirely devoid of furniture and decorations, but right in the middle of the floor, lying in a dark stain, was the lower half of a body, from just under its ribs down.

The legs, still wearing jeans, were askew as if they were badly broken and then tossed around. The feet were bare. The person had definitely been African-American, but I couldn't tell if it was male or female without checking, and I really didn't want to do that.

A similarly gruesome scene lay in the next small room, as well. I walked to the doorway to the bedroom, mouth and nose still covered, and leaned on the doorjamb to survey the carnage. The body was missing its arms, legs, and head, leaving behind only its partially clothed and badly mangled torso. A bloody, matted mess of long blond hair lay next to the body. This one was probably a woman.

As I made my way around the apartment, the only things I found were the remains of a destroyed cot in the bedroom and a camp stove in the space that served as a kitchen. There was one other doorway off the bedroom, which I assumed to be a bathroom, but I didn't bother to check.

I crossed back out into the main room and sat on my heels next to the first body for a solid minute, debating whether I wanted to search it for a wallet for the kid's sake. I finally decided I would check the pockets. I poked the front pockets with my gun, but they felt empty. I hooked a finger through a belt loop and rolled the legs slightly, and I could see the outline of a wallet in the right pocket. I set the gun down and reached for it.

From my left, I caught a blur of motion coming from the room with the blond corpse in it. Some creature vaguely resembling a massive dog slammed into me, sending me flying hard into the wall at the far side of the room, and then it crashed through the window, taking the curtain with it, gibbering a bizarre, high-pitched squeal as it ran.

I got to my feet as quickly as I could, scrambled to get my gun, and then ran to the window, but I was too late. The damned thing must have been hiding in the bathroom. It had taken out the window and the metal security grate that covered it from the outside without slowing down.

With all that noise, I was sure someone would call the cops, and I did not want to be here to explain these partial corpses, so I stuffed the dead guy's wallet into my jacket pocket, holstered the Sig, and hopped out the window in an attempt to follow any tracks that might have been left behind. Back inside, I could hear someone banging on the apartment door.

Whatever it was that had barreled through the window left a messy set of deep divots in the grass. I followed them around the building, back toward Dwight Street, and found the curtain lying on the ground just before the sidewalk leading to the building's main entrance. I continued to follow the trail of dirt and grass onto Dwight Street for about fifty yards until it finally petered out, and I lost it.

I hadn't had much of a chance to search the apartment, but it didn't seem like the bomber left much behind anyway. Other than being attacked by a giant dog, I had nothing but a corpse's wallet. That was real bang-up detective work. It was twilight, and activity along the streets and in the playgrounds had completely died out, making for a quiet evening — much quieter than I would have expected, but maybe that was just the way it was here.

Without any other leads at the moment and since the tracks led down Dwight before they disappeared, I decided to continue along the street to see if anything presented itself. As I walked past the park opposite the housing project, I got the distinct impression that I was being followed.

CHAPTER 19

I LEARNED LONG AGO TO TRUST my instincts, so even though I couldn't pinpoint anything specific, I walked purposefully toward several expansive open lots just down the street. I crossed the split between Dwight and Otsego Streets and tried to keep my pace even as I approached a strip mall with a sizable parking lot out front surrounded by a six-foot chain-link fence.

The shopping center consisted of a bank, several small stores, and a supermarket, which I decided to duck into. I paid for a bottle of water and then drank it just outside the store to see if I could make out what was following me. It was hard to see much because neither of the two lampposts in the parking lot was functional. Despite being focused and wary, I spotted only a few cars in the lot and the occasional shopper walking to and from a vehicle.

Being followed was nothing new, but I had to remain vigilant to avoid being ambushed. I preferred to draw out whatever was tracking me, but that took time and at least an inkling of where they might be.

As I stood there, waiting and watching, I took a minute to check the wallet I'd taken off the corpse. Sure enough, it held a driver's license for a Maurice Ingram, aged twenty-two, with an address in the Red Hook Houses. His ID put him at six-four, one hundred ninety pounds. Based on his remains back in the apartment, I never would have guessed he was that tall. Poor kid. I shook my head and put the wallet back into my pocket and refocused my efforts on spotting my tail.

After about fifteen minutes of garnering odd looks from a few locals and another bottle of water, I decided to keep walking in the darkness. That was when a group of guys about half a block away started making their way toward me from a side street just past the shopping center. In the moonlight, I could tell they weren't dressed in any gang colors I could identify, but they definitely gave off thuggish vibes. They ambled toward me as a loose group, laughing and making comments about how stupid I must be to be out here at night alone. A couple of them made jokes about why I'd be there at all and how I probably should pay to pass through.

Just what I needed. I continued on, focusing more on my surroundings than on them, but I'd only made it across the street in front of a school-bus lot ringed by an eight-foot-tall corrugated-metal fence before they closed in on me.

I was sure these thugs weren't what had been following me or what had attacked me in that apartment, and if either of those things showed up while I was forced to waste time dealing with these wannabes, the guys would likely just end up getting themselves, or me, killed. I attempted to push past, but they made it clear I was their target for the evening. I counted six men, at least four of them armed with guns. The oldest couldn't have been more than twenty-five, and the youngest probably couldn't even legally drive. All of them wore their pants so low they would have made Isaac Newton rethink his theories on gravity.

"I don't want any trouble," I said, dividing my attention between surveying my surroundings and trying to identify the leader.

"Trouble's all you got," said the tallest one just off to my right.

The others laughed and jostled around nervously while trying to act tough. I could see the fear in some of their eyes, but several others had the cold, dead eyes of kids who were used to violence. The nervous ones presented the real danger. They were unpredictable and often rash, the ones who shot people during a purse snatching because something startled them. And I wasn't wearing my cuirass.

"Why don't you pass over your wallet and anything else you got, before you make me shoot you," the talker said as he dramatically pulled a gun from the front of his pants. The talker was taller than the others by a few inches and beefier, too. He wore a white tank top with way too many gold chains at his neck and a ball cap turned most of the way around. I could also see a glint of gold on his teeth every time he talked—and he was the only one saying anything. He was undoubtedly the leader.

The gun he pulled was a Smith and Wesson M&P nine millimeter—a street gun, easy to obtain, easy to get ammo for, and powerful enough to kill. He pointed it at me and held it sideways, the ridiculous way they did in movies, with his last three fingers extended rather than around the grip. I could have slapped it out of his hand.

"Look, guys, just walk away now, and everything will be okay. I'm just passing through," I said as calmly as possible, turning myself so that I presented a smaller profile to the talker just in case he did pull the trigger.

That was when I got that paranoid sensation again: those guys definitely weren't what was following me. My feeling was substantiated by a horrible screeching noise and what sounded like a car crashing. Something was making its way through the school-bus parking lot on the other side of the tall fence to my left, and it sounded as though it was pushing buses out of its way. Then two distinct calls, similar to the high-pitched gibbering I'd heard from the thing that blindsided me in the apartment, emanated from the lot.

"You guys better run now," I said to the thugs as I pulled the Glock from my waistband and pushed through them to take cover behind some parked cars across the street. I was behind the car before they could even react.

The would-be gang members' heads swiveled around as they tried to figure out what was going on and where I'd just gone. The only light on the darkened street came from a single streetlight at the other end of the block, but the rending of metal, the scraping of steel on cement, the shattering of glass, and the grinding of the buses being shoved around was hard to miss. Several of the gang members took off back up the street at a full sprint, clearly terrified. The three that stayed behind were either too scared to move or too stupid to know better.

"What the fuck's going on in there? Where'd that dude get to?" one of them said with an audible tremor in his voice.

"You guys really should follow your friends — right now," I shouted from behind the car.

"I ain't runnin' from nobody," came the reply, followed by half a dozen quick pops from his gun as he fired into the car I was hiding behind.

"Suit yourself," I said, popping my head up just long enough to see what was coming from the lot behind them. I looked from the bus lot to my gun, noting that the weapon was going to be practically useless against something that could move a bus. I could have pulled one of my knives, but I really didn't want to have to get in close enough to something that strong and fight it with a knife—even a really sharp one—especially without my armor. At least with the gun I might get lucky and shoot whatever it was in the eye. More than likely, it would just irritate the crap out of it, but at least I could do that from a distance.

I poked my head out again just in time to see the two gang members who weren't focused on me get flattened by a section of the sheet-metal fencing behind them as it suddenly sheared loose with a deafening explosion and smashed into them like a freight train. Driven by something massive, the mess of metal and human bodies continued straight into the car I was hiding behind with a thundering crash that slid the car sideways and knocked me on my butt. I got back into a crouch and could see and smell motor oil leaking all over the street and realized that what had gone through the fence and crushed the thugs was a fifty-five-gallon drum full of it. It must have weighed over four hundred pounds, and whatever was out there had tossed it like a baseball through a metal fence. As I once again contemplated the usefulness of my gun in this situation, I found myself thinking we could really use a guy like that on the Padres.

The remaining gunman froze. I, on the other hand, quickly crawled behind the next car to my right. As I raced between cars, I could see at least three figures inside the bus lot through the gaping hole in the fence. One was gigantic compared to the other two, but they all appeared humanoid as they crossed the lot toward Otsego Street. The giant creature walked completely upright, but the smaller ones alternated between loping on all fours and standing on two legs as they weaved back and forth across the lot like dogs on a scent trail. In the darkness, I couldn't tell exactly what they were, and at three against one, I wasn't sure I wanted to stick around to find out, so I sprinted down Otsego Street as fast as I could go.

I easily covered a hundred yards in less than four seconds before a guttural scream that I assumed came from the last gang member echoed from behind me, followed by two of those bizarre gibbering howls. The more I listened, the more it sounded just like a damned hyena's laugh.

I stopped running right outside a fenced community farm across from a brightly lit furniture store and realized I had to lead whatever these things were away from any kind of crowded places. I grabbed the top of the farm's eight-foot chain-link fence and vaulted into the field beyond.

The farm was an open pasture a city block in size with a few small structures along its northern edge, which at least meant that whatever was following me couldn't sneak up on me. The land had been plowed and planted with a few dozen rows of several kinds of vegetation that were all about a foot tall or less except for two sparse rows of corn along the south side of the field. The furniture store was just beyond the corn and across the street. The corn stalks were a foot and a half taller than everything else, but none of the vegetation offered enough real cover to hide behind. Still, it was all there was apart from the storage building, which would be too obvious, so I chose to head across the field to crouch among the diminutive stalks of corn.

I felt for my Sig in its holster under my jacket and pulled my knife from its sheath on my calf. This was really going to be ugly. My only chance was to attack at least one of the creatures as hard and fast as I could and take it out, evening up the odds just a bit. I waited, breathing in the earthy smell of the small urban farm.

It took a long few minutes, but I noticed movement coming from back up the street. A pair of oddly shaped dogs approached the fence, then one of them barked that laughing cry. They really were freakin' hyenas.

The creatures stopped outside the fence where I'd jumped, and sniffed the air. The most massive of the pair tossed its head and let out a low laugh, and then the creatures leaped the fence in a single bound. In midair, they shifted into humanoid form, landing heavily in the tilled dirt, and the last piece clicked: they were ghouls—not just any ghouls, but Middle Eastern Ghilan, the least powerful of the various races of Jinn. Of course, that was still a relative observation. And while Ghilan may not have been the smartest kids in the class, they could not only shapeshift but could also assume the form of the last person they ate. In human form, the massive one had the appearance of a very stocky blond woman while the other looked like an African-American man.

The pieces began to fall into place. Those things had to be the Middle Eastern Parans Ned had heard about. They were likely the presence the old Lar had talked about feeling, too. The problem was I just couldn't see a pack, much less a pair, of Ghilan taking Oc and Dec unless they caught them completely by surprise. That was unlikely — unless, maybe, the giant bus-moving thing was involved, too. That thought made me feel all kinds of uncomfortable.

After they landed in the field, the pair of Ghilan began surveying the space, sniffing the air. I was sure they knew I was nearby. The blonde let out a soft, staccato call and then shook its head and shifted back into hyena form. The other stayed humanoid.

A Ghilan's resemblance to a hyena was about the same as its resemblance to its last human victim in human form, which meant only vaguely. They took on their victims' height, hair color, and general build, but their torsos remained thick and muscular. Their long arms ended in heavy claws, and their legs were short, thick, and muscular. Their stumpy heads sat right on their shoulders, and their eyes were large and dull, matched only in proportion by oversized mouths jammed full of massive, shearing teeth like a real hyena's, capable of cracking a human femur with ease.

In hyena form, they were huge, quadrupedal beasts with short back legs and long front limbs that ended in hand-like claws. The hairless and leathery skin was a mottled brownish gray, and their torsos were thick and muscular and gave rise to canine-looking heads. Their lower jaws protruded and could unhinge completely. Despite the size of their eyes, they were better suited to scent hunting, and they always hunted cooperatively. They were equally quick and deadly in either human or hyena form, and they were tough as hell to kill.

While I wanted to be preemptive, I decided to hold my attack until they'd separated themselves a bit to give myself a small cushion between assaults. I waited while the female began moving on all fours, occasionally rising on its hind legs, sniffing the air as she closed in on me down the middle of the field. Undoubtedly, she knew I was near, but I was sure she hadn't spotted me yet. The other Ghilan, in human form, began skirting the fence far to my right toward a little greenhouse, a dark-colored metal storage trailer of some sort, and a covered farm stand. He walked upright on stubby, bowed legs. He crossed into an open area, and I got a glimpse of his face. Eerily, it reminded me of the picture I'd seen on Maurice Ingram's driver's license. These creatures were definitely in that apartment, either searching for or working with the bomber, and one of them ran me over trying to get away.

Just as I was about to make my move on the female, the trailer's door opened, and out walked a small, hunched man carrying a heavy rake. I immediately recognized the protector of Brooklyn.

"You're a long way from home, no?" the Lar asked the surprised Ghilan.

Oh, hell yeah! The Lar's sudden appearance startled the pair of Ghilan so much that they froze. The male near the Lar glared back at the female and then cackled a creepy, soft version of their crazy laugh. I used the distraction to my advantage, shifting into a prone firing position and squeezing off three rounds at the female's head. All three rounds connected solidly but only knocked her off balance. Even if the rounds had penetrated her thick skull, I wasn't sure there was much inside it to damage. The only way to kill this thing was to rip it apart.

Across the lot, the Lar stood over the other Ghilan, pummeling it with his rake. *And I thought I was fast.* I stood up and charged the off-balance female, tackling her, but I had too much momentum and rolled past her once we landed. I was trying to get back to my feet and face her when something clamped down on my ankle like an iron vise and then slung me backward through the young corn. I landed where I began, about fifteen feet away, spread-eagled on my stomach with the breath knocked from my lungs. I did manage to hang on to both my gun and knife, though.

I pushed myself up to my knees and sucked in air. The female Ghilan threw her head back and screeched a long, piercing cry and then charged me in a loping gait, her massive jaws spread wide, slobbering as she closed the distance. I recovered enough to feign still being incapacitated, and I waited, making a show of breathing heavily. When she closed to within a few feet, I raised the gun and emptied the clip into her face and upper body, sending her into a face-plant and a skid that I had to roll to my right to avoid. Without hesitating, I discarded the gun and jumped on her prone form, impaling her in the upper back with my knife. As sharp as the blade was, it took all my weight to drive it through her musculature and heavy skeleton. As the blade bit, she bucked, throwing me off her back, but I managed to keep a grip on the knife with one hand. She thrashed, trying to reach me, ramming her heavy elbow into my ribs several times, but I wouldn't let go. With my free hand, I punched at the base of her neck repeatedly until the knife finally pulled free, and I rolled off into the corn stalks.

She was on me in an instant, pinning my legs and my left arm. I stabbed at her with the knife in my right hand, but she subverted the blow by grabbing my arm, trying to drive it back down to the ground. She glowered at me and roared in my face, showering me with hot drool and spittle and breath that could peel paint. Our arm-wrestling match was at a standstill. Suddenly, an inhuman piercing yelp from across the field drew her attention, giving me the break I needed. She backed off just enough that I overcame her strength and jammed the knife into the side of her head. She reared up, allowing me to free my left arm, and I grabbed her by the throat and rolled her to the left, driving her over with the knife in her skull.

Once free, I straddled her, pinned her jaw shut by shoving on her chin with my left hand, withdrew my knife from her temple, and then jammed it under her chin. Again, she started to thrash. I pulled the knife free, stabbed her again in the face, and left the knife imbedded just to the left of her nose. I shoved my left hand into the knife wound under her chin and grabbed on to her jaw and pulled with every ounce of strength I had until I pulled her lower jaw free, sending thick black blood flying everywhere. She lay still beneath me, but I knew she was a long way from dead. Hell, she'd probably even recover, given enough time.

"You better finish it off," the Lar said from across the field.

I pulled the Sig from inside my jacket, put the gun against the roof of the Ghilan's mouth, fired ten rounds into her skull, and then stood up and fired the remaining six rounds into her chest at point-blank range. Her body went into spasms and then went still. While she still may not have been completely dead, I was sure she wasn't about to pop up anytime soon.

I changed out the clip and put the Sig back in its holster then collected the Glock and replaced its clip and tucked it back into my pants. Finally, I grabbed the knife and wiped it off on the sleeve of my jacket. Weary, I turned back to face the Lar.

It turned out that his rake wasn't a rake but a spear, and his serpent was eating chunks of the male Ghilan's flesh as the Lar cut it loose from the carcass. It was kind of disgusting to watch as the snake thing threw its head back convulsively to chew and swallow, and the sound of the crunching bones made me wince.

Before I could even worry about the recent ruckus attracting unwanted attention, a series of rapid-fire gunshots exploded off in the distance, back in the direction of the Red Hook Houses. The Lar just leaned hard on his spear, closed his eyes, and shook his head, his thin lips pursed. *Inner-city life, I guess.* Of course, as soon as the farmers saw the garden in the morning, all hell would break loose.

"This one's done for," I said, breathing heavily. "If your snake is still hungry, send it over here."

"We're not done," the Lar said as he approached me, replacing the rake head over the spear's tip. "There's an Ifrit coming after you just up the street. I don't know why it didn't attack with these two, but it's coming now."

"Seriously? That's what shoved around those damned buses? An Ifrit? Shit. Given what just happened with the fucking Ghilan, I'm not sure if I can face their fire-wielding big brother with just my guns and a knife." I showed him the blade. "Everything is back in my room."

"I can get your gear for you if you want," the Lar offered. "No problem. Just take about five minutes."

It didn't take me long to decide. "Okay, go, but hurry up. I don't know how long I can hold this thing off with a gun and a knife."

There were five kinds of Jinn, including ghouls and Ifrits, and all of them were evil and nasty creatures. All of the types were said to have been formed from fire, and they were ridiculously strong. Ifrits were the most powerful—they could manipulate fire, and they were incredibly cunning. This was going to get nasty.

I watched the Lar go back into the storage shed then decided to draw the Ifrit farther east into a huge recreation area—and away from the furniture store and other people—in order to minimize collateral damage.

Without wasting more time, I vaulted the farm's fence and bolted for the open space down the street. I could hear the crunching of metal and glass somewhere behind me to my left, and it was getting closer. I ran along a sidewalk path through a thick stand of trees into the park and out to the most significant open space I could see—a football field in the middle of a running track. Once in the center of the space, I crouched into a kneeling position and tried to focus on any noises coming from behind me. The night was strangely quiet.

From what I could make out of my surroundings, the jogging track and football field was at the far northern end of the huge recreational area. Just to the south, a row of trees, denser at either end, stood between the track and another massive open part of the park. The farm and street lay directly to the west of me.

Finally, after what felt like hours but was really just a minute, a noise like a bull chuffing drew my attention toward something hurtling through the air from the farm, heading in my direction fast. Check that—it was heading directly at me like a guided missile.

I dove to my right, rolled, spun around, and fired three times at the object. It landed with a heavy, wet thump ten feet away from me. It was the remains of the talker from the street gang. He had literally been crushed before he was thrown at me.

I followed the body's trajectory to see if I could detect any movement, but I couldn't. Of course, in a major metropolitan area, like New York, the light pollution pretty much hampered night vision, and to make matters worse, I was looking back toward the furniture store, which was lit up like a football stadium. I decided to rely on sound.

As I strained to listen, a strong growing rumbling like a damned earthquake shook the ground beneath my feet. I got to my feet as the ground buckled in a straight line that was heading directly at me at incredible speed. Before I could move, the ground erupted beneath me and threw me ten feet into the air. I landed mostly on my back, but I managed to brace myself to lessen the impact then quickly got my feet under me. I ran off the football field to the south toward the open space beyond the trees. The Lar had said five minutes; it'd been three, and if the Ifrit managed to catch me, it would be over in one. Man, was he taking his own sweet time.

I continued moving at a steady pace, and I still couldn't see a thing for all the trees that surrounded the park, but I didn't stop. I figured it was safer to keep moving than to present a stationary target.

I changed directions every few yards to avoid being predictable, but it was hard to be unpredictable and move farther away at the same time. I finally decided to bolt for the denser part of the stand of trees just ahead of me. As I ran, the ground began to rumble again, so I swerved sharply and ducked through the trees and into the open space beyond. The expanse of grass on the other side was a huge, square field with a baseball diamond in each corner.

I watched the ground bulge behind me and then shoot past toward the far end of the park, where it buckled and collapsed a wide section of a brick wall at the park's far southern edge. I couldn't see the first furrow from my new position, but I could tell that this one didn't have the same origin. This one came from the trees across the field, somewhere between the farm and the furniture store.

The partially collapsed, ten-foot-high brick wall was about a hundred and fifty yards away to the south, and I couldn't tell what was directly on the other side, but I figured if I could make it over, I might be out of the Ifrit's view long enough for the Lar to find me and deliver my gear.

With my Sig in hand, I covered the field in just over five seconds. Moving as fast as I could, I scrambled over the debris and ducked through the gaping hole in the wall and took cover just inside.

Once on the other side of the brick barrier, I could see the space was an extensive parking lot for private tour buses and limos. With my view illuminated by a few lamps scattered around the lot, I took a second to survey the area. Thirty buses and limos of varying lengths were parked in several seemingly random rows. Most of the lot was empty and, luckily, entirely devoid of people. From what I could make out, the lot sat right on the edge of the Upper New York Bay, and I could actually smell foul, fetid water from what I guessed was the Gowanus Canal nearby, as well.

I slowly crept along the shattered wall, finally taking cover behind part of the fallen structure. The spot afforded me a view straight back into the ball fields I'd just crossed. The whole trip had taken me less than half a minute, so I was hopeful that the Ifrit had no idea where I was and that I hadn't covered too much ground for the Lar to catch up to me—which I was sure would be any second now.

After a few more minutes of scanning the area for movement, I saw a shape move from beneath the trees at the far side of the ball field. A figure crouched with one hand on the ground at the edge of one of the baseball diamonds less than two hundred yards away, and it was huge. It was possible that the zoo could have lost a gorilla, but at around eight or nine feet tall and humanoid except for its inky-black skin, it was probably safer to assume it was the Ifrit. The enormous Jinn also emitted some sort of strange red energy where its hand rested on the ground. I'd never seen that before in an Ifrit, so I had no idea what he was doing. However, it did give me yet another thing to concern myself with when fighting the damned thing.

I watched it rise from its crouch and move slowly south in my direction, moving its head purposefully from side to side. I doubted the Sig would do much to the beast even at close range, and at that distance, I knew it would be totally useless, so I holstered the gun and checked my knife out of habit. Where the hell was the freakin' Lar? I watched as the Ifrit crept across the infield of the baseball diamond, when it suddenly glanced back over its shoulder and then slunk quickly back into the trees from which it had emerged.

From my current vantage point, I had a clear line of sight to the Ifrit. What I wouldn't have given for a Barrett XM500 sniper rifle, or better yet, an XM307 fully automatic grenade launcher. Hell, I'd have settled for a piano to drop on it. I tried to assess my options, and none of them boded well with me armed only with a knife.

If the Lar didn't show up in the next minute, I decided my only option would be to try and escape. Without my armor and weapons, I was no match for this thing. And given the Ghilan had tried to kill me rather than question me—admittedly, a stretch for any kind of ghoul—I had to assume they wanted me dead because they thought I was on to something. At least there was that.

I hated the thought of leaving a monster like an Ifrit to wander around Brooklyn pissed off. Still, going up against it would prove little more than suicide at that point. As I continued to assess my pathetic tactical options from amid the rubble of the wall, a sound behind me caught my attention. It was the Lar, standing next to my heavy gear bags and the Pelian Spear. *About damned time!*

I crawled out from behind the debris and, in simple combat sign language, conveyed the Ifrit's position. I put my hand to my mouth and used my fingers to indicate fangs then pointed back across the ball field. The Lar shook his old head. To my surprise, he pointed off to our left. I couldn't tell if he meant in the bus lot or not, but it really didn't matter. I had my gear, which meant I could finally go on the offensive.

I geared up and pulled the Pelian Spear from its tube last. Its long, thin, bronze-colored head had a dull finish that didn't glint at all in the light given off by the security lamps, and it didn't appear nearly as special as it actually was. In addition to being indestructible and capable of piercing virtually anything if used with enough force, its ability to stop beings from teleporting or phasing in and out would come in very handy with this type of Jinn. While I hadn't seen this one do it yet, Ifrits were capable of teleporting to anywhere they could see. If I could nail him with the spear, I could level the field a bit. *If only I had that piano to drop on him, too.*

Once I was ready, I looked back to the Lar and shrugged.

"It moved into the far side of this lot," he whispered. This was his town. I was sure he always knew the position every living thing in it — even things that teleported. "I distracted him a bit earlier, but he has found your scent now."

"Once I see you are in range, I will draw its attention. From there, you are on your own. This one is strong — stronger than me — and he can control both fire and earth. *In bocca al lupo, custode,*" he whispered, patting my back, wishing me luck.

Fire *and* earth. That explained a lot.

"*Crepi.*" I began heading along the wall to my left. I had no idea where the Lar was, but knowing that Ifrits avoided water at all costs, if I could keep it with its back to the water, then the sonofabitch would have to pass through me to get away.

CHAPTER 20

I CREPT CAREFULLY ALONG THE WALL, the Pelian Spear in my hand, until I came to a series of long metal storage crates at the northwest corner of the lot. As quietly as I could, I climbed on top to lie in wait for the Ifrit. I didn't have to wait long. When it reappeared on top of a bus less than fifty feet away, it was facing into the lot.

The monster was huge, probably all of nine feet tall and four hundred pounds, with shiny pitch-black skin and glowing orange eyes and nostrils. It was vaguely human except for its leonine face, and a long mane of black hair was the only covering on its naked body. It stopped and sniffed the air, raising its head like a dog that had caught a scent.

"Hey, *pazzo*, come down from there, or I'll break your face," the Lar said from somewhere in front of it.

The beast shifted to peer down at the Lar and left his broad back facing me. That was my cue. I got to my feet on top of the crate, found my target, and tossed the spear lightly. The last thing I wanted was for the weapon to go straight through it. My throw impaled the monster in its shoulder and knocked it off the bus. It landed on the ground with a roar.

I drew my swords and began closing the distance as fast as I could, jumping from bus to bus with ease. By the time I got close, the Ifrit was starting to stand back up, wrenching at the spear, growling, and trying to pull it free.

I roared a battle cry and leapt down, aiming to land just outside the thing's reach, but it spun around and backhanded me in midair and sent me into the side of a bus. Luckily, it was one of those small tour buses with lots of windows along the sides. I crashed into but not through the tempered glass, breaking most of the windows, and landed on one knee, practically on the Ifrit's foot. Pain exploded

119

through my head, neck, arms, and hips from the impact, but nothing felt broken. When I recovered, its groin was right at my eye level — one of many things I wish I'd never seen. The Ifrit threw its head back and its arms wide and roared.

Fueled by adrenaline, I drew the sword in my left hand up and across the Jinn's thigh, cutting deeply, and lunged the sword in my right hand into its gut. I drew my right arm up with everything I had, dragging the sword through the creature's stomach and out just below its chest, cutting a gouge that began spraying lava that singed my face and forearm before I could back out of the way.

The howl that followed was deafening, and the Ifrit began swinging wildly. I rolled to my right, barely avoiding another collision with its massive right arm, and scrambled out from between the buses. The spear was still bobbing wildly from the Jinn's shoulder, the tip of the blade just visible in its upper chest. Grounded by the spear and unable to teleport, the wounded beast tore a massive gash in the bus to its left with a savage swipe of its immense claw and then focused on me again.

It let out another earsplitting shriek and then stretched its left arm toward me, and fire jumped from the flaming liquid gushing from its side straight at me. I dove left, but the fireball caught my legs and spun me around, setting my pants on fire with a rush of heat across my lower body and searing pain in my legs. I landed in a loose, awkward tumble that knocked the sword from my left hand, but at least I was out of the creature's line of sight.

I rolled and swatted frantically at my legs to put the flames out, sprang up, and ducked back. I tried to locate my lost sword as I watched the area back between the buses where the Ifrit was. I could hear its heavy breathing coming closer. I could smell the burnt flesh from my legs, but I couldn't feel anything yet. I knew the pain would come.

I ducked between the next pair of buses to my right and immediately rolled under one to get an idea of where the Ifrit was. I had to fight through the growing pain in my legs as they brushed the ground. The Jinn had slipped out to the space at the end of the buses where it had nailed me with the ball of flame. The area was now completely ablaze, and the creature was leaving a trail of flaming gore as it progressed among the vehicles. Directly under the bus in front of me, a glint of metal caught my eye in the glow — my other sword.

Several of the buses in the row I'd just run from were now fully ablaze, and a bus near the far end of that row was rocking side to side. I braced myself for the coming pain and rolled toward my sword as fast as I could. The second I grabbed it, the rocking bus tipped on its side and fell into the one next to it. The caustic smell of burning metal and rubber was thick. The Ifrit's roar drowned out the sound of sirens rising in the distance.

I climbed out from under the bus, swords in hand, and walked into the open area that was now ringed by burning buses. The Ifrit had its back to me, but I could see that the Pelian Spear was still firmly embedded. The wounds in its side and leg were oozing molten blood, sizzling as the flow dripped to the ground.

"You picked the wrong guy to chase, Torchy," I yelled as I walked, spinning both swords.

The Ifrit faced me in front of the wall of destroyed burning buses. Its voice was low and guttural but surprisingly understandable. The heat generated by the burning vehicles was tremendous, as was the growing pain in my legs, but I channeled it all to help me focus.

"You will die here in this" — it gestured toward the buses — "forsaken mess. And after I show it to her as proof of your demise, I will give your body to the wretched Ghilan to desecrate."

"Not likely. But if you tell me who you want to show me to, I'll take it easy on you, and we can both go see her now. I'll even let you live."

I had no doubt that the creature would reject my offer, but what did I have to lose? Ignoring the searing pain, I bent down on one knee, stuck both swords into the cement tarmac, spit onto the leather wrappings around my hands, and rubbed them, never taking my eyes off the beast. Its injuries and berserk attacks had clearly weakened it. I had taken several Ifrits before in straight one-on-one fights, and I was sure I could do it again as long as my legs didn't give out on me.

It laughed a horrible laugh and took a faltering step forward on its wounded leg. The hobble made me grin. In the distance, the sirens were getting louder. I figured we had maybe five more minutes at most. If I couldn't end this before they arrived, I had little doubt that this injured monster would attempt to take out as many humans as it could before I finally killed it.

"You will not kill me, Diomedes. You... are not strong enough," the beast said, laughing.

"Statements like that have a way of coming back to bite you in the ass, tough guy. I'll give you one more chance to answer my question, and then I'll finish my cut." I pointed at the oozing wound in its side.

"Insolent!" the Ifrit roared and then charged like a rhinoceros.

The beast's blundering attack was cliché. I grabbed my swords and took off, but instead of running straight ahead, I angled for the overturned bus to my right and used it to redirect a jump and flank the monster. It had moved first and predictably, giving me a slight advantage. The distance couldn't have been more than a hundred feet to begin with, and with our combined speed, it was practically past me when it realized my strategy.

The jet-black Jinn tried to stop and redirect its bulk but skidded several yards before it managed to whirl around and swing at me with its right arm, using its left to keep from falling as it twisted. I brought one sword up to parry and sliced right through its arm, severing it just below the elbow. The Ifrit's momentum carried it past me, and I ended up directly behind it.

It roared in pain and disbelief as I spun around and in a single fluid motion brought my other sword from overhead down in a wide arc at its other arm, which was braced on the ground. I connected just above its wrist and cut right through and into the concrete. The Ifrit toppled over onto its chest without its crutch, screaming in defiance, molten blood gushing from its severed limbs and puddling around the creature's prone form.

"Last chance," I said as I got to my feet. I pried my sword loose from the cement and took a few steps back to avoid the growing lava-like blood pools. My swords and the spear were unaffected by the fiery liquid. "Tell me who sent you."

The creature growled so deeply that I could feel it in my chest.

"I tell you what: just answer me this," I said, trying to compromise. "Was it you who killed the Spartoi?"

The beast rolled from its chest onto its side and began to get up, the hatred evident in its glowing orange eyes. It threw its head back and started to laugh then scowled at me as it pulled itself onto one knee. The Ifrit labored to speak as it tried to right itself. "They were weak and died like cowards. I let the Ghilan gnaw on their corpses."

It kept its left arm tucked close to its chest, and the stump of its right arm hung uselessly at its side. The Pelian Spear was firmly stuck in its back. The wounds in its thigh and chest leaked flaming liquid onto the cement tarmac, forming sizzling puddles at its feet.

The sirens grew behind us. The cloying smell of the superheated air and the burning buses was starting to make my eyes water, and the pain in my legs was becoming impossible to ignore. And with that last statement, the beast was just pissing me off.

The ground started to rumble around us, and the Ifrit began laughing again as the same red energy I'd seen earlier began to form along the creature's legs where they met the flaming, blood-covered tarmac. Without waiting to see what was about to happen, I closed the distance between us and brought my swords down on both sides of its head, meeting somewhere in its chest. The rumbling and the laughing abruptly stopped. I put my foot in its chest and pulled my swords free, pushing the giant body backward onto the spear, which sent the spear forward through its chest. The head separated from the torso, and fiery ichor spilled onto the ground, partly melting the soles of my boots.

The sirens were close now, probably just down the block, and their shrill wail snapped me out of my adrenaline frenzy. I sheathed my swords and walked around to retrieve the spear, kicking and shoving the Jinn's torso to wrench it free and melting the soles of my boots even more, nearly falling twice because of the pain in my legs. I was trying to locate the best way out, using the spear as a crutch, when the Lar came out from between some buses in front of me.

He waved me over urgently. "The police and fire be here in a moment. I have done all I can to slow their approach, but I cannot delay them any longer," he said, as if apologizing for not helping in the fight. "I have also collected and placed all your gear in a small inflatable boat tied up on Henry Street slip, other side of the building there." He pointed to a monolithic structure at the edge of the water. The stern set of his jaw suggested concern. "Also, I can help with the pain."

"Huh. Is it that obvious?"

He touched my shoulder, closed his eyes for the briefest of moments, and then smiled. "Go now. As long as you remain in Brooklyn, you will feel better and heal faster. It is the least I can do for your help. Go, go. I will take care of the Ifrit's body and give you time to leave the dock. And thank you, *custode*."

"You are a worthy protector for this community, and my success is in no small part your doing." I bowed my head just a little in gratitude. I limped for the slip and the boat as fast as I could, feeling the pain slip away with each step.

From the seawall, I could see that the bus yard was on fire and firemen were all over it. A news helicopter hovered overhead. I needed to get out of there fast. I found the boat with my two heavy gear bags and hopped in then noticed there was no engine on the rubber tub—just two oars. But the pain was all but gone. I stopped and shook my head. For that, I would gladly row.

CHAPTER 21

BOUT AN HOUR LATER, AFTER rowing from the mouth of the canal past what might have been two dead bodies and a load of stinking trash to an open lot at the Third Street Bridge, I grabbed my gear, ditched the inflatable dink, walked out to the street, and hailed a cab for my bed-and-breakfast. Twice, I felt like I was being watched again.

I had to have smelled as if I'd just walked out of a vehicle fire, complete with the unpleasant odor of burnt rubber, gas, and charred flesh. My hands and arms were smeared with soot and dirt, which I could only imagine covered my sweaty face and hair as well. Incinerated pants up to my knees and partially melted boots rounded out my ensemble. I did my best to ignore the cabbie's less-than-furtive glances over his shoulder at me.

I actually felt like I was making progress. Clearly, I had stirred up a hornet's nest—somebody knew I was getting close and had tried to deal with me directly, using goons. Ironically, if whoever was behind this whole mess hadn't sent the Jinn after me, finding the apartment would have been a bust and I would have been at a dead end. If I started poking around with an army behind me, whoever it was might just disappear. At least on my own I presented a target they felt they could come after, and I preferred to be bait rather than use someone else for that task.

Reflecting on all that made me realize how tired I was. I stared at my burned legs and my blackened right arm where the Ifrit's searing blood had landed on me. When I finally left Brooklyn, the burns were going to hurt big time. In the meantime, I poked at the burns on my arm and beamed at the complete lack of pain I was in, which almost made up for my near-total exhaustion.

Back at the bed-and-breakfast, I lumbered upstairs, luckily

avoiding any staff. Once I'd fumbled into my room, I put my gear down, pulled out a medical kit and a few towels, crept across to the shared bathroom, and quietly locked the door behind me. I took my pants off slowly and began the process of cleaning and debriding the burns. It wasn't as bad as I thought, but several areas on my upper shins were severely blistered, slightly blackened, and oozing. With the exception of my knees, which were covered by my kneepads, both of my legs were red and tender from mid-thigh down to mid-shin, and while it didn't hurt to move my legs at the moment—thanks to the Lar—they were stiff. I definitely wouldn't be wearing shorts anytime soon.

The debriding process was slow and tedious. All I could really do was clean the burns as best I could in the bathtub, bind them in fresh, clean gauze, let it dry a bit, and then remove it and repeat. Thanks to my immune system, I wasn't worried about infections, but I would certainly feel the brunt of the pain at some point. Finally, after three wrappings, I cleaned and dressed the worst burns and wrapped them loosely with more gauze.

Fortunately, the wounds on my face and arms were just contact burns, but I also had a shallow gash from my cheek across to my ear. Despite the Lar's help, my head and left arm still ached a bit, except where my left elbow was numb from ramming it into the side of the bus, and I was covered in bruises that were just beginning to turn a lovely shade of ugly. I took some prophylactic aspirin and hobbled back to my room. I looked like hell, and I could only imagine Sarah's reaction to me if she could see me now, but at least I smelled better.

I tugged on new clothes, feeling the stiffness now that I was slowing down, and started to piece together what I knew so far. It wasn't much, so it didn't take long. I knew the bomber was a nobody and that somebody wanted him to remain that way. I also knew whoever was behind this had to be strong enough to control Jinn, including Ifrits, as well as be magically sophisticated enough to create the explosion at the Met and use the Cup of Jamshid. Apparently, if Ned was right, the being in charge had terrorist connections, too. And it was a *her*.

The list of beings I knew that fit that description, not to mention had the *cojones* to try, was short. Of all of them, one stood out—Medea, a seriously nasty witch even older than I was. I recalled her being somewhere in Iran at some point, but I hadn't heard of her doing anything this far-reaching in over a millennium. Still, she definitely had connections in the Middle East. I decided to call Athena to run my theories by her. She answered so fast the phone never rang on my end.

"I hate it when you do that," I said, instantly annoyed. "But I think I may have an idea about who's behind this mess."

I explained to her what I had found and then listed my suspects, starting with Medea, while Athena listened intently. By the time I was done, she nixed all but two of them. Of course, as usual, she had information I didn't—like that one was dead. Of course, it had happened recently, and on a day when I was out fishing.

The only other likely suspect was Lilith—a fallen angel, the first of all known vampires, and supposedly, the first wife of Adam before Eve came along. She was a real piece of work and far worse than Medea, but for the last few centuries, she had been content to play Vampire Queen in Romania.

Of the two, Medea just made more sense. Born several centuries before my time, she was once the wife of Jason, of Argonaut fame. While she wasn't as powerful as Lilith, she more than made up for it in pure, unadulterated bitchiness—she'd actually killed two of her own kids, her second husband's fiancée, and the poor woman's father, too, before knocking off her uncle.

I found myself snarling as I recalled the last time I'd encountered her, just over a thousand years ago. She was calling herself Morgan le Fay—the nemesis of Merlin. Since the war between the nasty witch and the equally uppity half-demon, half-human wizard was causing all manner of collateral human damage, it was my job to stop it. Unfortunately, Medea managed to get away while I was rescuing some of King Arthur's knights who were helping me. She always was a slippery bitch.

Agent Wright beeped in while I was on the phone with Athena, but I let it ring over to voicemail. After a few more minutes of discussing our two suspects, I ended my call with Athena and left her to research the witch and her current whereabouts as well as Lilith's current endeavors, just to cover all our bases.

It was getting late, and I was exhausted, having not slept much in four days. The lack of sleep I could deal with—I'd trained for that my entire life, and my increased strength and stamina helped—but cap that with my evening's jaunt with the Jinn trio, and I was beat. Even so, I was too excited not to call Sarah back before going to sleep.

"Agent Wright? This is Steve, returning your call. Any news?" I figured it was best to play dumb. Explaining ghouls and Ifrits to a normal mortal would just get me an awkward silence or even hung up on.

"Haven't you listened to my message? All hell's been breaking loose in Red Hook. I thought you were going to be investigating out that way. I'm on my way there now."

"Um, no. I haven't heard a thing. I mean, maybe a few gunshots, but I figure, hey, it's Brooklyn, right? What's happening?" I wondered for a minute if I'd played it too coy, and I started to feel stupid. Part of me felt guilty for lying to her while the rest of me felt it was the prudent move. The prudent side won out—too much was at stake to allow my feelings to interfere.

"Some kind of gang war at a bus yard in Red Hook. Big shoot-out and fire. Half of Gowanus Industrial Park is burning. It's a mess."

Great. Now I really felt bad. "Well, that would explain all those sirens earlier. Are there many injured?" My job was to protect humanity, not chalk it up to collateral damage.

"So far, no. Kind of odd, actually. Not a single casualty, but there's a trail of damage all the way down Otsego and into the Red Hook Recreation Area down to where they set everything on fire at the bus yard."

Given the three dead gangbangers left in the wake of my fight with the Jinns, I guessed the Lar had done a little cleaning up for me. I would have to apologize to him later.

"Well, I'm glad that at least no one's been hurt. Oh, I did find one piece of information in my search for that cup. I think the bomber lived in those Red Hook Houses," I continued without thinking, mostly to keep the conversation going. I tried to convince myself that I'd said it because I wanted the police to find the two dead bodies in the apartment, but I was afraid that if they dug too much, they'd end up with a description that matched me. Still, someone really did need to inform the families of the two victims about their loved ones.

There was a long pause before she answered. "Really? Interesting..." She sounded a bit cagey all of a sudden. "I tell you what, I'm on my way there now. Why don't I come by and pick you up? Where should

I meet you?"

I could tell by the sudden change in her tone that she wasn't buying my clueless routine anymore, and the fact that she didn't give me much of an alternative to picking me up suggested she didn't trust me. Wonderful.

"Eighty Rutland, just off Flatbush. Gimme fifteen minutes."

I hung up. *Stupid me.* I sighed, and my stomach flopped. She knew I was lying to her. There went any chance at a relationship and any hope for sleep that night. I'd probably be in jail within the hour. I felt sick.

Just in case, I changed into a blue polo shirt and khakis that I hoped made me appear a little more respectable, and I fussed with the burn and cut on my face, hoping she wouldn't be freaked out. I holstered my Sig and tried to decide what to do with my knife. I sure as hell wasn't about to strap it to my leg. I decided to wear my tactical vest to blend in with the other law-enforcement types, which allowed me to store the knife in its usual place in its sheath on my upper chest. I took a few seconds to check and reload clips for the Sig, pulled on a light jacket, and then went down to meet Sarah — um, Agent Wright.

The moment I walked out of the bed-and-breakfast, I got that annoying tingly feeling again. I was a popular guy that night. At least I knew I was pissing off the right people. If I could avoid getting arrested as a suspect in the murders and mutilation of two bodies in the Red Hook Houses, I might actually be able to make some progress on finding this Cup and whoever took it.

As I stood in front of the building, a guy stepped partway out of the shadows of the building a few houses up Rutland to my right. I adjusted my jacket, pretending not to notice. Another figure approached from my left along the sidewalk about fifty feet away while two more stood around doing nothing across the street. The two across the street both turned their heads the moment I noticed them. Parked cars lined both sides of the street for the full length of the block, bumper to bumper, and all four figures kept to the shadows, including the one closing in to my left. For the moment, no cars were coming or going, and there was no one else along the length of the block. Since it was after eleven, most of the lights in the few houses not darkened for the night were coming from upper rooms. Overall, the street was quiet.

As I took stock of the situation, getting a sense of my surroundings, several small, quiet impacts on my back caught me by surprise. The chucklehead to my right had shot me. He'd actually tried to shoot me in the torso from thirty feet away. *Freakin' amateur.* I dove for the space between the two cars parallel parked along the curb in front of the bed-and-breakfast while pulling my Sig. As soon as I made my move, all four figures followed suit: the two across the street ducked behind cars, and I lost sight of them; the shooter to my right ducked back into the shadows; and the shooter to my left dropped to one knee, and I could see the glint of a silver gun in his hands. Based on the impacts of the bullets to my vest and the relative lack of sound, I guessed the shooter was using a silenced .22 or something equally small. The other shooters would likely be similarly armed. That meant they were going to have to get very close to do any real damage to me, even if they managed to shoot me in some spot not protected by my vest-covered cuirass.

Everything got quiet for a second.

"You get him?" a hoarse voice asked from behind a car across the street.

"I hit him, but I don't think he's dead," came the response from the guy up the street to my right.

"Can you still see him?" asked a voice from back down to my left.

Total amateurs. I now had a pretty good idea where they all were, even the ones I couldn't see.

"Hey, guys," I said. "Whaddya say you give up and go home? That way you might actually survive tonight. Just tell me who sent you, and we all walk away."

No one spoke for several minutes. While I was waiting for a response, the lights of a car coming up Rutland from Flatbush Avenue reflected off the other cars on the street. Crap. The last thing I needed was someone getting caught in the cross fire of idiots. I just needed to keep the situation calm until the car passed.

The car stopped right next to me, and a few seconds later my phone rang. I poked my head up to get a glimpse through the windshield, and my heart stopped. Sarah was sitting behind the wheel of the dark-colored Chevy Impala, holding a cell phone to her ear. *Dammit.*

My phone stopped ringing, and her car door opened.

"Sarah, stay in your car," I shouted.

"What? Where—" she managed to say before a bullet struck her windshield.

I popped up and fired twice up the street and twice down the street into areas where the gunmen were hiding, not really expecting to hit them but hoping they'd back off long enough for Sarah to take cover. The unsilenced nine millimeter sounded like a cannon on the quiet street.

"Holy shit!" she screamed. She ducked behind the front driver's side fender of her car — totally exposed to the gunmen on the opposite side of the street.

I fired two more rounds into the rear and passenger side windows of the car I was sure the two gunmen on the other side of the street were hiding behind, shattering the glass and sending it showering onto the sidewalk beyond. The instant I pulled the trigger the second time, I stood, took a step, and jumped, sliding across the hood of Sarah's car. I landed on the other side of the vehicle, just behind her, and immediately covered her with my body, turning my back to the gunmen behind us.

The maneuver brought a hail of quiet small-caliber gunfire from the pair behind us, with bullets ricocheting off every car around us. At least half a dozen bullets impacted my back as I covered Sarah and kept my head down. As soon as the shooting stopped, I stood up and spun around. Both gunmen were standing just beyond the cars behind me, frantically changing clips. I fired twice at each one, making them both drop, and then spun back to see if I could spot the other two who had flanked me to begin with. The one originally to my right was sprinting back up Rutland and away from us while the other just stood and started to fire his weapon. Sarah's car took the brunt of his barrage, with bullets shattering her passenger side and rear windows.

Sarah had pulled her gun. She stared at me, wide-eyed — not in fear but in incomprehension.

"Stay. Put." I spoke to her as forcefully as I could, ejecting my mostly spent clip and slamming home another. I ran around the back of Sarah's car and rushed the remaining gunman, vaulting the car he was behind as if it were a short fence. As soon as I cleared the rear bumper, the man threw down his gun and started to run toward Flatbush Avenue.

"Freeze!" I shouted, but it only served to make the guy run faster.

I could have shot him, but I wanted him alive. I took off after him, but whether it was fatigue or poor judgment on my part, the kid managed to stay just out of my reach. I chased him out to Flatbush, where he bolted into the street, and an old Cadillac promptly hit him with a bone-shattering thud. He flipped up the car's hood in a wild somersault and then smashed into the windshield. As the car screeched to a halt, his limp body rolled down the hood and off into the street. Tires screeched, and a car's horn blared behind the Caddy while another car traveling in the opposite direction skidded to a halt sideways to avoid running over the kid's body.

I ran into the street, up to the kid, and checked him for a pulse, but I could tell by the angle of his head, neck, and limbs that he was dead. I stood up with my hands on my hips and cursed my stupidity at not running faster. I could hear the drivers of the cars stopped around me asking me questions while a few of them got out to see. One even pulled out a cell phone to take pictures. I strode over to her, snatched the phone away, and tossed it onto the building on the other side of the street in disgust. Then I walked back to the street corner, upset with myself for not running just a bit harder to catch the kid.

I'd almost made it back to the sidewalk when a police car pulled up into the intersection around the stopped cars with lights flashing and siren blaring. Back up Rutland, I could see Agent Wright putting a flashing red light on the roof of her car as well. "Stay where you are, and put your hands behind your head," came a tinny voice over the police car's loudspeaker. "Do it now!"

I complied as I faced the cop. The officer threw his door open, braced himself, and pointed his service revolver at me. For the briefest of moments, I entertained the idea of running, knowing that I'd barely feel the impact of the .38-caliber shell on my armored back.

"Officer, wait!" Sarah shouted from behind me. "I'm Agent Sarah Wright of the DHS, and this man is working in conjunction with our department on a matter of national security."

I craned my neck just far enough to see her walking up the street in the glow of the red flashing light from her car, with her ID and badge in one hand.

"Hello, Sar—um, Agent Wright," I said sheepishly, hoping that maybe I was misreading her earlier tone.

"I'll get to you in a minute," she said in a low, serious voice, walking past me toward the cop as she presented her badge. The scowl on her face could have withered a cactus. I was screwed.

The police officer examined the badge and made a call back to his precinct to check the validity of her credentials while I stood around with my hands on my head. I felt stupid and tired, and I really wanted to search the guys who'd tried to ambush me. After another minute, he handed her ID back, and they had a conversation I couldn't hear but managed to get the gist of through their body language. Clearly, Agent Wright was pressing the cop into the service of the DHS, and she wanted him to secure the area.

Once they finished that conversation, she fixed me with the same intense expression she'd had before. It conveyed both disappointment and confusion. As she walked over to me, she pulled out her handcuffs. "Put your hands behind your back and turn around," she said, her voice devoid of emotion.

I just lowered my head and did as she asked. "Don't you even want to know what happened?"

"Depends on if you're going to tell me the truth this time," she said, cuffing me and then turning me back around. "Let's go back to my car." She nudged my shoulder to prod me along.

"Well, I was just walking out here to meet you, and I got jumped. That's the honest truth. You got there just as everything happened. Two guys are over there, and one guy is right here." I lifted my chin in the direction of the two guys I'd killed back by her car. "The fourth guy ran up Rutland and got away. The dead guy on Flatbush ran into the street before I could catch up to him."

She said nothing. As we walked back up Rutland toward her car, people were starting to poke their heads out of their windows, and lights were coming on as the neighborhood busybody patrol surfaced. People were gathering on fire escapes and stoops, and I could hear mumbling as people filmed us with their phones. *Fucking perfect.* I tried my best to keep my head down as we walked.

The entire length of Rutland was composed of apartment buildings and quaint old homes, but behind us, Flatbush was heavily commercial. The multicolored awnings on Flatbush were for hair and manicure salons, and the ones on the corner of Rutland were for deli markets.

That was when the smell of food caught my attention and sent my stomach into fits. I hadn't eaten much in days, and I was starting to feel that now, too. I'm used to little sleep and not eating for long periods of time, but it was all finally catching up to me.

We finally made it to her car, and I leaned against her front fender. She stood in front of me, hands on hips, eyeing me with an expressionless face that I couldn't read. After a long minute, she grabbed my jacket, pulled me to turn me around and then, to my surprise, took the cuffs off.

One hand back on her hip, she put her other hand out, palm up, and waved her fingers at me, indicating she wanted my gun. I handed it over to her slowly and deliberately, rolling my eyes.

"Now, explain to me exactly what happened again, slowly and in detail," she said.

I finally had a chance to take a good look at her. She was wearing a dark-colored pantsuit with a white shirt, her hair pulled back in a loose ponytail, much the same way she'd been dressed at the museum, only this time she was also wearing makeup. Despite the cosmetics, she glowered at me the same way she had the first time I'd met her.

She did a quick double take when she noticed the right side of my face. Her eyes softened for a second then hardened again.

"Look, I just told you. You saw everything that happened. Can we at least go get something to eat while I go over this again? I'm starved. And besides" — I tried to smile — "you owe me dinner."

At that comment, her face lost all expression again, and I could see the muscles in her jaw harden. "We can't leave until the police get here. Then we can go get something to eat. But they'll need your statement, too, and your weapon. I assume you have a permit for it?" She hefted my Sig. "Shit, you look like you're dressed for combat. What is that thing?" she asked, grabbing one of the Velcro tabs over one of my many vest pockets.

"It's my body armor," I replied curtly. "You said we were going to go where the bomber may have stayed, so I thought it best to be prepared. You know, an unknown enemy, hostile territory, IEDs, that kind of stuff." I was torn between trying to repair any damage I'd done to whatever chances I'd had with her and becoming irritated with her treatment of me.

She lowered her head and glowered at me from under her raised eyebrows as if I were talking about little green men and flying saucers. "You do know this is Brooklyn and not Baghdad, right? Is there something you're not telling me? Something I should know?"

"Nope," I replied brusquely. "I've just been doing this long enough to know it's better to be safe than sorry. We've got a probable Middle Eastern dissident who blew up some sort of bomb in one of the most prominent museums in the country. Something was stolen from that museum, and now I've been attacked. It's got to be connected. These guys were professional hitters. Well, semi-pro."

"Professional hitters?" she sneered and had to stifle a laugh.

"Okay, maybe talented amateurs," I quipped. "Still."

"That's not what I mean," she said, shifting her weight from one foot to the other, sighing heavily, and rubbing at her forehead. "You think these guys were hired to kill you? Why? You aren't the only one investigating this, and no one else has been attacked. Are you sure you aren't just being paranoid? And what happened to your face?"

I self-consciously reached up to touch the cut across my cheek. Luckily, just then the next group of cops arrived and began cordoning off both ends of the block with yellow tape. It wasn't long before a gaggle of cops and crime-scene investigators showed up.

I gave the exact same statement I'd made to Sarah to a detective, who was clearly annoyed with the task. I had to try very hard not to snatch his head clean off his shoulders several times, but I wasn't too snarky. These things usually went better if I wasn't a smartass.

As I was wrapping up my statement, a patrolman ran over to the detective and whispered in his ear. Detective Patience sighed with exaggerated exasperation. Whatever had been said, he was done with me. Before he left, he gave me the usual speech about being in touch and not leaving town without letting them know and needing my gun for ballistics purposes. I thought about how many of the damned guns I went through on a monthly basis, and I wondered whether SIG Sauer had a frequent-buyer's program.

The cop left, and Agent Wright came back over, arms folded across her chest and a tight set to her lips and jaw. She leaned on the car next to me and didn't say a word.

After an awkward two minutes of silence, I finally spoke. "Can we go get something to eat now?" My stomach growled audibly.

"Yeah, I suppose so. Let me just tell the OIC you're leaving with me."

I didn't move while she left to find the officer in charge. I wasn't really sure how long it took her. One of the downsides of being faster and stronger than normal was that while I had the stamina to match, when I hit a wall, I hit it hard. As of about an hour earlier, I'd not only hit the wall, but I'd crashed right through it. I needed food and sleep, and I needed them soon. Plus, for some reason I felt like a total rookie around Sarah.

I was so out of it that I nearly jumped out of my skin when she snuck up on me to let me know we could go.

"Jeez, jumpy much?" She laughed.

"Just tired and hungry. Food, now," I practically squeaked, completely embarrassed she'd caught me off guard.

"There's a pizza place right down the street. We'll have to take a different car since mine is now evidence in a shootout. I've arranged to borrow one of the unmarked police cars." She pointed up Rutland beyond the yellow crime-scene tape.

"Outstanding."

"While we're eating," she said as we walked, "maybe you can tell me why I have a description of someone who matches you at the Red Hook Houses earlier today snooping around an apartment with two mutilated bodies in it."

Suddenly I didn't feel so hungry anymore.

The pizza place was little more than a hole-in-the-wall local shop that was set up mostly for carryout orders with the full kitchen behind the counter. Fortunately, they had a single table up front near the entrance, and it was available, probably because it was close to midnight. The smells of tomato sauce, pepperoni, and baking bread permeated the small space, sending my stomach into spasms of expectation.

Ordering the third large pizza seemed to freak her out, but not nearly as much as when I finished it. She stared at me with wide eyes, starting about halfway through the second pie, and even the portly guy behind the counter was impressed. My heightened strength and speed came at the cost of an increased metabolism, so when I went without eating for a while, I tended to binge. It was even more extreme when compared to Sarah, who ate no more than two slices in total after she'd picked all the meat off them.

I started to feel a bit better and could finally concentrate on what she was saying. I tuned in to the middle of a story about how she'd decided she wanted to join DHS, and I became embarrassed about missing so much of her story so far. I thought it had something to do with being bothered by flies eating alphabet soup. I focused intently on what she was saying from that point on.

"I'm sorry. I've been talking incessantly for the last half hour, haven't I?" she said sheepishly. "I usually don't go on like that. You're looking better. That must have really shaken you up."

I nearly choked on the slice I was eating. "Nah, I was just really hungry. I haven't had time to eat today," I said between bites. "Or yesterday." I didn't mention that being attacked by milquetoast mortals, even armed ones, barely even raised my pulse. Somehow, I thought it would come off as a tad arrogant.

"Your face and hands look bad. Maybe you should have had the paramedics take a look at you." She reached out to touch the scabby cut across my cheek and ear.

I liked the feel of her hand on my face. It felt good to be touched. "Nah, I'm good. I'll be even better as soon as I get a little rest," I said, continuing to eat.

"So," she said staring down at the table. "Want to tell me about the Red Hook Houses and a couple of mutilated bodies?"

I put down the slice of pizza I was picking at, exhaled, and stared absentmindedly at the stock photos of Italy on the wall space near the entrance. There was no point in lying about it, though there were a few details I figured I could leave out.

I reached into my jacket pocket and pulled out Maurice Ingram's wallet, placed it on the table, and slid it across to her. She picked it up and examined its contents.

"That was in the male victim's pants," I said. "I think it's the oldest kid in the family that lives across the hall from the apartment his body's in. Young kid that lives there said his brother was missing. I didn't want him to find out on his own."

"So you were there?" she asked, sitting back hard in her seat.

"Yeah. Sorry I didn't call you first, but I was following a lead. I think that apartment is the bomber's." I picked over the remnants of the third pizza.

Sarah just sat there in silence for a few long minutes. I was afraid to make eye contact, so I just kept playing with a leftover crust on my plate.

Finally, she spoke. "You should've called me." It wasn't the admonition of a cop but rather one that suggested I'd let her down personally.

I nodded. "You're right, and I'm sorry, but once I saw the bodies, I figured it would be most expedient to get the hell out of there."

"You're lucky the ME says the bodies have been dead for at least twenty-four hours, or I'd have no choice but to haul you in as a person of interest," she said, her tone more stern. "I agreed to work with you as a favor to my boss, who owed a favor to the Metis Foundation, but if this is the way you guys operate, I'll tell you right now you won't be working with me again." She lowered her voice and jabbed her finger at the table as she said it. "Two-way street, Steve. I help you, you help me."

I couldn't say anything. She was right, but the truth was she had no idea what this whole situation was about. I probably should have called her immediately upon finding the bodies, but being run over by a Ghilan was kind of an extenuating circumstance and one that was hard to explain to mundanes. Still, she was just trying to do her job, and I'd betrayed her trust.

"I promise if we ever work together in the future, I won't do that again," I said finally, meeting her gaze. "Full disclosure." I raised my hand to swear.

I was torn about saying that because I knew it was a lie. I'd never be able to tell her everything, but I could tell her what she needed to know. That would have to be good enough. I yawned, suddenly very tired and not just physically.

"Ah, it's late," Sarah said. "Did you still want to go over to the Red Hook Houses with me? I need to check it out if it was the bomber's residence."

Her eyes softened, and the rigid set to her jaw melted away as she relaxed, and I had to smile. She grinned in return. If I weren't so tired, I might have jumped her right there. I'd say it was the gentleman in me that prevailed, but it was more likely the scared schoolboy.

"I tell you what: just drop me back by the hotel," I said. "You can go check out the Red Hook residences without me. I'm supposed to be flying out tomorrow. Just do me a favor, and watch your back. This case is far more than what it appears."

"I'm always careful, but there are over two hundred law enforcement officers from at least five different agencies involved in this. Why should I be singled out?"

"I'm not saying they'll target you specifically — just that they may target all of you or any one of you who gets too close. Just keep your head on a swivel is all I'm saying." I wiped my mouth on a napkin and then yawned again.

The expression on her face was a cross between confusion and worry. She either thought I had a concussion or that I was nuts. Given my present state, I was hoping she thought I was just concussed. *Whatever.* She didn't need to get dragged any further into this thing.

My problem was that whoever was behind this mess knew I was involved, and by now, they probably knew who I really was. My life was going to get a lot more hectic. Another thing that kept bugging me was how whoever was behind all this had found me so fast. They might have had the bomber's apartment under surveillance, but how did they find me at my lodging?

"Yeah, I should get moving," she said, frowning slightly.

Apparently, Agent Wright took my pensive moment and yawning as a sign of boredom. "Sorry, I'm just really worn out," I said.

"I understand." She threw seventy-five dollars onto the table. "I've never spent that much at a pizzeria before."

I finally took in the breadth of the carnage. The serving tray next to our table was covered in empty pizza trays and dishes. Not to mention that I was covered in crumbs. *Oops.* "Sorry. I'll make it up to you. I didn't mean to eat this much. Let me pay for it — I insist."

"Nope, I owed you," she said laughing. "Besides, a dinner in the city would have cost twice as much for a third the food. I'd just like to know how you keep the weight off," she said, joking, as we walked out to her car.

If she only knew...

"Next time is on me, then," I said, smiling.

She nodded, smiling back as she tucked her hair behind her ear. My smile broadened.

On the street, I began to feel a bit exposed. I'd left my vest in Wright's trunk to avoid coming off as a total paranoid delusional and to keep from scaring civilians. But I'd been in way too many scrapes in my life to ignore that feeling I got in the pit of my stomach when bad things were about to happen.

Something caught my attention as we walked: a massive bird that resembled a gigantic black owl was perched on a rooftop across the street. Not that there weren't owls around New York City, but this bird was about the size of small child, maybe four feet tall. Odder still was that even though it was in shadow, I could see its massive yellow eyes following us. Whatever it was, it wasn't normal.

When we got to the car, I walked around to the back and asked to get my vest out of the trunk. Wright obliged, but the set of her lips and the stiff way she shuffled through the keys indicated that she was annoyed. Once the trunk was open and partially blocking us from the owl's view, I quietly asked her for her sidearm.

"What? Why?"

"Just trust me. Give me your damned sidearm," I snapped.

I didn't want to tell her about the mammoth bird across the street, but I had a sneaking suspicion that it wasn't just hunting for stray cats. She reluctantly handed her gun to me. I took the safety off and opened the slide to see if a round was chambered. It wasn't. Clearly, she wasn't required to use it much.

I quietly chambered a round and brought the gun to bear on the last place I had seen the shadowy bird, surprising Agent Wright. The damned thing was gone. I checked the rooftops of all the buildings across the street before I caught the wink of something metallic straight overhead.

I swung around to check out the buildings next to us, but the bird had disappeared without making a sound. Owls flew eerily silently, even the largest species, but after seeing the metallic glint, I was sure this was a Strix, a gigantic, owl-like bird that made a pterodactyl seem like a baby duck.

Strixes inhabited the outer edges of Tartarus, the place where truly evil beings resided for eternal punishment. Their claws and beaks were some sort of metal capable of shredding plate armor or severing a man's leg. They ate people, too—as their primary food source. Legends said they were once men punished for acts of cannibalism. Strigoi, the true vampires, used them as scouts and security, as did some of the more malevolent Unseelie Fae and anything else that could control them. I was willing to bet that Strix was the thing watching and following me since I'd showed up at the Red Hook residences. Lilith employed Strixes, but she lacked the subtlety needed to send Jinn and mortal human assassins to take me out. The more I thought about it, the more I liked Medea for this whole mess. At least I wouldn't have to face a full-blown vampire army to get to Medea.

Sarah put her hand on my arm, gentle but steady. "Whoa, there. You okay?" she asked, snapping me back to reality.

"Uh, yeah. Just thought I saw something," I said sheepishly. "Sorry, it's a lot of years of training. It's hard to keep it in check sometimes. Thanks." Man, did I feel stupid. Not to mention excessively paranoid, too.

She never took her hand off my arm.

"Nice gun." I handed it back to Agent Wright, more than a little embarrassed. It was a Beretta Px4 Storm Compact. "Not used very much, though." It was a reliable and tough gun with little recoil. "Forty cal?" I asked, noting its shorter barrel length, desperately trying somehow to shift attention from my seemingly paranoid outburst.

"Yes," she said, reaching for the gun. "Uh, just target practice. We don't get into many shootouts in the DHS," she said wryly. "Part of the reason I left the FBI for it, like I was telling you earlier."

"Yeah, I suppose you're right," I said as I walked back to the passenger-side door. I had to try not to seem caught off guard by the FBI comment, which I'd clearly missed in the restaurant earlier.

"You want to explain to me what that was all about, or should I just chalk it up to you being tired?" I could see concern etched on her face.

"Could have been the pepperoni. Spicy food makes you see weird things," I replied without thinking. Stupid comment.

She stared hard at me for a solid minute across the car's roof then said, "Seriously, what was that?" as she opened her door and got in.

Once she was in the car I thumped myself in the head. "Nothing. I guess I'm just on edge."

"No kidding." She drove me back to my hotel. She didn't say another word the whole trip.

The closer we got to my lodging, the bigger an idiot I felt, especially as we wound our way among the crime-scene techs still working the site of the shootout. This was exactly why it was so hard for me to have a relationship with a mundane. But it didn't stop me from keeping watch over the rooftops as we drove.

"I'll stay in touch. And I'll be better the next time I see you, I promise," I said as I climbed out, vest in hand, before she could reply. I was too embarrassed even to say goodnight to her.

I ran into the hotel without turning back. Inside, I pushed through a few guests gathered in the salon to see what was happening outside, climbed the narrow staircase up to the second floor, and entered my room without turning on any lights. I crossed over to the window and pulled the blinds and curtains closed and then checked my watch. It was nearly one in the morning, and despite my near total exhaustion, I wasn't finished yet. I flipped the light on and grabbed my gear bags. I needed to call in backup.

Wrapped in a chamois inside a small compartment in the gear bag I kept my clothes in was a book-sized, brown-leather satchel that held a half-dozen arcane artifacts of a not-so-mundane-as-they-appeared nature. I pulled out a roll of parchment made from reeds from the River Styx and a writing quill from a roc feather and got my tanto knife from my vest. I sat down at the desk and began the fairy equivalent of a couple of e-mails.

True names were a powerful commodity among the fae and those beings that could use certain types of magic, and this type of communication was precisely the reason. I knew the full and true names of several fairy folk, and they knew mine. If I wrote them down, I could send a message to them wherever they were. I could do worse if I were so inclined, but the two fae I wanted to contact at the moment were friends, and right then, I needed them to watch my back.

When I finished writing the messages, I cut my thumb with the knife, squeezed a few drops of blood on the corner of each page, and murmured the incantation that would connect their names and my words. For all I knew, it was "Jimmy Crack Corn" in some archaic language. I wouldn't have put it past my friends, especially since they were particularly twisted Anseelie Fae called Peri.

The Anseelie—those of neither Light nor Dark—were considered traitors by the Seelie and Unseelie Courts and were bound by no agreements or accords with any beings. While both the Seelie and Unseelie Fae went to great lengths to maintain their codes of honor, formality, and behavior and had specific consequences for violations, the Anseelie were unburdened by such contrivances. As traitors, both courts had once hunted Anseelie Fae mercilessly for their crimes, and all but a few of the known types of the subversive races had been wiped out. Of all their kind, Peri were considered to be among the most feared.

The two fae I was contacting were some of the deadliest fairies around and as honor-bound and trustworthy as most humans—that is, not at all. Peri had no qualms about lying, cheating, stealing, and killing, if it served their purpose at the time, and my friends were no different. Luckily for everyone, there just weren't that many Peri left.

Like most fae, the two I was summoning were millennia older than I was. The brothers were as different as night and day. I'd met them several hundred years ago when I'd saved their lives. At the time, Duma was masquerading as a traveling court jester. His troupe of Peri entertainers performed a harlequinade, but in reality they were all mercenaries and assassins. Abraxos played the clumsy oaf Pierrot, and they even had a real wizard play the Fairy Queen and transform the players into the characters of the harlequinade.

The troupe got itself into trouble when it raided a Scottish castle for plunder during a secret meeting of the Seelie and Unseelie Courts that was presided over by Yngvi, a Seelie Elf noble, and Lord Rubezahl, an Unseelie ogre. Ab and Duma were the lone survivors of that offensive when I showed up, drawn by the bloodcurdling and grisly sounds of a horrific attack. I freed Ab and Duma, rescuing them from execution, and in return, they swore a blood oath to serve me. No fae can break a blood oath without dying.

One of my greatest regrets was that I was too late to save Duma's mate, the harlequinade's Columbine. Perhaps the last female Peri, she was presented, injured but alive, to Lord Rubezahl's vicious Cu Sith attendants. Those shaggy green dogs were the size of cows and significantly more brutal in a pack. After that day, Duma never spoke of her.

I didn't call on the pair very often because using them always led to death, destruction, and chaos. But together, we'd survived against overwhelming odds on more occasions than I could count. While our relationship was originally based on the oaths they swore, over the centuries it had developed into one of mutual respect and even trust. They had never let me down, nor I them. With all the creatures I'd dealt with chasing the damned Cup to this point, I knew I was going to need their kind of help if the trail indeed led me to either Medea or Lilith.

I finally fell into bed around two thirty — after I completed the incantation to send the messages and burned the papyrus with my blood on it — and got some fitful sleep that was more like passing out for short periods of time.

CHAPTER 22

AFTER I DRAGGED MY GEAR back through the Ways to the outskirts of San Diego and was crossing the casino parking lot toward my truck, I couldn't help but notice someone hunched over in my passenger seat. It was around five in the morning on the West Coast, and the sun was just breaking over the mountains to the east, but the lot was surprisingly full. I ducked behind a car, set down my bags, and pulled out my Glock. At this time of day, I assumed most of the cars belonged to casino hotel guests, and I didn't see anyone moving around the parking lot. I began circling around my truck, remaining several rows away, trying to get a better view of whoever was in it.

A dark-haired young girl lay against the passenger-side door of my truck at an odd angle. I started to approach the truck with a steady bead on the person inside, but rapid and furtive movements near the front of the vehicle caught my attention.

I stopped and listened, but I heard nothing. I dropped to the ground to look under the cars, causing me to bite back a groan from the pain that had returned to my legs since leaving Brooklyn, and noticed the feet and legs of someone straddling a prostrate form near my bumper. I pulled myself back to a crouching position and began moving to flank them. For all I knew, it was a robber mugging a lucky casino patron, but after yesterday, I wasn't about to take any chances.

When I was one row back but still several cars to the left of them, a soft gurgling sound escaped from the prone form on the ground. It was one I'd heard many times before: air escaping from someone's lungs without passing over vocal cords. Someone had been stabbed, and whoever had done it was a professional.

I still had the element of surprise on my side, so I watched for several seconds, trying to get a feel for what the killer was doing and which way he was facing. When I was sure his back was to me, I came out from around the car in a combat-ready firing stance.

"Freeze," I said calmly and quietly.

The killer was on one knee, stooped over the dying naked figure. He froze, dead still — too still, in fact, to be a human. "Can I at least scratch my ass? My underwear is riding up my butt." The voice was immediately familiar.

"What the hell? What are you doing? You know how close to death you just came?" I said, still aiming the gun. I was simultaneously relieved and irritated.

It was Duma, and as usual, he was dressed in some custom Savile Row tailored suit that cost more than my truck, his pale skin and bright-blond, shoulder-length hair a stark contrast to his black clothes and sunglasses, which he wore even though the sun wasn't up yet. He stood up and flashed a wide smile with a short, vicious, curved knife — reminiscent of a claw — in his left hand. The blade, a karambit with its hilt heavily bound in leather to protect him from the metal, was one of his favorite weapons, and it was dripping with green goo. At just over six feet tall, his clothes and seriously chiseled features would have made models jealous, despite the weapon.

"Not as close as this guy," he replied, gesturing at the corpse at his feet. The figure on the ground was not human at all. "How you been, D?" He smiled broadly and spread his arms like he was going to hug me.

I lowered the gun and laughed. As a rule, Peri were beautiful creatures, which was why they were originally thought to be the offspring of fallen angels. They were as varied in their appearances as people were with one exception: their eyes lacked all pigmentation. Like their Elven and Sidhe brethren, they were fair-skinned and tall and always slightly built. They were so fast that they were often thought to possess the ability to disappear at will.

"What's going on?" I jerked my head at the body in my car and the one on the ground as I put my gun away.

Having worked with him for so long, I just assumed Duma had the situation under control, including whoever was in my truck. The bizarre figure on the ground was humanoid in size and shape, but it was bestial, and its skin was grayish and sickly. It had no mouth or ears, only eyes, and slits for nostrils. It reminded me of a six-foot-tall, hunchbacked football player with long arms and nothing but eyes on his bald, wan head. Its fingers were misshapen claws at least ten inches long.

"Was that one of the Phonoi?" I asked, tapping its claws with the toe of my shoe.

"Yep."

That meant that the set of claws was only one of the many implements it might possess to inflict carnage. The Phonoi were the male embodiments of murder and violent death, and each one was different. It took one of the Old Ones to call them into being—or a damn powerful witch or wizard. The situation had Medea written all over it, and she obviously had a veritable Swiss army knife of Parans at her beck and call.

"This one was hiding over there behind that car," Duma said, pointing with his knife to a nondescript black sedan down the row. "But I don't think they were here just for you." Duma placed his knife into a pocket in his jacket and jerked his head toward the figure in my truck.

I looked through my windshield at the person inside. She was indeed a young girl no older than thirteen, and she was suddenly staring at me with wide eyes, her mouth agape. The moment I made eye contact, she began clawing at the door to get out, screaming something I couldn't quite understand through the closed cab. I stared at Duma in surprise to see if he had any idea about what was going on. He just shrugged and shook his head.

Before I could make it around to open it, the girl managed to get the door open, tumbled out onto the ground, picked herself up, and lunged at me—hugging me around the waist as if I were her long-lost father. She sobbed so hard that her shoulders heaved, and she mumbled unintelligible words.

Awkwardly, I patted her back and just kept glaring at Duma, who was doing his best not to laugh hysterically. I had no idea what this was about.

"Something I should know, D?"

He broke into laughter.

I pried the girl loose and bent down, enduring a great deal of pain to get a better look at her. She was dark complexioned, had short brown hair and light-brown eyes. She was covered in dirt and reeked as if she hadn't bathed in years. She could have been Hispanic, but the way she was dressed said otherwise. She wore a filthy red smock with a heavily stained white shirt under it, reminiscent of a uniform, and she held some sort of dingy scarf or kerchief in her hand.

She began talking again, rattling on like a freight train with no brakes, and it took me a second to realize she was speaking Farsi.

"*Aroom bash,*" I said in Farsi, telling her to calm down.

"Diomedes, I found you, I found you," she replied in her native tongue, repeating the words over and over. She pronounced my name *Dee-oh-me-dese.*

Finally, after a minute, she stopped, and her eyes widened with fear, and her entire body stiffened. She saw the dead creature on the ground behind me, and she screamed and began to run. Duma reacted before I could and caught her before she made it a full step.

I walked back over to her and knelt down again, fighting through the pain of the movement. I grabbed her gently by the shoulders. "*Negaranesh nabash,*" I said, telling her not to worry.

"It's dead," Duma said in perfect Farsi. He walked over and kicked at the creature a few times to prove it.

Still, the girl's wide eyes remained fixed on the dead creature. It took some effort, but I stood and walked her back to the door of my truck and helped her in. I closed the door, walked around to the driver's side, and climbed in with her, hoping she'd feel more secure. "See, we're safe in here now," I said, again speaking Farsi. "How do you know who I am?"

"She hates you," she said, tears drying on her face as she calmed down. Her whole body relaxed.

"Who hates me?"

"Medea. Medea. Medea..." she mumbled before she finally passed out.

I had assumed Medea was behind this, but now I knew. The revelation still caught me off guard. Leaving the girl to sleep, I climbed out of the truck and walked back over to Duma. "We need to get her someplace safe."

"Yeah, yeah. First, there's another one of these around here somewhere. Ab went after him." He came over to me and held out his hand, smiling. "Meantime, it's damn good to see you, my friend."

I took his hand, and it became a brief hug. I hadn't seen Duma in a while.

"How long's it been? A year?" I asked, recalling our scavenger hunt across half of Russia for the egg that held the soul of Koschei the Deathless.

He bobbed his head with a broad grin on his face and returned to the Phonoi to pull a wicked-looking kukri knife from its upper chest. The creature began shaking violently, and a horrible shriek erupted from the gash left by the blade and was followed by a thick green slime. The howl was the sound of the spirit tearing itself from the body it had been given and being pulled back into the nothingness it was drawn from. A violent feeling surged through my own body: I wanted to reach across and strangle Duma. The feeling was gone as quickly as it had come. It didn't affect Duma because he wasn't human.

Phonoi were made when the ill will and malicious sentiments that humans displayed were gathered and concentrated by those capable of summoning them. They were given a human form that was then perverted by the evil it contained. As they died, that energy got released back into the world. Their demise could easily cause nearby humans to enter into a killing rampage. I'd dealt with those abominations before, and I could resist the effects of one or two dying around me — but any more than that, and all bets were off.

"Beats me, but it sounds about right," Duma finally responded, trying to wipe green goo from his suit. "You know I have no concept of time. Sun comes up, goes down, the Earth spins around, whatever. Too long is all I know. What kinda crap you get yourself into?" He kicked the once-human shell the murderous spirit had left behind. "This was a twelve-thousand-dollar suit."

"Oh, you know, the usual. Supernatural bombers, wizards, Jinn, magic cups, assassins, Strixes," I said with a shiver, trying to shake the last of the murderous feelings.

I walked back to get my bags, and Duma followed without concern, as if I'd just mentioned a grocery list and not a litany of nasty creatures. The problem with him was I couldn't tell if his lack of reaction was because he was used to this kind of situation with me, or he just didn't view the creatures as all that nasty. I got the bags to my truck and threw them into the bed.

"What are we going to do with that?" I asked, hooking a thumb toward the body on the ground.

"Dumpster?" Duma asked with an unconcerned shrug.

Something heavy landed in the bed of my truck with a thud. I drew my gun and spun around to the truck's tailgate to see Duma's brother Abraxos grinning from ear to ear.

"Whatever you do, make room for another," Abraxos said. The pale hulk was wiping his hands as he stood at the rear bumper of my truck. He was monstrous, nearly seven feet tall, and dressed like his brother in clothes that had to be custom-made to fit his massive frame. Ab wore his pale hair close-cropped the way I did. While Duma pretended he never spent any time on his hair, Ab and I both knew he took an inordinate amount of time to achieve his disheveled style.

I walked around to see what Ab had thrown in the bed of my truck. In some respects, it almost resembled a human, but it was somewhat crushed, so some body parts were indistinguishable.

"Did you have to hit him so hard, Ab?" I asked, trying to identify the pulpy mush. This wasn't a Phonoi.

"It ain't a *him*," Ab said then grabbed me from the side in a bear hug that made me feel as though I'd just descended fifteen hundred feet underwater in two seconds. "Good to see you, D!"

It took me a few seconds to catch my breath after he released me and a few more to let the pain in my arms and back subside. I bent over to breathe, resting one hand on the fender of my truck, and eventually managed to sputter out, "Good... to... see... you... too, Ab."

The hulking Peri walked back behind my truck and bent down to pick up his massive war hammer. That explained the crushed critter in the bed of my truck. He lifted it to his shoulder, walked around to the rear of a boxy black Mercedes SUV a couple of parking spaces down, and frowned impatiently at Duma, who promptly punched a button on a key fob.

"I think it's one of the Androktasiai, the bitch." Ab said, looking down at his pants, which were torn over his massive right thigh. A pale yellow liquid stained the black material down to his foot.

Androktasiai were the female counterparts of the Phonoi, the very personification of manslaughter. Unlike their male brethren, they were as beautiful as they were deadly — except for this one. Hell, I couldn't even identify a head anymore.

"Jeez, bud, how far did she fly?" I asked, laughing a bit.

"Nah, it wasn't a broad stroke; it was pure overhand," Ab said, demonstrating the maneuver by lowering his hand in an arc from high overhead. "All I had, too. I had to pull her out of a two-foot-deep hole. She sank her damned claws into my leg before I finally nailed her, though." He pointed at the wound in his leg.

I craned my neck to get a look at the gash, but it didn't appear to be that bad. Besides, fae healed quickly, and they didn't scar.

"Awwwww... did itty bitty Abby get a boo-boo? Want big bruver to come kiss it and make it better?" laughed Duma.

"You can kiss my ass, Duma," replied Abraxos, pointing across the truck at his brother. "I ain't complaining, just telling you what happened, prick."

"Whoa, boys. Let's play nice. And let's get these things"—I pointed to the mess in the truck bed—"cleaned up before anyone comes around. And we gotta get this girl somewhere safe so we can talk to her. She knows who I am, and I think she knows who's behind all this." I focused on the mystery girl in the cab of my truck.

"Yeah, let's move before any more of these things show up, or your pinky police for that matter," Duma suggested. "I'll go get that one."

Duma and Ab referred to humans as "pinkies" because of the skin color. I didn't think they intended it to be derogatory, but it was hard not to take it that way sometimes. I'd learned to deal with it a long time ago.

He ran to the front of my truck to retrieve the Phonoi. He was a blur in motion, but we could hear him grunting as he moved the body. Ab and I couldn't help but laugh as we listened.

Duma, like most of his race, was faster than me but not nearly as strong. Ab was extremely odd for a Peri because of his strength and relative lack of speed. While he was stronger than me, he was nowhere near as fast, though he was still faster than any mortal human.

Once we had the remains of the two murderous beings covered with a tarp in the back of my truck and all my gear stowed, I hopped into the cab and watched the girl in the passenger seat next to me for a moment, listening to her quietly snore. She was clearly exhausted, and I couldn't fathom how she had found me. Duma and Ab climbed into their ugly black SUV that probably cost more than my boat and truck combined and pulled out to follow me. Cars were one of Duma's weaknesses. The other weakness was females—human ones in particular. The only thing that ever interested Ab, on the other hand, was combat.

I drove home, keeping an eye on Duma's SUV in my rearview mirror, feeling better that they were there. During the three-quarters-of-an-hour trip home, the kid twitched and mumbled occasionally as if having a bad dream, and I wondered where she came from and why she was so unkempt.

At home, I pulled my truck into the garage and closed the door then let Duma and Ab in through the front door. I asked Ab to put the remains of the two creatures in my truck bed into a couple of fifty-five-gallon drums I kept in my garage for just such a purpose while I carried the girl into my house and laid her on the couch.

CHAPTER 23

WHILE THE GIRL SLEPT, I called Athena to inform her about what had happened and to confirm my suspicions about Medea. She had very little information about Medea's current whereabouts, but even so, she wanted a full debriefing. That meant she was coming over. Given her dislike and distrust of Duma and Ab, a family reunion was the last thing I needed.

While I waited for Athena to arrive and the girl to wake up, Duma, Ab, and I sat in my living room, quietly talking about the last time we'd run into the Phonoi together. They were drinking the two-hundred-year-old cognac I kept just for them—I hated the taste and burning sensation of alcohol.

"Dude, you were about to get your head ripped off until I showed up," Duma said, laughing at my expense.

"What? Me? If I recall, it took Ab to pull out that boney blade thing that one shoved through your back... after I broke it loose from its arm," I reminded him. "Besides, there were only twelve of them. I could have taken them."

And that was when I sensed her presence. The proximity of her power—the source of my strength, stamina, and speed—eased the aches and pains in my extremities and even noticeably reinvigorated me.

"I see you chose to call these... traitors," Athena said from the kitchen, her voice dripping with disdain.

"You ever heard of a doorbell? Maybe you could knock. You guys"—I gestured at Duma and Ab—"might want to head to the back for a few minutes." The last thing I needed was any kind of confrontation.

"Not a fucking chance, D," Duma said, standing up defiantly. Ab stood up with him and flexed his hands in agitation. Both brothers' expressions were stern, though neither had drawn a weapon yet.

"Who is she to judge us? She isn't even from this world."

Shit. I could feel Athena's power start to gather, and I could see her blue eyes spark as her face became darker and her features more raptor-like. "Enough," I shouted. "From all of you." I walked purposefully straight up to Athena and met her gaze, nose to nose. "Not. In. My. Home," I said as forcefully as I could.

I turned enough so that I could also see Ab and Duma. "You are all *my* guests in *my* house. You will honor that," I said, pointing at the brothers. Then I turned back to Athena. "And *you* will respect those I *choose* to associate with, or you can leave." I jabbed my finger toward the door for emphasis.

Athena's power started to make the air in the house incredibly dry, and the hair on my arms and neck was standing on end. The glasses in the cabinet and the silverware in the drawer were jingling, and a light bulb in the kitchen sparked and then popped. The temperature dropped, too. I didn't falter. In fact, I narrowed my gaze at her, and suddenly everything returned to normal.

I walked back into the living room with my heart pounding in my chest. Ab and Duma sat back down in their chairs, though they were both still visibly tense. I crossed over to where Duma had placed his glass on the coffee table. I picked it up, downed the remaining contents, returned the glass, and then sat in my armchair with a flop. I was numb, pissed, and slightly afraid to look back at Athena.

"The company a man chooses says a lot about him," Athena said as she came into the living room, holding the bottle of cognac. "But the lengths he goes to defend them says even more."

Athena was dressed for business in another gray suit complete with wicked-tall spiked heels and her fiery red hair pulled back tightly into a bun. I could tell she was still upset because her blue eyes continued to glow as if reflecting firelight, and her face was slightly flushed. She placed the cognac on the coffee table next to Duma's glass. I didn't need her platitudes. I respected her, but I'd gotten over being intimidated by her countenance long ago.

"Why do you care?" I asked as she loomed over us. "I work with them—you don't." My heart was beginning to calm down, but I was still ticked off.

"Yes, but they are your associates, and you work for me. By association—"

"By association I get the job done. Sometimes with their help." I pointed toward them for emphasis. "Back off. I don't hang out with Peri. I choose to collaborate with Duma and Abraxos. I trust them more than any other beings alive. You trust my judgment on all other matters. Why can't you leave this one alone?" I was tired of this argument, and the more we had it, the more I refused to waver.

"We have more important matters to discuss."

"Yeah, we do," I said quietly, sitting forward in my chair.

"Such as, who is this?" Athena asked, her voice suddenly soft and lilting, almost motherly.

The little girl was curled into a ball in the corner of the couch, as still as stone with her eyes wide in fear. Holy crap. She had witnessed the entire argument between a godling, a mythic warrior, and two fairytale beings.

The girl's eyes darted around the room but mostly traveled between me and Athena, and then my benefactor did something I had never seen her do before. She sat on the couch next to the girl, reached her hand out to stroke her arm, and began to sing. I looked peripherally at Ab and Duma and then back to Athena, stunned.

The song was an ancient lullaby that I hadn't heard in millennia, but I watched as Athena's power washed down her arm like a rivulet of water rolling down a branch as it flowed into the girl. Within moments, the girl relaxed. Even Duma and Ab relaxed. When Athena finished singing, she folded her hands into her lap and just smiled at the girl. I had never see Athena appear more human. My mouth hung open.

The child's eyes met mine, and her smile grew, which in turn caused her eyes to light up. The sight instantly reminded me of why I did what I did. The girl hopped off the couch and rushed me again, grabbing me in a hug around my shoulders.

"The girl is a powerful claircognizant," Athena said, still smiling.

Again, I had to pry the girl loose from her hug. "Who are you?" I asked her in Farsi.

"My name is Fakhri Fawaz, and my brother is the one who blew up the museum in your New York City." Her face became a mask of sorrow, and tears began rolling down her face again. "He did it for us — my sister and my mother — but only because Medea deceived him."

Her wet eyes traveled from me to Duma and Abraxos and then

around to Athena, as if asking for forgiveness. I could feel the anger rising in the pit of my stomach.

I sat her down on the edge of my coffee table and then got her some water from the kitchen. Her weepy eyes followed me the entire way. I handed her the glass, and she drank it down without stopping. At least I knew how she found me, since claircognizants seemed to know anything they wanted to know. But I couldn't imagine how she got here and how hard that must have been — particularly if she was being pursued by Phonoi and Androktasiai. "How did she deceive your brother?" I asked her.

Her gaze vacillated between Athena and me. "Medea promised my brother, Mazeen, power and strength in return for doing this for her. She is a powerful witch. She said she needed him to do this so that she could make a statement to the corrupt nations of the world. That is what she told us all, but it was a lie. I knew she did it so she could have someone steal a cup — a magic cup that could tell her where something was. Mazeen wouldn't listen to me though." She started crying again.

Again, the four of us just traded looks, though Duma appeared entirely uninterested. He never cared about the details, only the point.

"How does Medea know I'm involved?" I asked.

"You took the Cup away from the one who took it for her. She cursed your name over and over that day. I escaped, and then I came to find you. You can stop her. You can make her pay for what she did to my brother. I know that is what my mother thought." Tears continued to roll down her face.

"Fuckin' A," Duma said in English. "Bitch must pay." His tone was flat and matter of fact and not driven by emotion — Duma's goal was now clear.

I gave him a look that suggested he needed to shut up. Now. He just sat back in his chair.

"You can do that?" the girl asked, addressing me as if she'd just asked me to buy her a balloon. "Stop her before she hurts my mother and my sister, too. And my friends. She is evil, and she lies. She needs to be stopped. My mother said so. She said Diomedes can stop her." Her eyes drifted from Athena back to me.

"I will," I replied, the anger inside me building. I agreed with Duma. She smiled, dug into a pocket on her smock, and held her hand out to me. In her palm were a featureless flat silver metal disk about the size of a quarter and a smooth river stone. "I stole these from her before I escaped."

I took the items from her, holding the disk between my thumb and forefinger, examining it. Other than being incredibly lightweight, it had the appearance of a slug used to fool coin-operated machines. The rock I recognized instantly as a Way Stone.

"Do you know what she wanted the Cup for?" Athena asked, now standing, her voice still soft and very feminine. She kept her hands folded in front of her and resembled a schoolteacher.

The girl thought about it for a moment, her eyes drifting up and then to Athena. "She wants to find a chain that once bound a giant from your world. He didn't do anything wrong, though. He was just trying to help people."

Her power was incredible. If she thought about it, she knew it, though from what I knew about claircognizants, the information had to be from the past or present—she couldn't see the future. And I couldn't see any sign of it the way I could with magic. Her ability had no obvious hallmarks at all. Her story sounded as if she were describing the tale of Prometheus, who was bound by a chain that couldn't be broken for bringing fire to humans. I got that the Cup could help Medea find the chain, if it still existed, but why would Medea need an unbreakable chain at all?

"I'll tell you what, Fakhri, why don't I take you some place where you can clean up and get something to eat and we can talk some more?" Athena said as sweetly as I'd ever heard her. "That way, Diomedes can get to work on stopping Medea and helping your mother, sister, and friends."

Fakhri eyed me tentatively, and I nodded. Then she glanced back to Athena and grinned.

"Actually, that's a great idea," I said, leaning forward in my chair. "She'll take very good care of you while I'm working."

I stood and offered the metal disk to Athena, who took it without saying a word or changing her pleasant expression. She put her hand out to Fakhri, and the girl took it without hesitation.

"You have an owl," Fakhri said to Athena.

"I do indeed," she replied. "Would you like to meet him?"

Fakhri nodded excitedly as they walked to the front door hand in hand. I hopped up as quickly as I could, given the stiffness in my legs, and opened the door for them. To my surprise, she had a black Mercedes limo waiting at the curb. That was new.

"Um, what about those barrels in my garage?" I asked quietly, rubbing my ear as she passed me. I didn't want those things hanging around my house any longer than necessary.

"I will send someone to deal with them immediately," she said in the same sweet tone of voice. "And I will pass this along for research." She held up the silver slug and then slipped it into a pocket in her suit jacket. Then her features hardened, instantly conveying she was serious and all business once again.

"You'll need help with this, and you must consider yourself under constant surveillance and a continuous threat of attack. I will gather as much information as I can about Medea's goals and whereabouts, but you will have to go after her to stop whatever she is planning. Stop her for good."

"That's my job," I replied with a sigh. "I'll be waiting to hear from you... with bated breath..."

I didn't need her to tell me that was my mission. I knew that the minute Fakhri started telling me about her brother. At this point, I just needed to know where to find Medea. I didn't even care what kind of army she had around her. It wouldn't be enough.

CHAPTER 24

AB AND DUMA PLAYED VIDEO hockey in my living room while I tried to wrap my head around the situation as I sat at my fly-tying desk, staring at different-colored feathers and fur. Since I had no clue about the battlefield yet, my primary issue was manpower. In a skirmish of Duma, Ab, and me against any mortal battalion, there'd be no contest. But over the last few days, I'd already encountered wizards, several flavors of Jinn, and most recently, the demented death spirits. Throw in the likelihood of encountering some human henchmen to round out the mix, and there was no telling just how sizable her army was.

To make matters worse, Medea herself presented serious problems. She'd been a stark-raving living nightmare the last time I crossed her path while she was taking on Merlin, and that was a long time ago. Who knew how strong or loony she was now? And other than using it to find the chain Fakhri had spoken of, I had no idea what else she could do with a cup that supposedly could show you the future. At that point, it became less about retrieving the Cup than stopping her from achieving her end goal, whatever it was. All I knew for sure was that sneaking up on someone who had a cup that showed her everything, and who knew how to use it, was damn hard.

"My biggest concern is support," I finally threw out to the Peris sprawled across my meager living-room furniture as they screamed at the game and each other like ten-year-olds.

"I got your back, D," Duma said. "You're a handsome, upstanding guy, capable of any task you put your mind to." He smirked at me.

"Not that kind of support, tool. I want to keep the assault team small, but we need tactical and technical support. You guys have any objection to working with more humans?"

"As long as they can handle themselves in a fight, and I don't have to bail them out, no. But there aren't going to be many of you that can go one-on-one with what we're likely to face," said Duma, shaking his head. "Unless they're like you."

"The guys I'm thinking of won't have to go one-on-one with anything," I responded. "Not closer than a thousand yards anyway. You remember Frigate, the sniper I served in the SEALs with? And Geek, the combat-electronics genius from Africa? They're both good in close quarters — for humans, at least."

"I think so," Duma replied, "but how much do they actually know about, um, you know, Parans, the Old Ones, and witches, and such? Just curious."

"They know there're more than humans in this world, but they haven't been exposed to much of it, other than a few nasties." I shrugged. "One has a family history with a loup-garou and the other met a wicked little redcap when he was a kid, but they should be mentally stable, combat-hardened enough to handle more than that."

I got hung up on the idea that they'd either be okay with finding out, or I'd be responsible for causing their mental breakdowns. But I kept telling myself that operators in Special Forces around the world were heavily psychologically vetted for stability, and I knew they'd be worth it if they could handle it.

"Whatever. They'll be dead before I learn their names anyway. You pinkies have such short lives." Duma shrugged. "Though, if the one guy really is as good with a rifle as you used to say, that'd be damn handy."

"Hey, maybe the other one can fix my laptop," added Ab. He looked ridiculous with the tiny game controller in his giant hands.

I glared at him, and he shrugged deeply and returned to his game. One guy lived in Mississippi and the other in England, and I figured it was going to be best to talk with them in person. I also thought it'd be best to take Ab with me. He could help validate my explanations about other beings as well as act as a second pair of eyes. Duma could stick around my home and keep his eyes open while we were gone.

I hadn't seen Geek or Frigate in a few years. That made the plan a little risky. My showing up out of the blue would likely raise suspicions among guys like these. At least Frigate and I shared a common bond as part of the SEAL Team DEVGRU, and we'd been close once — as close as I ever get to mundanes anyway. I hoped that Geek's service in the British SBS would carry the same weight, and he'd be receptive to me as one special operator to another.

Ab and I left early the next morning. Every time I traveled the Ways with Ab and Duma, I was constantly amazed. Humans were woefully limited to five measly senses while, as best I could tell, fae had dozens of sensory capabilities. Ab and his brother could feel and see the energy traveling along the Ways, where I was limited to barely seeing major intersections—and then only because of Athena's gifts to me. And I needed an enchanted key—a Way Stone—to open them.

Like all fae, Ab knew how to open a door onto the Ways even where one didn't exist. Every time I asked him how they did it, he couldn't explain. Ab once said it was no different than telling if something was rough or smooth and that opening a door onto the Ways was just like opening a normal door except that if you didn't open it, you could walk through it as if it wasn't there.

Fae also knew the simplest routes between any two points on Earth, sensing their path in a manner similar to migratory birds or sea turtles. The difference between the fae and me traveling along the Ways was the difference between knowing how to drive a car and being able to build one from raw materials and then race it at Le Mans.

Ab walked straight to the corner of my backyard, waved his hand as if telling someone to sit down, and the area in front of us lit up like someone had unzipped a cover over a spotlight. I followed him into the light. We walked less than fifty steps from my back door before we found ourselves on a sandbar in the middle of the Tchoutacabouffa River outside Biloxi, Mississippi, almost under Interstate 10. I pulled out my cell phone, switched it back on, and checked the built-in GPS. "Not bad, Ab. Frigate's house is on Brickyard Bayou, just a few miles from here. If we had a boat, we could pull up to his dock." I peered around to get my bearings. I hadn't been to Frigate's home since well before Hurricane Katrina, not since we spent time together at the Navy's Riverine Warfare Center on the Pearl River, just a few miles west of here.

"Want me to find one?" he asked.

"Nah, but we need a ride." I found the number for a taxicab on my phone.

Ab had left his hammer back in San Diego and brought only a pair of heavy dragon-skin gloves. I'd brought my swords and another SIG Sauer. Ab's gloves and everything except my gun were in a bag he carried easily over one shoulder. I was dressed in jeans, a T-shirt, and a light jacket, while Ab wore fatigue-style pants and a performance-type long-sleeved shirt with a gun manufacturer's logo on it. At size 4XL, it barely contained his biceps and chest. It was the closest he could probably come to blending in with the mundane world.

It took about thirty minutes for the cab to arrive. Meanwhile, we stayed on the bank of the river to avoid drawing attention to ourselves. Once the cabbie called to tell us he'd arrived, we crossed the sandbar and walked up the soggy riverbank and strolled straight across to the cul-de-sac where the cab waited. Nothing special — just a mythical Greek king from the Trojan War and a seven-foot-tall albino giant strolling out of the trees.

The tiny Vietnamese cabbie nearly fainted when he saw Ab. I had to sit in front because Ab barely fit sitting up in the back. During the entire half-hour drive, the cabbie kept taking glimpses of Ab in the rearview mirror. I had to work at keeping myself from laughing. I gave the driver a hefty tip when we pulled up in front of the house. He muttered something about Ab's size before he took off, spraying us with loose gravel. So much for Southern hospitality.

The house we stood in front of was beautiful and brand-new, a typical bayou waterfront home built up on wooden piers some fifteen feet off the ground in case of flooding. The house itself was a plain two-story design, painted pale yellow, with a giant wooden staircase leading up from the driveway to a porch that surrounded the main floor of the house. The front entrance sat at the top of the staircase in the center of the façade — ornate leaded glass and dark wooden French doors. Under the house sat a giant custom truck with dual back tires for increased towing capabilities, a bass boat, and a BMW. From the driveway, I could see there was someone out on a pier behind the house.

"Stay here till I call for you, okay? I don't want to scare the crap outta anybody yet. But keep your eyes open. If you see anything suspicious, do what you gotta do." I walked toward the pier.

"Can I help you, mister?" said a voice from above and behind me. The heavy southern drawl was unmistakable.

"I'm not sure. But could that southern accent get any thicker, Frigate?"

"Demo?" came the puzzled reply.

161

My nickname in the Teams was Demo because of my predilection for destroying things. Apparently, my skill set was fairly focused.

"Nice to see you again, Kyle," I said, turning toward the house with my hands on my hips.

"Holy crap, Chief—it is you, ain't it! I haven't seen or heard from you since that mess in Africa a few years back." He walked down the staircase to ground level.

I hadn't seen Kyle "Frigate" Sellers in four years. He still appeared young for his age, but his dirty-blond hair was longer than before and kind of frizzy, making him look like Gene Wilder in *Young Frankenstein*. His arms, shoulders, and chest were still muscular enough under his shirt, though he was somewhat leaner than I remembered. His lithe build emphasized the fact that he was at least four inches shorter than me.

When we'd first met about ten years before, he was significantly younger than I was supposed to be, a young pup just out of the Green Course and fresh from the Marine Scout Sniper School, where he'd graduated at the top of his class. He served six years in the SEAL Team Development Group as a sniper before quitting. His first two years were in my platoon, and I was his chief petty officer. I gave him his nickname because frigate birds had the uncanny ability to show up out of nowhere and pick off baitfish at the water's surface. They sat sometimes as high as a mile up, riding the jet stream, watching for prey. When they spotted it, there was no warning and no escape. Frigate was like that with a rifle.

"Yeah, it's been a few years. I live in San Diego now. I take people out fishing."

"No shit?" He eyed me skeptically.

Once he'd made it down the steps, he approached me and offered me his hand, which I took.

"If you take people fishin' in San Diego," he asked with a curious gaze on his weathered face, "then why you show up here? And carryin', no less?"

I gotta get a better tailor. Frigate always did have good eyes, and like most snipers, he saw everything from a tactical point of view. He never beat around the bush, and he never took his eyes off me.

"I'll be straight with you," I said. "I need your help. Weird crap like back in Africa, only weirder."

"Kurt," he called past me to the kid on the dock, "why don't you go up and help your mom for a minute." His voice was serious and his thick accent gone. The smile on his face was forced.

The kid's shoulders sagged, followed by his head, and he began mumbling. Frigate mussed up his hair as he walked past, and I could see the affection and pride take over Frigate's face as he did so. Suddenly, I couldn't help thinking that maybe it was a mistake to come here.

"Kid's your spitting image, only younger," I said, grinning.

Frigate just gave me a sideways glance as he watched to make sure his son was out of earshot. His brow furrowed deeply as his eyes narrowed, and his lips formed a tight line as if he were trying to determine whether I was serious. "How long's it been?"

"A few years — 2008, I think. Look, I need to talk with you for a few minutes. Preferably not someplace in the open," I said, pointing toward the house.

"Come on up to my office," he said, and I followed him back toward the house. "Why don't you invite your big friend there, too, before he scares somebody." He pointed nonchalantly toward the street out front where I'd told Ab to wait for me.

I didn't even realize he'd noticed Ab, but I should have known. It made me smile. I whistled to get Ab's attention and then waved him over. He gave me a confused frown and then started walking toward us.

Once on the porch, Frigate and I continued around to a side door that led into a small office filled with papers, filing cabinets, bookshelves, and a desk with two computers. The place was a mess. On top of one bookshelf were a revolver and six silver bullets, sitting on a book about lycanthropy. On the wall above it, under a mounted striped bass, was a photograph of a half-dozen guys out at a bar. Other than the haircuts on a couple of them, you probably wouldn't guess it was from our days in the Teams, taken just before I retired. Frigate and I were the only two in the picture still alive. The other four died in Afghanistan the next week. I'd pulled Frigate and our lieutenant, Matt Kane, out of a two-day-long firefight and carried them both for nearly twenty miles. The lieutenant didn't make it.

Seeing the image brought back memories of all the comrades-in-arms I'd watched die over the centuries — good men, just like Kane and countless others, dead at the hands of other men for reasons we never questioned. I didn't even want to think about the friends I'd lost in wars against Parans they weren't even aware they were fighting.

I missed the SEALs, as well as the other military units I'd been attached to over the centuries—not the mindless bureaucracy but the interaction, teamwork, loyalty, and connection to others with a similar drive and mindset. While serving as a soldier was the closest I felt to belonging to the human world, it was always bittersweet because I could never serve more than a few years at a time before my agelessness raised suspicions. That was probably why I got along so well with Duma and Abraxos. While they weren't human, at least they understood what it was like to live in my world.

I pointed at the photo, chuffed, and shook my head. "Seems like a thousand years ago."

He didn't respond. Instead, he just sat down heavily in an old wooden office chair and leaned back with his hands behind his head, watching me. The chair squeaked horribly.

"So... looks like you're a building contractor now," I said, hoping for some sort of response this time.

"Yeah, since I quit a few years back. Took over my daddy's business. You wanted to talk—about weird shit, I believe?"

Outside I could hear Ab clumping up the wooden staircase to the porch. I knew he was doing it on purpose. Big though he was, he could have walked across bubble wrap without making a sound.

I took a deep breath and let it out. "I need your help. I'm not sure how to explain this, but it's combat related and has nothing to do with any standing military you know anything about. It's... complicated."

"Chief, you aren't just beatin' around the bush—you're swingin' around some trees along the way."

"Look, I don't know any way to say this without you thinking I'm crazy, so..." I walked back out the door to check on Ab, who was now just a few steps away. I returned inside, and Frigate raised his eyebrows in anticipation. The chair continued to make its annoying squeak as he rocked slightly. "You remember back in Africa, that creature that had you guys pinned down for days until I showed up? It wasn't a genetic experiment or a freaked-out rhino; it was a chipekwe, and I killed it and the witchdoctor that controlled it."

I could tell by the sudden eclipse of daylight that Ab was at the door. "You remember my friend Ab?" I asked, gesturing at him. "He and his brother were helping me when we ran into you and that SBS squad. Ab and his brother are not what you'd call 'human.'"

Ab had to duck to get in through the door. He just grimaced and waved, and though I wouldn't have thought it possible, Frigate's eyebrows managed to climb even higher as his eyes got wider.

"He's the last of a race of beings called Peris, and he's one of many kinds of fairies that exist in our world. Wizards and witches exist. So do dragons and other so-called monsters."

Frigate swallowed hard and then shook his head slightly. I could tell I was losing him.

"Chief, you sure you're okay?" Frigate asked. "I mean, your friend is *big* and kinda odd-lookin', but I seen a few Marines that looked like him..." He got up and started to move uncomfortably around the small room, but there was no way out except through Ab. "And we all agreed that big creature was just some kinda rabid hippo or something," he said, rubbing at his forehead.

"My real name is Diomedes, son of Tydeus of Calydon. I fought alongside Achilles and Ulysses during the Trojan War. I'm thirty-two hundred years old, and I'm known as a Guardian, and I work for a being you'd know best as Athena, Goddess of Wisdom and Warfare. It's my job to protect human life from all nonhuman threats."

Maybe dumping all this information on him wasn't the best strategy, but it felt cathartic to tell someone who I really was. I would have kept going, too, but I could see Frigate eyeing the windows, wondering if it was worth the jump. I could see it in his eyes. I couldn't blame him, really.

"Just calm down, Kyle. I'm not lying, and I'm not here to hurt you or your family. Look at Ab..." I waved a hand toward the burly Peri then intercepted Frigate before he could work his way into a corner. I easily beat him, causing him to bump into me.

"How the hell—?" he stammered, pointing back to where I had just been then squinting at Ab.

"Sit down, please, before you fall down." I helped him to his chair, and he fell into it. "Look, I know it's a lot, but I'm not lying to you. I seriously need your help."

"If you're really what you say you are, why do you need my help?" Frigate put his head in his hands and rubbed his face with the heels of his palms.

"I need a sniper, one I can trust. We're going against a very powerful witch who likely has an army of creatures and an item that may give her the ability to see us coming."

"Oh. Okay. Sure," he said staring at the floor.

"Dammit, Frigate, I'm not making this up, and we need your help. You of all people have to believe that there are things that exist outside of the normal." I grabbed the lycanthropy book off the shelf, scattering the bullets in a cascade of metallic clanks and dumping the gun onto the papers beneath with a heavy thud. I tossed the book at him. "That stuff is real," I said, pointing at the book. "You recall all the stories you used to tell us out on the Pearl River during training about there being a Rougarou in the swamps around there? You said you and your father had even seen it while hunting and that the locals all whisper about it but no one openly acknowledges it. You used to joke we needed silver bullets in our guns as we ran the river." I bent over to snatch one of the scattered silver cartridges off the floor and then tossed it to him. "Well, you were right. Locals call it a Rougarou, but it's actually a loup-garou, a type of werewolf. A very nasty one. Hell, there's an entire clan of werewolves that have lived in the swamps along the Pearl River for over a hundred years. They use loup-garou for protection." I paused for a few minutes to let it sink in.

Frigate couldn't hide his confusion as he stared at me, clearly trying to make sense of what I'd just told him. Finally, he just started rubbing at his hair nervously.

"My point is, there's a lot more to this world than you know, and I need your help protecting it. Ab, hand me one of my swords," I said, hoping to somehow prove myself.

Ab let the heavy bag slide off his shoulder with a thump that practically echoed on the wooden floor, dug in until he found them, and handed me one.

"Look," I said, offering it to Frigate. "It's not made here on Earth. It's lighter than it should be, and it's incredibly sharp, and I can run it through the armor on an M1 tank. In fact, I have."

"You mean those slashes down the side of that one Abrams tank on the air base in Turkey?" he said, the recognition clear on his face. "They said they had you on surveillance video hacking apart someone or something next to that thing. I remember that. They couldn't figure out what you could have done to create the damage to the armor plating on the tank, and they couldn't find any remains, so they chalked it up to a computer glitch. You mean you really did hack something up there?"

"Yeah, a group of Moroi—mortal vampires that feed on energy. Four of them."

"Freakin' leeches," added Ab from behind me, shivering and making faces. "Gross."

Frigate just arched his eyebrows and nodded as if he agreed, his face a mask of total disbelief. "Well, if that's all true, then what good is a rifle gonna do at a thousand yards? Don't you need some kinda sword or magic weapon to kill things like that? Silver bullets and garlic and all that?" For emphasis he held up the silver bullet I'd tossed at him.

"Not really. A bullet from a fifty-caliber sniper rifle will rip pretty much anything apart, human or not. Some creatures can take more damage from a weapon like that, but hell, I bet even Ares himself would have an issue with a fifty-cal round in his ass."

Frigate's features had practically aged ten years over the course of our conversation, and I could see the disbelief etched on his face, but I could also see something in his eyes that suggested that at least some of what we were saying made sense. Part of me felt vindicated for dumping so much crap on him all at once.

"So, you aren't human?" Frigate leveled at me, his voice becoming calm and steady.

"Well, technically, yes. At least, at one time I was just as human as you are. Now I'm not really sure anymore. I'm rare. I am the champion of a dominant Protogenoi, the representation of its power and ethos here on Earth. There are a few of us, but I'm the oldest still around."

Having said all that, my brief catharsis from telling someone who I really was suddenly made me feel more like a freak and even less human. *Damn.* I couldn't even explain myself to a guy I'd shed blood, sweat, and tears with for years. How could I ever relate to Sarah? Maybe I was no different from the monsters from which I was supposed to protect humanity.

The sound of Frigate's voice brought me back to the conversation at hand. "And you want me to grab my gun and join you to run off and fight a witch?" he asked, shaking his head.

I grinned. "Well, when you put it that way, it sounds weird. But basically, yes. At a distance, if you still got it, you'll be safe, and you can offer my assault team the long-distance cover and support we're likely to need. It'll be just like old times. Well, almost," I said, my grin widening. "Look, Ab will pass back through here tomorrow at 1100 Zulu. If you're willing, he'll bring you to the staging site. If not, I completely understand. If you choose to help us, I promise you I will do everything I can to keep you safe. I'm also trying to keep my assault team safe, and you're my best option. Kinda flattering, if you think about it. All the bizarre and powerful creatures in the world I could work with, and I need *your* help." I pointed at him. "We aren't just fighting to save the American ideal anymore—this is to save the human ideal. And bin Laden and al-Qaeda are pansies compared to the bitch we're after."

"Enough, enough with the recruitment speech, Chief. I'll think about it. Right now, I need to think."

"Got it," I said, holding out my hand.

Frigate shook it, and I knew he was in. I could feel it in his solid grip and see it in his eye. It made me proud to know there were humans out there willing to face any enemy, even a supernatural one, without accolade, to preserve life as we know it.

"It is good to see you again," I said, chucking him on the shoulder. "Let's go, Ab."

CHAPTER 25

"**N**EXT STOP IS BOURNEMOUTH, ENGLAND, to find Geek," I told Ab as we left Frigate's home.

Ab stopped and surveyed the area as though he had lost something, changing directions every few seconds, and finally led us into the woods halfway up the block from Frigate's home.

"This way should be quickest. Should get us to a spot in Iceland, and then we can move on to England's southern coast," he said, pointing.

Among the moss-strewn oak trees, I could see the shimmering wave of energy that indicated a weak spot in the veil between our world and the Telluric Ways. Ab pointed it out as if a glowing neon sign marked it. He waved his hand as though shooing mosquitoes, and once again, a passage onto the Ways opened in front of us.

The first step was warm, muggy, and peacefully slow like the very atmosphere of southern Mississippi, but the next became cold and harsh. A few steps later, we emerged into a cold, cloudy, rocky wasteland in the middle of what I assumed to be some desolate part of Iceland. We ended up walking for around forty-five minutes before Ab repeated the lazy-hand gesture and opened another door onto the Ways, which was good because the uneven terrain was causing the burns on my legs to ache. A few steps later, we were in England.

Once we exited the Ways, I had to rest my legs for a minute, so I took the time to turn my phone back on and check its GPS to see exactly where we were. The cool, damp air made me shiver, and I could smell the sea nearby. I could tell by the manicured landscaping and open-grass field that we were in a park within some city's limits. The buildings I could see had the typical asymmetrical, cross-gabled, steep-pitched roofs, half-rounded doors, and oversized chimneys typical of English cottages, but for all I knew, it was Cornwall or Liverpool. Once the map came up, I had to admit I was impressed. We were in Meyrick Park, right in the middle of Bournemouth.

"There should be a country club that way." I pointed southwest as I consulted my phone.

"How'd this guy "Geek" get his name?" Ab asked.

I wasn't sure if he was genuinely interested or just trying to make conversation as we walked. "You know he was a former Royal Marine in the Special Boat Service and a hard-core electronics expert and computer nerd. He's also hardcore into cryptozoology. All those interests earned him his nickname. His name is actually Will Elmsmore, and he runs a seriously state-of-the-art, high-end electronic security consulting firm, and the Royal Marines are one of his clients."

"Ah, gotcha," Ab replied. "I was worried it was because he bit the heads off small animals for fun or something."

I glared at Ab.

"Hey, as bad as we Peris were, you don't see us doing that kinda crap. That was all human stuff," he said, dismissing the activities of my species with a wave of his hand. "I mean with animals, anyway."

I didn't want to know what he meant by that last part, so I just shut up and walked.

I needed Geek's help because I only understood enough about computers to play games and do my e-mail and maintain the website for my charter business, but Geek could practically build a city from his keyboard. Or destroy one. He knew electronic countermeasures, security systems, computer networks, and anything else that ran on chips, processors, and the like. Sure, I could have run the Op the way I used to, using only "eyes on" intelligence, but somehow, I doubted even Columbus would have refused a GPS if he'd had access to one. Plus, like Frigate, Geek had had his own encounter with a Paran, which he regularly wrote about on his cryptozoological website, and I was hoping that would make it easy to convince him to help us. By the time we got to his house, it was past dark. When I traveled by the Ways, skipping across time zones so quickly made jet lag seem like the changeover to Daylight Saving Time. A few hours ago we'd left San Diego at dawn, and now it was just past nightfall.

Geek's neighborhood sat right up against the southern edge of the golf course at Meyrick Park. Trees separated the links from the road on one side of the street, and stone and white-clapboard homes lined the other. Instead of front yards, driveways took up the space between the houses and the sidewalk, and low stone walls and various hedges separated the lots. The homes were all English-style cottages, and the wooden-shingled roofs lent them a classically English character. A few cars passed by on the streets, but other than a single jogger and an older couple walking their cocker spaniel, the neighborhood was quiet.

About halfway down the block, we stopped in front of one house that had a roof covered in solar panels. Small whip antennas and video cameras sprouted from each eave, and spotlights occupied each corner and even the space over the door. This had to be the place.

I could tell by the sensors underneath each fixture that the lights were motion activated, but I didn't expect to feel as if I'd just broken out of prison when they snapped on as I walked up to the front door. I told Ab to stay out of sight but to keep an eye out while I talked to Geek. I was worried about this conversation for the complete opposite reason I'd been concerned about talking to Frigate. This guy was going to eat up the idea of Paranthropoi and Protogenoi like a fanboy at Comic-Con.

"No solicitors, please," blared a tinny voice from a speaker hidden in the ivy next to the door even before I could knock.

"Um, I'm not selling anything. I'm here to talk with Will Elmsmore about an event in East Africa in 2008. I was there, too."

"What's your name?" came the metallic retort.

"He would know me as Chief Petty Officer Steve "Demo" Dore, of the US Navy SEALs, though I wasn't active when we met. Look, I just need to speak with him. I'll only be a few minutes." I was already tired of talking to a wall.

The door popped open. It was heavily reinforced and set in a seriously heavy-duty metal frame. *Yikes. Paranoid much?*

"Hello?" I called as I entered.

The dim hallway was about forty feet long and ran the length of the house. There were two archways off each side, and the one farthest back on the right actually had a door in it, which was closed. In the scant light, the walls were a nondescript white. Other than a single narrow table and a mirror midway between the archways on the left, and a series of historical prints of mythical animals on the right, there were no decorations. Even the floor was bare wood. But there were more than a dozen video cameras set at all angles to record every inch of the space. I waved in no specific direction, figuring one of the damned cameras would get me head-on.

"Back here," came a disembodied voice. The lone door down the hall popped open with a slight hiss.

I walked toward it, and lights I hadn't seen at first popped on and off as I passed. The hum of electronics and a hot breeze around my head and shoulders and freezing cold around my legs assaulted me as I approached. As I pushed the heavy, reinforced door open, a wave of frigid air instantly chilled me, and the eerie sight of blackness lit up by video screens everywhere stopped me from entering further. It was a disturbing, unnatural light. Behind a desk on the left side of the room, a man with a pencil jammed between his lips was clicking away at a keyboard, his face lit up by the monitor in front of him. Every square inch of wall space was taken up by metal frames, wires, and electronic devices, all of which emitted tiny pinpoints of red and green light and a soft rhythmic hum.

"You're Demo?" he asked as he spit his pencil out and glowered at me through the eerie and indistinct glow of his computer monitor. "What about that day in Africa, mate?"

"Can you turn on a light? This place is like a neon tomb."

"No, but we can go into the parlor." He got up and grabbed a cane. He hobbled toward me, and he stopped when he noticed my surprise.

Geek was just about my height and built like me, with sandy brown hair kept in a low-maintenance crew cut, like mine. He was dressed in khaki pants and a dark-colored polo shirt, and nothing about his appearance suggested computer nerd. He'd played rugby all through his days at university and at one time had actually entertained the idea of going pro, but for some reason joined the British Marines and then the SBS instead. But he'd had both legs the last time I saw him.

"Caught an IED in Afghanistan two years ago. Blew my lower leg off. This is my light-duty prosthesis." He rapped his left shin with the cane, producing a hollow tap.

"Well, this changes things a bit," I said, following him out of the dark, icy room across the hall to a comfy sitting area that lit up as we entered and resembled a drawing room out of a Victorian grandmother's house. He flopped into a plush, high-backed armchair and pointed me toward an exceedingly formal couch on the other side of a rectangular coffee table. A matching chair sat to his right on the other side of a small table. He looked as out of place in that room as he did behind a computer.

I sat down on the couch. It felt like wood covered in cement. "I was going to ask for your help, but..." I gestured at his leg.

"I believe that's called discrimination, Demo." He flashed me a wry smile.

"You're right, but I need you for a combat op. Electronic support."

He eyed me suspiciously as I continued. The conversation progressed much as it had with Frigate, at first. Understandably, Geek thought I was pulling some kind of elaborate prank because of his belief in odd and unexplained things. Even my explanation of the situation in Africa that he and Frigate and their respective squads were involved in was met with skepticism. It struck me as incongruent, considering the guy had Web pages devoted to the existence of garden fairies and the Loch Ness Monster.

"So, you're saying that thing back in Africa was a supernatural creature?" he asked, squinting his eyes at me.

"No, it was real enough, just not normal, and it was being controlled by a wizard. I know this because I was there to kill it and the wizard when I ran into you guys," I said, starting to regret my decision to recruit him.

"But do you have any *proof*?" He suddenly sat up and leaned forward, jabbing his cane in my direction for emphasis and staring at me intently. "And what do you mean, *wizard*?" His eyes opened wide as he said the word "wizard," and he cocked his head and sat up ever so slightly straighter.

"Proof?" I tossed my hands up. "No, not really. And by 'wizard,' I mean exactly what you think. A person who manipulates energies for various purposes, including throwing fireballs, if he wants." I rolled my hands around absentmindedly as if would somehow help me explain what a wizard was.

After trying to stem the inevitable inundation of questions that followed the attempt to establish my genuineness, I finally managed to turn the conversation to the bombing in New York and the theft of the Cup. Geek instantly insisted that he had picked up chatter that an obscure terrorist group out of Iran had carried out the attack, and he dismissed the theft as a simple consequence of opportunity. Once I brought up Medea's name in connection to the terrorist cell, however, he practically buzzed at the idea that a mythological figure could be real.

Then he asked me who *I* really was, and my truthful response prompted him to suggest I somehow prove it. That was precisely the reason I hadn't revealed my identity to more than a handful of normal humans—ever. They'd either think I was nuts, or they would go nuts. Frustrated, I screamed for Ab at the top of my lungs. Given that I was known as the "Lord of the Battle Cry" at Troy, I knew my voice would carry.

Predictably, Ab assumed there was trouble. He smashed into the armored front door so hard that part of the wall around it collapsed in a deafening blast. The door landed just outside the entrance to the parlor with an impact reminiscent of a three-car pileup on a freeway. Geek's eyes were wide with a mixture of shock, disbelief, and amazement, and his mouth hung open like I'd just whacked him with a bat.

"Back here, Ab. We're safe," I called.

"Shit, D, I thought you were in trouble. Don't do that again, please," he said, walking into the sitting room and examining his dragon-skin gloves to make sure they were unharmed.

"Bollocks," mumbled Geek. He stared, slack-jawed. His eyes traveled back and forth between Ab and me repeatedly as if he were watching a tennis match, and his face was drained of color and devoid of any emotion. For a moment, I thought he was going into shock, and then his face flushed with excitement.

"Oh, I'm in, mate," he screamed. "Whatever it is, I. Am. In."

"Great!" I said, and Ab shrugged and arched one eyebrow, clearly not understanding a thing that was happening.

"So, when do we leave?" Geek asked excitedly.

"We're moving out within twenty-four hours," I said, crossing my arms over my chest. "I'll need to know the gear you'll require ASAP. Communications, surveillance—the works. But seriously, knowing what I told you about us going after Medea, if you think that leg is going to be an issue, then I'll find someone else. It's just I know you're the best at this stuff."

Geek's shoulders sagged and his smile disappeared, replaced by an expression of serious intensity, though his eyes were still alive with curiosity. "Like I said, I'm in, mate, but on one condition: you gotta answer some questions."

"Fine, but off the record only, or you can kiss your already unstable reputation goodbye."

"Ah, right," he said, suddenly sheepish. "A list of gear it is, then, yes?"

He walked past us through the parlor back toward his darkened office, pausing briefly to assess the damage that Ab had caused in the hallway. He looked back at Ab, grinned, and shook his head as if he had just discovered an unknown vein of gold in his backyard.

I followed him back into the warren of electronic machines and computers. When I crossed the hall and noticed the damage, I frowned at Ab and hung my head, shaking it. I grabbed the contorted metal door, wrenched it free from the wall it impaled, and handed it to Ab while I silently mouthed "clean this up," pointing from the Peri to the hallway. Ab's massive shoulders sank, and his chin fell to his chest.

Just inside his office, Geek stood watching me, wide eyed and slack jawed once again. "That door weighed nearly two hundred kilos…"

"Yeah, substantial," I said while dusting off my hands. "Sorry. Ab'll clean this up some before we leave."

"No, mate. I mean, you just pulled that thing out of the wall like it was a piece of plywood," he said, fawning.

"Right. Uh, the list of gear, please?" I didn't know what else to say.

Suddenly animated again, Geek scooted around to the chair at his desk and started typing. A few seconds later, a printer whirred and he stood up, grabbed the sheet, and handed it to me.

"Excellent," I said, examining the page.

"Standard communications and electronics package with a few optional extras. Some of that stuff may be bloody hard to come by. I may have access to alternative gear if needs be." Geek was all business again.

"Not a problem. I can get it. And, uh, again, sorry about your door and the hall, Geek."

"No worries, mate," Geek said, the cold blue glow of the light from his monitor gleaming off his white teeth. "Ab is bloody strong, isn't he? That door was supposed to withstand nearly thirteen hundred kilos of force. And you! You picked it up like it was nothing!"

"Sorry. I'll try to stand it back up for you," Ab shouted from down the hall, amidst sounds of rending metal and falling bricks and clatter.

"We'll see you tomorrow at roughly 1200 Zulu. Meet us in Meyrick Park, on the southeastern edge. It'll either be me or Ab, and we may have an American with us you may remember from Africa. No one else." I headed into the hall.

Geek followed. We watched with amusement as Ab tried valiantly for a few minutes to stand the rent door back in its twisted reinforced frame, but the best he could do was lean it against the wall.

Ab and I took a more direct route home and made it back to my house in less than twenty minutes without incident, just after two in the afternoon. That gave us about twelve hours before we needed to head out to my staging area to prepare for our assault on Medea.

CHAPTER 26

BACK AT MY HOUSE, I told Ab and Duma to get their gear ready while I talked with Athena about what she'd discovered about Medea. Then I collected the equipment Geek had requested. I knew the brothers would have their armor and weapons in that ugly SUV Duma drove, but I wanted them to make sure they were ready, too. I was tired of playing catch-up. It was time to go on the offensive.

While I collected the needed gear from the Dvergar quartermaster at one of the Metis Foundation's storehouses in Mission Valley, Athena informed me of what she'd learned about Medea and her whereabouts. Fakhri had told her that Medea's base of operations was indeed in Iran, on Mount Alvand, outside of Hamadān. The Old One whom I knew as Hecate, the Goddess of Witchcraft, was helping Medea with a complicated ritual to harness the power of chaos and then unleash havoc in a directed attack.

According to the wizards Athena had on staff at the Metis Foundation—all full members of the Hermetic Order of the Golden Dawn—our entire universe tended toward chaos, making its energy readily available, but disruption of a system's equilibrium created significantly stronger forms of power. Riots, arson, terrorist attacks, or anything that caused hysteria among people could generate massive amounts of localized chaotic energy, but any attempt to harness enough of it to use as a weapon would first require capturing the energy in a vessel strong enough to store it. Fortunately, the Metis wizards couldn't identify any container on Earth strong enough to do so—outside of Pandora's Box, which was actually a bronze jar that had been, fortunately, destroyed. Of course, they also couldn't conceive of how she could direct such an attack efficiently. No offense to the wizards, but I was more concerned with making sure we didn't find out.

Unfortunately, the girl couldn't help us locate the chain she said Medea wanted. Apparently, its location changed constantly, and her ability only allowed her to divine where it was at the present moment or where it had been in the past. While I desperately wanted to throw a kink in Medea's plans—and finding that chain before she did would definitely do that—I had to settle for hitting her as hard and as fast as I could before she could accomplish her goals.

Fakhri also confirmed my suspicions that Medea had an army of Phonoi and Androktasiai and Jinn at her disposal, as well as an army of fanatical human zealots dedicated to or duped into her cause. As a result, when Athena offered her Spartoi this time, I gladly accepted them to augment my small squad.

The last item we discussed was the metal disk Fakhri had brought us along with her Way Stone. According to Athena, the disk was some sort of magic-based incendiary device that drew energy from anything that generated an electrical charge within a given radius and then used that energy to create a kind of gravitational singularity. In essence, the disk created a small, short-lived black hole. Athena said this type of device was activated by reversing its polarity, using a strong magnet, but that it would need to be isolated from human contact to become live. Fortunately, the one Fakhri had stolen was now deactivated.

Athena said that, overall, Fakhri was doing well but that she was physically and emotionally worn-out and concerned about her mother and sister, so—in an uncharacteristic display of empathy— Athena didn't push the girl to give us the layout of Medea's base of operations. Instead, she used her government contacts to get me full access to satellite imagery, spectral analysis, geology, and topography of Mt. Alvand and its surroundings. She promised to keep me updated on any additions Fakhri could help with while the operation was underway.

With the intelligence in hand, I loaded the gear I'd requested. Of all the stuff Geek wanted, the only thing I recognized was an updated version of the satellite communications system we used in the Teams—an AN/PSC-5 Spitfire SATCOM and its KY encryption set. There were also two things that I assumed were heavy-duty laptop computers encased in metal housings, but they might have been used for carrying important documents for all I knew.

Among all the other thoughts that raced through my brain, something about the constantly moving location of the chain struck a familiar chord, but it sat at the back of my mind and gnawed at me like a rat chewing through wood. *Screw it.* It would have to join the club of other details that bothered me about this whole frigging mess.

As I pulled into my garage back at my house in Roseville, Duma met me with an expression that jumped from confusion to amusement to concern. "We got a problem, D," he said softly. He had his karambit in his hand. "I was thinking I should kill her, but..."

"Kill who?" I asked, totally confused.

"Her." He pointed through the garage into the house to a woman seated in my living room.

All I could make out from the doorway was her shoulder-length dark hair, which was wreathed in a haze of some sort of greasy magic that gave off a sinister gray energy.

"She's hot, and she says she's a friend of yours and that you worked together recently in New York on the bombing thing, you dog," he said wryly. "Showed me her DHS badge. Looked real enough to me... but she ain't exactly dressed for business, if you know what I mean," he whispered out of the side of his mouth.

Sarah. Holy shit.

"Something's not right." Several odd things about the situation raced through my mind, including the fact that she was clearly under some sort of spell and probably, thanks to me, in danger. Even so, I could feel my pulse quicken and my palms began to sweat.

"No shit, Sherlock. She's a hot chick, and she's interested in you," Duma smirked.

"Fuck you. I mean, she's been touched by magic. Did she say why she was here?" I couldn't help jumping back and forth between being excited that she'd come out here to see me and dismayed that she wasn't here under her own volition. My world sucked sometimes.

"She just said she's here to see you, and she insisted on waiting till you got home. Tell me you tapped that, please."

"Would you control yourself for a minute?" I snapped. "If she's being manipulated, we have to help her." I caught myself running a hand through my hair and brushing dirt off my long-sleeved T-shirt. Another second, and I probably would have checked my breath.

"Oh, so you do have the hots for her." Duma smirked again as he watched me.

"Would you grow up?" I quietly said over my shoulder, embarrassed as hell, as I walked cautiously into the house. "But if she attacks me, and it seems like it's going badly for me, just make sure I'm dead, okay?" I whispered through clenched teeth, trying to make a joke. Then it dawned on me to whom I'd just said that. Duma might take me seriously. "Or maybe just knock her out, instead," I said out of the side of my mouth.

She got up and spun around to see me. It was definitely Sarah Wright, and she was definitely under some sort of spell. And she was definitely not dressed for work.

I had to pick my jaw up off the floor before I tripped. I found myself unable to say much. "H-H—uh, hi," I finally managed.

She was dressed in a low-cut, tight-fitting blue minidress that set off her hair, her gray eyes, and her long, lean legs. She was in shape. She hadn't said a word, and I was already distracted with blood flowing to parts other than my brain.

It took me a second to get past her physical appearance and notice the murk around her head. It was reminiscent of the haze on the mole people down in the caverns under Central Park, only much stronger and far more focused. It also didn't turn her into a listless zombii, but I could see she wasn't entirely herself. Medea had to be behind this, which immediately put me on guard. I couldn't fathom a single scenario in which the old witch would send Sarah here for a less-than-nefarious purpose.

"Steve," she said, smoothing out her dress. The name practically poured out of her mouth. "Sorry for just dropping in like this, but" — she started to walk over toward me—"I've missed you."

Medea's intentions be damned. The thinking part of my brain got stuck in neutral, but luckily, Duma bumped me from behind and snapped me back to reality. His presence stopped Sarah in her tracks, too.

"Uh, oh, did you meet my friend Duma?" I asked, trying to regain control over my brain.

"Yeah, we met earlier," said Duma as he walked around me and stood roughly between us within arm's reach of both of us. He had his hands behind his back, and his eyes were locked on Sarah, but he still had the same shit-eating grin on his face.

"Is there some place we can go that's... a bit more private?" she asked, cocking her head to one side.

"Um, now is not really a good time," I said, trying to defuse the situation a bit despite the protestation of a few body parts.

"But I have information about the bombing." She ran her middle finger along the neckline of her dress.

"Is it hot in here?" I could feel the sweat dripping down the side of my face and hear my heart pounding in my ears. I didn't recall being this nervous my first time in battle.

Duma just grinned back at me, enjoying my predicament entirely too much.

"We ID'd those shooters from Brooklyn," Sarah said. "I'm just not at liberty to discuss things in public." Her eyes traveled quickly from me to Duma and back to me again.

My brain kicked back in again, and I shook my head to clear it. Obviously, she wasn't herself because she wasn't even fazed by Duma's pure-white eyes. The Sarah I knew would have noticed that trait from twenty yards off.

"Are you feeling okay, Sarah?" I asked, stepping closer to her. I stopped just outside of what I estimated to be her reach. If she had a gun, I reasoned, she would have used it by now. Besides, I had no idea where she could hide one in that dress.

She stepped closer in response to my movement, and I freaked out. "Now!" I shouted to Duma and backed up.

Duma's hand flashed so fast I didn't see his blow to the back of her head. She just collapsed on the floor.

"Jeez, man. Did you have to hit her so hard?" I asked, kneeling down at her side to cradle her head, checking for blood.

Despite the fact that she was unconscious, the fog surrounding her head remained intact. I felt bad about having Duma knock her out, but despite panicking, I really did think it was the safest thing for her. At least, that way, she couldn't do anything to hurt herself or me.

"Wow, you really do like her," Duma said, kneeling down to search her.

I slapped his hands away. "Knock it off, would ya? Hey, Ab, get in here!" I was sure Ab was engrossed in some video game on the TV in my bedroom. The plinking and beeping noises down the hall stopped.

"Is that babe gone?" he called back. "She was hot, man. Oh…" He stopped when he saw us both kneeling over her prone body. "So, we had to kill her?"

"She's not dead," Duma replied. "I just smacked her on the back of the head and knocked her out cold. And from what I can see up close, she's clean. She's got nothing dangerous—" He stopped himself, examining her rear end as I tried to maneuver her to pick her up. "Well, nothing that *looks* like a weapon, anyway. Mmmh, and she ain't even my species."

"Holy crap!" I shouted. "Can't you control yourself at all? Ab, help me get her into the chair, and Duma, go get the rope from the garage." I pushed Duma away from Sarah.

While I knew all too well that Duma was a real Lothario when it came to females of virtually any humanoid species, I also knew he was playing his attraction to Sarah just to get my goat. And while I normally didn't let his antics get to me, in this case he was succeeding.

"Ooh, bondage, I'm all over it, D," said Duma.

"Just get me the damned rope." I shook my head as I lifted her.

Her hair was incredibly soft as it fell across my arm, and I couldn't help but notice how smooth and silky her legs were.

Though I didn't really need his help, Ab bent over and grabbed her feet and helped me set her down in my leather easy chair. Duma came back in with a length of rope, and I tied Sarah's arms and legs securely then noticed that the pendant on her necklace was all too familiar—it was one of those implosive disks. I hesitantly poked at it. I tried to grab the pendant nestled in her cleavage without being too ham-handed before Duma impatiently stepped in.

"Oh, for the love of all that's normal." He reached down to grab the pendant.

I slapped his hand away, glared at him, and snatched it before he could grab it, keeping it wrapped in my hand, remembering what Athena had said about the device and human contact.

"I need one of you to search her thoroughly for magnets of some kind." I glanced between Ab and Duma.

Duma was amused by the entire situation, standing with his arms crossed and a wide grin etched across his face, while Ab was serious and concerned about what I was doing.

"Ab, you do it. Be respectful, please."

"Magnets? What for?" he asked, holding his hands up as if surrendering. "I mean, I'd rather not, D. That means using metal."

"See this?" I held up the necklace with the pendant in my palm.

"According to Athena, it's an incendiary device created to go off in the presence of magnets when not in contact with human skin. I don't know if Peri skin will suffice, and it's a bad idea for me to chance getting this thing close to the magnets. She has to be carrying them. Just use your gloves, and go get a nail out of the garage."

"Makes sense." Ab shrugged. He walked back down the hall toward my bedroom. He reappeared pulling his dragon-skin gloves into place, flexing his fingers, and then walked into the garage.

"Man, that toolbox is a fae's nightmare," Ab said upon returning, shivering as if he were cold. "It's like a portable torture chamber. If I didn't have my gloves on..."

I stood up and stepped back while Ab walked over to Sarah with the nail in his gloved fist. Duma just lounged on the couch behind me.

"Just use it like a wand," I said, rubbing at my beard nervously. "Wave it over every part of her, and see if anything reacts."

It took less than a minute to identify her earrings as magnets — strong ones, too. They practically pulled free from her ears as Ab passed the nail near one of them.

"Grab those, and make sure they're the only ones. I'll figure out what to do with this." I shook the necklace in my hand.

The scenario these were supposed to work under suddenly played through my head. Maybe the necklace and earrings would come off as we climbed into bed together, or perhaps it would fall away from her body as we rolled around. *Either way, talk about going out with a bang.* Then it dawned on me: I might be able to use this thing to my advantage.

I walked out to the garage and got the nonsticky, self-adhering tape I used for wrapping the arbors of my fly-fishing reels and some lead tape with which I occasionally covered my knuckles. I wrapped the necklace around my wrist, bound it with the tape, wrapped over the pendant with the lead tape, and then added more tape to secure it. My hope was the lead would keep the pendant from reacting to anything magnetic I might run into. When I was done, I walked back into the house.

Ab was standing next to Sarah, taking off his gloves, while Duma remained reclined across my couch, eyes closed as if napping. I knew better.

"That's all I found," Ab reported, pointing to the nail on my kitchen counter. "You can put that away if you don't mind."

"And not for a lack of looking." Duma sat up, waggling his eyebrows and smiling.

I grabbed the nail off the counter and tossed it at Duma, who easily dodged it and laughed. "Man, you're going the right way for an ass kicking. Give me those magnets."

Ab brought them over to me, cradling them in his left hand, bundled inside his removed gloves. I took them and passed them over the wrappings on my wrist at full arm's length, cringing just in case, but nothing happened. "Good. It works."

"What the hell?" Duma demanded. "Were you just testing to see if those things would go off? Man, that's not cool, D. You coulda blown us all up."

I took as much pleasure in his concern as he was taking in ribbing me about Sarah. I considered it a bit of payback. "Nah. It's actually not an explosive; it's an implosive. It creates a gravitational singularity. We'd get sucked into it," I responded, smiling, probably smugly, at him.

Duma just shook his head.

"I wouldn't have done it if I didn't think it was safe. Besides, it's in contact with my skin." I brandished my lead-covered wrist. "And I might be able to use this in our favor when we run into Medea."

"Great. Now what about her?" he asked, pointing at Sarah.

I shoved the magnetic earrings into my pocket and walked back over to Sarah, where she was tied in the chair. She was still out, but the magical haze around her head persisted just as intensely. I thought that most spells to control or manipulate dissipated if either the target or caster was knocked unconscious. I was great with battlefield tactics, a whiz at reading the water when fishing, and I even understood a little about combat magic, but what I knew about this kind of magic would fit in a thimble and roll around like a BB in a boxcar. Even so, I knew I had to help her.

The only magic user I was on anything close to good terms with worked at the Metis Foundation. I was pretty sure his name was Voerig, and he was a Magister Templi of the Hermetic Order of the Golden Dawn, which meant he was a powerful innate.

"I need to make a quick call," I said, pulling my cell phone out of my pocket.

After a few minutes of careful pleading, I convinced Voerig to come over, and more importantly, not to tell Athena where he was going. I was going to owe him, not only for his help but also for his discretion. I couldn't even imagine what this was going to cost me. Wizards and witches were as devious at deal making as the fae, but despite the potential cost, I thought it prudent to keep my boss out of this since her reaction to the situation might be a little harsh and more strategic than humane. I waited and watched as the wizard arrived in less than thirty minutes in one of those odd little hybrid cars. It figured.

I'd never really spoken with Voerig much, and I remembered him reminding me of Walter Huston in *The Treasure of the Sierra Madre*, smelling like prunes, and having the personality of a dead fish — pure milquetoast. His appearance as he walked up to my front door didn't surprise me at all.

He couldn't have been taller than five-foot-two at best. He was dressed in pink Bermuda shorts and a white Cuban shirt with black knee socks and Birkenstocks. He was mostly bald, but his ratty gray beard reached down to his waist. He carried only an old-fashioned leather doctor's bag that required him to use both hands, like a small child carrying something too heavy. I shook my head as I watched him lurch up my front walk, lugging the bag.

I had no doubt that Athena surrounded herself with the most competent people she could find, but his physical appearance was uninspiring. His magical aura, on the other hand, was downright intimidating. It appeared as an intense, coruscating green glow that surrounded and permeated his entire being, with tendrils reaching out toward every surface he approached. His aura acted like a living creature rather than a passive veil of energy. I couldn't help but be impressed as he reached my door. If anyone could help Sarah, it was this tiny little wisp of a man.

"Thank you for coming so quickly, Magister Voerig. Please, come in." I watched as the tendrils of his aura entered first, reaching out to the various surfaces inside as if testing them before he entered.

"You are welcome, Tydides. I am glad I could be of service to one such as yourself." He inclined his head in a lieu of a formal bow. "Now, where is the unfortunate victim?"

I directed him over to my easy chair. The tendrils of his aura began exploring Sarah before he was close enough to touch her. The ropy green energy recoiled as it met the greasy gray haze engulfing her, and Voerig winced. He set his bag down with a jingling thump and then bent forward as if to stare at Sarah up close, his hands behind his back. His eyes were actually closed, and he was mumbling. His aura coalesced into a sheet that began to envelop Sarah's entire form. At first, the green energy scattered like water from oil as it touched the haze around Sarah's head. I watched as the wizard's face strained and his mumbling became more determined. His aura flashed and then fully surrounded her.

My intention was to leave him to work while I finished my preparations for our assault on Medea, but as I began to walk down the hallway to join Duma and Ab in my bedroom, the wizard cleared his throat behind me. He was standing upright next to the easy chair, hands still behind his back.

"Certainly, you don't expect me to do all the heavy lifting myself, do you?" the wizened little man said, peering down his nose at me.

"Ah, well, I don't really know much about magic."

"Well, I assumed that's why you called me," he said with a chuckle. "That doesn't mean I won't need an assistant who is capable of doing as I say."

I couldn't tell if he really needed my help or if he just relished the idea that he might have a chance to boss me around like a lowly apprentice. I looked at Sarah's unconscious form in the chair and then back at the old wizard. "Whatever you need," I replied, throwing my hands up in surrender.

"Excellent," he said like a professor who just got his point across. "Please lay her on the couch, and then bring me my bag."

I complied, and then the wizard began digging into his leather satchel, placing liquids and items on the coffee table next to him, some of which gave off small amounts of magical energy.

"Ah ha!" he finally said excitedly, holding up what appeared to be simple cotton rope. "Remove that one and use this to bind her legs and wrists, and then bind her arms at her torso. Tie her tightly."

I took the rope and did as he said, noticing a few delicate veins of copper running through the white strands as I secured them.

"And then place this over her eyes," Voerig said, holding out a black satin sleeping mask.

"Um..." I took the mask from him, confused.

Voerig squinted at me. "Let's just assume that I know what I'm doing here, shall we?" He chuckled again.

I couldn't help but think he was trying to make me feel like an idiot. Putting up with his condescension was probably just part of the price I'd have to pay, so I gave him a half smile and put the mask over Sarah's eyes as requested.

With a wave of his hand, the wizard's aura leaped toward the rope binding Sarah, turning its entire length the same bright green and tightening her bonds.

"All I can tell is that this is a very old spell. Not simple or outdated, mind you, just ancient. It is, in fact, very efficient and quite effective, but the hold on her mind is minimal, so it should be *simple* to break without harming her." He smiled smugly, emphasizing *simple,* and gave a flourish with his hands.

"Ah," I said, as if anything he said made much difference to me. I understood the parts about "simple to break" and "without harming her," and that was all that mattered.

"I will let you know how I need your help as I work, understood?" He grinned at me for the briefest of moments and then began.

The first thing he did was grab one of the little vials of liquid from the coffee table and unstopper it. He then passed it under Sarah's nose and returned the bottle to the table. A second later, Sarah arched her back, her arms and legs gave a spasm, and she inhaled deeply. The instant she tried to move, Voerig placed both hands, claw-like, over her body. The magic in the ropes flared brilliantly, and she became rigid again, though she was clearly awake and struggling.

He began speaking what I could only assume was some sort of incantation in a language I didn't know or even recognize. His voice began low, but as it increased in volume, it also increased in strength. I watched as his aura surrounded Sarah, stopped pulsing, and then began glowing brighter and brighter with the volume of his voice. I could see Sarah trying to speak, but I couldn't hear her over Voerig's thundering voice. The lights dimmed, and the temperature in the room began to drop rapidly as all of the ambient energy was sucked into Voerig's aura.

All at once, an explosion of green light blinded me while every light in the house exploded, sending us into utter darkness. The sensation was staggering, and I had to bring my hands to my eyes.

When I opened them, my vision was wrecked with floating green spots in the blackness, but I could hear Ab and Duma grousing about the power outage from the bedroom.

Out of the darkness, a single flame jumped to life, and it took me a second to see that Voerig was the source. With the conjured flame, he lit several candles from his bag as my eyes adjusted.

"What the hell, guys?" Duma said gruffly through the darkness.

"That was most interesting," Voerig said, lining up a series of crystals on the coffee table. Once he had them lined up, he blew on them, and they began to glow. "Oh, you can do better than that." He addressed the crystals directly, egging them on with his hand, and they glowed even brighter until the entire room was well lit. "Much better."

As the light increased, Duma stood right behind me while Ab leaned against the wall where the hallway met the living room. Duma pointed toward Sarah, and his eyes widened. She was sitting upright, straight as a rail, moving her head as if surveying her surroundings. Even Voerig recoiled at the foot of the couch as he noticed her. The haze around her head was so intense it was hard to make out the finer features of Sarah's face. Voerig's green tendrils had coalesced back into a solid mass close to the wizard's body.

"Ah, is she supposed to be doing that?" I asked.

Voerig scowled at me and put a single finger to his lips.

"Diomedes? Is that you? I know you're there, Diomedes." The voice sounded like Sarah and came from her body, but it was definitely not her talking.

No one moved or spoke, but we all traded furtive glances as Sarah kept turning her head mechanically from side to side.

"Come now, Tydides, I know you are close. I just wish to speak with you," Sarah's body said.

Duma stepped silently next to me, holding his karambit in one hand and one of his kukri knives in the other. I grabbed the front of his shirt and held him fast, slowly shaking my head. His body relaxed slightly, and I let go.

"Why, Medea, it's been a long time," I said, deciding to see where this was heading.

The moment I said her name, Voerig's eyes widened, and his mouth opened slightly. After another second, he scrambled off the couch as fast as his little old body could move him, and he ducked in behind Duma.

Holy crap. If this guy was that scared of her, we were screwed.

"Ah, so nice that you remember me," said Medea through Sarah's body as her head turned toward me.

"How could I forget?" I moved Duma so that I could see Voerig behind him. "Get her out of Sarah — now," I whispered hoarsely, trying to keep my voice low.

"Now now, Diomedes, whispering isn't fair," Medea said. "But who are you talking to? Most certainly, I felt another mage. A member of the Order, no doubt..."

"Well, sure, why not? We were having a party, and everyone loves magic tricks." I widened my eyes at the wizard and jabbed my finger toward Sarah.

Voerig suddenly snapped his fingers and became animated. He glared at me and rolled his hand around at the wrist, urging me to keep the conversation going. Then he grabbed Duma's sleeve and tapped Ab on the elbow, and they disappeared down the hall into darkness, leaving me alone with Sarah, who was possessed by the nastiest witch in history. *Just one of the perks of being me.*

"Come now, let's not be coy," Medea said. "We both know you're going to try to save this woman for some reason. I simply wish to tell you to desist."

"Desist?" I said, walking closer to Sarah. "I don't follow. Was our party so loud that it was bothering you in your cave? I mean, the magic tricks were great, but we were just about to bust out the polka music."

"Enough!" Medea screamed. "If you choose to pursue me, I will be forced to end you this time. If I must prove my point, I will start with killing this woman."

"Whoa, whoa, whoa." I guessed that Voerig was working on a solution, but I had no idea what or how soon he'd be ready. "No one needs to kill anybody here. I don't even know what you're talking about."

"Don't lie!" Medea shouted again. "I know you killed my Ifrit and Ghilan in New York, and I know that little waif found you before my servants could stop her. I also know you took Jamshid's Cup from that pathetic excuse of a shaman I hired to steal it in the first place. After I had the boy blow himself up for me, of course. And, of course,

I recovered the Cup, didn't I? So I'll say it again. Desist. You cannot stop me, Diomedes. You never could."

Damn, this witch was nuts, and she really needed to die. Where the hell was Voerig? I really had no idea where to take the conversation with the crazy lady in order to draw it out. I thought about telling her I knew she was after the chain that bound Prometheus, but it wasn't as if I knew where it was, and I preferred to have her guessing at just what she thought I knew.

"Stop you? I wasn't trying to stop you," I said, turning and speaking a little louder so they could hear me down the hall. "I was just trying—"

"No matter. I know you are coming. It is in your nature, and besides, it is inevitable. You and I have been absent of blade for far too long. Meanwhile, I will show you what you can expect..."

At that, Voerig came shuffling rapidly down the hall toward his bag at the foot of the couch, and Ab walked over to grab the coffee table next to it. Duma stood next to Ab, focused on Voerig.

"Wait, wait, wait," I said. "Why kill her? She's irrelevant. You don't have to do this. If this is about you and me, then let's just settle this between us."

While I spoke, Ab grabbed the coffee table with one hand as if it were a small box, spilling all the objects on it onto the floor, and lifted it out of the way. Voerig threw a fist-sized glass vial at Duma, who caught it and instantly flew into a blur of motion in the space the table once occupied. Voerig tapped me on the shoulder and pointed at Sarah and then onto the floor where Duma worked. Through the Peri's blur of motion, I could see a circle forming on the carpet. I got it: Voerig was going to use a conjuring circle to isolate Sarah and sever the connection with Medea.

"Oh, always the hero. Poor child. Heroes always die alone," Medea said, and then Sarah's body began to tremble violently in her restraints as if she were having a grand mal seizure. Blood started to run from Sarah's nose.

"Guys, anytime now," I said to no one in particular.

The blur that was Duma stopped and rolled to get out of the way. "Now, D—do it," he shouted.

I scooped Sarah up, which was like trying to hug a thrashing, hundred-pound tuna, and stepped into the middle of the circle Duma had formed, careful not to smudge or smear the design. The instant I cleared the border, the slightest hint of a wall of energy surrounded us, and my ears popped as the world became silent. Sarah's body fell limp in my arms. Through the slightly murky barrier, I could see Voerig clap his hands in triumph, though I couldn't hear anything beyond my own breathing. I felt like I was in a glass jar. Sarah was back to being unconscious again, her breathing steady but shallow. I exhaled heavily. Even the haze around her head was gone.

After a solid minute contemplating what had just happened, I finally stuck my foot over the circle on my carpet and slid my foot back, smearing the circle and releasing its energy, popping my ears again. I laid Sarah back down on the couch and looked from Voerig to Duma to Ab, my hands on my hips. "Thanks, guys," was all I could manage to say.

Voerig was the only one who chimed in. I knew Duma and Ab wouldn't say anything, nor did I need to thank them, which was exactly why I did.

"You are quite welcome," the wizard said excitedly. "We bested Medea, did we not?"

"We severed a link to her from four thousand miles away." Duma snorted derisively as he threw me a wet rag.

I laughed as I wiped the blood from Sarah's face and removed the mask. And then something dawned on me. Why did Voerig have me tie her up and place the mask over her eyes? He must have known this could happen. I wondered if I should be pissed off or just happy we saved her. I decided I had enough to deal with. I didn't need to start a fight with a wizard, too.

"You saved the girl, though, right? She'll be okay?" I asked the mage, handing him back the mask.

"I shall make sure of it," he replied, smiling broadly, clearly pleased with himself.

Voerig began untying Sarah, and I walked mindlessly to the garage to check on the circuit breakers and to get more lightbulbs. However awkward I was with the mundane, this was precisely the reason I couldn't get involved with them. Sarah had nearly gotten killed by something she didn't even know existed. That would be her life if she stayed anywhere close to me. And I couldn't do that to her — not if I really did care for her.

After throwing the breakers and gathering all the extra bulbs I had in the garage, I returned back inside. In my living room, Sarah was lying on the couch, covered with a blanket. Voerig was in the kitchen, brewing something that reeked—it smelled like a combination of skunk, licorice, and mint. Ab and Duma were leaning against the kitchen counter, laughing. All at once, a sound like a chainsaw ripping through aluminum, wielded by a grizzly bear with sinus issues, erupted from the couch. Duma pulled his knife, and I fumbled with the box of bulbs I carried, and then we realized it was just Sarah snoring. I say *just*, but she'd actually rattled the windows. Sonic booms were more subtle than that. I had to laugh, relieved she was okay.

"Holy crap!" laughed Duma next to me, curved knife in hand. "I thought a dragon farted or something. Speaking of which." We both frowned at Voerig, who was swirling the rank liquid in a small copper pot over one of the gas burners on the stove. He was disheveled. Even his aura was severely diminished and inactive. "What is that stuff you're making?"

"Oh, it's my own special concoction," the withered old man said, smiling. "It's like a sports drink for wizards." His smile grew, and he began humming to himself.

"Well, how'd the rest of it go?" I asked as I walked into the kitchen, waving my hand in front of my face to ward off the smell.

"Fine, fine. She's sleeping now. Short of the bump on the back of her head, she'll be right as rain when she wakes up. I have no idea how much she'll remember, though, poor girl. Where do you keep the cups?"

I grabbed the closest thing to a teacup I had—a mug with a fish tail for a handle that a client had given me. "It's all I have. Sorry, but I don't drink tea or coffee."

"Heathen," he replied under his breath as he snatched the mug from me. He stared at it intently for a few seconds.

"What was all that?" I asked.

"Well, in the beginning, it was a thought-implantation spell. It didn't need to be complicated, because the basis for the action already existed. It just"—he waved his hands around—"enhanced them. Reinforced them, so to speak. You can't really make someone do something they wouldn't be willing to do, without dire consequences."

The impact of that statement was jarring. It made me even more melancholy, given that I knew there was no way I could allow any kind of relationship to develop between me and Sarah.

"But—" I had to stop to clear my throat. "Um, what about the rest of it?" I finally spit out.

I could hear Duma snickering over my shoulder. That was followed abruptly by another riotous blast of sound from the direction of the couch. I could have sworn the dishes in my cupboards rattled.

"Oh, my," the wispy little wizard said, clearly still on edge, spilling the stinky tea all over himself. Once he gathered himself, he continued. "Medea is wickedly powerful. I could barely penetrate her spell at all. Of course, no one bothered to tell me it was her we were dealing with." He peered at me again from under his bushy eyebrows. "The moment I did permeate it, she knew it and was able to project herself through her connection to the girl. Unbelievably strong." He shook his head and stared into his cup of tea. "Many of the so-called fairy tales about nasty, evil witches were based on things Medea did during her time in medieval Europe. The Order even commissioned two men, Jacob and Wilhelm Grimm, to create and spread stories about her—and others—as a kind of warning. There are those among the Order, the Ipsissimus included, who believe that her power exceeds the collective capabilities of the entire Third Order."

"Seriously?" I asked, unsure of how to follow up his statement about Medea's strength.

Voerig just bobbed his head without taking his eyes from the cup.

The Third Order included the entire upper echelon of the most powerful group of mortal wizards and witches on the planet. The Ipsissimus was the head of the whole shebang and widely considered the strongest wizard among them. I was in way over my head.

"In the end, the only thing I could think to do was isolate the poor girl," Voerig continued after a few silent moments. "Fortunately, I was proved correct in my assertions." He smiled broadly at us all.

The wispy little wizard may have saved Sarah, but I still didn't trust him. He obviously knew whoever had control over Sarah could act through her. We bound her and covered her eyes, but we left her free to speak. Wizards and witches, and even witchers—those who weren't born with it, but learned to use magic—were tricky folk, and they always seem to be playing their own games. But it was clear that he and the rest of the Third Order and members of the Hermetic Order of the Golden Dawn were afraid of and flummoxed by Medea.

I always knew she was strong, but I never had a magical baseline to judge her against. No matter. Using innocents as unwitting assassins put her firmly at the top of my shit list, and I didn't care how powerful she was—I wanted to watch her try to outrun a fucking bullet.

CHAPTER 27

SARAH WOKE UP A SHORT time after Voerig left, predictably and understandably out of sorts and in some pain from the knock to the head. In the first few minutes, she kicked Ab in the groin and came close to cracking Duma's skull with my fly-tying vise, but she eventually calmed down enough to recognize me. The moment she saw me, she stopped flailing and began breathing so shallowly and rapidly that she began hyperventilating. I walked over to her with a dishtowel full of ice for her head and helped her sit down. She focused on me with wide, confused eyes. She tried to talk in between quick, panicked breaths. "I... I... I... remember..."

I didn't have a paper bag to offer her, but Sarah was obviously experienced enough in crisis situations that she managed to regain control of her breathing and calm herself down on her own. After a few minutes of deeper, more relaxed breaths, her eyes traveled from me to Ab — leaning against the living-room side of the kitchen counter — and then to Duma, who was absentmindedly picking at his nails with his karambit as he sprawled over my easy chair. She took a deep breath, and then her gaze drifted back to me, her face full of confusion.

She gingerly touched the knot on the back of her head and then put the towel full of ice over it. "I... remember everything," she said slowly, staring down at her free hand, which she kept in her lap. "I just don't understand any of it." She shook her head, and tears began to roll down her cheeks, though she didn't make a sound.

"It's over," I said, hoping that the words would somehow make things easier. I leaned forward and rested my elbows on my knees, staring at the remnants of the conjuring circle on my carpet.

Sarah sniffed her runny nose, and I could see her wipe at her face out of the corner of my eye. No one said anything for a few minutes. I got her some tissue from the bathroom, which she accepted with a weak smile. She wiped her eyes and nose and was briefly startled again by the sight of the blood left over from Medea's attack.

"Who the hell is Medea, and why was she calling you Diomedes? I thought your name was Steve Dore. And what was that... thing I passed through to get from New York to here?"

"It's a long story. Like three thousand years' worth."

"I'm not going anywhere yet," she said, readjusting the icepack on her head, fixing me with the eyes of a highly trained observer in the drawn face of someone who had just been through the wringer.

I tried to explain everything to her as simply as I could—who Medea was and what we thought happened, from the bombing in New York until she showed up here. I didn't mention the various beings and creatures that existed in this world. I just didn't think it was wise after finding out all she had in such a traumatic way. And I didn't really say much about me, other than my real name was Diomedes and that dealing with trouble like this was my job. She didn't say a word the entire time. In fact, even her expression remained constant— and full of uncertainty. I hated having to tell her this stuff, but she had experienced it, and I owed it to her. And I wasn't about to lie to her again. Not after what had just happened to her.

When I was done, she just nodded slowly. "Um, do you have anything to drink?" she asked after a minute of silence. "Maybe some aspirin?"

"Sure." I hopped up and headed toward the kitchen. "Water, juice, soda—what would you like?" I was thrilled to hear her finally talk again. Given what she'd just gone through because of me, I'd happily have given her anything she asked for.

"Anything with alcohol."

Yeesh. She was not taking this well. As I was about to pull my bottle of scotch out of the cupboard, Duma held up a finger, walked out the front door to his truck, and came back holding a bottle. Meanwhile, I grabbed a few aspirin for her from a bottle I kept in my kitchen cupboard.

"Try this." Duma walked over and set the bottle on the counter.

I grabbed a glass and poured her a couple of fingers of the pale green liquid and presented it to her along with the painkillers.

She took them, sniffing the drink. "What is it?"

"Just try it," Duma responded.

And she did. "Wow, is that good." No hack or cough, no hoarse voice — nothing. "What is it?" she said, holding her glass out for more.

"Nope. One is more than enough for a pinky," he said, putting the stopper back in the bottle. "In case you don't remember, my name is Duma. I assume you are Sarah Wright of the Department of Homeland something or other, yes?"

"Oh, sorry," I said, feeling like an idiot that I hadn't formally introduced them since she'd woken up as herself. "Sarah, that's Duma and his brother, Abraxos, but we call him Ab. Guys, this is Agent Sarah Wright of the Department of Homeland *Security*." I squinted at Duma as I gave him the official title.

"What are you? And what did you mean by 'pinky'?" She shook her head as if trying to clear it and winced.

"Ab and I are... not human, as you obviously noticed," Duma said, drawing his hand outward for emphasis. "We are fae or fairy folk. Peri, to be more precise. And by pinky, I mean *your* kind." At that, he waved his hand dismissively.

"Nice, dipdunk." I glowered at Duma in a way that I hoped conveyed my desire for him to shut up. "They are my friends," I said to Sarah, who sat on the opposite end of the couch.

Sarah bowed her head as if processing the information, and then her brow furrowed deeply. "So, 'pinky' is some kind of derogatory term for a woman?" she asked with a slight edge in her voice.

"Whoa, relax," Duma replied. "It's a derogatory term for your race."

"What?" Sarah was suddenly standing, a bit shaky but holding the shot glass as if she were about to throw it at Duma. She was acting outraged but was on the defensive, as if she were trying to fight her way out of a corner she felt she'd been backed into.

"Not your color, woman," Duma said. "The fact you are *human*." For reasons I couldn't fathom, he closed the distance between them faster than she could blink.

She dropped the ice pack, scattering cubes everywhere, and practically fell back onto the couch, but I raced to catch her before she did. Startled, she gawked at me and at Duma and then pushed herself loose from my grasp and back to her own feet.

"The drink is diluted and fermented wyvern blood with a touch of single-malt scotch." He was being uncharacteristically brash.

"Whoa, just relax, Duma," I said, trying to step between them. "What crawled up your butt?"

Whatever was going on was completely unlike Duma. In fact, I had never seen him act like this before unless he was trying to bait someone into attacking first. He winked at me and gave me a wry half smile. I shook my head slightly, letting him know I had no idea what he was up to.

Sarah straightened, pushed me aside, and stepped up to him till their faces were inches apart. "I may not have a clue what the fuck is going on here, but I will not stand here and be insulted by some kind of... whatever you are," she said with a gleam in her eye. She poked him in the chest repeatedly with her finger. "And hey, aren't you the one that hit me in the fucking head?"

Her tenacity and tone, especially the last comment, actually backed Duma up a step toward the conjuring circle in the middle of the carpet as she railed at him, but she wouldn't let him get far. That was when I finally figured out what he was up to. He wanted to see how she'd react in the face of adversity, given what she'd just learned. Would she fold, or would she keep moving forward? Clearly, she wasn't about to fold. I just stood back and started to laugh.

Stupid move. Her attention shifted to me. Her eyes got wide, her brow raised, and she pointed her finger at me.

"And you..." She started in on my erratic behavior and how I'd lied to her back in New York, used her, and then assumed she wouldn't understand what was really going on. She backed me across the living room and into the kitchen counter. Twice, I thought I might actually have to physically defend myself, and I had to fight my instincts to keep from doing so.

I was way out of my element. Duma began to laugh uncontrollably. Again, Sarah redirected her attention.

But before she could fully engage Duma, he held up his hands in surrender. "Oh, I like her!" he managed to say in between laughs.

She froze. I tried to stifle a snicker for fear of her wrath.

And then she started to laugh. "None of this makes any sense. I woke up this morning and everything was normal. Now, everything I thought I knew..." She sat down in the easy chair.

"Look, I know it's not easy to believe, but it's the truth," I said. "The world is bigger than you know, but it's also rife with creatures and beings so foul that the evil that men are capable of pales in comparison. True nightmares. That's where I come in."

She definitely was handling things better now that she had vented a bit. "So you guys are some kind of troubleshooters. I get that," Sarah said, standing. She folded her arms across her chest and made direct eye contact, her focus laser sharp and her expression resolute. "I want to help."

Duma and I both replied at the same time, trying to stop her from going any further with the thought. She held up her hand to shut us up. Beyond her, Ab appeared from down the hallway. I was so wrapped up in our conversation that I hadn't even noticed he had left the room.

"Hey!" Ab shouted over Duma's and my chorus of reasons that she couldn't help. "What the hell is going on in here?"

We all stopped instantly. His brow was knitted, and he scowled as he watched us. With his white eyes, he appeared rabid.

Sarah was the first to speak up. "I'm going with you guys."

"Cool. The more the merrier." Ab reversed direction and disappeared back down the hallway.

"I don't think Athena will like this very much," Duma said.

"Frankly, it's my team, and I can add anyone I want. If Athena doesn't like it, she can kiss my ass." That was me: defiant to the end.

Duma smiled at me. He had baited me right into that one.

"Wait," said Sarah, whipping her head back and forth between Duma and me, her eyebrows raised and eyes wide. "*The* Athena? Goddess of Wisdom and Warfare?"

"Yeah," I responded. "That's the one. Why?"

"She's actually *real*? I used to pretend to be her when I was a girl!" She threw her hands up. "She was the coolest Greek god! Goddess! My brothers used to pretend to be Greek heroes, like Hercules and Achilles—"

"Of course they did." I rolled my eyes and sighed.

I could see something dawn on her as her eyes got even wider, and her mouth fell open.

"And wait, Diomedes—no! Are you *that* Diomedes? The one from the Trojan War? You can't be. No way. The one who beat Ares and Aphrodite?" She sounded like a kid who'd just found out she was talking to a movie star.

"Yep. That'd be me," I said, focusing on the ground, waffling between being thrilled she knew the stories about me and embarrassed she was fawning over me. Who knew she was a fan girl?

"Un-freaking-real," she said, sitting back down in the chair. "You guys were my heroes as a kid. I even dressed up as Athena for, like, five years in a row at Halloween."

"I suppose your brothers dressed as Achilles." I stared at my shoes and crossed my arms over my chest.

"Well, one did, once, but no one knew who he was supposed to be."

"See!" I shouted. "If it weren't for Brad Pitt, no one would even remember his name."

Sarah just looked at me, confused.

Duma shook his head, holding up his hand to stop her. "Long story—don't ask."

"Athena runs the Metis Foundation," I said.

"You're kidding me!" she said. "All the years I consulted for them, I never had a clue."

"Why would you? No normal mortal knows. Most of her employees don't even know. Sarah, look, I know you want to help, but the guys on the team all have years of training and backgrounds in small-group tactics and assault operations. I've worked with all of them before in combat situations. I just don't know how you'd fit in. I'm not trying to insult you, but DHS isn't exactly a high-speed combat unit. You even told me back in Brooklyn that you rarely used your gun."

"Look," she began defensively, "I told you at the pizza place that I *requested* to be transferred to DHS from the FBI, where I worked on the counterterrorism Fly Team. I've worked all over the world, and I speak three languages. I've even trained with the Green Berets for counterterrorism combat ops."

FBI. Fly Team. That was why I had hazy memories of insects eating alphabet soup from of our conversation at the pizza parlor. It explained a lot.

"I can handle myself in combat," she said. "The only reason I left the Fly Team was because I wanted to settle down." She stared at the ground sheepishly. "Guys don't like women who can kick the shit out of them. Besides, running all over the world at a moment's notice is hard on relationships."

I snorted. *Add being immortal and chasing monsters for a living, and see what that does.* "Sarah, this is different. These aren't just terrorists we're dealing with. They aren't even all human, for Pete's sake."

"Yeah, but it does explain a few things I saw when I was with the Fly Team, not to mention all the crap I've gone through since you showed up a few days ago. And I know it sounds idealistic, but I like the idea of protecting not just the US, but the world. I can handle it. I won't let you down. Please give me a chance."

I eyed Duma. He just shrugged. Some help he was.

I shook my head and exhaled deeply. Her statement about the trouble she'd endured since I showed up was painful, but the tactical part of my brain pushed through to overrule my emotions. Clearly, she was qualified, and now that she knew, she could make up her own mind. Besides, if she knew everything and could handle it, what did that mean for us?

"Okay, you're in. But dammit, you do exactly what I say, no questions asked, understand?"

She nodded her head only once, her expression deadly serious, and I could see the same resolve in her I had that day at the museum. This chick would have given Penthesilea, Queen of the Amazons, a run for her money.

CHAPTER 28

A B, DUMA, SARAH, AND I spent the next few hours gathering and preparing gear before heading to my staging site on the southern end of Andros Island. Before we left, I made one quick phone call to tell Athena to send the Spartoi support team she'd offered me earlier as soon as they could be ready and asked that they also stop by my house and pick up the excess gear. When we were ready, I sent Ab to gather Geek and Frigate as planned while I traveled to the site with Duma and Sarah.

My staging area was mostly a shanty in the Bahamas that also doubled as a good place to hole up and chase bonefish when I had the time. It was isolated and difficult to get to and was bounded on one side by the ocean and the other sides by thick mangroves, sea grape, gumbo-limbo, and palm trees. Sneaking up on the site was nearly impossible.

Ab arrived with Geek and Frigate in tow about an hour after we got there. Both Frigate and Geek were a bit uneasy from their first trip through the Ways, though it didn't seem to hamper Geek's enthusiasm. I could hear him barraging Ab with questions as they approached the shanty through the mangroves. Ab shuffled through, his face drawn and haggard, threw down the gear bag he was carrying, and kept walking down the beach without saying a word. Geek didn't miss a beat. He immediately began to question me, and I knew exactly how Ab felt.

I spent a few minutes introducing the rest of the team and then called Ab back in to help me open my armory for everyone to gear up. While my shanty was little more than a few rough walls and a thatched roof, I had spent a decade, nearly half a century ago, carving an underground storehouse out of the coral of the island. I had enough weaponry to equip our team sufficiently and then some, all stored right below their feet.

The human part of my team stared in surprise as Ab and I opened the heavy reinforced-steel vault door set into the ground under the floorboards. As soon as the door was completely open, a white light lit up the hole, followed by a series of electronic thunks from the fluorescent ballasts turning on below.

"Get moving. Each of you will pack your own gear, so check it, then check it again," I said and then got out of the way. Geek, Frigate, and Sarah all peered down into the hatch, wide-eyed and mouths agape like kids gawking at store windows at Christmas time.

About an hour after the human contingent of my team began outfitting themselves, Athena's presence on the island became obvious to me. I encountered her and her Spartoi retinue in a clearing fifty yards from my shanty. Her dragon's-teeth warriors, a dozen of them, carried all the gear from my garage plus their own. Athena wore her hair in a loose braid over one shoulder and dressed in knee-high leather boots, tight gray pants, and a matching athletic top. Her brow was heavily creased over her squinted but intense blue eyes. Something was clearly bothering her.

"Let's walk," she said without stopping to wait for me as she headed back up along the beach away from my shanty.

My first reaction was that she was pissed about me dragging Sarah along, and all I could think was that I would not enjoy this conversation. Reluctantly, I jogged to catch up to her.

"Look, it's my team," I said before she could start talking, "and I'll choose anyone I damn well want."

"I'm not here about Agent Wright, and I approve of her addition. Things have escalated."

Her reaction stopped me in my tracks for a second, and I had to jog to catch up with her again. "Things? What things? What do you mean, 'escalated'?"

"There are reports of a hijacked passenger jet having crashed in a remote region of Western Bulgaria, in the Balkan Mountains near the border with Serbia. Jundullah is taking credit for it. The plane originated in Tehran. All passengers and crew are assumed dead." She listed the details as if she were reading a menu. "Fakhri confirms Medea is behind this and is now on site as well. She says the chain is there."

"A hijacking? How is that—" I stopped myself in midthought.

"You said Jundullah, right? Of course. They're based in Iran and trace their roots back to the Medes, don't they?"

I had only dealt with Jundullah as part of the Teams and never thought about them much beyond that, but their involvement made perfect sense. They were a known terrorist organization that traditionally only operated within Iran. It was small-time compared to the Muslim Brotherhood, Hezbollah, or al-Qaeda, but they did have a unique history that connected them directly to Medea.

"Correct. And the founder of the Medes is historically credited to Medus, Medea's son." She stopped and smiled at me without amusement.

"The chain is definitely there?" I asked, my mind racing for a plan of action. *Screw it.* If she was there now, I didn't have time. My plan of attack would be simple: attack.

"Exactly," she responded, handing me a piece of folded paper. "You need to leave now for Bulgaria. When you arrive, you'll meet a Sânziană called Gali. That paper should give you rough directions via the Ways. You'll arrive in a wooded area outside the village of Stakevtsi, close to the wreck site. It's not very remote, but the local village is small, so there shouldn't be too much interference from rescue workers or governmental agencies yet. But you need to move now. Once they get on scene, more lives may be lost if Medea is still there."

Her eyes flashed electrically, and she walked off into the mangroves. I sprinted back down the beach to my shanty and dug through my gear bags to find my weapons and armor while everyone eyed me as if I were crazy. The human operators on my team wouldn't be ready for a skirmish this quickly, and I couldn't leave them alone, either. Ab wouldn't be fast enough to keep up, nor was he social enough to help the others if I took Duma. I also didn't have time to think up any small-group tactics, and without a plan, Duma would do what he did best—kill everything indiscriminately—and while not a bad idea, it wasn't always the smartest strategy. I was going to have to fly by the seat of my pants on this one, and that was something I accomplished best on my own.

"No time to explain. I'll be back as soon as possible," I shouted to no one in particular as I ran off into the mangroves. "Gear up, and be ready to leave when I return."

I stopped just long enough to strap on my vest and armor before opening the Ways.

CHAPTER 29

USING WRITTEN DIRECTIONS TO NAVIGATE the Ways was kind of like using a cleaver to do brain surgery, but whoever had composed them for Athena was remarkably detailed, which really helped. I ended up in a peaceful valley in a pristine old-growth forest. It reminded me of something out of a fairy tale—and probably was just that.

Many of the trees were gigantic, but even the shortest had high canopies that cast ominous shadows. A beautiful mat of brown leaves covered the forest floor, which was broken only by an occasional stand of scrub brush or sapling growing in any light that made its way through the canopy above. It was cool and earthy and entirely medieval.

This region of Bulgaria had given rise to legends of vampires and werewolves, and I knew the birthplace of Vlad the Impaler wasn't far away. There were more Moroi, or energy-sucking mortal vampires, in this region than in any other place on Earth, but it was still remarkable and serene.

As I got my bearings, a striking young woman with a greenish hue stepped out in absolute silence from behind a massive silver fir tree—definitely a Sânziană, one of the local fairy folk.

"Hello." I waved then corrected myself. "*Zdravei.*"

I didn't know much Bulgarian, but it usually didn't matter with fae. They seem to understand all forms of communication, including among animals.

At my greeting, the fairy suddenly stood a bit straighter and cocked her head inquisitively, and it occurred to me that she must have been using a glamour to try to hide herself from me.

"Yes, I can see you. Gali? Pallas Athena sent me."

With that, she relaxed a bit and scrutinized me from head to toe. "Yes, I am called Gali. You must be Tydides." She held out her hand stiffly as she approached.

"Yes, but call me Diomedes." I took her hand and gave it a brief shake.

It was awkward and rigid. Some fairies tried hard to fit in with humans when they had to interact with us. Our customs, such as joining hands when we met, were bizarre to them.

"Very well, but we must move now. A small group of humans is quickly approaching the wreck site, and a Căpcăun named Targoviste is already there, searching for something. Can you keep up?"

A plane crash would provide a veritable buffet for the local variety of ogre. Căpcăuns were massive, nasty, and prone to violence, and they liked to eat people, too. Dead or alive.

"I'll do my best," I replied, taking in the hugeness of the valley. The forest was too thick to see much beyond the dense foliage, but I could smell the acrid odor of burning fuel and rubber. I followed Gali, who was moving slowly for a Sânziană in her native realm. Alternating between running bipedally and quadrupedally and occasionally bounding between trees like some kind of lemur, she could have probably moved up and down these slopes through this forest faster than most cars could run the Autobahn. She seemed to be keeping it down to city-street speeds for my sake, constantly checking for my presence over her shoulder. We got to the crash site within fifteen minutes.

While I recovered from our brisk woodland jog, Gali, who showed no signs of fatigue or even exertion, led me to a stand of trees that grew denser as we approached it. She placed a finger to her lips and beckoned me forward with the other hand. As I got to the trees, I could see smoke filtering through the scattered sunlight in the dark forest. But there was far more sunlight than there should have been. The smell of burning flesh and wreckage became oppressive the closer I got to the edge of the clearing. I could hear lots of movement—heavy, metallic banging and scraping, along with the teeth-grinding sounds of bending metal from up ahead—but couldn't see what was making all the commotion through the smoke and bright sunlight. A gruff voice was bellowing in a language I didn't know.

I pointed at my ears and shook my head, trying to indicate to Gali that I didn't understand. She shook her head and pointed in front of us. It took a second to adjust to the light and get into a good position to see the wreckage—mostly a massive dirt hole in a clearing of broken and twisted trees. Over the crater's edge, I could just make out parts of an immense wing and the blue-and-white tail section decorated with a winged horse. Dense smoke billowed from the wreckage, and the caustic smell of burning metal, rubber, and flesh clogged my airways.

The more I studied it, the more the sight struck me as odd. Very little of the wreckage lay outside the crater except part of a wing, and it appeared that the entire fuselage was crushed inside it. The tail section was sticking straight up as though planted in the earth. It was as if the plane had fallen out of the sky straight down to this spot.

There were no survivors, bodies, or even body parts—not that an ogre would pass up the opportunity to finish them off if it had enough time. I did see a few crimson smears of blood along the visible parts of the white fuselage, but nothing that led to anything I could see. The only thing I could figure was that this crater was deep—far too deep for a passenger-jet crash.

Based on what Fakhri had told Athena, Medea had Jundullah hijack the plane and then purposely crash it here in order to recover the chain she needed. Crashing a plane to get what she wanted was right up Medea's alley off Crazy Street. What stumped me was where the chain would be located that she needed to do something so extreme to get to it.

I quietly crept along the clearing's edge to my right, trying to get a better view. Several people emerged through a furrow in the crater's edge about a hundred yards in front of me, carrying out bright golden chests from somewhere inside the wreckage.

Well, sort of people. The odd creatures carrying the chests quickly drew my attention away from the gleaming golden crates. They walked upright, but they were misshapen and malformed, and none of them projected any kind of magic or power of their own, but some sort of magical energy enveloped them all. They weren't possessed by it like Sarah or the zombiis had been, but rather, the force played over and around them like the exploring tentacle of an octopus. The ones carrying the chests had massive torsos and arms, but their legs were all different lengths and builds. Others had only one arm, some had shriveled and withered arms, and some even scrabbled rather than walked, hunched over on all fours. They wore little in the way of clothing except for loincloths or ragged pants. Many were so skinny you could see bones under their skin, but the ones carrying the crates were heavily muscled. And there were a lot of them.

Gali was gazing up, sniffing the air, her face unreadable. Within the span of a heartbeat, I could see her expression change to one of urgency and concern. She mouthed something and then a soft voice like a breeze whispered in my ear, "There is a *mag'osnik* here, also." Gali pointed to a spot on the other side of the crater. "A powerful magic user."

The sorcerer's power washed over me as soon as Gali said it. The hair on the back of my neck and arms stood up as my eyes were drawn to a hooded figure with a long staff who was just emerging from the furrow. I hadn't seen her for a while, but I never would have forgotten that kind of evil. It was Medea. *Son of a bitch!*

She had always been tall for a woman—nearly six feet—and her fiery red hair flowed out from her stark-white, hooded heavy cloak. I couldn't see her face well, and she used the staff for support as she limped along, but there was no mistaking the black aura that surrounded her. It was her aura's shimmering haze that extended to and fully enveloped every creature I could see around the crater.

She screamed at the beings carrying the chests as if they were cattle, stopping briefly in front of several others, who instantly cowered at her feet. I could see her aura pulse and change to a bloody red, and without saying a word, she raised her staff and brought it down across the head of one of the creatures with a sickening crunch. It crumpled limply to the ground, and the other two scrambled away. She'd always had a short temper.

I pulled out my Sig, chambered a round, and made sure my spare clips were handy. I quickly looked around the wreckage to make sense of the landscape and get a feel for how many I was up against. I counted at least twelve of the misshapen humanoids, and Medea. That was what I could see. I knew there was an ogre somewhere nearby, probably in the crater having a nosh, and I still had no idea what else was down there. Apparently, recovery of the chain was important enough for Medea to show up in person.

"This area lies over the top of many *peshteri*—um, caverns. The airship's impact must have penetrated them," Gali said in her breezy whisper before gliding in silently next to me, flitting from tree to tree in a blur.

"What are they taking out?" I asked quietly.

They were placing huge, golden chests decorated in all manner of reliefs and designs at the edge of the trees less than seventy-five yards away, just off to our right. Medea began digging through the gilded coffers with the end of a staff as bloody red energy began to overwhelm her aura again. She was searching for something and not finding it. I felt a brief moment of joy.

"I do not know," Gali answered. "It does not feel like it belongs to this region, and it is not of this plane."

"What do you mean, doesn't belong to this region?"

More of the misshapen creatures were emerging from the wreckage, carrying golden chests, when a louder, more animated chatter and sudden increase in speed of movement ran through their ranks.

"I mean that whatever they are removing was not in those caverns until just before the airship crashed here," Gali said in a short, terse tone and with a stern cast to her face.

I couldn't tell if she was upset with me or with what was happening to her forest. Then two Ghilan and a pair of the humanoid figures emerged with a stone case that emanated a forcible and pure blue-white energy that I had only seen from items created in the home world of the Protogenoi toward Medea. The case was little more than three feet high, but it was immense in breadth and width, easily eight feet by twelve. It appeared to be made of some sort of smooth, pale stone-like marble, and its faces were carved with figures and symbols I couldn't quite make out at that distance. Based on the effort expended by the creatures hauling it, the case was heavy as hell.

Medea's seething aura calmed back to a uniform black instantly when she saw the container. She limped heavily toward it, forgetting to use her staff in her excitement.

I searched for a better vantage point from which to attack, but this was the only area that offered any cover at all without a person having to run from tree to tree. I was seventy-five yards away from Medea, which made a round from my Sig pretty useless. I was sure I could hit her, but at that distance, it wouldn't do much damage, and with a witch as powerful as her, I would have to make every shot count — especially without backup.

Gali was watching the situation intently. Medea attempted to open the chest while her Ghilan and other creatures stood aside, gibbering and bobbing. Then the giant ogre approached from the back of the crowd. The massively built and slightly hunchbacked Căpcăun carried a mangled human arm in one hand and an immense log in the other. His bald head was small on his broad shoulders, and the most notable feature on it at this distance was a single giant tusk projecting up from his lower jaw. He wore pieces of greenish-colored animal-hide armor over his shoulders, waist, and thighs.

Whatever I was going to do, I needed to do it then before the kitchen sink showed up. The only advantage I had was surprise, and for maybe a few seconds after that, I'd also have the benefit of them not knowing how many were with me. I figured I'd have the upper hand for about thirty seconds at most. There was something to be said for shock and awe. To quote one of the greatest military strategists of the late twentieth century, "Yippee ki yay, motherfucker."

Gali stared at me with her eyes wide as I pulled one sword, kept the Sig in the other hand, and charged from the brush at full speed, roaring a battle cry at the top of my lungs. At least I had the shock part in my favor.

Thanks to the clearing and the fact that the wreckage had gone straight down, I only had to hurdle a few broken tree trunks in my path on the way to Medea. I'd closed to within fifty yards before her creatures even turned around, and I opened fire with the nine-millimeter Sig P226, aiming for the densest mass of humanoid figures. I emptied the clip ten yards from them, dropped the gun, and pulled my other sword.

The group had just begun to react by the time I assaulted them, and I tore through most of the oddly shaped creatures with ease, killing or incapacitating eight of them. The two Ghilan were significantly faster than the others, and they split up to flank me. The ogre was still farther back toward the wreckage.

I tried to bank toward Medea before she could act, but the footing on the leaf litter and the loose dirt from the crater proved too unstable, and I ended up rolling about fifteen feet to her right. I used my momentum to carry me into a position on one knee, holding both swords down at my sides. The maneuver nearly brought tears to my eyes because of the burns on my legs, but the pain helped me concentrate. I focused on her as I came to an abrupt stop less than five yards away.

Medea took one look at me and practically hissed. Her face

contorted. She'd been a remarkably attractive woman when I first knew her several thousand years ago, but millennia of hate and evil had perverted her beauty. Her nose and high cheekbones were sharp and angular while her sinister eyes sat in heavily creased slits beneath a wrinkled brow. The skin of her lower face sagged into jowls and a turkey-like neck. There was no wart that I could see, but that was all that was missing.

I needed to act before she could draw enough energy to attack, so I lunged at her, ready to bring my swords down. I made it about half the distance before I hit something I couldn't see and caromed off, flying just over and behind her, landing with a jarring impact that sent waves of pain through my burned lower body. Whatever I ran into was stationary, like a wall or some sort of shield. Considering that it had been less than thirty seconds at that point, it was damn fast for a defensive spell.

"Now that's just not fair," I leveled at Medea as I stood up and got into an attack position. But before I could think of anything smarmy to say, the pair of Ghilan closed in on me from both sides. They were covering ground at a frightening speed. I took a half step back with my left foot to avoid the left-hand Ghilan's collision and swung my left sword in a wide arc at about waist level, right to left, then down toward the ground. I used the momentum from the attack to tuck into a roll and prepare for the second Ghilan.

The first Ghilan landed some ten feet away, and its body tumbled in two different directions. The second one closed in on me from behind simultaneously, but I was expecting it. It was committed to an airborne attack but had aimed for me while I was still standing. I came out of my roll sideways and raised my right sword to impale the creature as it tackled me. I used the momentum to roll us farther behind Medea just in case she was readying an attack.

The speared Ghilan was scrabbling to stop our movement and unpin itself when I punched it with my left fist, sword still in hand, in the side of its bulbous head. Something in its skull cracked, but all types of ghouls can take an enormous amount of physical punishment. The thing screeched and pulled free of my sword, swinging its long, sinewy arms wildly. I broke focus for less than a second—always a major no-no in combat—to relocate Medea, and the Ghilan nailed me across the chest with its claws in a blow that nearly took my breath away.

I reacted before its swing was complete, bringing the hilt of my right sword down on the other side of its skull with a heavy thud. The blow disoriented the creature just enough, and I pulled my left sword up through its midsection. My blade traveled up and out just beside the screaming beast's head. The howling stopped instantly.

When I returned my attention to Medea, she was hurriedly directing the last few mobile humanoids to grab the massive stone box, and then I caught more movement to my right. The ogre was barreling down on me, swinging its tree-trunk club over its head. The damned thing probably had spikes sticking off it, too. Ogres were so cliché.

I set my feet, readying myself to deflect the impact of the makeshift club, when the monstrous creature fell with a yowl as something impaled it from behind. It skidded and slid headfirst through the dirt and leaf litter.

I took advantage of the situation and turned my attention back to Medea. The air around me began to crackle with motes of energy, which I took as a sign she was about to unleash hell on me. Without thinking, I hurled my right sword at her as hard as I could, just as one of the humanoid creatures dragging the chest crossed between us. The blade caught the creature square in the back, causing it, and then the others, to drop the box with a jarring thunk. The container remained sealed. The impaled being tumbled into Medea, and the energy dissipated as quickly as it had appeared.

"Damn you, Diomedes," came Medea's curse as she shoved the dying form away. The witch held her right hand out in my direction, fingers splayed widely, and I could see and feel the field of bloody red energy pop to life just beyond her reach. In my peripheral vision, I could see the ogre getting to its feet to my right.

"Diomedes, watch out!" Gali screamed from somewhere well behind me.

Medea was levitating a twisted piece of wreckage. She sent it flying in my direction. I dove straight ahead, landing hard on the remains of several of the humanoid creatures I'd shot and hacked. A thunderous crack from somewhere in front of me made me duck my head instinctively, delaying my recovery just another second, but I scrambled to my feet to face Medea again. I got my feet under me just in time to see her stepping into a dark, fire-lit cavern that had somehow appeared at the edge of the wreckage. She disappeared the second she stepped through it. It was as if someone flashed a picture on a screen and simply walked into it, and then the screen shut off. I didn't even have enough time to think about following her before the portal closed.

The stone case sat, cracked open like an egg, where she'd been standing moments before. Its otherworldly aura had vanished, and it was empty.

CHAPTER 30

A SHARP, PAINED GRUNT CAME FROM behind me. The ogre was impaled in its chest by the piece of wreckage Medea had thrown at me. Disappointed but relieved, I walked over and pulled my sword free from the back of the creature I'd unintentionally speared, and then I went back to the ogre, whose right leg was seeping black, thick, smelly blood. A long, slender green stone dagger protruded through its leg from just behind the knee. The ogre spat a gobbet of black goo in my direction and unsuccessfully tried to shift himself. Behind him, Gali peered down into the crater from its edge.

"Don't go anywhere, ugly," I said to the ogre.

I met Gali at the rim of the crater and followed her intent gaze down a good seventy-five feet into the stinking, burning wreckage, dozens of charred bodies... and at least twenty golden coffers full of treasures in some kind of massive cavern ripped open by the plane's crash. That explained why the impact crater was so much deeper than it should have been.

Along with the coffers, within the cavern were all manner of jewels, jewelry, trinkets, weapons, armor, and gold and silver coins scattered about by the crash. Some of it had a faint magical aura, but most did not. One thing was for sure: there was a lot of it.

"There are at least fifty more chests down there. I do not know this trove of riches. It should not be here," Gali said, her brow furrowed.

I approached the ogre. "What is this cache?"

He just sneered, black blood coating his lips and the one protruding tusk. He coughed a few times as he tried to laugh, spitting up more stinky black slime.

"Sure you don't want to answer?" I asked, dragging my sword along the piece of wreckage that impaled him, watching as the supernaturally fine edge peeled the metal in curls.

The creature flinched but not much. I thought about heading back to my team and leading an attack on Medea right then, but for the moment, I knew where she was. I had a live prisoner of war, and I was hoping he might give me some insight into the witch's plans. At worst, it would cost me a few minutes of time.

"I can make this end faster if you'll just answer the question."

"No," came Gali's voice from behind me. "Targoviste will not be made to suffer any longer, and you will not threaten him with torture."

I took this to mean she was going to help the smelly ogre. My mistake. She took her stone dagger from his leg and slit his throat as calmly as if she were slicing a piece of meat for dinner.

"Well, now how am I supposed to find out what this is and what Medea is up to?" I said, irritated and surprised, gesturing at all the chests around us.

"You will leave now," she said, without any tone or inflection in her voice as she wiped the black goo from her blade with some leaves. "I will find out what this is and report to Athena. She will report it to you if she deems it knowledge necessary for your current situation."

"Oh, I will leave now?" This fairy chick was really starting to piss me off. "Really? Look, Gali, I appreciate your help with the ogre earlier — really, I do — but I need to know what this is and exactly what Medea is up to. And our one and only living accomplice is now no longer living. Granted, I would have done the same thing, eventually, but at least I would have had some information before I killed him."

As I railed a bit, something shifted in the wreckage behind me. For a brief second, I thought maybe there were survivors from the crash. The sound was coming from one of the humanoids who wasn't quite dead yet. Gali noticed it too and followed me over.

"Whoa. If you kill this one, you and I are going to have serious issues, Gali," I said, walking up to get a better view of the misshapen dying form.

"This one is only human. You may do to it what you wish," she said in the same annoying toneless voice. "I simply will not allow a human to torture one of the fae, Unseelie or otherwise. Regardless of the reason." She was practically glaring down her nose at me, which was hard, because she was easily a foot and a half shorter than me.

"What? Look, you green twit, on a battlefield, I do not discriminate, and I treat all opponents the same, human or nonhuman."

"Your actions and behaviors on the field of battle are well known to me, Tydides. Indeed, they are well known to us all." She stared directly at me, chin slightly elevated in defiance, as she put her blade away.

Well known? She made it sound like it was a bad thing.

I hung my head for a moment, trying to figure out her point, but then the more primitive part of my brain kicked in. "Just kiss my ass, you hoity-toity little wench," I practically spat. I walked over to get in her face, and she met my gaze unflinchingly.

"You may want to spend your time questioning that," she said, pointing at the dying form beside us, "rather than waste your breath on me. You will not sway my opinion of you."

I was just about ready to take her head clean off, but she was right. The thing she called human that was lying at my feet was in bad shape. I bent down to get a look at it. It was so badly deformed that I couldn't immediately tell its gender, but since nothing on it appeared overtly feminine, I made the assumption it was male.

He didn't have a magical aura, nor did he give off the feel of one of the fae, or any other Paranthropoi, for that matter. He had human features so grossly distorted that he resembled something I'd expect to see in Tartarus, ripping apart those doomed to an eternity of pain. One of the creature's arms was at least twice as long as the other, and twice as muscular. His legs were human enough, but his feet were misshapen and only bore three giant toes each. His torso was thick but lopsided, increasing in bulk as it reached the larger arm. He was also incredibly hunchbacked and had no neck, just a stumpy bald head set right onto his shoulders. His face was distorted, but his eyes were very human. He had two bullet holes in his muscular upper chest and a deep gash across his abdomen from my swords, and he lay in a widening pool of blood.

"Who are you?" I asked as his eyes opened slowly and fixed on me.

He responded in Farsi, but I couldn't understand him as he tried to talk through the blood in his throat.

"What were you doing here?" I asked in Farsi.

I pitied the person—not because he was dying or because I had been the one to injure him. My pity stemmed from the fact that his life to this point could not have been easy or anything close to normal, and not just because of his deformities. Somehow, Medea had gotten to him, and whatever she'd done to him had to outweigh the burden of his twisted features.

He tried to laugh and then began to speak. I could only make out a few words here and there, but the strain eventually proved too great, and he died. All I got was something about a queen, chaos, and the names Perses and Croesus.

I drew a hasty conclusion that the queen he spoke of was Medea, and as for chaos, well, I knew that was part of her plan. What I didn't know was how the names were connected. The only Perses I knew of was a Protogenoi that was known as a destructive Titan in Greek myths, but the name Croesus, on the other hand, explained a lot. This treasure trove had to be King Croesus's fabled fortune, the Qarun Treasure—the real one, not the one sitting in a museum in Turkey embroiled in a legal battle between countries.

Croesus was a king during the fifth century BC who was renowned for his wealth, which consisted of not just gold and jewels but also items considered magical in nature and supernatural in origin. Apollo helped him hide his treasure by keeping it in perpetual motion far beneath the surface of the Earth. Supposedly, there was no way to predict when or where it would appear. By today's standards it would be worth billions, with some artifacts probably classified as priceless relics.

I had no interest in the treasure or in the magical artifacts that it might contain. I had lost and gained many fortunes in my lifetime, and none of it ever mattered to me. Gali would inform Athena about the cache, and she could deal with it. I knew Athena would distribute the wealth among various nonpolitical causes worldwide—poverty, disease, hunger, and the like—and that was good enough for me.

As I contemplated what all this meant, the steady sound of a helicopter in the near distance rose over the forest. I tried to locate Gali, but she was gone. I needed to follow her lead, and fast.

I took one last look at one of the greatest treasures in the world as I secured my swords, and then I grabbed my SIG Sauer from where I'd thrown it down and bolted back the way I had come.

CHAPTER 31

AS I ENTERED MY SHACK back on Andros, everyone was at the table, talking and eating cracked conch and lobster salad. They hadn't even set a plate for me. To make matters worse, they'd put all my fly-tying stuff in a heap in the corner.

Sarah was the first to notice that my shirt was partly shredded around my vest and that I was covered in blood. "Yikes! Did you piss off a lion?" she asked, suddenly getting to her feet.

That pretty much got everyone's attention.

"No. Ghoul. Well, two ghouls, a dozen mutated human things, and an ogre, to be exact. Oh, and Medea herself."

"What?" Duma replied, stunned. "Where did you run off to so fast?"

A chorus followed. "A ghoul?" said Sarah.

"Really? A real live ghoul and an ogre?" said Geek.

"Sounds like something knocked the chickens loose from your henhouse, Chief," said Frigate.

"Hey, hey, HEY!" I shouted over the din, staring hard at Frigate for his comment about my sanity.

I took the next few minutes to explain what had happened and what I'd discovered, while I cleaned and dressed my wounds with Sarah's help. I was so engrossed with explaining my theory about how everything fit, from the bombing to the Cup and now the treasure, that I didn't notice she was helping me until Duma winked at me and gave me a slight nod with a broad shit-eating grin plastered across his face.

I completely lost my train of thought and could feel myself flush with embarrassment. It took me a minute to recompose myself. I got strange looks from Frigate and Geek. Duma left the shanty stifling his laughter. Ab sat stoically, seeming not to notice any of it.

"Why'd she need the Cup to find the chain, Chief?" asked Frigate. "Surely, something else might have helped her do that. Maybe even that kid who found you."

"Fakhri is a claircognizant," I replied shaking my head. "She only knows the past and the present. She can't see the future. Besides, I'm not sure if Medea even knew about her abilities. Also, other than the Cup of Jamshid, I don't really know of any crystal ball-type artifacts that would be powerful enough to pierce Apollo's enchantment on the Qarun Treasure."

"Well, why crash a plane to get to it?" Geek asked as he opened a small folding dish antenna and connected it to a laptop. "Certainly there are more covert ways to go about it—excavation equipment, hell, even dynamite. The plane crash is already all over the global news."

"Her timetable is truncated." I shook my head again. "She just stole the Cup, and I took it back, and she got it back only a few days ago. And she knows we're on to her. No time to set up an excavation. Plus, from what I saw, the caverns where the treasure was at the time of the crash were under dozens of feet of rock and sediment. Even a major excavation would have taken days. A hijacked plane full of explosives pushed into a full-on kamikaze nosedive did the trick in seconds."

"Not to mention if her intention is to create more chaos, hijacking and crashing a plane is a good way to do it. Especially in light of what the world *thinks* happened in New York," Ab said matter-of-factly while staring down at the floor, his massive forearms resting on his knees.

I arched my eyebrows at him. I hadn't thought about that. Leave it to a Peri to understand how to incite terror and panic.

Through the entire conversation, Geek typed furiously on his laptop. Finally, he looked back at me and rubbed his face and shook his head.

"What?" I asked him, wondering what had him so concerned.

"I've been looking for information on the Qarun Treasure and Perses, cross-referencing every related key word I could think of. I got nothing that connects the two to explain why that thing mentioned the name Perses."

I stood up and began to pace, trying to figure out why the deformed minion would have mentioned him. Maybe I'd misheard him.

"Hey, did you know Perses was a Titan and a God of Destruction?" Geek asked after tapping on his keyboard again. Geek's fingers flew across the keyboard in a series of clicks and clacks that would have made a machine gun jealous. He only paused long enough to curse the slow response time of his satellite receiver while he muttered to himself about various permutations of the terms he searched and which databases he should be hacking.

"Yes, yes I did," I said. "He is a nasty bastard but pretty much long resigned to his native realm, as far as I know."

"Bugger," came Geek's response over the top of his screen. "But did you know he had a daughter?" He squinted, clearly hoping to stump me.

"No, I didn't."

"Ha! Yes, he did," he said, pleased with himself. "Hecate, Goddess of —"

"Witchcraft," Duma said, walking back in to the shanty.

I really didn't like that connection. Medea had been the chief priestess of Hecate thousands of years ago, and according to Fakhri, the Old One was still helping her. While Hecate was never that powerful a Protogenoi, her help would still make Medea much stronger than she would be on her own — the way Athena strengthens me. Throw Hecate's father — a Protogenoi known for causing destruction for kicks — into the mix, and things go from bad to worse.

"We need to get busy here," I said, glancing around the group. "Geek, according to Athena, you should have access to some information on our destination. Maps, recent satellite and thermal imaging of the area — a full intelligence package. Bring that up, and let's figure out a plan of attack."

I pulled a dry-erase board up from my armory, leaned it against the wall, and we spent the next few hours creating a plan based on what we knew. According to the maps and the limited information we had received from Fakhri so far, our most troublesome issue was that much of Medea's operation took place inside a convoluted system of tunnels inside a virtually unexplored mountain. The witch's current base of operations was near the top of Mt. Alvand in the Zagros Mountain chain separating Iraq and Iran, at nearly eleven thousand feet. Alvand was also a nexus point for the Telluric Ways, meaning the amount of energy that flowed through that mountain was incalculable.

Luckily, some of the shallower ends of the tunnels near the rocky, snow-covered surface showed up on thermal-imaging scans, but old geological surveys suggested that the cave complex, connected to at least four distinct tunnel mouths, could cover as much as ten square miles. It was a logistical nightmare.

The thermal scans weren't detailed or even recent enough to give us any real idea of the size of the population within, either. The entrances always showed a few random humanoid heat signatures, and our only solid piece of information on the numbers we might be facing was that one particular cave mouth had significantly more traffic than the others. Still, all they showed were a few dozen of Medea's creatures. Fakhri made it sound like she had hundreds.

To press the issue of urgency further, now that Medea had the chain she was after, I had to assume she was capable of carrying out her plan immediately, so whatever we did had to happen very soon.

"Can't we just get the girl to tell us more about the warren of tunnels and her army?" Frigate asked, leaning back in his seat.

"As much as I would like her to, no," I replied, shaking my head. "We don't have the time to wait for her to recover enough to help us out, and I will not allow anyone to push her beyond her capabilities, especially after all she's been through."

"You're aware that Medea knows we're on to her," Duma added, flipping one of his smaller stone knives in his hand. "And if she uses the Cup, she might know everything about any plan we devise."

"So be it," I replied. "We need to attack so quickly that even if she knows our plan, she won't be able to respond to it in time. Terrorist cells are often poorly organized and ill equipped for rapid response or defensive campaigns. Plus, Medea, while undoubtedly a brutal despot and a powerful sorceress, is not a battlefield general. In fact, her favorite tactic always seems to be to run away."

I was convinced our only real option was to hit her hard and very fast. And I was good at that. I continued outlining my plan, sketching a few ideas on the board as I went.

"Based on our intelligence, our best bet is to break into one support and three assault units and cover all the known entrances into the tunnels. We enter the three less-trafficked caves simultaneously and then conduct a coordinated search, remaining in constant communication while we move quickly, clearing any resistance as quietly as possible. This approach should allow us to find Medea and then converge on her as expeditiously as possible."

"Why not just have one team create a distraction to clear the way for the other teams?" Sarah asked, pointing at the board. "Might make it easier for the other teams to advance."

"Couple of reasons," I replied, leaning on the table. "First, I'm not crazy about sacrificing any of the lives of my team, including the Spartoi, in a forlorn-hope operation. Second, I'm afraid that the distraction would alert Medea to our presence and allow her to escape before we can get to her."

Everyone nodded in response.

"The two heavily armed Spartoi squads and my team with Ab and Duma will breach," I continued. "Frigate, Geek, and Sarah, you will, from a distance, watch the main cave entrance, directing Frigate as he takes out any targets of opportunity. You will move in only after we find Medea."

"Accordin' to these topographic maps, Chief, looks like there's an ideal sniper's roost among the rocky outcroppings just opposite the high-traffic cave mouth," Frigate said, bending over the map with a steel ruler he'd picked up off the table to make a few measurements. "Looks like it's just over six hundred yards out. Should be doable, even in the high winds, altitude, and cold conditions."

"Perfect," I said grinning more than smiling in response.

Even Duma cocked his head and arched an eyebrow, clearly impressed with the statement.

"Um, only one issue, Demo," Geek said sitting back in his chair and crossing his arms. "How are we supposed to stay in constant communications *inside* a mountain, mate?"

He had a significant and valid concern I hadn't really thought of until he mentioned it. Of course, I'd never had to plan an assault on a mountain while directing a team, either. Our normal Spitfire SATCOM setup would be a satellite-UHF-VHF-based encrypted system, which wouldn't work underground, making remote communications in a cave all but impossible. "Well," I said, throwing my hands up.

Before I could even muster a response to his concern, he piped up excitedly with a solution that took him nearly twenty minutes to explain. Once he was done with his dissertation on satellite – and VHF-based communications gear in underground situations and had outlined his solution to the problem, Geek gazed at us animatedly, clearly expecting a similarly enthusiastic reaction in return. We were all stunned into silence. Or boredom. One or the other.

"Ah, yeah. Sounds thrilling." Duma yawned and got up to walk around.

"Just in case any of y'all wondered why we call him Geek," Frigate said, stretching his arms and legs.

Ab's head was down, and his chin was resting on his chest. I decided he was checking his eyelids for leaks.

To make his solution a reality, Geek needed dozens of extra AN/PRC 126 radios to set up as relay units and enough time to reconfigure them, or we would be going in deaf, and that was unacceptable, not to mention idiotic. Aside from the fact that Medea knew we were coming, we were already compromising the assault by rushing my timetable, and that was the *only* concession I'd make.

"Look, I need to debrief the Spartoi and contact Athena about getting the radios Geek needs. Don't waste the time. Make sure you're geared up and ready to roll when I say. Geek, in the meantime, any help you need, just ask. There should be a half-dozen of the radios in my armory. That should start you off."

I walked back outside. I'd barely made it around the corner of the shack when I ran into one of the Spartoi.

At my presence, he came to a rigid halt and bowed his head slightly. "General Tydides, please, if you will follow me," he said with his head still bowed.

"Of course," I replied, taking a deep breath. "I need to update your team, as well."

The Spartoi encampment was down the beach in a clearing among some sea grapes and coconut palms. It looked like the military camps I remembered from my youth: simple tents with several cooking pits and a longer central tent for storage and arms.

The Spartoi all were identical in their khaki fatigues and standard Combat Integrated Releasable Armor System, or CIRAS body armor, and tactical holsters strapped to their thighs. They could have passed for giant Marines, which was actually comforting. Each one was a near-replica of the other: six and a half feet tall, well built, with short-cropped sandy hair, a square jaw, and brown eyes. Their skin was as pale as dried bone. Their only distinguishing features were the scars they'd accumulated. With few exceptions, they lacked individual identities, and preferred things that way. The leader who stepped forward when I arrived had three stripes tattooed across his cheek.

Before I could say a word, I felt Athena's presence, and then she stepped out from the supply tent dressed exactly as she had been earlier. Instantly, the Spartoi came to rigid attention as a group, standing as stiff as the teeth they came from.

"Good," I said, pointing at her. "We need to talk."

"Indeed. You were correct. It is most certainly Croesus's treasure that was unearthed by the plane crash, and Medea now has *Alysideus Prometheus*."

"Hey, she had a dozen minions, a few ghouls, and a freakin' ogre," I said, trying to defend my failure to stop Medea in Bulgaria. "And — wait. Ally who?"

"Alysideus Prometheus," Athena replied, standing a few feet in front of me with her hands held loosely behind her back. Her eyes were an intense blue but not flashing. Her face reminded me of a porcelain mask except for the slight crease between her brows. She didn't appear perturbed, just concerned.

"It is the name given the chain that bound Prometheus at Scythia. It cannot be broken by whatever is bound by it, and it can only be broken by one with unselfish motives. Lest you forget, it once held a Titan for millennia."

Heracles, one of the earliest Guardians, broke the chain to free Prometheus. He did it in defiance of his benefactor, Zeus. His actions, though noble, did not bode well for him, and he died a treacherous death a few years later. While he died hundreds of years before my time, I was sure he would have argued it was worth it.

All this talk about Titans got me thinking about the other name the deformed creature had mentioned. "So we know what Croesus means, but what about Perses? I know he's Hecate's father."

"Yes, he is, but fortunately, he is no longer as strong as he once was," Athena said, turning out toward the beach. "And now Medea has the chain that once bound his cousin."

"Okay, I get it." I crossed my arms over my chest. "But why bind a Titan at all? Zeus did it to punish Prometheus, but I doubt he was a willing captive. Surely Medea isn't strong enough to hold Perses down and bind him even if he is weakened."

"I don't know, but Hecate has always despised her father, and with her help, Medea just might have the strength. With the rise in the popularity of the various witch religions, Hecate has become stronger over the past half century. The situation worries me. I fear that Perses's penchant for destruction and disorder may make him a vessel powerful enough to contain the entropic energy that Medea is gathering for her ritual. I can foresee no acceptable outcome, either here on Earth or in our own realm, if you do not stop her. Members of the Golden Dawn suggest that the energy could be used to start or prolong wars in already unstable regions or destabilize tentative peace accords. Its effects could even undermine the détente between the Seelie and Unseelie Courts, which would disrupt the natural order of the world."

Her statement about human wars bothered me, but the comment about the fae had the impact of a Mack truck. My understanding of the fae was that Queen Mab of the Unseelie Court and Queen Titania of the Seelie Court were once, in fact, the same being. A schism caused by the appearance of humans and an argument over what to do with our emerging new species resulted in the ruling entity splitting into two separate beings — opposite sides of the same coin — and led to the formation of the two separate Courts. It was said that neither side could hold sway for long without upsetting the balance of nature and that those swings in the balance brought about climate changes, pestilence, and even plagues. In the past, when those wars occurred, the fledgling human species wasn't very numerous, but entire populations were still lost as collateral damage. A full-scale war between the Courts now would be devastating to the vast human population.

"Can't someone warn Perses?" I asked, contemplating the ramifications of Medea's plan.

"Even now, I have messengers attempting to do so," she said, avoiding eye contact. "But our realm is not like this one. Finding him could take some time."

"Forgive me, my lady." The leader of the Spartoi took a few rigid steps forward to approach her before bowing his head in deference.

"Speak," she said without looking at him, either.

"Perhaps you should join us in this fight. Surely, then—"

As he spoke, I shook my head vigorously and drew my hand across my throat, hoping to deter the guy from continuing down that thought path. To my surprise, Athena just exhaled heavily. In the past, when people had suggested Athena enter the fight, the consequences had been swift and quite visually stunning — and utterly final.

"Master-at-arms Icosa, I cannot fight this or any other battle in this world," she replied, her eyes losing their glow. "This is not my world, and I cannot in good conscience continue to help here if I choose to interfere any more than I already do. And it would be hypocritical for me to do what I so vociferously try to keep my brethren from doing. That is why I charge Diomedes with such tasks here. In him, I will be with you. I trust in him. You should as well." Her face showed no sign of emotion, and her eyes remained flat after she spoke.

The Spartoi thumped his chest in salute and then returned to his previous post. Her disheartened response worried me. She said she trusted me, but I couldn't help but feel she thought we were outmatched.

Without warning, four of Athena's personal guards ducked out of the supply tent behind us, carrying four wooden crates. They were the best of her Spartoi, and they were outfitted with golden armor and weapons fashioned by Hephaestus himself. Not that she needed their protection, but she always traveled with them. The gilded soldiers — I liked to think of them as gold-capped teeth — set the crates down and then stood at attention. "AN/PRC 126 radio units" was stenciled on the sides of each one. Given that I desperately needed the radios and time was of the essence, I decided to forgive her this one time for actively being inside my mind.

She glanced back at them briefly without changing her dour expression and then placed her hand on my shoulder. The gesture struck me — not just because she never allowed physical contact but also because I could feel her energy surge into me through the connection. Her eyes flared electric blue once again, and her face darkened into the sharp, raptor-like features of her warrior-self. Strength and confidence washed over me, and the pain caused by the burns on my legs subsided completely.

It was easy to see why humans had worshiped the Protogenoi throughout history. The Old Ones were powerful beings even on Earth — and even more so when they were surrounded by those who believed in them as deities. I no longer believed in beings like her as I once did — she didn't need me to. There was a great difference between believing and knowing. Belief was one of the most powerful forces in this world, and her kind fed off it and used it to augment their strength. It was a dangerous situation for humans as a race, and it had been abused many times — hence my job.

"You must stop her, Diomedes. I am sorry to rely on you once again, but I have no choice. I fear for your safety and the safety of those who fight alongside you. The Spartoi will not let you down." Her eyes continued to flare as she spoke, but her face changed back to that of a beautiful woman.

It was not lost on me that I was the only human that she had ever allowed see her in her true form. Even Odysseus, whom she favored almost as much as me, saw her only in disguise.

"I bid you strength and honor, my warrior," she said, lowering her hand from my shoulder as she walked back toward the tent.

Her guards surrounded her, and they disappeared back into the supply tent. Her presence, but not her energy, simply evaporated.

CHAPTER 32

AFTER ATHENA LEFT, I EXPLAINED our plan of attack to the Spartoi and had them help me carry the crates of radios back to the shanty. As we walked through the mangroves in the failing light of evening, I could hear the thundering report of what was unmistakably a fifty-caliber rifle from up the beach. Frigate was sighting in his weapons. Fortunately, the nearest neighbor was twenty miles away.

The Spartoi waited with the crates outside while I entered the shanty. Duma and Ab were sitting around the table, checking over their own gear. Geek was sitting in a corner of the shanty at a table brought up from my underground armory, and he was working on our radios under my fly-tying lamps. He had a throat mike on and an earpiece in one ear and was peering through my magnifying glass from under a bizarre visor with lights and lenses as I approached him. His eyes were distorted to an enormous size, and the lights practically blinded me.

"How's it going?" I asked, holding my hand up to shield my eyes.

"Sorry." He reached up to switch the lights off. "Bang-up, actually. Got four done already. Everything seems to work just fine."

"Good work, Geek," I said, buoyed by his progress. "The rest of your radios are just outside with the Spartoi. Tell them what to do, and they'll help. Where's Sarah?" I glanced from Geek to Ab and then Duma for an answer.

Nobody responded for a few long seconds.

"Down the beach... with Frigate," Duma finally said, raising his eyebrows, trying to get a rise out of me.

"Knock it off. We leave as soon as Geek's finished," I said and then hiked down the beach.

It wasn't hard to find them, even in the darkness of the early evening. In the bright moonlight, unimpeded by the light noise of any cities or towns, I could see Frigate lying on a mat, snuggled up to a massive Barrett M107A1 rifle with his face right behind a Leupold Mark 4 scope fitted with a night-vision attachment. An MK 13 Mod 5 sniper rifle lay next to him. Sarah sat cross-legged next to him, peering through a spotter's scope, giving him information about windage and range at a target way out on the flat. She had a Kriss Super V Vector across her lap.

"Interesting choice," I said, intrigued by her weapon.

They both looked up at me, and Frigate switched on a small red LED light so he could see and still preserve his night vision.

"Yeah, I was surprised you had it, actually." Sarah patted the gun. "I used one in the Fly Team as part of a test group, but it had the short barrel, not this long one. I really liked it."

I was impressed. Maybe even a little turned on. She was perfectly at home helping Frigate sight in his weapons.

"That longer barrel makes using a suppressor easier," I said. "Plus, it uses the same clip as the Glock twenty-one, so I suggest you pull that as a sidearm. The forty-five ACP round has good stopping power, too."

She pulled the forty-five-caliber model Glock from the holster on her hip. "Done," she said, frowning at me with one eyebrow arched as if I'd just insulted her. "I like to keep things simple."

"How goes?" I asked Frigate.

"All good, Chief. We're just waitin' for the green light." He gave me a thumbs-up.

"Well, once you're done, head back to the shanty. As soon as Geek finishes his science project, we're Oscar Mike," I said, using military speak for "on the move," feeling myself become more uptight. "I'm headed back."

About halfway back to the shanty, heavy footfalls in the sand came up from behind me. They were too heavy to be Sarah, so I didn't stop or turn around.

"What's up, Frigate?"

"Chief, lighten up on Sarah, would ya'? She's tryin' real hard to impress you," he said, holding the Barrett over one shoulder while the MK 13 hung from a strap from the other. "And she likes you, too."

"I can't lighten up. You know that. We got one speed on this, and it's flat-out. She either keeps up, or we cut her loose. If we fail, we won't be the only ones dying, you get that?"

"I get it, but she knows her shit, Chief. You just gotta give her a chance to show you. Plus," he said, waggling his eyebrows, "she *likes* you."

It was a pleasant enough idea. I let myself linger on it for just a second, but all the reasons why it wouldn't work—my immortality, my job, putting her in constant danger—crowded in, along with the reality of the current situation. I'd have to deal with my feelings about Sarah later. If we lived.

Back at the shanty, Geek had set up an assembly line using every surface in the house's only room and employing half a dozen Spartoi as helpers. Each one of the giant warriors worked on a different aspect of Geek's radio reconfiguration project. When I walked in, things were humming along efficiently, although the sight of the imposing Spartoi hunkered over tables and working with tweezers, tiny wire snips, and soldering irons looked positively absurd. Geek moved purposefully from Spartoi to Spartoi, correcting or approving each one's actions like a teacher in a lab.

Geek stopped what he was doing and came over with a smug grin plastered across his face. "Almost done, Demo," he said proudly. "Won't be more than two hours to wrap things up."

I left them to it while I gathered my gear, methodically checking and double-checking it all. While it didn't need it, I retaped the disk on my forearm, just to make sure it was secure, and put the magnets into a pocket on my vest. I was still determined to use that thing as payback for the two attempts on my life, and for all those people back at the museum. As I pored over my knives and swords, Sarah and Frigate came in and began to watch. Geek followed as soon as he noticed them gathered beside me.

"I take it those are special," Geek said, referring to my swords. "Made by Hephaestus, or something?"

"Actually, they are. But that"—I half grinned back, pointing at my spear where it leaned against the wall near Ab's hammer—"specifically, is the Pelian Spear."

Geek's eyes widened. He looked especially ridiculous with the stupid magnifying-lens goggles pushed back on his head. "Really?" he asked, reaching toward it. "Can I see it?"

"Sure, just be careful."

"What in the Sam Hill is the Pelian Spear?" drawled Frigate.

"Achilles's spear, given to him by his father and made by Hephaestus," Sarah responded, smiling at me. "Was said to be able to penetrate anything." She leered at me.

The knife I was holding slipped through my fingers. "Well, uh, almost anything in the right hands," I said, trying to recover my composure as I grabbed the spear from Geek before anyone got hurt. The second I touched it, the spear virtually came to life, the metal of the shaft and head shimmering.

"Whoa! Brilliant. Hey, was Achilles really killed by an arrow to his foot?" Geek asked, unfazed by me snatching the weapon away from him.

"No, he wasn't." I checked to make sure the clips for my sidearms were loaded. "Paris did shoot him with an arrow, but Apollo guided it, and it stuck him in the chest, under his arm. By the time we got to him, he was dead. However, the little prick did shoot me in the foot once. Paris, not Achilles. Then he ran away."

"Paris, not Achilles," Duma threw out, partly to poke fun at my long-standing irritation with Achilles's fame.

"Yeah, the punk," I replied, ignoring Duma's goading.

Geek led them in a barrage of questions about mythology and the Trojan War, and I indulged them for about thirty minutes because some of what they were asking might actually serve to prepare them for the coming fight. Still, after a while, I had to throw my hands up in surrender. Luckily, one of the Spartoi came over before I had to get violent, and announced that they were finished with the radios. It was close to midnight.

"Let's move. Gear up and reassemble out front in ten." I grabbed my vest, and everyone scattered.

Three minutes later, a dozen Spartoi were gathered along the beach in front of my shanty, grouped into two squads of six soldiers. They stood stock-still in formation, two rows of three each.

The Spartoi were dressed in an odd combination of gear, sort of Marine Corps meets the Middle Ages: desert camo fatigues, metal breastplates, and what have become known as Illyrian helmets. One of them even had a red crest of horsehair down the crown, probably to distinguish himself as the leader now that his face was covered. It was like watching the clones from *Star Wars* meet *300* and *Black Hawk Down*. They were armed with swords, shields, and a variety of assault rifles and machine guns used by modern militaries.

The rest of the group gathered off to one side. Duma leaned against the shanty wall next to Ab, whose arms hung over the hammer across his shoulders. Neither had their helmets on yet, but they were in full armor.

Ab's armor consisted of full-plate adamantine arm coverings connected to a breastplate made of layered titanium plates sandwiched between ceramic and Kevlar. For good measure, he'd added a layer of dragon scales. Similar plates covered his thighs. His adamantine helmet resembled an oversized skull with a long black plume of hair from a manticore's mane.

Duma's armor consisted of a hauberk of some kind of black-scaled animal hide and was topped with a leather cuirass dyed in the traditional red-and-black diamonds of the harlequin character he used to play. He wore long black leather gloves and boots and had a helmet that resembled a highly stylized laughing skull, half-red and half-black, with a black Mohawk from its crown to its base. While I felt their armor was too showy and archaic, I knew part of their visage was to inspire fear on the battlefield.

Frigate sat on his heels, holding the Barrett, while Geek knelt on his good leg next to him using an M4 rifle for support. Sarah was the only one standing, shifting from one foot to the other. She was also the only one already wearing her pack, but all three of them wore PT Special-Ops body armor.

Spear in hand, I addressed my team stiffly. I had gotten used to working alone again over the last few years, and I wasn't used to giving motivational speeches. "Everyone needs to make sure to grab at least one thermite and one white phosphorus grenade each. Flash bangs and frags are up to you. Just remember, we'll be in tight quarters. We leave together, we come back together, but once we arrive, you all know where to go. Geek has explained the radio relay system, and each group has forty relays. Use them. We do not know for sure what we're going up against in these caves. I've seen Ifrit, ghouls, and a variety of mutant humans. There will certainly be Phonoi, Androktasiai, and at least one witch of immense strength. There may be others, but the witch is our main objective. Spartoi, your secondary objective is the Fawaz family. I will recover the Cup and chain. Anyone with an opportunity to take Medea out, take it. Do not hesitate. We do not know her full capabilities, nor do we know numbers. Make no mistake—we will be grossly outnumbered, and this will be difficult, and we will get bloody. We take no prisoners and do not expect to be afforded that dignity in return. I will offer no quarter; you do so at your own risk."

I focused on the human contingent of my team pointedly as I said the last part. Geek and Frigate's expressions remained unchanged, but the muscles of Sarah's jaw tightened for a second before I continued.

"We fight to the primary target at all costs. If we do this right, no human but those fighting with us will ever know it was done. If we fail, the consequences for all races and creatures could be incalculable. We must not and will not fail. I bid you all strength and honor." I crossed my arm over my chest with a closed fist and bowed my head briefly.

"Hooah!" yelled Frigate, and the Spartoi began a primitive and chilling war chant. Duma and Ab just glanced at each other and shook their heads. Sarah was a bit pale, even in the moonlight, and her eyes were wide, but there was resolve in them.

"Ab, get us to the jump point," I said and then walked next to Duma. "I need you to take Sarah on a special trip first and then meet us at Alvand," I whispered. I quickly explained what I needed.

He just laughed. "She's gonna kick your ass, you know that?" Sarah scowled at both of us. "Let's go, little lady. You and me got a hot date." He wiggled his eyebrows at her.

She reluctantly fell in with him, flashing a confused look at me as they left the group trekking into the mangroves for the Ways. Duma was right. I was going to pay for this one, but it was mission critical.

It had been a while since I'd led any kind of team into any sort of skirmish, but this one had the potential to do some serious damage. I'd pit us against any human force on the planet, but I still had my doubts about facing Medea. If my team could just give me a small window of opportunity, it would be all I needed—me being humanity's fist and all.

As I walked behind the group, I again got that odd feeling in the pit of my stomach that someone, or something, was watching me. Over on the beach, a squat figure walked up out of the water. The moon was behind his body, so I couldn't make out any details—except a garish Hawaiian pattern on a shirt. Surprised and pleased, I told everyone to continue along while I walked down to meet him.

"What the hell are you doing here?" I asked.

"Dude, bad news I thought you'd want to know," Ned said, his eyes anxious, though the full expression was hidden behind his bushy beard.

"What's so important you came here to tell me in person?"

"Perses disappeared from the other side," he said quietly, leaning in. The "other side" he was referring to was their home plane, the plane that all Protogenoi normally existed on. "He's here on this side now, but I hear tell it wasn't his idea. That ain't cool, man. That dude is all about bad vibes, destruction, and chaos, and if he ain't here of his own will... shit, I don't even want to think about it." He shook his head.

"Dammit. Medea has the, ah, Ally-whosits Prometheus..." I couldn't remember the freakin' chain's name.

"The Alysideus Prometheus? You screwin' with me, dude?" came Ned's response. His eyes widened and his body stiffened. "Don't even joke about that, man. That's like that green rock stuff for that super dude in them comic books to us, man." He suddenly appeared drawn.

"I'll stop her and whatever it is that she's doing to or with him. I'm leaving now, so is there anything else I should know?"

"Nah, ain't that enough? Oh, some dipdunk did run into your boat down at the dock, though," he said, snapping his fingers.

"What? Are you kidding me?" I screamed, surprised and pissed off all at once.

"Nah, I'm just messin' with ya, dude. You know I keep an eye out for your boat, man. No worries." I could see the twinkle return to his eye as the moonlight glinted off his broadly grinning teeth. Nothing kept Ned down long. "Hey, you got any beer in that shack before I leave?"

"No, you know I don't, old man."

"Wishful thinkin', I guess." He shrugged, waved, and strolled back down the beach.

He held up his fist with his pinky and thumb extended and shook it as he walked.

I gazed out over the flat at the moonlight reflecting off the shallow water. The world was peaceful and serene. Things were going to get nasty with Medea in her caverns, probably the worst mess I'd been in in a while. I hoped I was making the right decision bringing Geek, Frigate, and Sarah — mostly Sarah — into my world and into this mess. Mostly, I just hoped we'd kill the bitch.

I listened to the waves lap along the beach. *If we survive, I gotta let Sarah know how I feel.*

If we survive...

CHAPTER 33

THE PATH WE TOOK THROUGH the Ways to arrive on Mt. Alvand in western Iran was deliberately obscure, just in case. Alvand was an energy nexus, and my guess was that Medea had tapped right into its power — I would have done the same thing in her position. She'd probably even chosen the location for its energy. We could have just opened a Way right into her living room, but that would have made Custer's plan at Little Bighorn seem like genius by comparison. Of course, that would also assume she didn't have some sort of lock preventing that particular Way from being opened, too.

The roundabout trip took us less than an hour, and with the time change, that had us arriving in Iran at midmorning. We might have made it a little faster, but Geek and Frigate still had trouble adjusting to traveling the Ways. Fortunately, like motion sickness, their trouble only lasted while they were in transit. A few moments after they stepped out of the Ways onto Alvand, they were okay.

We exited at a snow-covered, mountainous ridge about eight thousand feet above sea level because I wanted a safe staging area as high as was prudent. At that altitude, a relatively thick layer of icy, frozen snow covered most of the uneven and rocky terrain, making footing treacherous enough without also requiring us to dodge potential wandering sentries the minute we emerged. I had purposely chosen to come through the Ways on the windward face of the mountain because I figured it would be less patrolled. It was below freezing, and the wind whipped around the mountain so fiercely at times that we had to scream to communicate face-to-face. Still feeling the surge of Athena's power, I was pleasantly surprised not to be bothered by the weather conditions at all.

Once we reached our rendezvous point, we had to wait about thirty minutes for Duma and Sarah to catch up to us, and when they did, Duma was right: Sarah was pissed. But she realized I'd sent her off with Duma to get something we would need and, short of the brief glare she gave me when they first arrived, she handled her anger stoically. She crossed to her team silently, without meeting anyone's gaze, her face intense as her hair whipped around. Duma was all smiles.

"Get it?" I asked, speaking into his ear once he was close enough.

"Of course," he screamed over the wind, patting a small leather satchel at his waist. "And so will you... later."

I faced the group to address them. All eyes were on me, and everyone acted impatient and eager to move. There were no signs of the fatigue or illness associated with altitude sickness in the human operators, which was encouraging.

"This is rendezvous," I said, pressing the sending switch for my throat mike to speak more easily to the group. I took my Way Stone and stuck it in among some rocks along with some food and ammo. "In the event everything goes sideways, those who know how can use this key. For those who can't or don't want to use it, head down the mountain to the town of Hamadān. Athena has a contact there."

They all nodded at me, their faces showing no emotion.

"From here we break up. Each team leaves in twenty-minute intervals. My team will take final position. Radio when you're in place, and I will give the go. If you run into sentries, take them out as quietly as possible and keep moving. If you encounter issues, fall back to the nearest team, or call for backup. You three," I said, singling out the humans again, "white out, and move out first. Sniper team is designation Nest. And remember, there is no radio contact until you're in position. Report what you see at the main entrance. Frigate, watch out for Medea—she is primary Tango. If you see her, do not hesitate to take the shot. Other targets are at your discretion. Otherwise, you are strictly support until you move in."

Next, I turned my attention to the Spartoi. "You are Eagle One and Eagle Two," I said, pointing at the two squads, "and my team is designation Talon. Clear?"

Everyone nodded.

"Let's move." I gathered my gear and pulled on a pair of goggles.

Like me, the entire team was fitted with LASH II throat-mic headsets, and each group had a bag full of Geek's modified radios.

Frigate's team pulled out ponchos patterned with white-and-gray camouflage, covered themselves, and took off up the mountain. Frigate took point, carrying the MK 13 with the heavier sniper rifle slung over his back, followed by Sarah and then Geek. They'd all fitted suppressors to their primary weapons. Despite Geek's prosthetic leg, he managed to keep up. His extreme-duty prosthesis was damn impressive and would have made Steve Austin jealous. I tried not to be too obvious as I watched Sarah disappear up the mountain.

The two Spartoi teams left at their specified intervals quickly, quietly, and without incident, and my team was underway when we got the first radio report.

"We are in position, ready to broadcast and receive," Geek reported, "but there is no entrance. Repeat, we see no cave into the mountain."

"I expected this," I replied. "Nest, switch to thermal imaging and reverify."

"I'll be damned," Geek responded after a minute. "There you are, you beauty. I have a visual on the entrance. I can see the cave mouth with thermal, just not with regular optics."

"All teams, be aware that entrances are shielded from view," I said. "They are there, but approach with extreme caution until you can confirm."

Thermal and infrared imaging couldn't be fooled by simple cloaking spells or fairy glamours, so I didn't know if the entrances would be visible to the naked eye until we were on site. It wasn't a major issue, but it was going to make sneaking up on any sentries behind the veils very tricky.

Later, radio checks confirmed that the teams were closing on their positions. Geek confirmed everyone's movements via thermal imaging from his satellite feeds when he could, and Frigate kept watch on the main entrance using an infrared spotting scope. According to Frigate, he had a good view nearly seventy yards into the tunnel, but so far, he hadn't seen anything specific except the occasional humanoid form.

My team was making excellent time climbing the mountain without issue when Geek broke silence again, about ten minutes later. "We have two bogeys ahead of Eagle One, moving between you and your point of entry. Be advised that I also see several large birds circling the main entrance, and I have heat signatures for additional sentries at each point of entry."

"How many at the cave mouths?" I inquired.

"The number is unclear," Geek replied. "Each entrance has a minimum of one, but assume more. Will advise when possible. What are those birds?"

"How close are we to the rovers?" came the response from the team leader of the first Spartoi squad.

"Eagle One, you are approximately half a klick from their position and closing. There are two rovers. Happy hunting. Repeat, should we be concerned about those birds?"

"Tell Frigate to consider the birds target practice. They're sentries," I replied. The birds had to be Strixes, and I figured the owl-like creatures couldn't cause us issues if they were dead.

We climbed as quickly and quietly as we could — which was far easier for Ab and Duma than for me, though I'm no slouch — and got to our position outside the highest cave mouth. We made it in just over an hour and took cover behind a snow-covered landslip with a good view of the entrance about twenty yards away. Despite the terrain and the conditions, we'd covered the nearly three-thousand-foot climb to eleven thousand feet with ease.

As I ducked my head around the landslip to get a glimpse of the cave mouth, Duma grabbed my shoulder and pointed off to one side of the ten-foot veiled opening then held up two fingers. I craned my neck just a bit to locate the two decidedly human guards and noticed two more just inside the cave's entrance. I pointed at the cave and held up two fingers, but Duma shook his head, indicating that he couldn't see what I pointed at. It was definitely magic, and not fairy glamour, that shielded the entrances — otherwise, Duma would have seen through it, too. The trick was going to be attacking the two separate groups in such a way that neither had time to raise an alarm.

Communicating by throat mics had the distinct advantage of whispers still being clearly audible even in windy conditions, but since talking face-to-face over the wind required screaming, I used hand signals instead. I pulled my MP5SD-N submachine gun up to a ready position and thumbed the selector switch to fire three-round bursts, making sure the gun was ready. Then I looked at Ab and Duma, held up a tight fist, and pointed to my ear, letting them know that we wouldn't move until we heard from the others. I indicated that Ab should stay put and Duma's target was the pair of guards he could see. I would take the two just inside the cave. The Peris acknowledged my order, and Duma drew his two kukri knives. Meantime, we waited — and watched.

Within twenty minutes, Eagle One confirmed they had taken out the roving sentries and were now at their appointed entry at about ten thousand feet. Shortly thereafter, we got word that the other team was also in position.

"Team, this is Talon," I radioed. "We wait until next radio check and then advance. Nest, hold tight until I give you the signal to travel."

It took less than ten minutes for the guards to radio in their situation reports, and then we made our move. I pointed at Duma, and he took off in a blur. I bolted upright behind our snowy hiding spot, took a tight bead on the first guard just inside the cave, and put three rounds into his chest with a muffled metallic spitting sound. He crumpled to the ground, and I closed in on the surprised second guard without hesitating and targeted him before he knew what had happened. I fired three rounds into his chest, putting him down as well.

By the time I got to the cave, Duma was next to me, bright-red blood dripping from his knives. The only sound came from the soft, metallic slide of the bolt on my gun moving with each shot.

I waved Ab forward, and as he loped up the hill toward us, I looked at the mess Duma had left behind. Blood was everywhere, staining the snow. I stared back at him hard with my lips drawn into a tight line and shook my head.

"That's why I shot them," I yelled, pointing down at the two I'd killed and back at the carnage he'd left behind.

He just shrugged. We had no time to cover them up. We needed to move.

A pair of kerosene lanterns lighted the mouth of the cave, and only the first few feet of the tunnel were natural. Farther on, the roughness of the gouges showed that the rest of the digging had been done by hand rather than machine. The barest hint of light from somewhere down the tunnel in front of us cast a meager glow but afforded us enough illumination to see our surroundings.

Before we advanced, I bent down to get a quick look at the guards I'd killed. They were, by all indications, normal humans. They weren't wearing any kind of armor over their outdated army-surplus olive drab fatigues, and not surprisingly, they were carrying Iranian-made KLS versions of the AK-47 — the standard weapon used by terrorists and wackos throughout the world. They were cheap, easy to get, easy to maintain, and simple to use.

I searched the guard for his radio, turned the volume way down, and jammed it into a pocket on my vest. From what we'd observed, they checked in about every thirty minutes, which meant we'd have at least that long before an alarm was raised, if the broken veils hadn't alerted them to our presence already.

CHAPTER 34

A B REACHED INTO A SMALL gear bag, pulled out one of Geek's reworked radios, and propped it on a rock next to the cave's entrance. Not the best hiding spot, but we had to leave it uncovered to relay the signal.

In the ambient light, there were no signs of high-tech surveillance equipment, or even electricity, as we snuck down the ten-foot-diameter, rough-hewn tunnel. I took point, with Duma right on my heels and Ab bringing up the rear. The farther we advanced, the warmer and more humid the air became. Initially, the only smells were of rock and earth, but sharper smells of body odor and wood smoke began to permeate the air as it warmed.

The second Spartoi team reported that they'd found a branching tunnel off the main shaft of their point of entry with noises and food smells coming from it, but no one had encountered anything living yet. While it was good for our recon work, it likely meant everyone was gathered elsewhere, and I didn't like what that might mean.

"We have encountered the entrance to a massive cavern," came another transmission from the second team, "a thousand yards across and forty yards high. Crawling with numerous unfriendlies. They appear to be occupied with some sort of group worship or ritual. No sign of primary Tango. We are returning to the fork and will establish a two-man overwatch and continue reconnoiter down adjacent shaft. Over."

My team continued along the tunnel, leaving relay units as we went, until the rock walls became smoother and appeared more machine cut than dug by hand. I held up my hand in a fist while I crawled forward to check what was ahead.

The light in front of us was bright, and I could hear voices—lots and lots of voices in some sort of rhythmic cadence. The smell of human body odor, wet rock, and a mixture of burnt things, including flesh, became so thick I could taste it. I could also feel a palpable, tingling energy that made the hair on my neck and arms stand on end the closer I got. The voices rose and fell in concert, though I couldn't make out any specific words. It was definitely some sort of ritualistic chant and exactly what I feared — Medea was starting her witchery.

A side passage carved out of the rock face branched off to my right as I continued to creep forward. It was nearly at the junction of the main passageway and a massive cavern, which I assumed was the one reported earlier by the Spartoi squad. I stopped just shy of the cavern's mouth and listened. The noise from the gathered mass of people was so loud that I couldn't distinguish any other ambient sounds. At least they wouldn't be able to hear us, either. That meant we didn't need to be as quiet, but we still needed to move quickly and maintain a low profile until we found Medea.

From my vantage point near the tunnel junction, I could see a small part of the massive cavern with some sort of a stone dais at the far end. The stage-like structure was huge — easily a hundred yards across — and surrounded by stalagmites and rubble. The cavern was brightly lit, but I couldn't determine the light source. From my position, all I could see were humans — lots and lots of humans. It had to be the same crowd the Spartoi reported seeing. To Athena's soldiers, anyone who wasn't us would be an "unfriendly."

I lizard-crawled to the mouth of the main shaft, past the side tunnel, to get a better view and then waved for Ab and Duma to move up to the carved side tunnel behind me. Across from me, and on the other side of the dais at the opposite end of the massive grotto, was another cave mouth, but I couldn't get a good view of the rest of the space without exposing myself to the throngs of chanting people.

I ducked back into the shaft, and Duma beckoned me. He pointed down the carved side passage, and I could see light and shadows from the giant cavern illuminating an area about a hundred yards farther down the passage — another entrance into the huge space.

I held up a fist to Ab. He acknowledged it, and then I directed Duma to follow me down the side tunnel toward the light. I tapped Ab's shoulder and indicated that he should keep an eye on us for further signals.

I took point, holding my silenced submachine gun with both hands just in front of me, under my face in a combat-high position as I'd done before in countless close-quarter battles. Duma crept silently behind me. The ambient light in the side tunnel increased as we approached the next opening to the massive cavern. Over the clamor emanating from the cavern to our left, I could just make out the faint sounds of scraping and shuffling, along with muffled voices and the occasional laugh echoing from even farther down the passage.

I crept up to the near edge of the cavern and peeked into the grotto. From this secondary entrance, I could still see the tunnel on the other side of the dais across the cathedral-sized space, but now I could also see a passageway on the near side of the dais, as well, and another, significantly broader passage midway across on the right. Including the two we'd found, that made five separate entrances into the giant stone hall. All of the passageways into the enormous cavern were rough textured and possibly even natural, but the most significant opening into the cavern—the one on my right—was far more intricately worked, and its mouth was carved with geometric shapes and all manner of symbols that I didn't recognize. It was also flanked by a pair of ten-foot-wide caves about twenty feet off the floor above it.

From this position, I also had a pretty good view of the chanting crowd. There were easily a few thousand of them crammed into the very center of the mammoth space. Some of the people were kneeling while others stood and swayed, but all of them had their arms stretched overhead and were dressed in loose white robes that resembled long nightshirts. I could see quite a few children as well as I tried to take stock of the situation. What a mess this was going to be.

Duma placed his hand on my back and thrust his chin in the direction of the two caves halfway up the walls on either side of the intricately carved tunnel to our right. At the edge of the farthest one, a huge Phonoi crouched like a monkey, watching over everything that was happening below him. From what I could see, he had four arms — one pair heavily clawed and one pair more humanlike, though only barely. Taking up most of the opening, he was enormous compared to the ones I'd encountered in the past.

I backed up to safe cover and gestured to Duma to head down the passage to see if he could identify the source of the noises I'd heard a moment ago while I remained where I was. Duma was far stealthier and faster than I could be.

Duma crept farther down the passageway, and the first Spartoi team reported that they were now holding position just inside one of the caves leading into the massive cavern and confirmed what I was seeing. According to their description, they were in the tunnel on the nearside of the dais, off to my left.

A report from the second Spartoi squad followed immediately, relaying that they had killed several hostiles and discovered an unoccupied living space and that they were continuing to search. The overwatch contingent of the team had nothing to report.

After his reconnoiter, Duma returned to my position. He held up his hand and flashed all five fingers at me four times, indicating there were twenty people farther down this side tunnel. I nodded and was about to start figuring out a plan when a thundering scream rocked the cavern, literally shaking the walls, followed by absolute silence for the briefest of moments. Duma and I looked at each other, his skeletal mask revealing nothing of the surprise and urgency I knew, like me, he had to feel. Within seconds, the wild chanting from the main cavern began again, increasing significantly in intensity and volume. Several less intense shrieks followed.

"I've got movement in the main tunnel heading deeper inside," Frigate reported over the radio. "I cannot make out the origin or any further detail, but whatever is moving is big."

The chanting in the cavern was reaching a fevered pitch. I poked my head around just enough to see what was happening and was surprised to find the crowd had separated into two groups, creating a clear path roughly east to west from the elaborately carved tunnel to our right toward the dais at the far left corner. An involuntary shiver crept up my spine, and I could feel the crispness of the air as the atmosphere became more and more alive with energy.

"I have a visual on two Ifrit and six Ghilan dragging something massive by chain," said the voice of the Spartoi leader over the radio. "They are coming through the main cavern entrance to the east. Phonoi and Androktasiai are appearing in cave mouths along the eastern wall, approximately five yards above the same entrance."

From my vantage point, I could not yet see the Jinns, but it was impossible to miss the seven Phonoi and Androktasiai now clinging to the mouths of the caves up the wall like spiders waiting in their web.

I watched as three more of the death spirits gathered at the cave mouths to join their brethren. With all that was going on, we needed to find Medea soon — not to mention Hecate. But I needed to know where they were before we advanced. I didn't want to attack this crowd only to have Medea show up behind us — or worse, sneak away.

All of a sudden, a lot more frenzied movement echoed up the side tunnel from the area Duma had reported seeing twenty people. I pointed at Duma and then hooked a thumb down the tunnel. At that point, we couldn't risk encountering anyone or anything, innocent or not, that might raise an alarm and give us away. I drew my thumb across my throat. I couldn't see his face behind his mask, but I knew he was smiling.

Back up the tunnel, Ab tightened his grip on his hammer and shifted in anticipation as his brother took off down the passage. Peri were like sharks with blood when it came to battle — they could smell it coming. I followed on Duma's heels as he ran off, swiftly and eerily silent.

The tunnel ahead of us emptied into a smaller cavern, maybe fifty yards across at its widest, where people in the same outdated fatigues as the other guards were running to gather things off bunks and from around tables. It was significantly warmer in here than in the tunnels and stank strongly of body odor with a slight tinge of rotten eggs. The space was some sort of barracks, with most of it taken up by four long rows of bunks, stacked two high, and metal lockers around the edges. A series of ten rectangular tables and benches split the room down the middle. At a glance, I counted at least twenty targets moving through the space. Duma quickly covered the ground between the cavern entrance and the nearest group to our right, and he began his deadly dance among five people caught completely off guard by our presence.

I took aim with the MP5 at the closest group to my left and fired as I advanced, weaving among the bunks, putting three bullets into each target before moving to the next. I didn't even stop to see what or how Duma was doing. When I ran through the clip, I ejected and replaced it and continued firing as I encountered targets.

I had eliminated eight targets before the distinct metallic rattling of one of the knockoff AK-47s erupted from my right, followed by two solid impacts on my cuirass as hay from the mattress on the upper bunk to my left scattered through the air. My attention shifted to the shooter, who was standing just on the other side of a set of bunks. His eyes grew wide when I faced him, and he dropped the gun and ran. I shoved the bunks at him before he got very far, and the rickety wooden framework knocked him down and then fell on top of him as the impact took down the next three bunks, as well, like falling dominoes. The sound of the falling beds echoed off the rock walls inside the cavern but was still only barely audible over the chanting that echoed from the main cavern.

Before I could continue my advance, I took the butt of a rifle to the face, instantly causing my eyes to water. The blow stunned me and blurred my vision for a second, and I could feel blood run through my moustache and into my mouth, but in the hands of a mundane, the attack didn't have enough force to do much more than that. Still, it hurt like hell. Again, the attacker gaped at me when I didn't go down, and he began trying to back through the bunks. Before he took a step, I reached for his rifle, seized it by the fore grip, and jerked it from his hands. I threw it away over my shoulder and slowly shook my head at him. Predictably, the guy ran, pushing past the few comrades still left standing in a total panic. I let him run rather than shoot him in the back. Duma intercepted him before he made it twenty feet.

I shook the cobwebs from my head and continued my advance through the room. The remaining guards were in the process of fleeing as we took them down. In less than three minutes, thanks to our preternatural speed, nothing was moving except Duma and me. I replaced the clip in my Sig and took another few minutes to complete the grim and unpleasant task of making sure that any still alive did not suffer any longer than necessary.

I stopped to wipe the blood from my nose, bringing tears to my eyes again, as Duma approached me. He cocked his helmeted head as he looked at me, held up a single gloved finger, and then bent it at the knuckle.

Great. Just what I needed—a broken nose.

At its far end, this barracks cavern opened into another tunnel leading farther north. Duma took up position on the right side of the passageway, and I ducked in along the left. I ejected the partially used clip, inserted another, and quickly surveyed the room we had just crossed. Weapons racks ran along the near and far walls. Luckily, the racks were mostly full, loaded with the cheap copies of AK-47s. *Better here than in hands.*

I poked my head around the edge of the tunnel to see where it led but could only see that it extended another hundred yards and had no visible signs of life. I was getting ready to let Duma know there was nothing down that way when another scream, more like a roar, shook the walls again. The chanting changed into a raucous cheer. As fast as we were moving, it just didn't seem fast enough.

A voice came through my radio—a transmission came from the second Spartoi unit. "We have come to a junction that intersects the main entrance tunnel—well lit, and lined with columns. Another passage continues on the opposite side of it. All tunnels clear to this point."

"Mark the intersection so we don't overlap, leave a relay, and then return to the opening into the central cavern off your original point of entry and await the order to advance," I replied.

Duma and I kept moving farther down the tunnel, and the smell of rotten eggs became stronger. Less than twenty yards down the northern passage, we came to a tunnel that branched off to our left and sloped downward. A smooth yellow substance coated the walls of the tunnel, and the odor of rotten eggs—burnt rotten eggs, to be precise—issued from it in a haze of intense heat. At least now I knew where that odor was coming from. I gestured for Duma to stay put while I continued exploring the previous passage, moving to the north. He threw up his hands in protest and then made an elaborate show of placing his fingers over the mouth and nose of his helmet.

Less than ten yards farther along the northern passage, the path intersected with a brightly lit, well worn, and precisely carved tunnel, about twenty feet in all dimensions, lined with colonnades on both sides. The air coming from the finely carved tunnel to my right was cold and crisp, and the blaring chants, cheers, and screams were coming from the left. This had to be the main cavern entrance to the outside. Another passage continued directly across from me, and I could see the letters "EII"—the mark left by the second Spartoi unit, Eagle Two—scratched into the edge of that tunnel at about head height. We had come full circle, and no one had found Medea or Hecate yet. *Sonofabitch.*

I returned to Duma at the mouth of the side passage and figured it was time to bring Frigate's team through the front door and close off any known nonmagical escape routes. Frigate, Geek, and Sarah needed to move in closer because they had no real line of sight from outside the cavern. Fortunately, this area of the cave system was currently cleared, so they'd be safe for the time being.

"Nest, advance to the tunnel entrance and proceed until the first intersection, approximately seventy-five yards in. Hold a position with eyes into the central cavern, and rig the secondary passageways to blow remotely on my signal." I waited till they acknowledged my order, and then I met back up with Duma to check on what was down the stinky, dark, yellow-walled pathway. The surfaces of the hot, reeking passage were smooth, curved rather than flat, and the floor sloped steadily down. The farther down we traveled, the stronger the smell became, bringing tears to my eyes and burning my nose. The temperature continued to rise steadily, as well. This passage was isolated enough that even the raucous sounds from the central cavern fell away. I finally began to hear indistinct voices coming from in front of us, and a faint glow from up ahead cast eerie shadows into the tunnel as the temperature increased rapidly.

I swung the MP5 behind me on its strap, choosing to draw out my swords instead. The tunnel jogged sharply to the left, and I couldn't see what was beyond the bend, but the sulfurous smell became cloying, and the light was brighter. The heat was stifling, and I assumed we were close to whatever it was. Given that I already knew Ifrit were present, and that they were creatures born of fire, I had my suspicions about what we'd find.

We continued to move cautiously but quickly. As soon as we rounded the bend, I could see a small cavern with no other exits that was immensely tall—easily a few hundred feet high. At its center was a massive fire that erupted right through the floor and practically roared on its own. The room was so hot it shimmered like asphalt in summer. Just to the left of the pit stood an Ifrit with its back to us, staring down into the conflagration. As we watched, another pitch-black Jinn began climbing out of the fire in front of it.

Shit. My legs hurt at the thought of the burns I'd gotten in Brooklyn. "Hamstring that one—I'll take his head off," I whispered, pointing at the Ifrit with its back to us.

Duma nodded, and we both took off at full speed. Duma was a blur as he did a baseball slide right between the Ifrit's legs, slashing its knees with his curved blades and severing the proximal heads of its massive calf muscles. The beast bellowed and fell to its knees.

I ran between the Ifrits, slashing at the one climbing out of the pit with my right hand while using the impact to slow me enough to swing backhand with my left, hoping to connect with the hamstrung Ifrit's neck. But the creature writhed in pain and ducked, so instead of slicing through its throat, I caught it square in the face, cutting the top of its head off at the nose. It slumped to the ground with a thump, and flaming blood covered the floor with a sizzle.

Duma was trying to flank the Ifrit that had emerged from the fire. It watched me cautiously and kept turning to keep Duma from getting behind it. There wasn't much room to move, between the fire pit and the dead Ifrit oozing burning blood all over the ground. My blow had sliced deep into the Ifrit's massive left shoulder, making the arm nearest Duma all but useless. We flanked the monster, and it bobbed in surprise, desperate for a plan. Unfortunately, the fire pit partially blocked my path to the creature. Only Duma had a clear line of attack.

When the Ifrit feinted toward me, Duma leapt. Since I couldn't have run directly at it anyway, I jumped in the opposite direction, back toward the entryway, and the creature disappeared. I guessed that it would teleport as far as it could see, and I was right. It reappeared in front of the entryway, just where I'd thought it would. I landed on its back just as it materialized, plunged my swords through its torso, and twisted violently to drag the cut through the beast's chest. The Jinn never knew what happened and was dead before it fell, spraying sizzling blood across the ground a good ten feet up through the tunnel.

"Fuck!" Duma shouted behind me. "How'd you know it was gonna do that?" He walked over to me, shaking his head, as I removed my blades from the hulk, feeling a bit smug. It wasn't often that I got to show up Duma with a fancy maneuver like that.

"Luck, actually, but it was surprised, wounded, and outnumbered. I'd have made a run for it, too." I shook the flaming gore from my blades and wiped them off on the rock wall before putting them away. "Now, let's get outta here. But before we go" —I reached into my vest pocket and pulled out a thermite grenade—"let's plug that hole."

We started up the sulfur-filled tunnel, and I tossed the grenade toward the fire pit behind us without bothering to pull the pin, figuring the heat would be enough to detonate it. We bolted back up the passage as fast as we could run and felt, more than heard, the explosion. It was a muffled *whump,* and the pressure wave that chased us up the tunnel knocked us forward but not off our feet. The last thing I needed was more Ifrits joining the fray, and given how quiet it was down there, I figured blowing it up was worth the risk. If we couldn't find Medea, though, it wouldn't matter in the least.

CHAPTER 35

BACK OUT IN THE BARRACKS cavern, the relatively cool air felt good as we dashed toward Ab at full speed. He was still crouched where we'd left him, but as soon as he saw us, he shrugged his shoulders and held up his hands to ask what was up then jabbed a finger in the direction of the cavern, which was now positively alive with energy and screaming bodies.

I crept up and peeked in. It was pure frenzy. Hundreds of men, women, and even children were swaying and roiling across the giant cavern's floor, chanting something in unison that was still unintelligible. The pathway that had split the crowd earlier had disappeared, creating a single mass of human bodies again. Most of the people had the dark skin, hair, and features common in southwestern Asia, but there were a few with lighter coloring. The faces of those closest to us were expressionless, but many of their eyes were rolled back and white as they swayed and contorted. The sound was a united cacophony, but the entranced movement struck me as random and agitated.

I could see no sign of any magic controlling the people or even in the air at the moment, but the energy was escalating at a frightening rate. Way above the crowd near the cavern's ceiling, the air was alive with the waxing energy levels, forming a sea of sparks or burning embers that didn't fade or even move. The individual motes of light just intensified as more and more appeared by the second. Despite the brightness emanating from them, the sparks weren't the source of the light that filled the immense space, so I just chalked the phenomenon up to something I could see that wasn't readily visible to others. I had never seen anything like it before.

At the other side of the grotto near the dais, I could just see the naked shoulder of a huge, hunched figure radiating the forceful blue-white aura of an Old One. The being was gigantic compared to the humans around it, but the power it gave off was weaker than I expected for a Protogenoi—down on a level similar to Ned's. That had to be Perses. On either side of him stood a massive black-skinned Ifrit, each far larger than any I'd ever seen before—half again as immense as the ones we'd just taken out but only slightly larger than the one I'd faced in Brooklyn. How many of these damned things was I going to have to deal with?

As I assessed the situation, absolute pandemonium began to break out in the crowd around the main entrance to our right. The riotous and rhythmic chanting became a wild and uproarious cheer. All I could see through the jumping bodies and waving arms were tendrils of black energy that faded to a brilliant blood red as they played over the turbulent crowd like a piano player's fingers touching keys.

"Frigate, where the hell are you?" I whispered hoarsely as I mashed the mic button. "Does any team have a visual on who or what just came into the cavern?"

All the responses came back negative. The crowd was too thick, and the entity was too short to see. With that unique aura of energy, though, I was sure it was either Medea or Hecate.

"Moving into the tunnel now," said Frigate's voice, finally. "Sorry, but we don't move as fast as you guys."

"Everyone stay focused. I'm pretty sure that was our Tango that just entered," I said over the radio.

The throngs of people slowly began to turn their attention to the source of the black tendrils, following the progression of whatever projected them as it made its way through the writhing mass of bodies toward the dais and the hunched figure at its base.

"Frigate, are you in position yet?" I asked. "Everyone else, stand fast."

Whatever was happening, I definitely needed to make sure that intense energy was Medea before I acted, or she might get away—again. When we attacked, it would have to be simultaneous and swift and focused on containing Medea. At least we had most of the exits from the cavern covered.

"We have visual on the Tango. She is progressing toward the rock platform through the center of the crowd," the leader of the second Spartoi squad said over the radio. "We will engage when target is clear of the crowd."

That squad was at the entrance directly across the cavern from my position, on the other side of and nearest the dais. If that was Medea, and the stage was her destination, then that position would be the closest point of attack and the best place for me to be when we did. It would take far too long and cost way too many human lives for me to fight my way across the crowd from where I currently stood. Given Eagle Two's recon, I knew the tunnel system Duma and I had worked through joined up with the one the squad had come through at the main passage, giving me a path around the crowd to reach them.

"Negative, Eagle Two. Stand fast. I'm coming," I said. "All teams, on my signal engage all hostiles, with priority being all nonhumans. Be advised: the humans inside do not appear to be under any sort of magical control. If they attack you, do whatever is necessary to protect your team. Frigate, when I pass your position, move forward to a safe distance and detonate the charges to close the side tunnels off the main entrance exactly one minute later. The explosions will be the signal to begin the assault."

Closing those side passages would keep any combatants from coming in behind my team as they advanced into the crowd. If we could attack them from all sides with our backs protected, then our small assault team stood a better chance while I took care of Medea. The only wild card was that I still hadn't seen Hecate, not even in disguise among the crowd.

One thing at a time. I knew where Medea was, so she was first.

I gave Duma and Ab a thumbs-up and took off through the side tunnel as fast as I could run. As I approached the passage where Duma and I killed the Ifrits, I unsheathed my swords. I slowed just enough approaching the main entrance that I could stop to alert Frigate's team to my passing without scaring them or breezing by without them noticing.

I stopped only long enough to signal as I passed them, waving a sword at Geek, who was the only one of the trio not glued to a scope. Frigate was standing behind one of the columns along the right side of the tunnel facing into the cavern, resting his cheek against the stock of the heavy sniper rifle, moving it among potential targets and, I assumed, taking stock of the situation. Geek, who acknowledged me as I passed, was on one knee behind a column on the opposite side of the passage with a mini laptop propped on his thigh. Sarah stood next to him, surveying the cavern with a spotter's scope.

Despite what they were dealing with, the team of mundanes came off as remarkably calm and ready for action. I resumed running, beginning a countdown in my head. I cleared one cavern and raced through a smaller, secondary one that was likely a mess hall and prep area. As I ran, I passed several groups of unarmed dead people in loose-fitting robes, and I noted the tight groupings of bullet holes in their backs and chests. The Spartoi were as efficient as Duma and me, though they had shot people in the back. I had no time to contemplate their less-than-honorable methods. Forty-five seconds to go.

I slowed down when the light began to increase at the end of the tunnel. "Eagle Two, I am approaching your position," I radioed ahead. Thirty seconds to go.

The din of screaming and cheering from within the main cavern died down as the energy changed from random and driftless to much more concentrated, sending a pain through my head like a hot lance, causing me to falter as I ran at top speed. As I regained my focus and my footing, a familiar, gravelly female voice began to echo through the caves as the noise from the crowd suddenly died away. I couldn't make out what she was saying yet, but I didn't stop to find out, either.

Just ahead of me, I could see the two Spartoi keeping an eye on the junction between two tunnels to make sure no one snuck up on the rest of the team from behind. Both soldiers knelt on the rocky floor, aiming their M4s in my direction as I approached.

"Coming through." I sprinted through the junction past them toward the rest of the squad waiting in the northern entrance to the main cavern.

"Falling in behind," responded from the pair, as they rose up from their kneeling positions on either side of the tunnel and followed me.

Fifteen seconds to go. Having reached the rest of Eagle Two, I crouched just inside the mouth of the tunnel, opposite Ab and Duma's position at the entrance across the enormous cavern, and took a quick survey of the situation from this new vantage point.

Medea was standing on the dais less than fifty yards to the right, just inside the cavern. Perses lay in a heap on the ground just in front of the stone platform. Six ghouls stood between Medea and Perses, bobbing wildly as they watched the crowd, while the pair of gigantic

Ifrit stood stolidly on either side of the once-mighty Titan, seemingly unfazed by what was going on around them. I was slightly behind and to Medea's left, and if Perses's eyes had been open, he would have been staring directly at me. As it was, he appeared unconscious, and his aura resembled a dying fire, sputtering and softening its glow.

Medea, on the other hand, was channeling the sparks of energy that were floating high overhead, the tendrils of her sanguine aura extending up to corral it. She was dressed in a floor-length, blood-red robe that was adorned with gold embroidery, and its hood was pushed back to reveal her wild red hair. She was wreathed in a magical energy that took the form of a cloud of pulsating, multicolored light that became brighter the more energy she gathered from above. As she raised her hands above her head, the chanting rose to a deafening crescendo, and the sparks of energy began to disappear into the fingers of her bloody aura, turning them a brilliant electrical red. The power began to course from above through her aura and into the magical cloud of energy that surrounded her in waves, coming faster and faster.

Her voice boomed out in a language I was unfamiliar with, but the stepped cadence that echoed through the cavern definitely felt like a ritual or a spell, and I knew that she was gathering the energy she needed.

I checked my watch. When the thunderous explosion echoed through the cavern, and dust and debris flew into the chamber from the main entrance—a few seconds later than I'd anticipated—the once chaotic space was plunged into a sudden eerie silence. Even Medea stopped midsentence at the explosion. On cue, gunfire erupted from across the cavern, sending an instant panic through the chamber. High-pitched shrieks pierced the air as bedlam broke out within the crowd, and the continuous metallic rattling of machine guns and automatic-weapons fire echoed around the chamber.

I ran into the cavern and crept among the rubble between the chamber's back wall and the rear of the dais to avoid having to push my way through the dense, and now terrified, crowd. I really needed the Pelian Spear, which I had cleverly left with Ab. Nonetheless, I closed the distance between me and Medea as fast as I could.

She disappeared before I was halfway there.

"Medea just teleported," I screamed into my mic. "Do not let her leave this cavern!"

The half-dozen Ghilan, who had been bobbing their bulbous heads below Medea and laughing to each other, climbed up to take her place on the dais. The pair of giant black Ifrits roared a challenge in no particular direction and threw their arms out wide, searching for enemies. Out of the corner of my eye, I watched Phonoi and Androktasiai pour like ants out of the high tunnels that flanked the cavern's main entrance, now directly across the cavern from my position by the dais. The freakish Phonoi skittered, many on more than two legs, while the decidedly female and mostly nude Androktasiai spilled across the floor like liquid, oozing among the screaming people. Both types of creatures reveled in the chaos, slicing throats and ripping abdomens as they pressed toward the dais. In Medea's absence, the creatures had reverted to their baser instincts.

It was hard not to watch the chaos the creatures caused as I continued to close in on the dais, moving more carefully, trying to sneak up behind the Ghilan to take out at least one before they realized where I was. It just wasn't right. The Androktasiai were beautiful, down to the last murderous succubus. It was like seeing a *Victoria's Secret* catalog come to life — if the models were members of the Manson family. Most were dressed in rags that barely covered their bodies — highly distracting, to say the least. Fortunately, I was a consummate professional, and those things didn't faze me. If it weren't for their fingers ending in razor-sharp claws and their teeth like piranhas', it would probably be a pleasant way to go.

Their male counterparts, on the other hand — the Phonoi — were as hideous as they were stunning. None had mouths or ears on their featureless bald heads, only slits for nostrils and a pair of beady black eyes. The similarities among them stopped there. Each of the Phonoi was unique with regard to its armament.

The human voices continued to rise again, only this time discordantly and in absolute hysteria. Steady gunfire rang all around, echoing along with the screams and roars, creating a deafening dissonance. I paused briefly in an attempt to locate any members of my team within the fray, but I couldn't. I would just have to trust in their skills and determination. Besides, I had issues of my own to contend with.

In a sudden burst of speed, I charged ahead and plowed, slashing, right into the heart of the six Ghilan on the dais. I took the first two apart and cut the right arm off a third before they could even react to my presence or form up to defend themselves. I stopped to face them and watched the one-armed Ghilan run away into the crowd, gibbering wildly.

Two of the creatures attempted to flank me, and one stayed directly in front. But before any of us could act, one of the Ifrits teleported just behind them and let out an earsplitting roar.

Fuck me. The lion-headed black Jinn was huge, and its smaller ghoul cousins suddenly began cackling their horrible laugh, bobbing excitedly and lashing out at me, emboldened by its presence. I braced myself for the onslaught and pressed my mic button with the heel of my hand.

"Frigate, I need a little help. I'm on stage," I all but screamed.

Before I could wonder whether Frigate was even alive, the beast's chest exploded in a cloud of flaming orange mist that looked like embers. The rupture of the creature's chest showered everything on the dais, including me and the three remaining Ghilan, with fiery gore, but the sight of the gaping hole in the dead Ifrit's ruined chest buoyed my spirits so much I completely ignored the pain.

The massive black hulk toppled over on the stone dais with a meaty thud, stopping the Ghilan in their tracks long enough for the report of the Barrett to echo through the chamber above the crowd's din like a peal of thunder in the enclosed cavern. I couldn't help but grin. Then I roared a battle cry and snapped the confused and frightened Ghilan back to attention. I had the initiative, so I didn't waste time searching for the other Ifrit. There was an old fishing saying that suggested fishermen shouldn't leave fish to find fish, and the same wisdom applied to enemies on a battlefield.

I attacked the closest Ghilan first. It tried to lunge as soon as I moved, throwing its long arms out wide while rapidly covering the short distance between us. I stepped to my left, and it sailed past me to the right as I brought both swords down on it in a wide arc. The impact of my blow and the creature's own momentum sent its body sliding off the rock stage behind me in several different pieces.

I spun to face the Ghilan to my right and was blindsided by the one behind me. I landed in a flop with a human-sized Jinn on my back trying to rip through my cuirass with its razor-clawed fingers. It failed miserably, though it shredded the back of my vest.

Before I could push myself up to turn over, the distinct metallic chattering of a machine gun split the air as the Ghilan slumped and fell across my back. I lifted my head in time to watch several of the Spartoi move beyond the dais, guns sweeping past my position.

I flipped the wounded creature off me, got to my knees, and drove the blade of my sword into the side of its head as I spun around. I wrenched the blade free, taking most of its head off with it, while searching for the last Ghilan. I caught sight of the creature, which was fleeing past the prone Titan chained to the floor just in front of the stage. As the Ghilan neared it, the Titan's arm lashed out to the end of its chain and seized the creature by the head, crushing it like an overripe tomato. Suddenly Perses's eyes were wild, and he let loose a roar that shook the cavern, causing stalactites from the ceiling to crack loose and fall into the crowd. I had to dive across the dais to avoid one particularly hefty formation as it exploded on impact with the stage.

I pushed myself up and tried to take stock of the situation. The grotto was pure chaos. Most of the remaining few hundred people were crowded into the center of the cavern. Only a few dozen of those in the center were armed, and they were firing randomly at my team as well as the Phonoi and Androktasiai that were still attacking them. Here and there, however, small, well-armed pockets of Medea's human followers were forming up ranks, trying to hold out against the Spartoi.

Back across the cave, I could see Ab, head and shoulders taller than most everyone around him, swinging his massive hammer in wide arcs while bodies—plural—flew. I quickly lost sight of him. Pairs of Spartoi fought through the crowd, firing their assault rifles or hacking with their broadswords. There were dead bodies everywhere, and for the briefest of moments, knowing that neither Duma and Ab nor the Spartoi would distinguish between armed and unarmed, I felt remorse for their deaths. But I couldn't dwell on that now.

Continuing to search the crowd, I couldn't see Duma, nor could I see Frigate's team, presumably still back up the main tunnel, but every so often the report of the huge sniper rifle would echo through the cavern. Luckily, the numbers of Phonoi and Androktasiai were dwindling, but the surviving ones still appeared, alone and in groups, ripping into anything they met. What bothered me most was that I couldn't see the other Ifrit or find Medea or Hecate in all the ruckus. I knew neither the Ifrit nor Medea could teleport without line of sight, which severely limited their range underground. They couldn't have gone far yet.

In front of the stone stage, the naked Perses, entirely human looking though ten feet tall, was chained with the gleaming, mercurial Alysideus Prometheus, hand and foot to the floor, as some sort of energy cloud gathered above him and began to envelop his body. In addition, he was bound within a circle of barely glowing symbols and writing carved into the stone floor. My heart sank. I jumped down to get a closer look, and he tried to grab me.

"I'm trying to help you, you bastard," I screamed as I dodged out of his shortened reach.

Perses roared again, his face contorted with rage and his eyes and hair wild as he pulled and thrashed at his bindings. The chaos of the situation around us was making him lash out, but unless something got within his reach, the restraints prevented him from doing much. I guessed that the cloud that surrounded the bound Titan was probably the chaotic energy that Medea was harnessing, aided by the glowing writing on the floor. Even more alarming, the havoc my team was creating with our attack had to be adding to that energy. The Phonoi and Androktasiai might well have been left to their own devices on purpose for the very same reason.

I couldn't let myself dwell on thoughts like that. I needed to find the bitch and stop her before it was too late. The world's chaos would be of no use to her if she were dead. To that end, retrieving my spear from Ab would be extremely helpful.

"Talon Three, this is Talon One. I need the Spear, and I'm coming to you. Can you give me a sign of your current location?" I called over the radio.

"Am I Talon Three?" said Ab's voice. "I thought I was Talon Two."

"No, you tool," cut in Duma. "I'm Talon Two; you're Talon Three."

"Why do I have to be Talon Three?" Ab actually managed to sound dejected in the middle of battle.

"I don't give a fuck if you're both Talon Two," I screamed over the radio. "Ab, just let me know where you are so I can find you, dammit."

All of a sudden, one of the Phonoi launched fifteen feet into the air, spewing green slime about a hundred yards farther south toward the mouth of the tunnel my team would have entered. Under it, I could make out Ab's hammer as his massive head and shoulders suddenly bobbed above the crowd.

"Good enough." I ran as fast as I could, shoving through the crowd, ducking and dodging attacks as I ran toward him. I needed to get the Pelian Spear from him as quickly as possible. As I approached, I could feel the nasty sensation of violence creep into my very being. Apparently, more than a few of the Phonoi had died at Ab's hands.

"Whoa, D—here," the big Peri said, dropping his hammer and holding up one hand to stop me as he tossed the Pelian Spear toward me. "Keep your distance. I've crushed about six of these things, and you know how pinkies get when they die."

He held one hand out to stop me while he bent down to grab his hammer again. In a single fluid motion he grabbed the hammer and swatted backhanded at a crazed charging robed figure and sent its crushed form flying into another small berserk group of Medea's followers.

I'd dealt with these death spirits more than once and could normally control myself, but if there were many more of them, I'd only be able to hold out for so long. If I couldn't, I might lose all control and attack anything in my path, including my teammates if it got bad enough.

I caught my spear and ran back into the fray to work out some of my Phonoi-induced violent ideas while I could still think clearly. I charged directly into a frenetic group of five of Medea's human acolytes. In seconds, I killed three of them and then managed to control myself enough to disable the remaining two before moving on again.

"I've got eyes on the Tango but no clear shot," Frigate screamed. "She's in the northeast corner surrounded by some freaky lookin'... things. Oh, fuck—" His comlink went silent.

"Frigate, respond. What is your status? Respond!" I shouted as I ran at full bore across the cavern toward the main entrance, where the sniper team was supposed to be holding position.

The fact that Frigate screamed while reporting scared me as much as being unable to raise him after he cut out. In all the years we served together, I never saw his heart rate get much above room temperature.

I slashed and stabbed my way through several small crowds of the same type of malformed, mutated humans I had seen at the crash site in Bulgaria, as well as mundane people, without a second thought beyond my team's wellbeing. Bullets ricocheted off my cuirass as I pushed my way through. I didn't care.

Several Spartoi were firing into the passage at something I couldn't yet see as I approached within a hundred yards of the tunnel mouth. I raced to close the distance, and the three dragon-tooth warriors were suddenly thrown backward toward me some twenty feet, as if an explosion had gone off at their feet. The hazy remnants of a burst of magical energy hung like a cloud of smoke where they had stood.

I ran in a wide arc, trying to bring myself around so I could head straight down the tunnel, fearing for my sniper team's lives. What I saw first just inside the mouth of the passageway surprised me: a smallish old woman in a plain dark robe.

The robed figure was pivoting away from the Spartoi and peering down the tunnel, lowering her right arm as she kept her left raised and pointed down the passageway now less than ten yards in front of me. While I could tell from her aura she wasn't Hecate, I could see and feel the greasy black magical power she wielded — like Medea's, only significantly weaker. I just couldn't tell what she was doing with her left hand.

I shifted my weight as I ran, turning the spear in my hand, and I threw it as hard as I could at the old witch. The spear struck her in her upper back and continued straight through her. She staggered, and I watched the greasy energy she controlled scatter like oil from a drop of soap. Before I made it another ten feet, a burst of machine-gun fire from in front of her tore into the witch, jarring her body like a spastic puppet. I stopped short as she keeled over.

Once I was close enough, I could make out Geek sitting in a pool of blood against one of the carved stone columns. He was pale, and his pants were shredded where his prosthetic leg had been. Frigate was getting back to his feet using the Barrett as a crutch. Sarah was changing out clips on the other side of the tunnel, holding the Vector in front of her face in a combat-high stance. A wave of relief washed over me, stopping me abruptly for a second as I took a deep breath.

When I saw blood on Sarah's face, I ran over to the group. All of them had bloody noses. Sarah's face was hard and her hair matted with blood, but I could see the muscles in her jaw tighten as she looked past me into the cavern, keeping watch.

Frigate grinned lopsidedly, hopping on his left leg but far from done. "Glad you could join us, but we got a party to get back to," he said, moving farther into the tunnel's mouth to get back into position.

"Find Medea," I said to him. "Now."

"On it."

Geek grimaced as I bent over to check on him. Sarah pushed in right behind me now that Frigate was up. She knelt at his side, her eyes moving quickly between checking Geek over to keeping watch into the cavern behind us.

"I'm okay," he croaked as he tried to move into a more comfortable position. "I hit my head after one of those mutant thingies grabbed my leg and wrenched it free. By the time I came to, there was an old biddy waving at us, and I couldn't breathe."

Sarah checked his head. "Just a scalp laceration." She patted him on the shoulder. Her face was drawn and streaked with dust and blood, but her eyes were lively and intense. "She put us in some kind of vacuum bubble. Felt like we'd just descended a few hundred feet underwater. The Spartoi tried to take her from behind, but they were less than sneaky about it. If your spear hadn't distracted her, we'd have been goners in a minute."

She wiped her nose with the back of her gloved hand and sniffed, smearing blood across her face, which made her look even hotter.

"Soon as that magic bubble popped, Sarah put a few in her," Frigate said over his shoulder, positioning his rifle on some rubble for support. "Geek fell on my damned leg, and I twisted my ankle." Suddenly his tone changed from friendly to urgent. "Uh, Chief, I found the Tango. She's over there, near that stone stage, doing something with that big guy chained to the ground."

"You guys stand fast." I watched as Sarah's eyes opened wider at the mention of Medea. I pointed at Geek as I spoke to her. "Make sure he's okay. And keep kicking ass."

The tight, thin line formed by her lips curled up at one corner into the slightest of smiles.

CHAPTER 36

COULD SENSE THAT THE PELIAN Spear was farther back down the tunnel somewhere. It felt like a slight buzzing in my ears that became louder the closer I got to it, like a metal detector. I found the spear embedded in a pile of rocks with less than a foot of its length sticking out at the back of the rubble-filled passage. I grabbed it and pulled as hard as I could to free the weapon then took off with it back into the fray, heading straight for the dais and Medea.

I spotted her on the far side of the cavern near Perses, exactly as Frigate had said. She was manipulating and directing the flow of energy from around the cavern toward Perses, who was thrashing wildly within his restraints. The writing on the floor around him began glowing brighter. To those who couldn't perceive energy, Medea's movements would have looked like some sort of martial-arts kata.

I charged through a small group of the mutated humanoids, using the shaft of the spear to shove them aside as I ran. Automatic gunfire erupted all around me, but before I made it halfway to Medea, a blood-curdling, bestial howl stopped me in my tracks. Two hundred yards away to my left, Ab was going toe-to-toe with the last giant Ifrit.

Time slowed as I watched. Ab landed a vicious blow with his hammer, catching the monstrous Jinn under its left arm and sliding it sideways. That blow would have driven a rhino over the centerfield wall at Petco Park, but the Ifrit just trapped the hammer under its arm and teleported twenty feet behind Ab and that much farther from me, with Ab's hammer to boot. I took a step to throw the spear and help Ab out when a black-and-red blur zipped toward the Ifrit from my left. Now weaponless, Ab whirled around and charged without a second thought, racing like a linebacker with a clear bead on the quarterback—if the quarterback were ten feet tall.

The Ifrit tossed the giant hammer aside as if it were a toy, snarled, and threw a gout of yellow flame a yard wide at Ab. It engulfed his entire upper body in fire but hardly slowed his advance. Several of Medea's followers, a little too close to the fight, burst into flames, screaming in agony before they died.

Someone screamed, "Ab!" above the din of battle. I couldn't tell if it came from me. By the time my head cleared, I realized I hadn't thrown the spear, and the red-and-black blur was flying through the air toward the Ifrit's back.

It was Duma. When he slammed into the beast that had threatened his brother, Duma rammed his curved kukri knives down to their hilts into its broad neck, flipped off its back, and landed in a low crouch with two more knives in his hands. The creature bellowed in pain, and I began running again, but as I closed into within fifty yards of the fight, three mutated humanoid creatures with swords cut me off.

I didn't have time for this. In one motion, I swung the butt of the Spear around, cracking the brute to my right across the head, then pulled the weapon back, rammed the butt into the next one's face, and spun around and jammed it into the third creature's chest. I disabled all three in seconds.

I watched Ab tackle the Ifrit with a thud I could feel in my chest. Smoke rose around them as he grappled the thing to the ground. By the time I'd made it the rest of the way over, Ab was pummeling the Ifrit mercilessly with his armored fists, the long black plume on the crown of his helmet gone but for a smoldering wisp, his upper-body armor and helmet blackened by the fire.

While the Ifrit wasn't quite dead by the time I arrived, it was damn close. I picked up Ab's hammer and threw it next to him with a resounding *thunk* on the stone floor of the cavern. The giant Peri continued to wail on the Jinn, sending sizzling blood flying with each blow. Ab calmly rose, picked up his weapon, and tossed it onto his shoulder. With his free hand, he took off his helmet and let it fall to the ground. His normally white eyes were a sickly yellow, oozy and swollen from the heat, and his face was blistered. He walked over to stand beside the Ifrit's head, grabbed his hammer with both hands, and spun it so the point on the rear of its head was facing up. When he brought it down, it drove the Jinn's head into the cavern floor, spraying flaming blood in all directions. I was getting damn tired of these flaming things. Blood landed on Ab's bare face with a sizzle but didn't faze him. Duma came over, clapping his gloved hands, and then removed his helmet and tucked it under his arm.

"I didn't need help, brother," Ab said crossly as smoke continued to rise from his charred armor.

Duma and I just laughed. Behind the humor, I could see the relief etched on Duma's face and in his eyes because I felt it, too. I hung my head, shaking it. Battle with these two was always different.

"Boys, we got bigger issues yet," I said, gesturing with my head over my shoulder back at Medea, who was still engrossed in directing energy into the thrashing Titan. "Make sure she can't leave this cavern."

I made my way through the remaining groups of humans and creatures, using the spear to dispatch would-be attackers as I tried to close in on Medea without drawing her attention away from her spell work. Gunfire was becoming less and less frequent, but an undeniable feeling of power was growing within the grotto, stemming from Medea and Perses. Perhaps fewer than thirty of Medea's armed followers remained, and I could make out a few small groups of Spartoi amid the fracas. I could also still see quite a few of the death spirits, both male and female, gleefully ripping apart anything with which they came into contact.

I was still several hundred yards away from Medea and the chained Titan when I noticed another figure on the dais behind Medea. It wasn't huge — less than six feet tall — but it was completely covered in a dirty, bulky gray cloak and hood. I couldn't see its face, only green, glowing eyes within the hood. A pair of boney grayish hands protruded from the sleeves. The being projected immense energy toward the witch, far greater than her own and much older but in the same greasy black form as Medea's. In addition to the power she cast toward Medea, the being gave off the distinct, pure aura of the Old Ones. She had to be Hecate.

She was augmenting Medea's energy to achieve their goal of harnessing the power of chaos. I had little doubt that Hecate had her own twisted agenda for using her father to achieve their goal, as well. It made sense that it would take Hecate to help a human, even one as powerful as Medea, harness and use the power of a Protogenoi — namely, her father, Perses. Whatever their reasoning, Medea — backed by Hecate — took crazy to a level that I could only imagine would make nightmares seem like an amusement park.

Up on the dais, Hecate was raising her palms upward and chanting in an unintelligible language as the wave of energy flowed like a power cord into Medea. Near Perses, the physical signs of magical power were beginning to germinate like sparks and fluorescent motes, playing around Medea's form as she mimicked Hecate's movements. The energy flowing into Perses was becoming a nearly opaque cloud that surrounded him, contained within the glowing writing on the ground.

I broke into a trot, keeping low with the Pelian Spear in my hand, as two Spartoi closed in on Hecate from just off the dais to her left. One of the soldiers trained a hefty M249 SAW machine gun on her, and the other had his M4 assault rifle in firing position less than twenty yards away.

Hecate paid no attention to the fact she was being flanked and continued her odd synchronized ballet of hand gestures and arm movements with Medea. All at once, the pair of Spartoi opened fire on her, the SAW rattling like a freight train, drowning out the lighter M4. The gunner with the M4 ran through his clip, ejected it, inserted another and kept firing while the box-fed M249 just kept rattling.

They had to have thrown a hundred rounds at her before they stopped, probably to keep the weapons from overheating. Hecate's only acknowledgment of their existence was a slight wave of her left hand, as if she were shooing away flies. Energy left the Spartoi like a fan blowing loose dirt around, and the warriors collapsed as if they'd been deboned.

"Frigate, take out the target on the stage. Priority One," I said, pressing the talk button on my chest as I scrambled across the cavern with greater urgency. I was now within a hundred yards of the pair and within my effective range with the spear. My only concern was that it was a one-shot weapon, so I had to make sure that one attempt counted.

Seconds later, something exploded near Hecate's head in a shower of light, and the thunder of the Barrett filled the hollow cavern, but again, she was unfazed. That was the problem with using mortal weapons against immortal creatures—they didn't always work the way they were supposed to. Even the armor-piercing, explosive Raufoss Mk 211 rounds that blew a hole through an Ifrit did no damage to her. It was worth a try, but I was hoping Frigate's attempt would at least distract her.

Meanwhile, the greasy, amoeboid energy wave Hecate produced continued to grow more concentrated. Before I got close enough to take my chance with the spear, a magical convulsion surged from Medea's hands and spread out in every direction through the cavernous space. Every human it reached slumped over, and the air became palpable with energy.

I could feel the wave wash over me, trying to invade my mind. I had a vision of Medea telling me my usefulness was past, that it was time for the Happening, and my reward would be a swift and painless death. Suddenly drowsy and comfortable, I had to dredge up a force of will to drive the image and feeling from my head. The mental invasion made me stumble a bit, but I quickly regained my balance and shook my head clear. Noting all the fallen humans, and given what I'd just experienced, I had no doubt my sniper team had suffered the same fate. I had to stop her before she killed them all.

At that point, the only thing separating Medea and me was a distance of about fifty yards, but a troop of Phonoi and Androktasiai surrounding the enormous, four-armed Phonoi skittered in to act as a blockade around her and Perses.

There were maybe three dozen murderous spirits in total, each of them following my movements like a cat watching a mouse. Some of them had natural armor like that of insects or turtles. The ones with bodies wore armor, and those with hands held weapons, but most possessed appendages that were lethal in their own right: scorpion tails and, for arms, everything from crab-like claws to barbed spears.

The four-armed Phonoi at the back of the group had silvery skin that gave the appearance of tight-fitting metal plates. Two of its appendages were like claws, each with four digits ending in massive metallic nails. The lower pair of arms was human enough and held an acinaces—a short sword originated by the ancient Medes—and a threshing sickle. I kept a close eye on him as I slowly continued to approach.

I stopped fifteen feet from the bad guys and rammed the Pelian Spear into the stone floor, sending sparks flying. I'd done it mostly for effect, but the horde of murderous beings didn't seem impressed.

"Medea!" I shouted. "What are you up to, you crazy witch?"

Out of the corner of my eye, off to my right, I could see three groups of Spartoi moving to back me up, but Medea didn't respond to my question or even acknowledge my presence. She just kept on chanting in a frenzied, stepped cadence that matched the intensity of the rising energy being pulled from the fallen human bodies. Behind her on the dais, Hecate continued to match her movements. The entire cavern was buzzing with an energy that felt like being outside during an electrical storm wearing a metal suit, and the air was filled with billions of tiny fireflies rising into the air from the collapsed people.

"Come on now, Medea. Let's be adult about this," I shouted, trying to break her concentration.

She still didn't respond. *Time to change from passive to much more aggressive.*

I pulled the Pelian Spear from the ground, and all at once, the group of Phonoi came to life, moving agitatedly in place, claws clacking and weapons clinking. The Androktasiai began chittering and hissing through their pointy little teeth. I almost took a step back at their display of aggression, but I was far too brave to be intimidated.

"Ooh, hot crowd, hot crowd," I said, mostly to myself, and then I noticed Duma on my left, shaking his head at my stupid commentary. "What took you so long?"

"Oh, you know, the usual. Killing bad guys." He was using the edge of one of his curved knives to scrape black blood from the other.

Off to our right, the Spartoi were forming up into ranks. I counted six of them as they broke into two groups and started slamming their giant shields together in unison, forming a wall between them and the murderous entities, sending a deafening metallic echo through the chamber.

They began to beat the backsides of their shields with their swords, chanting a thunderous "ah-ooh!" and keeping the din going. It didn't surprise me when the Spartoi began the clamor. It was a mainstay of their primitive tactical repertoire. What did surprise me, however, was that the trick worked.

The Phonoi and Androktasiai shifted their gaze toward the Spartoi, suddenly confused about whether they should direct their attention to the noisy soldiers or me and Duma. The pounding and rhythmic droning probably would have scared the snot out of most mortal units, but the United Nations of Death troops were entranced by it. In fact, it just excited them more, probably raising their anticipation of the carnage to come. That was the problem with spirits of manslaughter and death.

Hecate and Medea were clearly deep into some incantation that was drawing in and focusing enormous amounts of entropic energy to unleash some sort of hell on Earth. Meanwhile, approximately three dozen homicidal spirits, some drop-dead gorgeous and all as ramped up as kids on a sugar high, stood between the evil creatures and us. On my side, I had six members of the musical *Stomp* pounding away at their shields, and one refugee from a renaissance festival. I had no idea where Ab was or whether he was okay, and no clue about Frigate, Geek, and Sarah. *Go, Team Diomedes!*

CHAPTER 37

ALL AT ONCE, THE SPARTOI stopped chanting and banging, leaving only the low, steady rhythmic cadence of Medea and Hecate's spellcraft and the clicking and hissing from the death spirits. The quiet was as loud as the noise had been.

"Last chance, Medea," I said, tossing up the spear in order to shift from a stabbing grip to a throwing one.

When she didn't respond, I looked over at Duma then back at the Spartoi. Then I threw the spear as hard as I could, pulled my swords, and ran straight for the wall of death spirits and the colossal, four-armed Phonoi.

I aimed my throw at Hecate, precisely because I was hoping Medea wouldn't expect it—assuming in her focused state she even knew I was there. In the instant that I released the spear, Duma and the Spartoi charged the death brigade with me. The Spartoi were screaming as one as they closed the distance, and the spirits responded in a frenzy, moving to meet them head-on. I came in low and sliced the first Androktasiai I encountered across her abdomen, nearly cutting her waif-like body in half. Continuing to move, I spun around her as she began to collapse, and embedded my blade deep into the skull of a small Phonoi just to her left. Wrenching the blade free, I faced the next one, murderous rage growing inside me. Other than Medea, I was the only conscious human within the entire cavern.

As I spun from the female death spirit toward the Phonoi, I watched the Pelian Spear pierce some sort of barrier around Hecate then pass through in a shower of sparks and stab her dead in the middle of her chest with the slightest of thumps. The Titan Goddess of Witchcraft staggered and began to fall. In a massive implosion, the greasy black cloud of energy that Hecate directed at Medea broke loose and recoiled back on its source, accompanied by a deafening

271

crack like a sonic boom. Numerous smaller Androktasiai and Phonoi with their backs to the dais were pulled over backward. For the rest of us at the edges of Hecate's violent departure, it felt like getting caught in the surf as a wave ebbed. Hecate was simply gone, but the area of the stone dais where she stood was little more than a crater.

Duma, a handful of the Spartoi, and I managed to remain upright — though my head was ringing — but only a few of the Phonoi, including Four Arms less than fifty feet away, kept their footing. The Spartoi, still on their feet, slammed into the bad guys, using their shields as battering rams.

The rage building within me shoved aside the ringing in my head, and I stalked directly for Four Arms. Duma waded back into the fray next to me, both of us slashing as fast as we could. The high-pitched shrieks of spirits tearing themselves from their mortal shells were eerie. I could feel their hatred and viciousness seep into me. Reason and purpose left me. All I could think about was how badly I wanted to rip all four of the arms off the giant Phonoi that was currently tearing into what was left of the Spartoi. I forced my way through the melee, hacking and slashing as I marched in a deliberate path toward the beast.

The vacuum effect of Hecate's disappearance and the absence of her power seemed to break Medea's concentration. She nearly collapsed, and her scream of agony and frustration rose above the battle as her complex spell fell apart. The failed spell released the pent-up energy without focus, rendering it as harmless as air let out of a balloon.

Many of the unconscious people began to stir on the cavern floor, but with the rage building in me, all I cared about was getting to Four Arms. As I hacked at the creatures in front of me on my way to face the giant Phonoi, Medea looked around frantically and then moved away from the fight, maybe in an attempt to flee again. I didn't care. I just wanted to kill Four Arms, who was now less than ten feet in front of me.

"Kesed, kill him!" Medea hissed, pointing at me from what was left of the dais as she tried to regain her composure.

The creature's head whipped around in my direction. Four Arms pulled its sword from the neck of a Spartoi and withdrew one of its claws from deep within the soldier's side then threw the warrior's helmeted head to the floor. It ran toward me at frightening speed.

My bloodlust drove me toward the charging monster without fear or concern. The giant Phonoi was fast, almost as fast as I was. Moving at full speed, it tried to spear me with one of its clawed hands, its talons closed tightly into a wicked point, but I pivoted slightly, shifting my weight to the right, and the blow glanced off my cuirass and tore through the ballistic nylon of my already tattered vest. I parried a blow from the sickle in the demon's left hand and thrust my sword into its side and out its back. The brute howled. I sneered and screamed in response. I wrenched my sword from its metallic skin, and we spun around to face each other head-on.

We eyed each other for a second. Four Arms clacked its metallic claws loudly, still holding the short sword in its right hand and the sickle in its left. Tremendous heat and the smell of burning meat billowed from behind us, along with the screams and shrieks of the reawakening crowd, and my rage continued to rise. Every muscle in my body was tensed to the point of snapping as I gripped my swords so hard my knuckles turned white.

All at once, the massive Phonoi raced forward with its claws poised to spear me again. I crossed my swords tight over my chest, ducked down to avoid the talons, and lunged up within the massive Phonoi's reach, spreading my arms and drawing my swords outward with as much force as I could. I cut clean through its left claw, severing it above the elbow with a satisfying metallic ring. But the Phonoi deflected my blow to its right claw with its short sword, and my sword jabbed upward and lodged in its plated upper chest. I ducked, letting go of my sword, and the monster's sickle caught the middle of my chest while I was extended. The curved blade wrapped around me in a blow that knocked the air from my lungs and probably would have cut me in half if not for my cuirass — instead, it just threw me sideways like a ragdoll.

I tucked into a tight roll and came out of it in a low crouch, catching my breath. Wounded and moving more slowly, the Phonoi hesitated for a few seconds, bobbing, before lunging at me. It swung with its sickle and sword in a wild scissor, but I stepped back and let its arms swing past me. Something — the tip of the short sword or maybe the sickle — slashed into the back of my right arm as I jerked backward, and the sudden shock of pain made me drop my sword. I staggered back and ran my left hand under my arm to check the damage. It wasn't bad, but my hand came out covered in blood. My rage was so complete I had no idea where anyone else was, what they were doing, or even if they were alive.

Encouraged by my injury, the beast threw its head back and charged at me with its remaining arms splayed wide. On instinct, I ran straight at it, dove between its legs, and tried to snag my fallen sword along the way. Luckily, my speed caught the beast off guard enough that the bizarre maneuver actually worked. I got to my feet, sword in hand, and spun around to attack.

Before I could follow through, an intense heat radiating through the area behind me and to my right drew my attention. From her place on the dais, Medea's right arm was engulfed in and projecting a brilliant yellow-white flame. She directed it into the melee, continuing behind me like a flamethrower, wielding it with precision and incinerating everything in its path. The heat she generated even cracked rock.

Unconcerned with those being burned, I snarled at Four Arms and charged. I pulled the tanto knife from my vest with my left hand and raised that arm up as a shield as I ran. I kept the sword low to my right, ignoring the pain from the gash under my arm.

The monster lunged at me and swung low with the sickle, trying to catch my leg. I jumped the blow, but its remaining clawed arm caught me across the shoulder and head, sending me sprawling. I landed hard on my injured arm and lost my sword again, but I hung onto my tanto knife.

Bloodlust drove me to get up and return the favor, but my injured and overworked body wasn't reacting efficiently. Before I could get back on my feet, the Phonoi was standing over me. It reached down, grabbed the remains of my tactical vest, and lifted me to its face, breathing raggedly through the jagged nose slits while staring at me with its beady, dead black eyes. It hissed in my face, spraying me with gobbets of green slime, and then reared back its remaining claw to spear me.

I drew the tanto blade up across the thing's face, but the blade, as well made as it was, could only scratch its armored hide. Still, the Phonoi jerked its head back, giving me just enough time to pull out the sword I'd impaled its chest with and jam it under its chin into its skull.

Remarkably, it didn't fall. It didn't even drop me. It just stood there, unblinking and unmoving. I bellowed a bestial cry in victory, pulled the sword free from the creature's head, and hacked through the arm that held me. I dropped to the ground and pushed the monster onto its back.

The scream that erupted as the spirit tore itself loose was deafening. Rage unlike anything I had ever experienced before permeated every fiber of my being. I dropped my knife, wrenched out the arm still clinging to my vest, and used it to bludgeon the next thing I saw—a pair of Androktasiai tearing apart a dying Spartoi. I ripped into them with gusto, clubbing them with the severed arm and hacking them into pieces within seconds. Their death throes were eerily similar to an orgasm, their faces contorted into cruel mockeries of a smile. If I weren't so happy to see them die, it might have freaked me out a little.

Standing near the collapsed part of the dais where Hecate had been, I searched for the next fight, exhausted and breathing heavily. Some ten yards away from me, Duma was tangling with a few Androktasiai of his own. I only saw three Spartoi still fighting, giving as good as they were getting from the murderous spirits. Several bodies were burning—human, Spartoi, and demon alike—while others had been reduced to charred piles or ash. On the other side of the chained Titan, out of its reach, Medea had retreated to cover but was gathering sparks of energy about her hands as she prepared some sort of spell. My rage was subsiding only because I was too tired to act on it. I fell to one knee, trying to recover enough to move on Medea.

"Duma!" I yelled and pointed back behind the dais with my sword.

He hacked through a female demon's head with a downward blow and then tracked where I was pointing.

"My spear!" I yelled, pushing myself back to my feet.

He took off in a blur, running for where the Pelian Spear had stuck into the wall behind the dais, where it had passed through Hecate. Meanwhile, I found my other sword and skirted around the bound Titan to face Medea. I approached the violently thrashing Perses as cautiously as I could—which, given my current mental state, might have amounted to stomping along, screaming. I tried to focus on Medea.

I passed around the bound Titan's enormous shoulders, willing myself to concentrate on Medea, through my rapidly returning rage, as more of the spirits of manslaughter and murder perished around me. I tried to keep my distance and stay out of Perses's tethered reach, but Medea was waiting in ambush on the other side of him. As soon as I could see what she was up to, she nailed me with a ball of energy that knocked me over into Perses's range, and the Titan's arm lashed out and backhanded me, sending me fifteen feet through the air, out into the cavern, and away from the dais. Once again, my cuirass saved my life. I pushed myself up and got on my feet, feeling a renewed surge of urgency and rage. I looked at Medea and spun my swords at my sides.

I could see the same murderous look in Medea's eyes that I felt. As a human, these dying spirits were affecting her, too. It made me smile a bit, but it probably came off more like a sneer. "You sure you want to end it this way?" I growled as I squared off with her. "We've been around a long time, you and me. It's a shame one of us has to die here today."

"It's taken me hundreds of years to develop a ritual capable of gathering and binding chaos — not to mention locate the Cup of Jamshid and use it to find Prometheus's bane — and once again, you've interfered." She scowled. "You will not survive to do it again."

She tried to direct a spell at me, but I was expecting it and easily avoided the blare of green light. The bolt of energy exploded against the cavern wall hundreds of yards behind us. I batted the next blast back toward her with my sword, sending it crashing into the face of the stone dais, then walked slowly and deliberately closer to her, watching her movements, getting my second wind. She limped heavily as she tracked my movements. The once-beautiful woman was truly haggard and worn, her face drawn and her hands twisted into claws. Her red-and-gold cloak and her stringy red hair made her light skin appear even more pale and wan. There was no way she could continue to throw magic around for much longer.

As we faced off, I could see Duma creeping up onto the dais behind her with my spear. Ranged weapons were not his forte, but all he needed to do was distract her long enough for me to act. I didn't know where the sniper team was, but given that most of the mundanes in the cavern were still just gathering their wits, I doubted they would be of much use. The remaining Spartoi were still battling with death spirits, and I had no idea where Ab was. As far as I could tell, Duma was my only backup.

He drew back to throw the spear, but just as he let it go, she thrust out her left arm behind her as if to punch him. A bolt of erratic green energy lashed out from her hand and from a bracelet around her wrist and smacked him in the chest, throwing him into the cavern wall, twenty yards behind, with a sickening crunch. His body fell limp to the ground. The Pelian Spear flew weakly past Medea and skidded to a stop at the base of the chains holding Perses. The Titan of old ignored the spear and continued to thrash erratically, struggling against his restraints, the once-glowing writing that encircled him now dark.

"I will kill you and your comrades," Medea said, turning back to me with a vicious scowl, "while you watch. That will be nothing compared to my efforts here and the indignities I have suffered at the hands of these execrable god-things and impuissant humans."

"*Imp* what?" I asked, mocking her. "What kind of humans?"

She glanced from me to Perses and back, grinned a toothy smirk, and made a sudden move with her bony left hand that mimicked pulling something toward her. I dodged to my right, but the band of energy she'd loosed flew well behind me and would have missed me even if I hadn't tried to avoid it. My first thought was that she had rotten aim — but I could feel that the blast she projected didn't dissipate.

"Do you know how it feels to be betrayed by the very beings you once worshipped, only to find they are as petty and pathetic as mortals and still presume to use you like a plaything? That wretched beast we called Aphrodite destroyed my life twice out of petty jealousy. The nonhuman freaks feel this world is rightfully theirs. They can have it after I've destroyed it! All my life, weak, intolerant, covetous mortals have attacked me out of fear! These same wretched, gullible mortals choosing to believe in such contemptible gods, bent on destroying each other in homage to them, are unworthy to exist alongside those with true power. And you — you are their lapdog! You beings have ruined this world! If you are all so bent on living in chaos, then I am only too glad to give it to you!"

She was ranting. I had to do something fast. I shifted subtly, tightening my grip on my swords. At once, Medea twisted her left hand, and a female voice cried out in pain behind me. I froze.

Medea raised her right hand toward the ceiling and made a motion as if she were picking fruit from a tree, only more violently, and screamed, "*Apolyo!*"

The cavern began shaking, and small rocks fell around me like a hailstorm. Above me, stalactites began to shake and shear loose along with substantial chunks of the cavern's ceiling. I jumped away, avoiding most of the falling rubble, but the stalactites exploded on the floor, sending razor-sharp shards of limestone and rock in all directions. I let go of my swords and curled into a ball, throwing my arms over my face and head for protection as the debris pelted me and tore into the unarmored parts of my limbs, exacerbating the pain from the wound under my right arm.

As soon as the deluge let up, I got back to my feet and faced Medea again, anger welling deep inside me. She had killed to get the Cup of Jamshid and used innocent people to achieve her goals, luring them with false promises. She had lied to and abused the people she'd frightened into following her, using them as little more than human pawns in her twisted scheme. She had likely just killed my best friend and had used Sarah to get to me. She'd even killed her own children to get even with her ex. She needed to die.

Medea was laughing, but it was definitely more of a deranged cackle than a sound of mirth. Fueled in part by the malice that the dying Androktasiai and Phonoi had infused me with, I'd had just about all I could stand, and I finally snapped. Ignoring my swords just a few feet away, I roared a battle cry and rushed her with every ounce of built-up hatred and violence I had. She raised her free hand and held it up at me, palm outward, like a policeman stopping traffic. Fifteen feet from her, I struck a sheet of energy as solid as a wall and nearly blacked out from the force of the impact. She flicked her wrist and sent me flying sideways ten feet through the air while I fought to remain conscious. I skidded through the stalactite rubble toward the dais in a semi-conscious heap.

Medea cackled maniacally, and her eyes were wide and wild. She twisted her left hand slightly, and I could hear something sliding through the rubble from behind me. The closer it got, the clearer I could hear weak moans. Through the pain and exhaustion, some compulsion inside me kept driving me to get up. I blinked hard a few times, starting to move. As my wits returned, I rolled over to get a glimpse of whoever was moaning behind me, but by the time I'd gotten onto my back, Medea had dragged the figure close enough for me to see: Sarah was hovering a few inches off the floor, limp as roadkill.

CHAPTER 38

"**N**o!" I screamed.

Medea laughed even more wildly, and I pushed myself up to one knee. I had to save Sarah. I spotted my swords lying fifteen feet to my left as I did. I knew Medea was strong, but she couldn't keep throwing around this kind of magic for much longer. I grabbed for my Sig with no idea if it would even kill her.

The nine millimeter got tangled in the tatters of my vest as I struggled to draw it, and I saw Medea flick her hand in my direction. I flew off the ground once again. This time, she jerked me through the air to my left. I managed to free the weapon from its tangle and braced myself for the impact on my left shoulder. As I landed, I tucked my head and rolled into a kneeling firing stance within a yard of my swords. I aimed and pulled the trigger as fast as I could, watching as each round struck some sort of barrier around the witch in a shower of sparks and dull *tink*s. I tossed the gun aside and scrambled for my swords.

Medea cackled again, and just as I recovered the weapons, I jerked backward, landing hard on my back a few yards from Sarah's suspended and unconscious form. The witch was playing with me, though it didn't escape me that her attacks now mostly consisted of tossing me around. I started toward Sarah, but before I could take one step, Medea shrieked wildly and sent Sarah's limp body flying sideways and away from me a few more yards. Sarah moaned at the sudden sharp movement but remained passive.

I feigned a charge at Medea and instead threw one of my swords at her. I didn't expect to hit her, but I was hoping it would be enough to distract her so that I could grab Sarah and get her to safety. Apparently, it worked. The witch flinched, throwing her arms up as if to block the attack, and I began running.

The magical energy around Sarah's body dissipated as Medea recoiled, and Sarah collapsed to the ground with a grunt. I grabbed her by the front of her vest and carried her easily as I ducked around the dais for cover. Just as I made it, Medea screeched "*Apolyo*" again. Only this time, no stalactites fell, just smaller rocks and rubble. I hunched over Sarah, using my armored back to protect her. Several baseball-sized chunks of stone bounced off of me, but this attack was nothing compared to the earlier one. Medea was definitely weakening.

I shoved Sarah against the backside of the dais to protect her and raised my head just enough to peer across the stone stage toward Medea. The moment I did, a small green ball of energy came flying at me. I ducked, but the glowing projectile caromed off the edge of the dais, and the force of the impact knocked me over backward and sprayed me with debris.

I had only one option left: a direct attack. So far, I hadn't been able to make so much as a step toward her without being tossed around, having projectiles thrown at me or the ceiling brought down on my head. The only upside was that the force of the attacks was steadily decreasing. I was exhausted and in pain. I figured I had one good attack left in me, and I'd have to make it count. I crawled back around to the front of the dais to give myself as clear a sight line as possible to Medea and poked my head around to see where she was.

As she limped closer — to less than forty feet away — a bellow that sounded like the combination of a lion and a freight train came from out in the cavern to my left, and something flew toward Medea, though it was slightly off target. One of Ab's long-handled battle-axes crashed into the dais, well in front of the witch, with a clang and a shower of sparks.

Medea's head whipped around toward Ab, and she immediately cupped both of her hands in front of her, gathering energy into her palms. The bracelet on her right wrist glowed brighter and brighter as the ball of energy grew. She jerked, releasing the green light, now the size of a bowling ball. It flew like a comet toward Ab. For a split second, I thought about throwing my sword at the projectile in an attempt to deflect it, but given its speed, I decided that would be futile. I watched helplessly as the green orb collided with Ab in a dull impact that elicited a loud, pain-filled grunt and sent the massive Peri tumbling backward twenty feet into a bone-jarring flop.

Medea grinned and then chuckled as she once again began to limp toward the end of the dais I was using for cover. The closer she got, the more I could see her features darkening. She appeared gaunt and ancient.

"Your friends are going to die trying to save you, Diomedes. How noble." She sneered coldly and began to gather another ball of energy in her hand, staring out at Ab. The bracelet on her wrist barely flashed at all, and the ball of energy sputtered to form in her hand.

"*Erre es korokas*, bitch," I snarled.

She tilted her head, sneered at the old Greek curse, and laughed as she continued to limp closer. There wasn't going to be a better time. I launched myself like a sprinter leaving the stocks, and surprise registered on her face as I came around the edge of the stage, moving as fast as my injuries and exhaustion would let me. It was fast enough.

In her astonishment, the old witch released the orb of energy haphazardly, and I batted it aside with my sword without slowing my charge. I bellowed furiously as I ran at her, covering the twenty-five feet between us so fast she had no time to do anything else. I rammed my sword into her chest, and her face was a mask of bewilderment as I struck her. I lowered my head to gaze into her dark, uncomprehending eyes.

"That's what you get for fucking with my friends," I said through clenched teeth then roared at the top of my lungs and pushed her body back off my sword and into a heap on the ground. "Not to mention my world."

CHAPTER 39

A T ONCE, THE FEW REMAINING Phonoi and Androktasiai collapsed, the magic that had bound them to their forms suddenly exhausted. A few yards to my left, a massive chunk of rubble from Medea's first ceiling collapse grabbed my attention. I walked over, picked up the three-foot-long hunk of rock, and walked back over to Medea with it. Shouting, I raised the boulder overhead with every intention of dropping it on the old witch.

"Do it," a weak voice said from out in the cavern behind me. The voice was gruff and filled with pain, but it was unmistakable. Ab was still alive.

Sudden visions of me standing over Aeneas at Troy flooded my mind. Holding the rock high overhead, I glowered down at the impaled and withered old woman. She was shaking and struggling to breathe. Whatever it was, this was different. I used the boulder to try to kill Aeneas because it was all I could find on the battlefield. This old hag was all but gone, and dropping a rock on her now would be an act of pure anger and hatred. Those were Medea's motivating emotions, not mine. I screamed again in frustration and then tossed the rock on the ground next to her. I shook my head, the anger subsiding as I breathed.

Remembering Sarah, I ran back around the dais to where I'd laid her. She was breathing. Blood crusted her nose, minor cuts and bruises covered her arms, but I saw no serious injuries. Still, she was unconscious. I scooped her up and began wandering around. I didn't know who or what I was searching for, but for the first time in perhaps thousands of years, I felt panicked. My heart began to race, and I felt sick to my stomach. Sarah was hurt, and I had no idea where Frigate and Geek were, or if they were even still alive. For all I knew, Duma was dead, too. To my left, I saw a pair of wounded Spartoi checking among the numerous bodies for their brethren.

Fifty feet away, toward the center of the cavern, I saw Ab slowly getting back to his feet. Nothing else in the cavern was moving. The area around the dais was mostly filled with rubble, and there were lifeless bodies, heavy scorch marks, piles of burning ash, and blood everywhere. The smell of cordite, burnt flesh, and ozone hung heavy in the still, fetid air. Even Perses was unmoving in the aftermath.

"Ab!" I screamed at the top of my lungs, heading toward him with Sarah in my arms. Seeing him moving after Medea's attack gave me hope that everyone else might be okay, too.

"I'm okay," he managed to say, standing bent over, breathing hard, and giving me a thumbs-up.

"What about the others? Frigate! Geek!" I called but got no response.

Still straightening up, Ab just pointed back toward the main entrance tunnel I'd left them in.

"Ab, come take Sarah. Duma's back there." I motioned with my head behind me toward the dais. "I don't know if he's okay."

While his face was still swollen, blistered, and oozy, Ab's eyes registered the same concern I felt. I saw what had happened to Duma, and the thought of it scared me, so instead, I focused on the humans in our group. I handed Sarah off to Ab and ran back to the collapsed main tunnel on legs that burned with exhaustion. I searched frantically for Frigate and Geek along the way but saw only dozens of dead bodies and unconscious and injured people.

My nose hurt, my arm stung where it had been sliced, and I had more random aches and pains than I could count from being thrown around. Even the burns on my legs were hurting again, but I continued searching, undaunted.

I ran into the main passageway and finally found them both there—slumped over but alive, and both, thankfully, beginning to come around. I was relieved and elated. Frigate's dirty-blond hair was crusted with blood on the left side of his head, and his face was covered in crusty, bloody dirt, but he was otherwise okay. I helped Frigate get to his feet and made sure he was okay. Then, feeling guilty, I ran back to find out about Duma.

I found Ab next to Sarah and Duma along the back wall of the cavern behind the collapsed end of the dais. Duma was sitting upright, slapping at Ab's hand as Ab poked at his brother's head. I stopped and breathed deeply for a second and watched the two brothers, relieved beyond words to see Duma still alive. Sarah's unconscious form lay next to him.

Unsure what to do, I bent down to check on her, taking her hand, fearful because she wasn't recovering from the spell like everyone else. I tried to wake her up gently by talking to her. Finally, after a few minutes, her eyelids fluttered, but she still didn't wake. I wondered what I had gotten her into as I held her hand and tried to brush her hair back from her face. I was wiping some of the dirt from her cheek when Frigate limped across the cavern toward us, lending an arm to Geek, who hopped along next to him. I could only manage a half smile as they approached.

"Ow," Geek groaned. "What the bloody hell happened?" His shredded pants hung oddly where his prosthetic leg had been ripped loose, and dirt and dust covered him from head to toe. His face was caked with dried blood, and his right cheek was swollen and purple, but his eyes were wide and lively.

I turned back to Sarah, who had awakened and was watching me with the same kind of expression a person would have the morning after an alcohol-induced blackout. She winced as she rubbed her furrowed forehead. The pupils in her gray eyes were dilated. "What happened?"

"Magic," I responded, too happy to hide my grin.

I just sat there for a long moment, holding her hand, looking across the cavern at the destruction. By this time, many of the prone figures around the cavern had started to stir. I assumed they were Medea's surviving human minions and devotees—the ones stalwart and zealous enough not to flee.

"I'll be right back," I said, finally letting go of Sarah's hand. I'd just realized my job wasn't over yet. I rose to my feet with grim determination, grabbed the one sword I still had, and trudged back toward the nearest group of survivors—two men and a woman in white robes, about fifteen yards away. Human or not, my intention was to kill all that hadn't run away.

Before I could raise a sword, Sarah spoke in a weak voice from behind me. "Wait—you can't." There was a combination of urgency and concern in her voice. "I thought you were sworn to protect us... all of us humans."

"It's not safe to leave them alive," I responded, propping the sword on my shoulder, unable to meet her gaze, afraid she'd see me for what

I truly was. "Even though she intended to kill them all, zealots are hard to predict. They could have viewed death as their destiny, and having been denied their rightful reward, they may want revenge. These people may still pose a threat."

"They're just people. How can we be a threat to you?"

"It's not me I'm worried about," I said, finally looking up at her. She was on her feet and walking unsteadily toward me.

"Steve... Diomedes," she said shakily, "most of these people are frightened and innocent. Most of them never even lifted a weapon against us. Who knows what Medea did to get them to stay? Look what she did to Fakhri's family — and to me. You can't..."

I lowered my sword, my shoulders sagging. Maybe she was right. The concern on Sarah's face lessened when I lowered the sword, though it didn't disappear entirely. More importantly, her comment about Fakhri reminded me of the promise I'd made the girl. Right now that was more important.

I stood there for a second and then walked off to check on the Spartoi and remind the surviving squad members of our secondary objective of finding the Fawaz family. I would not leave without them. And meanwhile, I had to locate and recover the Cup and then figure out the best way to free Perses without getting my head ripped off, and I had to get the Ally-thingy chain back. Then I would decide what to do with these survivors.

Back along the far side of the dais, the Spartoi were gathering their dead and wounded. Only a few of Athena's mercenaries were still alive, and only two were fully ambulatory. These creatures were soldiers, so while their injuries or deaths from helping me bothered me, the fact that they had done so honorably outweighed the guilt. Combat was the only life they knew or understood.

The most fit of the survivors was their leader, who had a nasty gash across his face that ran through his nose, nearly severing the tip. The cut was deep and gaping but bloodless, making it only slightly less gory than it appeared. These beings bore even the most intense pain with ease, marking injuries as badges of honor. To them, death and injury were as natural as eating and sleeping were to mundanes.

The warriors were tending the injuries of those who would live and helping to ease the passing of those who wouldn't last much longer. Finally, they gave all their dead brethren the equivalent of last rites in a quick but respectful ceremony. All of it was done with the stoicism I'd expect from an emotionless creature whose life revolved around battle.

I could relate to their view of life more than I liked to admit, and I'd seen their post-battle ritual before. This time, the ritual reminded me of just how human I still was. My life was about more than fighting and death, even though that made up the bulk of it. For me, mortal combat served a purpose, a means to an end. I did what I did to protect humanity.

As I silently watched the warriors honor their fallen comrades, I thought of Sarah and realized that I hadn't allowed myself to really care for anyone for nearly a thousand years because... well, just because. But it occurred to me that without a connection to other people and without caring for someone, I might as well just be one of the Spartoi—a hollow tin soldier.

When the Spartoi were finished, I reminded the squad leader that we still needed to locate the Fawaz family, alive or dead. He made a curt bow of his head and then rallied his men without hesitation to continue their mission.

Back behind the dais, Ab was helping Duma to his feet. Both were looking better, but Duma was still far from being able to move unassisted, and Ab moved slowly and deliberately but with determination. They argued about the Ifrit Ab had tackled and killed. When I walked up, they just stared at me and exhaled heavily with the corners of their mouths turned up in the barest hint of smiles. The expression was nearly identical for both, demonstrating the depth of their familial bond. I'd seen it too many times before.

"Um..." I tried to clear my throat and then turned away, catching sight of Perses as I did. "You got the pouch, Duma?" I asked, eager to change the subject.

"Yeah, on my belt," he said, coughing. "But you'll have to get it yourself."

Ab grabbed the pouch from Duma's belt and threw it to me, and I returned to Perses's prone form. The Titan was quiet, as if asleep. His naked body was covered in dirt and soot and surrounded by rubble and a few dead bodies. There wasn't going to be an easy way to do this. I started by kneeling next to the chain that held the giant's feet, since it was out of range of his hands. I dug into the pouch and pulled a little of its contents out into my palm. It was an herb called raskovnik that resembled a four-leaf clover.

Raskovnik, or razkovniche, was a remarkable plant with the unique property of being able to unlock any lock, magical or otherwise. The problem was finding it. Basically, there were two methods: lock up turtle or hedgehog babies and wait for the mother to gather the herb to release its offspring — which seemed cruel and tricky — or chain up a maiden and have her walk through a field. If she came out the other side unchained, the herb was in that field.

Sarah had helped Duma find it for us, and I had no doubt I would hear about him surprising her with the undignified field task once this was all finished. I wasn't looking forward to that conversation with her, but my options for opening the locks on Perses's chain were limited — I could either use the herb or break the lock. Though my motives were unselfish enough, I didn't want breaking it to be our only option, so we needed raskovnik, and Sarah had been our maiden fair.

I crushed the plant into my palm and sprinkled it into the keyhole. The lock snapped open with a resounding *snick*, and the Titan God of Destruction stirred only slightly.

"Perses, I'm trying to help you get free," I said calmly, hoping to keep things from getting out of hand. This being was known for creating havoc — on the order of natural disasters — for kicks, and I was about to set him free. He just lay there, breathing steadily. I gave him a wide berth, now that his legs were free, and walked cautiously back up toward his head. His eyes were closed, and his face was peaceful enough, so I took out more of the herb and crushed it between my fingers, keeping a watchful eye on his face. I quietly crept toward the lock on the chain holding his arms, which were as long as I was tall and as broad as my torso. Being this close to the lock on his arms also put me within reach of the Pelian Spear. It had ended up by the chain after Duma's wayward throw. I quickly but quietly kicked it out of the way to avoid the possibility of being skewered with it. It impacted the dais with a clank that echoed through the now quiet chamber. I squeezed my eyes closed and froze in my tracks.

I was well within Perses's reach, but he didn't move. I breathed a heavy sigh of relief, and as I opened my eyes, I saw him focused intently on me.

Oh, shit. "Relax, Perses," I tried to say as soothingly as possible, holding my hands up, one palm out and the other holding the herb pinched between thumb and index finger. "I'm just trying to help you. I just want to set you free. This is raskovnik. It'll open the lock." I wiggled the hand holding the crushed herbs and kept my other hand up to show I was unarmed.

The giant's softball-sized brown eyes just followed my movements as he breathed heavily through his mouth.

I slowly crept forward, holding my breath once I got close enough for him to either rip my head off or kill me with his stinky breath. I had no idea what the beings back in his realm ate, but it stank like week-old garbage and rotten fish mixed with Limburger cheese. It made my eyes water.

As gingerly and overtly as I could, I ground the herb between my fingers, sprinkling it into the hole in the lock. Sure enough, as soon as the tumblers in the lock snapped open, Perses surged to his feet and howled loudly enough to rattle the cavern again. I dropped and tucked into a fetal position near his feet, half expecting to become a soccer ball.

Surprisingly, the Titan stepped over me to where I'd stabbed Medea and then approached the crater in the stage where Hecate had been. "Where is the lying bitch?" Perses screamed. He picked up the carcass of a Phonoi and threw it against the far wall with a wet thump that echoed across the cavern. His eyes tracked around the cavern then back to the crater, and he screamed in anger. "And where's my daughter?"

I immediately got to my feet behind Perses, expecting to see Medea's dead body. I had stabbed her right where he was standing. I had seen her dying. There was no way she could have survived. Someone had to have taken her body. I didn't know if I was more confused or pissed. I felt sick.

"Medea was right there, I swear!" I shouted, holding up my hands in surrender. "But I sent your daughter back to your native realm."

I bolted around Perses to pick up my spear and get on the dais, in case of further violence. The position also gave me a more elevated view of the cavern. Part of me was hopeful I might actually spot someone dragging Medea's body off. *Damn.* Even in death, she was a sneaky bitch.

"Very well." Perses watched me intently. We stood eye to eye now that I was on the elevated stone stage. "I am in your debt, Guardian."

With that, the Titan simply disappeared without as much as a sound.

I hopped down from the dais, walked back to my team behind it, and sat down heavily next to Ab and Duma with the Pelian Spear in hand. I practically fell over backward out of frustration, with the spear across my chest. The brothers just stood there, wide-eyed. Everyone gawked at me with equally astonished expressions.

"Dude, you got balls as big as church bells," Ab said, making Duma start laughing before breaking into a raspy cough. Even I laughed for a second.

"Did any of you see where Medea went?" I asked, sitting back up, hooking a thumb over my shoulder toward the spot where I'd stabbed Medea.

Everyone shook their heads. I ran the whole scenario over again in my mind. I'd stabbed her right through the chest. There was no way she could have gotten away on her own. *I stabbed her right through the freakin' chest.* When I tracked down her shriveled old ass, I'd definitely drop the damned rock on her head, put a stake through her heart, *and* bury her upside down, too, just to make sure.

I shook my head. "Crap. When you're ready, get your asses to the rendezvous point." I patted Ab on the shoulder and got back to my feet. "I'm not done yet."

CHAPTER 40

NEEDED TO LOCATE THE SWORD I'd hurled at Medea trying to save Sarah. It took me a few minutes, but I found it stuck in some rubble near the crater Hecate had made when I speared her. I couldn't help but smile when I saw the depression the so-called goddess had left behind. At least I knew *she* was gone.

I glanced back toward Sarah, Frigate, and Geek, who were sitting against the cavern wall and talking, and I exhaled heavily. Then I watched as dozens of Medea's followers continued to wake throughout the cavern while others began to stagger around, shocked and confused. Sarah was probably right. I didn't need to kill the survivors.

Those followers that were now on their feet lurched around aimlessly, tripping over dead bodies and live compatriots who hadn't woken up yet. They displayed no regard for the dying and wounded among them, and they ignored my team completely.

It bothered me that Medea had intended to kill them, but I also wasn't at peace with the idea that many of these people were probably here willingly. Even if Medea had lied to them, it was likely that the only part she lied about was the necessity of their deaths. Worse, she might have told them they would die for the cause. In that case, their survival made them unfulfilled martyrs. It was hard to stop people who were willing to die for their beliefs — that was exactly the kind of zeal that could drive one of those people to drag Medea's body away someplace where a person could spend a lifetime trying to resurrect the old biddy. That kind of unquestioned devotion was what worried me most.

As I walked across the cavern toward the main entrance, I saw the Spartoi leader come out of a partially hidden tunnel at its mouth. He carried a little girl in his arms. Behind him, another of the dragon-tooth mercenaries carried a dark-haired old woman. The woman and the girl were both dressed in filthy, tattered robes. I felt a small sense of relief as I approached them.

Up close, I could see that the woman wasn't as old as I'd first thought. Her physical condition made her appear much older. She and the child were cadaverously thin, covered in sores, caked in dirt, and reeking of their own filth. The woman's legs were withered and useless, and her taut skin gave her an ancient, almost mummified appearance. The Spartoi were unfazed by both their appearance and smell.

In Farsi, I asked them both if they knew Fakhri Fawaz, and they almost imperceptibly bowed their heads in affirmation. The young girl couldn't even lift her head from the squad leader's chest as she did so. Despite the filth and the emaciated features, I could see the resemblance to Fakhri.

Satisfied these were her mother and sister, I spoke to the squad leader. "Have your men ready to leave as soon as possible. And I need to ask you to carry the Pelian Spear for me. I don't want to take it with me while I locate the Cup and finish looking around."

He took the spear and tucked it under the girl. As useful as the spear was, it was unwieldy in tight spaces, and I didn't want anything slowing down my search for the Cup, Medea's body, and whoever had dragged her off.

"General Diomedes, you should begin your search down that tunnel," the squad leader said without expression, tossing his head back in the direction they'd come from.

"That's where you found them?" I asked, gesturing at the woman and child.

"Yes, but it also seems to be some sort of living quarters and work space with many books and papers, as well as devices of magic and sorcery," he replied in the same deadpan tone of voice.

I clapped the squad leader on the shoulder, and the Spartoi continued back toward the rest of the group. As the Spartoi left, Sarah and Frigate passed them, moving in my direction, propping Geek up between them as they walked. Geek, despite his battered and bloody appearance and the loss of his prosthetic leg, was grinning like an idiot and jabbering on about Jinns and witches. Sarah and Frigate just smirked and tolerated it, shaking their heads as he droned on.

"Head back to rendezvous. Ab and Duma will follow along with the remaining Spartoi and the Fawaz woman and child." I pointed toward the Spartoi they'd just passed. "Just make sure you're prepared for anything that may pop up along the way. Some of the survivors may still be looking to become martyrs."

"What about you?" Sarah's brows were tented, and she frowned at me.

I didn't want to remind them that Medea's missing body could mean that she was still alive in there somewhere, requiring me to find her. The last thing I wanted was for them to feel as if all this had been for nothing. "I need to find the Cup of Jamshid and make sure everything is secure, and then I'll follow shortly. It won't take me long. I just have to check out a few more things."

"Be careful, Chief," Frigate said, his expression solemn.

"I'll be fine. Just clear out. Oh, and leave me your grenades, just in case I need to plug any holes when I leave."

"Grenades are in our gear bags with our guns where we left 'em," Frigate said, pointing up the entrance tunnel.

The wounded trio limped back to the rest of the group, and Sarah glanced at me over her shoulder and flashed me a suspicious grimace as they hobbled off. She knew I wasn't being completely honest with her. If it kept her safe, I didn't care.

I headed for the spot down the main entrance the sniper team had used. I threw their gear bags and grenades into a single bag and then returned to explore the passage where the Spartoi had found the woman and child.

The passageway lay concealed behind a rockfall just to the north of the junction between the entrance tunnel and the main cavern. Everything about it was different from the others. Like the entrance tunnel, this passage's curved rock walls were completely smooth, and the floor was dry and level — not naturally formed. It was evenly and brightly lit, but as with the main cavern, I couldn't determine the source of the light, which was a warm, pleasant glow that seemed to emanate from the rock wall itself. The smell wafting up from farther inside was musky, woody, and very exotic. Though I could smell a wood fire, the scents were more of a pleasant woodsy or earthy smell and not burnt at all. All of it was totally out of place in a rock cave.

The featureless tunnel continued straight for twenty yards, widening as it progressed, until it reached a turn that jogged to the left. I stopped to listen, swords at the ready, but the only sound I could hear was water dripping from around the corner. I had no idea what I might encounter given that the Spartoi had already been down here. There could be other prisoners, but because they weren't ordered to free anyone but the Fawaz family, the soldiers would have ignored them. Part of me hoped I'd round the corner and see Medea standing there.

I cautiously poked my head around and saw a spacious, well-lit room, thoroughly decorated with magnificent rugs and tapestries and beautiful modern furniture. There was a sleeping area with a four-poster bed, a comfortable living area, and an extensive workspace complete with a giant, boiling cauldron. *Hey, clichés are clichés for a reason.* Several of the floor coverings didn't appear to be carpets. A few were animal hides, including a shaggy pelt next to the bed, which had to have belonged to the most massive golden bear in history. The open central space in the room was devoid of any floor coverings, though some type of writing obscured part of the ground in a manner similar to what had surrounded Perses.

I came around the corner and into the mouth of the room. If I hadn't known it was in a cave, and if it weren't for the even illumination that came from no visible source, I might have thought I was in a Victorian home in New England. It had to be Medea's personal chambers.

I worked my way along the far left side of the room, where a good-sized cage held a nasty-looking salamander — not one of the slimy little amphibians kids kept in bowls but a fire elemental, three feet long and, well, on fire. It was banging around in its cage as I approached to get a better look. A long, low workbench was covered with papers and books filled with notations in writing I couldn't identify and symbols I couldn't decipher. I set my swords down and began searching for the Cup of Jamshid.

I rifled through the seemingly random collection of papers until I came across a torn page that contained a partial list of names of some of the nastiest dictators and most unstable countries around the world, including Assad from Syria, Gaddafi from Libya, Mubarak from Egypt, and Kim of North Korea. There were also names of leaders of various Paranthropoi races, some of whom I recognized. Each one had a unique symbol or some sort of sigil next to it. A chill traveled up my spine. I recognized some of the symbols from the circle of writing that had surrounded Perses back in the main cavern.

Some of those leaders were so deranged to begin with that it would only take a slight push to send them completely over the edge. If that happened to even half of the names on the list, the world could be at war for decades. And if she really could affect the various races of Parans around the world... I didn't want to think about it, so I stuffed the stack of papers into my bag and kept trying to locate the Cup.

I shoved books off shelves and opened cabinets until I came across a small bronze vessel sitting in the center of an elaborate, narrow, chest-high table that looked somewhat like a lectern. Next to the table was a workbench. I recognized the Cup's fluted shape and etchings instantly. I grabbed it and stuffed it into the gear bag with the papers and then shifted my attention to the rest of the room, determining what else I should check out before I left. As I looked around, the writing on the floor farther back, near the center of the room, caught my eye. The more I studied it, the more I realized it was more than just writing.

I approached and circled the spot cautiously, examining it. It was a circle of symbols set in the floor like numbers on a clock. Each symbol was connected to the other by a series of fine inlaid lines, and all of them were surrounded by another circle that was about fifteen feet in diameter. Each symbol was made of a different material — wood, bone, and various stones and metals — and the connecting lines were copper. The outer circle was a bright metal that could have been silver, nickel, or even platinum, for all I knew. I could feel a potent but subtle vibration of power emanating from it, but I couldn't see it, which suggested to me that it was some sort of portal or doorway that wasn't currently in use. Unlike the circle of writing out in the cavern, I didn't recognize any of these symbols from the pages I'd taken.

I didn't know much about magic, but I knew that when someone surrounded symbols with a circle like this, the perimeter would contain and isolate whatever the symbols conjured or created. This one was elaborate, to say the least. The conjuring circle was probably Medea's, which meant that its purpose, whatever it was, was evil. And if it was hers, I wanted to destroy it. I retrieved my swords from the table and dragged them through the sigils. The supernatural blade gouged through the stone floor and materials that made up the inlaid design, ruining it as if I'd dragged my foot across a circle of salt. As I scarred the circle, a slight pop went through my head like an altitude drop as the power was released and the circle was ruined.

That'll show her. Maybe I could leave a burning bag of poop on her doorstep, too.

After my wanton vandalism, I returned to my inspection of Medea's opulent chambers. I recognized one of the tapestries from the keep she'd been holed up in when I attacked her with two of Arthur's knights, almost a thousand years ago in England when she was calling herself Morgan le Fay. The tapestry was beautiful and close to thirty feet long. It depicted a fight between an enormous green dragon and knights led by a golden-armored warrior.

That was the last time we'd faced each other, and she'd managed to escape then, too. The reminder of yet another failure to destroy Medea just pissed me off. I grabbed a clay pot from a nearby shelf and threw it at the tapestry, shattering the vessel. It didn't really make me feel any better, but the action did draw my eye to a series of dog-crate-sized cages hidden behind another tapestry that featured a battle with which I wasn't familiar. I ducked behind the tapestry to view the cages. All of them were full of human waste, dirty rags, and maggot-ridden food. Several still held the desiccated corpses of prisoners. The cages couldn't have been more than three feet cubed, and I knew instantly that at least two of these had held Fakhri's mother and sister. Medea's inhumanity knew no bounds.

Turning in disgust, I began searching the living space at the rear of the chamber, where several massive bookcases were jammed with tomes, baubles, and curios. Some emitted weak magical auras, but most did not. A prodigious cabinet of curiosities among the shelves housed a freakish collection of skulls, both deformed and normal, and preserved specimens that in normal circles might be perceived as oddities but that weren't, in my opinion, all that strange. Where I came from, three-headed dogs just weren't that unusual.

Over near the cauldron in her work area — over a fire that produced no smoke, only heat — was yet another workbench that held containers of some kind of liquid metal, and simple molds for quarter-sized disks. Several dull metal slugs lay on the desk. I searched around for magnets and didn't see any.

I put my swords away and quickly undid the strap on my greave to get at the pendant taped to my forearm. I pressed that disk into a mold, careful not to remove my finger from it. It fit perfectly, verifying that the device was indeed one of Medea's designs. I twined the live pendant's chain around my hand to secure it and tucked the disk under the leather wrappings on my palm. Then I picked up one of the lifeless blanks and stared absentmindedly at it. And that was when an idea came to me.

I could throw all my grenades onto the sigil on the floor, along with the magnets I carried in my shredded vest, then chuck the disk at it and run like hell. Since the disk wouldn't implode until it got near the magnets, I should be okay as long as I threw it from far enough away. Besides, if the size of the vortex created by the device was related to the power of the magnets, then the ones I had wouldn't create that large a singularity until the first one set the grenades off. Still, the implosion-explosion should serve to obliterate most of the stuff in the room and set the witch back a few years until I could find her again. It beat leaving a bag of poop, anyway.

I set to work on my plan and placed the collection of grenades, including flash-bangs, white phosphorus, thermite and frags, as well as Sarah's magnetic earrings, at the center of the ruined sigil. Then I revisited the worktable for one last search of Medea's papers. I wanted to grab as much as I could for the Metis Foundation to analyze. I was making a valiant effort, riffling through page after page of unintelligible writing, until I got an odd sense that I was no longer alone.

"Did you really think I'd die that easily, Diomedes?" said a cracked and ragged voice. Medea was scowling, her eyes wide and crazy and her robe shredded and bloody, but she was very much alive and using Frigate as a shield.

"Honestly, I was hoping. Don't you know when to give up and die?" I tried to hide my surprise. I tossed the book I'd been holding back onto the table. "I like what you've done with the place. Nice and homey... if you're Voldemort." I snickered.

She just glared at me. Frigate stared dully off into the middle distance and was incoherent.

"You know, the bad guy from *Harry Potter*? Don't tell me—"

"Enough!" she shouted. "I told you I would kill your friends and let you watch, but he will have to do. Then I will finally kill you."

"Whoa, whoa, whoa," I said, raising my hands in surrender.

"Just relax."

The chain from the necklace I'd wrapped around my hand came loose, dangling from the disk I'd tucked into the wrappings around my palm. I could see recognition register on her face as her eyes shifted rapidly between the necklace and me.

"Oh, this?" I said, holding the hand with the disk up slightly higher. "It's just a souvenir. I have the earrings that match, too. Well, had, at any rate. They're over there with the grenades." I jerked my head toward the pile I'd made. "If it's yours, I'll give it back," I said, holding the disk out toward her.

She backed up, dragging Frigate with her by the throat. He was being very compliant as all this happened.

"Frigate! Hey, Frigate!" I shouted. "You okay?" *Dammit.* The last thing I wanted was to put anyone back in danger.

"He is for now, but his mind is mine," Medea said, sneering. "You will watch as I destroy it."

"Not if I destroy you first." I tossed the dud disk I had kept toward the grenades in an elaborate show.

"You fool," she shrieked and let go of Frigate, who collapsed. She held out her arms toward the conjuring circle and murmured. When nothing happened, her eyes became wide. She jerked slightly and then faltered back a few steps.

The instant she threw her arms up toward the conjuring circle, I made my move. I pulled out a sword with my free hand and vaulted over the table, landing between her and Frigate. Her confusion at the lack of an explosion or the lack of a spell going off — or both — combined with my sudden movement had her totally off balance, and in her weakened state, she nearly fell as I landed in front of her. I swung my sword, aiming for her outstretched right arm, and took it off below the shoulder.

She collapsed on her knees, screaming, and I brought the hilt of my sword down on her head as hard as I could with a resounding crunch that instantly deformed the shape of her skull. She crumpled silently to the floor, blood running down her face onto the ground around her crushed head. This time she was done, but to make sure, I removed her head with a single blow across her neck and then threw it into the pile with the grenades.

"Let's see you walk away from that one." I walked back to help Frigate, who was beginning to wake up.

"What happened? Where am I?" he asked, obviously bewildered.

"It's okay. We're getting out of here right now." I put the sword away and offered him my hand.

I had to fight a sudden sense of panic about the safety of the rest of the team since Medea had managed to get to Frigate. Since she was definitely dead now, I was better off working on my plan to destroy everything she'd left behind. Even with Medea dead, the last thing I needed was for some wannabe to find this place.

Frigate was wobbly, but he was able to stand on his own. He shook his head violently, as if clearing it of cobwebs, and then focused on me with relief. "I remember thinking you were in trouble and needed my help, so I left the others and ran back and then... are we back in the damn cave?" He looked around.

"Yeah, I'll explain later. Meantime, move that way as fast as you can," I said, pointing to the tunnel behind him.

I walked back over to the worktable and grabbed another pile of papers and books and shoved them into the bag before checking to make sure Medea was still dead. Even with her head fifteen feet away from her, I wouldn't have put it past her to survive somehow. Of all her skills, she was most adept at survival. I glanced at her crushed and severed head among the grenades and the dead, lifeless eyes within and felt reasonably sure even this was beyond her resurrection capabilities. I tossed the little metal disk toward the pile in the center of the room and ran.

The implosion rocked the cavern, and wind rushed past me, tugging me backward, which was an altogether different sensation. Medea's chamber began to collapse behind me. I cleared the tunnel and sprinted into the main cavern just as the ceiling began to fall in, which caused a chain reaction, bringing down stalactites that exploded all over the cave like carpet bombs. I had to block the flying shrapnel from my face with my armored left forearm as I ran. The grenades had a bit more punch than I'd expected. Medea's remaining followers were panicking again, running around and knocking each other over, trampling those who fell.

Somehow, though, through the confusion, I managed to find Frigate heading for the opening my team had originally entered through, limping along at a fair rate for someone with a twisted ankle and a head full of dust bunnies. When I caught up to him, much to his embarrassment, I grabbed him, tossed him over my shoulder in a fireman's carry, and kept running as fast as I could, dodging half-crazed people as I went. The cavern behind us continued to collapse, sending a thick, choking cloud of dust and debris through the tunnel as I ran with Frigate over my shoulder. I didn't stop until I made it to the snowy plateau outside.

Once we were clear of the cave system, I put Frigate down, and we both began trudging down the mountain to find the rest of our team without saying a single word. An hour later, Frigate and I finally caught up with the surviving members of our group. Sarah was the first to see us. She and Geek were at the back of the ragtag team — she supported him on one side while he used the Pelian Spear as a makeshift crutch. She let Frigate take her place helping Geek and then smiled at me in a contentious way that I didn't understand and strode toward me purposefully. I gave her a weary half smile as she stopped in front of me. Then she punched me. Right in the jaw. Hard.

"What the hell?" I said, rubbing my jaw, holding my arm out to keep her from closing in again. The blow hurt but not nearly as much as the surprise of her punching me.

"What the hell?" She gestured wildly with her hands. "What the hell? Exactly. What the hell were you thinking?" She was still ranting as she stormed back toward the rest of the group farther down the mountain. "That was for that shit with Duma in freaking Serbia looking for that fucking plant! I suppose you know what he had to do — what I had to do to find that stuff!"

I just rubbed my jaw, shook my head, and fell in behind her. She was probably right. I deserved it.

I flinched when she turned around again, still glaring at me, her mouth pressed into a small, thin line. She walked back to me and climbed onto a rocky outcropping to reach my eye level. I flinched, readying myself for another assault, but this time she leaned in and kissed me.

I didn't remember much after that.

CHAPTER 41

A COUPLE OF DAYS AFTER WE got back, I was on my way to the Metis Foundation yet again. Athena had placed Fakhri and her family in a private hospital, and they were doing remarkably well, considering what they'd been through. I had returned the Cup of Jamshid and the Chain to Athena the minute we returned. My entire team had been debriefed, and I'd been round and round about everything multiple times, so I wasn't sure why she wanted me to come in.

Ab, Duma, Geek, and Frigate were staying with me, and Sarah was staying in a nearby hotel. Even after kissing me, she was still pissed at that whole raskovnik thing. I couldn't really blame her. It *was* kind of demeaning. I still wasn't sure what that kiss was all about. At least I understood the punch.

Ab was pretty much recovered from his burns, and Duma was going to be fine. They were planning to leave the next day, though I didn't know where they were going. *Damned Peris heal so fast it's sickening. My burned legs will hurt for days. And Ab and Duma won't even have any scars to show for it, either.*

Frigate was leaving that day to go back to his family. It had been good working with him again, but he was a family man, and I hated involving him in my world. It changed everything. He took things in stride and was behaving exactly the way we always did after a tough op. He was trying not to dwell on the specifics of the mission and acting slightly more boisterous than normal. I could imagine that he was also somewhat relieved to find out that the dealings he'd had in my world as a kid were real and that he wasn't crazy. He was a good man and a good friend. And I would never forget the image of the Ifrit's torso exploding from the impact of the Raufoss fifty-caliber round he fired to save my ass. That was a first for me.

Geek had been at the Metis Foundation offices every day since we'd returned. In fact, when I walked in, the first thing I saw was Geek inside the Bullpen, pointing and gesturing wildly at some data on a few of the monitors on the back wall while half a dozen people watched and took notes. Apparently, Geek had endeared himself to Athena by belittling the Metis Foundation's security setup the moment he entered the offices two days earlier. I'd tried to warn her. To my surprise, she took him seriously and had the staff working with him to redo most of the security protocols. Of course, his expertise was invaluable, and I got a feeling I was going to be seeing much more of him in the future. The sight of him holding court, droning on and on about some technical minutiae without the fear of his audience falling asleep, made me smile.

I crossed straight over to the stairs without stopping to address the annoying receptionist. I'd been at the offices many hours over the last two days, so I was pretty sure she knew who I was by then, stinky or not. Besides, I was still convinced she wouldn't be there much longer.

The door at the top of the stairs opened and closed behind me, and I walked straight past Brey without saying a word and right to Athena's office.

"You should know—" Brey said. After two days of debriefings, I wasn't in the mood to stop and find out what it was she thought I should know. The door slid open, and I walked in.

To my surprise, there was another person already there, though no one was talking. In fact, the way Athena smiled at me, I got the feeling they were actually waiting for me, which immediately put me on the defensive. Since Athena never revealed her true self to normal mortals, having another person in her office also meant I needed to check the nameplate on the desk.

I should have stopped and talked with Brey. I sighed and eyed the marble plaque at the front of the odd desk. The name "Sebastian W. Exley" was embossed in gold above the title of Senior Intelligence Analyst, whatever the hell that meant. Great, today she was "Exley," the uptight, arrogant British prig she used for seriously high-ranking officials.

I saw Athena dressed simply in a gray suit with her hair pulled back. I was told she usually projected her Exley persona as dressing in expensive suits with perfectly coiffed salt-and-pepper hair and drinking tea with his pinky extended.

The other person in the room was a very tall, bald, middle-aged man who probably was regularly mistaken for a pro basketball player. His age could have been anywhere from thirty-five to fifty-five. He was dressed in a black-on-black suit that must have been very expensive and fit him like a glove.

"Diomedes, this is Gregor Chahine," Athena as Exley said, standing to introduce us.

"Pleased to meet you, Gregor." I presented my hand.

"A pleasure to make your acquaintance as well, Tydides," he said with a heavy accent that suggested an origin in Sub-Saharan Africa.

While he may not have known he was sitting in front of Athena, he certainly knew who I was. As he reached for my hand, a pinkish energy surrounded his fingers and engulfed my hand with a noticeable chill before receding. I peered at him sideways because, other than that, I saw no sign of an aura, nor could I feel any supernatural power. He chuckled at my confusion. Athena was also smiling, clearly pleased to have me off balance.

"Mr. Chahine is the Ipsissimus of the Hermetic Order of the Golden Dawn," she said, sitting back down.

He bowed his head at the formal introduction, and I shook my head in acknowledgement, raising my eyebrows as I did so. Out of respect, I sat after he did. The man sure didn't look as silly as his title sounded.

"I asked the Ipsissimus to join us because we are still having trouble deciphering some of the materials you brought back." Athena leaned forward onto the desk. "And he has some questions for you, as well."

I nodded and leaned on one elbow.

"We feel confident that we understand the 'what,'" Gregor said. "It is the 'why' that still troubles us. Perhaps if you go over it again with me, we might glean some sort of an idea. The fact that she could harness that kind of energy at all is... incomprehensible." He spread his hands as he finished.

I immediately became suspicious. It was human nature to push our boundaries, and now that magic users knew harnessing chaos was possible, of course they wanted to "better understand it." That was the origin story of every revolutionary technology-turned-weapon that had ever been created.

In the core of my mind, something made me feel my suspicions were well founded. I saw Athena's eyes flash blue only for an instant, and I knew the sensation came from her. She distrusted the Order's motives, as well. That meant I needed to proceed cautiously.

"As I said in my report, Medea needed the Cup of Jamshid to locate the Qarun Treasure, which apparently contained that Ally-whatever chain. She used her human connection to the terrorist organization Jundullah to carry out the necessary attack to recover the relics and probably because she enjoyed the chaos terrorism created. Attacks like that likely helped her keep her followers united for a modern cause. Of course, that's just speculation because I didn't exactly ask her before I cut her head off." I leaned back in my chair, trying to decide how much to say.

"How did she expect to harness and then release the energy?" Gregor asked, shifting in his seat so that he could place his hand on his chin. I could see the barest hint of his pink aura flash in his eyes as he watched me.

"Can't really say for sure," I said, shrugging. "I'm not much with magic. That's why I brought back those papers and books." I gestured over to a table in the room's corner that held the stack of materials I'd brought back.

"Very well." Chahine tented his hands in front of him, staring down into his lap. "The only other precedent the Order can find for harnessing and controlling chaos is Pandora's Box, given to humans as a test by Protogenoi—one that we, as a species, failed. The Order are operating under the assumption that Medea was trying to create a similar device, this time using Perses as the vessel, likely because she could not create one powerful enough to contain that amount of power on her own. We have no idea why she chose to use Perses as the vessel, nor what damage a device like that could have wrought had the ritual been successful."

"Medea likely chose to use Perses because of his penchant for destruction," Athena said, sitting back in her chair. "As a Protogenoi he would have thrived on chaotic and destructive forces here on Earth. Hecate, as his daughter, would have had a blood bond with him, allowing her to manipulate his energy in our world, especially if they had physical control over him. Or so Athena says."

"Right," I said, trying not to sound totally out of my depth. "I can't speak much from a magical standpoint, but I do know that chaos begets more chaos. If her intentions were to destabilize already shaky governments, as some of the information in those papers suggests, then the potential for long-term, virtually self-perpetuated worldwide conflict was very real."

No one responded to that statement for several minutes. Smugness crept over me for bringing up such a profound statement—especially in front of the most powerful mortal magic user on the planet. I wasn't about to bring up the symbols connected to the various governments and rulers that had encircled Perses. Athena said that since the symbols could represent those people in a spell, then a wizard, or witch in this case, could use them to form a direct link to those people, allowing Medea to direct all that energy like water through a hose, right where she wanted it.

Chahine eyed me suspiciously, and then his eyes drifted to Athena as Exley. He could tell there was more we weren't telling him, but he was unsure what to do about it. "It is a good thing for humanity, and indeed all the beings of this world, that we have such a Guardian as you to help us," Chahine finally said, *almost* without any hint of derision.

That was enough for me. I shifted in my chair as if to get up, and the Ipsissimus put his hand on my arm to stop me. "Before you go," the Ipsissimus said in a much more genuine tone, "I would very much like to have a chat about your dealings with Medea in the past, so that we may update our archives, if that would be acceptable to you."

My eyes wandered to Athena only briefly and then back to Chahine before I sat back in the chair, getting comfortable. I knew Athena would want me to do it under the guise of keeping up good relations. "Sure, no problem."

"I shall leave you two to talk, then," Athena said. "If you'll excuse me?"

Chahine got up when Athena did. They shook hands and she left, glowering ever so briefly at me and inducing a slight pressure in my head. I took her silent admonition to mean, "Play nice."

After about an hour of storytelling, Chahine thanked me and then left. I followed him to the outer office with every intention of harassing Brey but instead ran into Athena.

"Thank you for your willingness to talk with the Ipsissimus," she said, standing in front of me with a file folder full of papers.

"No problem."

She smiled for a second before I saw something else on her face, something I had never seen before until a few days ago — motherly concern. The corners of her mouth turned up, she pursed her lips, and her eyes softened as she looked at me.

"Diomedes, Son of Tydeus... my Guardian," she said, using about the most formal reference for me I could think of short of my real full name. "Please be careful."

"Always," I said, surprised by her tone and the formal address and apprehensive as a child about to be punished by a parent.

"With Sarah."

"Oh."

"I do not have to remind you that she is mortal," she said, shifting into a tone that suggested a lecture was coming, "or that what you do for the sake of humankind in my stead is inherently dangerous —"

"Then why did you?" I asked, annoyed that *she*, the virgin goddess, was going to lecture *me* about my love life.

She held up a hand, and her smile grew. It was warm and genuine. "I do not want this to become a conflict between us. I merely want you to think about her in all of this. Clearly, your affections for her are stronger than you have felt in a long time. I will not tell you no, nor will I give my blessing."

"Good thing I'm not asking, then," I said, now fully pissed off that she wanted to interfere in my life.

"I am not just concerned for you, but her as well, Diomedes."

Before I could respond, Brey walked in through the outer door. I walked out past the Elf without saying a word.

Rather than head home and deal with a houseful of guests, I drove to the dock to do some work on the boat and get my mind off of that conversation. The plan worked for about three minutes before I began obsessing. Not about my relationship with Sarah — that was too hard. Instead, I kept thinking about the scrap of paper I'd found back in Medea's chambers along with the list of names and countries.

At the very top of the scrap, and partially obscured by a tear in the paper, was part of a word circled in blood. All that was legible was "rcalegon," followed by something written in an odd format with Greek and Arabic letters, dots, and funky symbols I didn't understand at all. Athena had sworn she'd have her people check into it, but it still bugged me. I'd seen something like it before, but I couldn't recall where. It might have been meaningless, but I didn't want to think about Sarah, so it was all I had until the phone rang.

Mercifully, the caller was a client upset with my sudden cancellation of a fishing trip. After making amends, I spent another hour calling other clients and apologizing for standing them up, as well. I promised free makeup trips to all of them, and I expected Ned to help make sure they'd be good ones.

Once I'd finished my calls, and to further avoid thinking about Sarah, I began the mindless task of scraping bird crap off the cap rail. I was mumbling to myself about the diet of a sea bird when the repeated wooden creaking along the dock behind me drew my attention.

It was Sarah. She was wearing jeans and a light jacket and had her hair pulled back. There were bruises on one cheek and cuts on her hands and neck, and I knew they covered her arms and legs, too. I could feel my stomach flutter and my pulse quicken the second I saw her. Despite my confusion about what to do with our relationship, and my attempts not to think about it, I was actually happy to see her.

"Nice boat," she said. "Not much room to sit down, though."

"It's a fishing boat. I had her custom built to keep the deck clear of obstructions. Seats and chairs just hang up fly lines and get in the way."

She pursed her lips in assent. I knew she hadn't come down there to see the boat. She climbed on board and sat on the bench seat under the T-top.

I threw my brush and rag into a bucket of soapy water. "You doing okay?" I asked, afraid to bring up the subject I knew she wanted to discuss.

She nodded.

"I'm really sorry about the whole raskovnik thing. I should have told you—"

"It's okay," she said, holding up her hand to stop me. "Well, not really, but I'll get over it. I understand that we needed it and that it was the best way to get it. Duma didn't have to be so happy about it, though." She shook her head. "Look—"

"I know," I said, keeping my eyes on a stain on the cap rail, scraping absentmindedly at it with my thumb. "I don't even know where to begin."

Athena was right. I hadn't had a real, serious relationship in hundreds of years. It just wasn't fair to anyone, not even me. I wanted to think it was for some romantic reason, like not being able to grow old together, but the truth was it was simply too dangerous—for both of us. Caring for Sarah was a weakness—one every one of my enemies would gleefully exploit.

I liked her a lot, and I could even tell she liked me, but we both knew a relationship between us had disaster written all over it. How effective could I be if I was constantly worried about her well-being? Sarah looked out at the boats docked in the basin as we sat there in silence for a few long minutes, both wanting to say something but afraid to speak.

"There's something else, too," she finally said with conviction after breathing a heavy sigh. "Now that I know what you are and what you do, I can't just turn my back on it. On you. I can be an asset, and I can help. Frigate and Geek, too. You don't have to do this alone. It's us you're protecting, so let us help you. And frankly, I thought we did pretty well back there."

She was right. She was an adult and could make up her own mind. It didn't hurt that she was highly trained, as were Geek and Frigate. If they wanted to help, I of all people knew I could use it from time to time. I just inclined my head a little.

I saw Ned heading down the dock to us with a bag of chips in one hand and a beer in the other. His shirt was a combination of metallic blues and yellows in a pattern that took serious concentration to identify. Of course, concentrating on it would probably cause a seizure.

"Hey, Ned," I called out.

Sarah pivoted in the seat, shielding her eyes to get a better look.

"What the hell is that shirt made of? It looks like an oil slick."

"Nice to see you too, dude. I'm payin' homage to the Chargers, man," he said holding up his beer in a mock toast. "But enough about my shirt. Tell me who this is."

"Sarah, this is Ned. Ned, this is Agent Sarah Wright of the Department of Homeland Security."

"Aw, shit, dude. *The* Sarah?" Ned asked, giving me a sideways grin.

"One and the same," I said, suddenly embarrassed.

"Happy to meet you, pretty lady."

She laughed.

"Did our friend here tell you anything about me?" he asked, pointing at me with his beer.

"No, not really, sorry," she said, smiling broadly while she watched him.

I shrugged. Ned was hard to explain. "Ned is actually a Protogenoi in self-exile. He was once a Sea Titan known as Nereus."

"Really?" Her eyes widened.

I liked that. I would have thought nothing would surprise her anymore.

"That's me, pretty lady," he said with a grin. "'Course, now I just surf a little and tell him where to fish. In exchange for beer and chips. Speakin' of which, dude, there's a big school of 'cudas off Imperial Beach here to get busy with each other, and them damned greedy white sea bass are plannin' on crashing their party, man. I say we go teach 'em a lesson."

"I'm all over it. You want to learn how to fly fish?" I said to Sarah, waggling my eyebrows, only half flirting.

"Sure, but bring a regular rod just in case." She grinned.

"I'm surrounded by heathens." I laughed and shook my head as I ran back up to my truck to get some rods.

Still, she had potential.

ABOUT THE AUTHOR

Brian S. Leon is truly a jack-of-all-trades and a master of none. He began writing in order to do something with all the useless degrees, knowledge, and skills–most of which have no practical application in civilized society–he accumulated over the years.His varied interests include, most notably, mythology of all kinds and fishing, and he has spent time in jungles and museums all over the world, studying and oceans and seas across the globe chasing fish, sometimes even catching them. He has also spent time in various locations around the world doing other things that may or may not have ever happened. Inspired by stories of classical masters like Homer and Jules Verne, as well as modern writers like J.R.R. Tolkien, David Morrell, and Jim Butcher, combined with an inordinate amount of free time, Mr. Leon finally decided to come up with tales of his own.

ACKNOWLEDGMENTS

Several people made this book possible, and without their constant help and support, it would have remained little more than an idea. I have to thank Teri for her encouragement and willingness to allow me to pursue this nutty endeavor. Without her, nothing would have ever been written. This book is because of and for her. I also have to thank Kathe and Glen Goddard for their willingness to be my beta readers when no one else would.

Many thanks to Meghan Pinson at My Two Cents Editing. Her invaluable input, editing, professionalism, and enthusiasm for this book helped me actually get it out.

Lastly, I have to thank Alyssa Hall, my editor at Red Adept Publishing. Her coaching, comments, and suggestions really helped me improve the story in so many ways I cannot enumerate them. Her constructive guidance taught me more about writing than any class I ever took. And she made the editing process enjoyable.